THE
LAST DAY
IN PARIS

BOOKS BY SUZANNE KELMAN

SUZANNE KELMAN

THE
LAST DAY
IN PARIS

bookouture

Published by Bookouture in 2024

An imprint of Storyfire Ltd.
Carmelite House
50 Victoria Embankment
London EC4Y oDZ

www.bookouture.com

ISBN: 978-1-83790-523-2
eBook ISBN: 978-1-83790-522-5

This book is a work of fiction. Whilst some characters and circumstances portrayed by the author are based on real people and historical fact, references to real people, events, establishments, organizations or locales are intended only to provide a sense of authenticity and are used fictitiously. All other characters and all incidents and dialogue are drawn from the author's imagination and are not to be construed as real.

Dedicated to the memory of Rose Valland, a humble art historian who became a courageous spy, risking everything to rescue tens of thousands of invaluable works of art during the darkest days of the Second World War. Her unwavering dedication and bravery in the face of unimaginable danger serve as a timeless example of the indomitability of the human spirit. May her memory shine as brightly as the masterpieces she helped preserve, inspiring hope and admiration for countless generations to come.

PROLOGUE

PARIS, AUGUST 1943

With her heart pounding in her chest, and her arms straining with the weight she carried, Isabelle sprinted through the shadows, focusing on the back of the darkened building. Her breath fogged in the chilly air as she raced through the door and bounded up the stairs two at a time, her lungs burning with exhaustion as her trembling hand fumbled in her pocket for the key. The sound of Nazi boots thudding up the steps below caused her stomach to tighten as the key slid into the lock, and she flung open the door and raced inside.

The cloying stillness of the house cloaked her in a bone-chilling cold, and she stood motionless for a few moments, the picture grasped in her hands. The feeling of emptiness took her breath away, not only the lack of heat and light, but of the lives that would never return here.

Placing the picture down, her fingers fumbled along the wall until they located a lamp, which she lit up with trembling hands. It was well past midnight, and she knew what she had to do. Rushing to the bedroom, her best friend Brigitte's dying words still echoing in her mind, she scanned along the wall until she found the thumb mark she remembered. Carefully, she pulled down a section of plasterboard to the ground. An icy fear gripped her as she heard loud shouts of the enemy reverberating through the building, knowing that Jewish families were being dragged from their beds in a frenzy of terror and panic. She fought to keep herself composed as anguished cries of children pierced through the walls.

She frantically lifted the precious piece of art and lowered it carefully into the gap, where it fitted perfectly. Swallowing down her tears, she noted the letter on the back that had already been placed there as she thought of what those heartbreaking words could say and gazed at the beautiful picture one last time. With trembling hands, she hastily covered it over with sacking; she prayed it would never be discovered, and she could only hope that all would be well. As her fingers scrambled to replace the section of wall, heavy fists pounded on the door. In a flash, a horde of grey uniforms burst through the doorway and seized her by the arms, dragging her from the room screaming.

ENGLAND, SUMMER 2010

Esther

Esther had been struggling to serve up the kids' dinner when she received the call. She answered sharply, more clipped than she had intended, as she wedged the phone under her chin and tried to mash potatoes in the saucepan.

'Chop it,' her son Henry whined as he looked down at his dinner. 'I can't eat it like that.'

She drew her head close to his, placing her hand over the receiver. 'I'll do it in a minute.'

Henry, who had little understanding of the concept of time, harrumphed and folded his arms.

'Chop it, now!' he insisted.

She raised her eyebrows, a warning.

'In a minute,' she ground out as she continued mashing. She had taken the potatoes off the boil too early, and they were giving her triceps a workout.

The voice on the other end seemed to sense the tension and spoke tentatively. 'Is this Mrs Harrington? Is this Mrs Esther Harrington?'

She caught her breath; it still hurt even after three years. 'It was,' she responded tersely. 'I'm divorced. I've gone back to my maiden name. It's Esther Walker, now.'

She glimpsed Henry from the corner of her eye. His little fists balled up on the table. He was building to a full-blown tantrum as his brother glowered at him. In response, she sighed as she placed the pan of potatoes back on the stove and stalked over to his plate, then began cutting up his sausages as he wiped the tears of anger from his face with the back of his chubby, pink fist. Daniel, his older brother by two years, looked across at him with disgust.

'He'll be a baby forever if you keep doing that for him.'

'I'm not a baby, I'm seven!' Henry spat out.

Esther, caught up in controlling her frustration, ignored them as she became aware of someone else speaking. She realized with surprise her phone was still tucked under her chin. It had to be a sales call; no one called her by her married name unless they wanted money. She was just about to hang up when the person on the other end continued.

'My name is Édouard Dupont. I'm an art dealer and I'm calling you from Paris. I have something sensitive to talk to you about. Have I picked a good time?' The voice was smooth and heavily accented, and she had visions of Peter Sellers in one of the *Pink Panther* movies.

'This is as good as it gets,' she responded wearily as she gripped a second pan. Walking back to the table, she ignored Henry, who was picking out lumps from his mashed potatoes with revulsion and dropping them in a pile in the middle of the table.

The voice continued. 'We have something we believe belonged to a Brigitte Goldstein here in Paris and were trying to track down her daughter, Sophie Walker. We found her in a nursing home, and they gave us your number.'

Esther stopped wrangling vegetables, her slotted spoon of bright green peas held in mid-air.

'Sophie Walker is my mother; Goldstein was her maiden name,' she responded, carefully. This obviously wasn't a sales call. 'She left Paris as a little girl during the war.'

Her mother's own face flashed into her mind, all the pain she saw there whenever someone mentioned Paris. How, back before the dementia, Sophie's mouth would tighten with regret, her eyes filled with tears of pain from still missing her own mother. She had never opened up to Esther about any of the details of her life and mother's death before she left France. Whenever someone asked her about her history, Sophie would just shake her head aggressively, squeezing her eyes shut, muttering the word *'horrible'* under her breath, one of the only times she would revert to her native tongue.

'Brigitte was my grandmother,' Esther continued. Saying those words brought a lump to her throat. Just the thought of the grandmother she would never know...

She exited the kitchen and walked into the hallway to concentrate. Esther surmised she might have about two minutes before Henry hit his stride in one of his complete dinnertime breakdowns. The voice on the other end became uncomfortable and quieter as the voices in the kitchen escalated. Trying desperately to hear, Esther walked straight out the front door and hovered on her doorstep. She shivered as she battled the blast of cold air that hit her; she just needed to concentrate on his words.

Her own mouth tightened as she shifted to defensive. She didn't want her mother upset. She was so fragile now.

'What is this to do with?' The irritation was obvious in her tone.

The voice on the other end didn't seem at all perturbed.

'Someone has been renovating a house here in Paris and has

found something we believe belongs to her. Would you be willing to come and see it?'

'What do you mean, come and see it?' Esther responded incredulously. 'Come to Paris?' He may as well have said come to the moon. She had a full-time job, two kids, and was one parent with a waste of space for an ex-husband. If she was going to Paris, she would have gone long before now. And with somebody hot and handsome.

The voice was speaking again. 'It's a very sensitive situation, difficult to describe over the phone. So, it would be better if you came here.'

'You can't have someone bring it to me?' she enquired, blowing out frustrated air, the thought of a weekend with someone hot in Paris consuming her thoughts until with a bump down to earth she realized the reality of her life.

'No, I'm afraid that's impossible.'

As if to punctuate that point, from inside the house there came a bloodcurdling scream, more for show than any actual emergency, but the voice on the other end sensed the tension.

'Why don't you call me back when you have had time to think about it? I promise you it will be worth your while.'

He hung up the phone, and she stood staring at the yellow streetlamp that had just flickered into life on the quiet street in the little Cotswold village she lived in. One neighbour walking her dog waved to her and smiled, making out as if standing on your step, with one hand on a phone, a tea towel over your shoulder, and a pan of lumpy mashed potato in your other hand was a normal phenomenon.

Hours later, after the boys had gone to bed, she thought about the phone call again. She thought about her sad family history. Her grandmother had been Jewish and lived in Paris, killed during the Holocaust. Going into her bedroom, Esther pulled down the box she kept in the top of her wardrobe and sat with it on the bed. She searched through it until she found what she was looking for, the only photo she had of her grandmother.

The picture had been taken outside a grand-looking stone building, beautiful pillars framing the young woman. She wore a dark A-line skirt and a flowing light-coloured blouse. She was medium height, probably around five foot three or four, but with determined eyes and a beautiful mane of black hair. By her side was another woman, taller and elegant with light-coloured hair swept up in a neat chignon. Her arm was draped around her grandmother's shoulder, hinting at their friendship. On the back of the photograph, scribbled in an unfamiliar hand, were the words 'Brigitte Goldstein', and though it was obvious which of the two was her grandmother, since she had the same-shaped face as Esther, and also Daniel's eyes, she had no idea who this other woman was.

She had asked her mother once, but she had just shaken her head, unable or unwilling to remember. So, the photo's date and time was a mystery. As she stared at the woman in the picture, whose determined expression she so often saw in her son, she tried to imagine what it must have been like to be living a normal life until she had been hauled away and presumably killed by the Nazis. Had her death been swift? Or had she suffered? All that Esther knew, she had found out on the internet a few years before: the date of her grandmother's death in Paris. The thought of this made her shudder. Her family had understood that all of her personal things had gone. Ransacked and stolen by the Germans. So, what on earth could be there that was hers? As she ran a finger down the tiny figure, she suddenly felt an overwhelming urge to find out what that object could be; but still the whole idea seemed so impossible.

2

PARIS, SEPTEMBER 1939

Brigitte

The moon hung low in the dark Parisian sky, casting a soft, silvery glow across the forget-me-not wallpaper on the back wall of Brigitte and Samuel Goldstein's bedroom. The night was serene, and the city outside lay still, wrapped in the embrace of slumber. Brigitte, cocooned in a tangle of soft blankets, stirred in her bed as the soft rustle of linen announced the arrival of her husband, Samuel, his touch sending shivers down her spine as his warm breath tickled her ear.

'Brigitte, my love, it's done.'

Her heart quickened at his words, anticipation and excitement swirling in her chest. Samuel's latest picture had been a labour of love, hours of meticulous strokes on canvas; she blinked open her eyes as she turned to face him, her hand gently caressing his cheek, feeling the slight roughness of his unshaven skin against her palm. The scent of paint and turpentine clung to his favourite blue shirt, a fragrant reminder of his tireless dedication to his art, and with the moonlight streaming through the window creating a soft, ethereal glow, she thought he looked like an artist straight out of a romantic painting. She yawned, as Samuel led her by the hand. Brigitte's breath caught in her throat as they reached the living room. There, bathed in the gentle moonlight, stood Samuel's picture – *The Hayfields of Paris*. Brigitte's eyes misted with pride as she took in its beauty.

The colours seemed to come alive, shimmering and dancing before her. In the centre of the canvas, a golden sun hung low on the horizon, its rays stretching like welcoming arms. The hayfields below were awash with an array of warm golds and rich reds as if the setting sun had painted them with its very last breath. The painting seemed to come alive to her, its colours vibrant with movement. But it was not just the landscape that captivated Brigitte; it was the spirit of the people, their silhouettes scattered throughout the painting. Farmers worked diligently, their backs bent in labour, while children chased each other through the fields with playful laughter, free of worry and fear. There was a sense of unity, hope, and defiance against the oppression that threatened to engulf their beloved city.

Her husband's voice was filled with passion as he spoke. 'This painting, my love, reflects all that I hold dear about France – the beauty of its countryside, the resilience of its people, and the hope for a future free from war. It's a symbol of our love and the dreams I have for our family, for Sophie... This is my love letter to Paris, to our home, and to you,' he murmured, his fingers gently brushing the side of her face. 'And it's also a promise – a promise that no matter what darkness befalls us, we will find the light, and we will rise again.'

Brigitte turned to Samuel, her eyes brimming with tears of awe and love. 'It's magnificent,' she whispered, her voice barely audible above the thumping of her heart. 'It's a masterpiece, Samuel.'

As the young couple returned to their bed, she reached for him, needing to be close. Encircling her arms around him in a tight embrace, she drew him down to her for a kiss, the fear and uncertainty of this threatened war stirred up by the resilient spirit she had seen in his canvas. As she did so a deep longing came over her, and she sensed the same in Samuel as he responded to her touch, building the heat between them that grew more intense as their lovemaking became urgent and passionate; their desire for each other seemed unquenchable as each one sought to take solace in the other's touch. As if for just a few perfect moments, they could be safe from the world around them.

Later, they lay together in blissful exhaustion, their breaths mingling in the stillness of the night.

'Do you ever worry about what might happen to us if this war is announced tomorrow as people believe it will be? What would happen if the Germans occupied Paris? The way Hitler has treated Jewish people even in his own country has been awful,' she whispered, the fear evident in her tone, 'you read such terrible things in the newspapers about what happened in Poland. I couldn't bear anything to happen to you or our sweet Sophie.'

He drew in a slow, ragged breath at the mention of their six-year-old daughter. Samuel traced soothing circles on Brigitte's back, his touch a gentle balm to her fears. As he listened to her words, the weight of their mutual concern was palpable in the hushed night.

'We can't ignore the reality of what's happening,' he admitted, his voice tinged with solemnity. 'But we must also find the strength to fight back, to protect our family.'

'This war, I believe, would be unlike anything we've seen before,' Brigitte mused.

He stroked the side of her cheek, looking deeply into her eyes. 'We are not alone in this struggle; there are others who are not Jewish who will share our fight. Together, we will find the strength to endure.'

Brigitte nodded, her tears now mingling with the sweat on her cheeks. His lips met hers in a tender kiss, conveying all the love and determination he felt. 'We will take each day as it comes, my love,' he whispered.

As she fell into a fretful sleep, a nagging fear haunted her dreams; what if Hitler came to Paris, and they were taken away or worse still, killed just for being Jewish? Who would protect their sweet girl?

As the first rays of dawn began to paint the room with soft shades of pink and gold, the Goldsteins embarked on their day – a home filled with love and creativity. The walls of their little sanctuary bore witness to Samuel's artistic journey, adorned with canvases capturing the essence of Paris – a vibrant tapestry of life and love.

Brigitte watched her husband from the kitchen as Samuel went to rouse their six-year-old daughter; he gently brushed his fingers through Sophie's hair, a loving caress.

'Wake up, my little princess,' he whispered softly, leaning down to place a butterfly kiss on Sophie's forehead. 'It's a brand-new day full of adventures.'

Sophie stirred, her eyes fluttering open with a sleepy smile. 'Papa,' she murmured, reaching out to hug him tightly.

With a playful glint in his eyes, Samuel opened her curtains. 'Rise and shine, my brave explorer. Are you ready to conquer the mysteries of the day?'

Sophie rose from her bed, and the apartment was filled with laughter and the sound of their footsteps as she and her father danced and tiptoed through the rooms, pretending to be explorers in search of hidden treasures.

In the small kitchenette, Brigitte greeted them with a warm smile. The aroma of freshly baked bread mingled with the scent of coffee, creating a comforting nest of domesticity. Entering the kitchen, Samuel spun Sophie around in circles, her giggles like music that chased away the shadows of fear that still lingered from the conversation from the night before.

Over breakfast, Samuel listened attentively as Sophie chattered about the dream she'd had and her anticipation for the day ahead at school. But amid the lighthearted banter, Sophie's innocent eyes clouded with worry.

'Papa, I heard Mrs Badeau saying that the soldiers are coming here and they will take away Paris. Is that true?'

Brigitte's heart clenched, realizing they couldn't keep the harsh realities of the world from their daughter forever. Samuel crouched down to be at eye level with her, his voice gentle but honest. 'Yes, my brave explorer, the Germans might come here if the war progresses, but we won't let them take away our Paris, the one we love; we will keep it hidden in our hearts, our little secret Paris.'

Sophie's small hand gripped his tightly, seeking comfort in her father's words. 'But what if they hurt us, Papa? I heard Mrs Badeau say they want to hurt people like us.'

Samuel hugged her close, his reassurance steady despite the tremble in his voice. 'No matter what happens, we will always be together as a family. And that is all that matters.'

Sophie nodded, her fears momentarily appearing to be eased by the love that enveloped her. As Brigitte poured Samuel's coffee, she too knew that their family's love would be their anchor, and that is what she would focus on.

Samuel's artist's eye never missed a detail as they strolled along the narrow streets to school. He pointed out to his daughter the intricate beauty all around them.

'Look, Sophie,' he said, his voice filled with awe. 'Do you see how the morning sun's golden light sparkles off the Seine's surface like glittering diamonds? It's as if it is inviting us to explore it.'

Sophie's eyes widened, and she nodded eagerly. 'Yes, Papa, it's like a magical river leading us on an adventure.'

He smiled at her, 'And one of these days, I will take you on a magical boat trip down that river to seek that adventure.'

Brigitte smiled to herself; she knew Samuel was doing his best to distract his daughter from all the fear surrounding them this morning, with the imminent news of the war to be declared. In every café they passed, people huddled over newspapers talking in hushed voices about the striking news of the day.

'Look at these cobblestones,' Samuel said, noticing as Sophie stopped short, shocked at the sight of a woman sobbing as she read from her crumpled newspaper.

'They've seen so much history; think of all the amazing people who have walked these streets,' he continued, distracting his daughter by pointing down at their pathway. 'So many stories. Each one a thread in the fabric of our beloved city.'

Sophie was immediately pulled back to the magical world her father created for her. 'I wish we could explore all the stories, Papa,' she mused, her eyes sparkling with wonder as they arrived at her school. 'All the hidden secrets of Paris.'

Samuel wrapped his arm around his daughter encouragingly. 'Oh, and we will, my darling, every last one of them, but right now, you have to fill your mind with learning; that is the truest adventure of all.'

He kissed her on the cheek, and she skipped into school with a wave and called out her goodbyes. Brigitte turned to her husband and brushed his cheek with a tender kiss. 'Thank you for that,' she said softly.

He raised an eyebrow in response, looking at her questioningly.

'For keeping Sophie from being scared,' she clarified, wrapping her arms around his waist and leaning in close.

Samuel smiled and gave her a gentle squeeze. 'That is why I am here, my love,' he said, gazing into her eyes. 'I could paint a thousand masterpieces or be more famous than da Vinci, but if I wasn't there for you or for Sophie in any way, then I have failed to be the man I strive to be. You two are my world.'

As the couple strolled home to start their day, Brigitte wondered how long she could stay wrapped in her husband's blanket of security before the reality of an oppressive force came in to rob them of all they had built.

3

2010

Esther

When Esther told Janine about the call from Paris at work the next day, her best friend stared at her in shock over the rim of the paper cup containing the remnants of her latte.

'You've got to go,' she stated definitively. 'You can't just not go. It sounds so intriguing. When was the last time you pursued anything exciting?'

Esther racked her brain. Exciting? How about interesting, or about her? She didn't remember the last time she had even had a moment of mild amusement.

'But how can I? And raising two children on my own is enough of an adventure for me, thanks.'

'Okay, not an adventure, perhaps, but you ought to look into it. At least for the sake of your mother. Think of what she went through. What they all went through.'

Guilt, every woman's dark friend, hit a chord in her. Janine was right. She couldn't let this go. What if this was something important? Maybe even some clue to what had happened to her grandmother Brigitte. Esther was due for some time off, usually only doing that when one of the kids was sick. What if she went to Paris?

When she got home, Esther called the art dealer and left a message and then made the call she was dreading.

'I'm sorry, you want to go to where?' James, her ex-husband, retorted with a distrustful air to his tone. 'To Paris, with who?'

'Not with anyone,' she responded, holding back her temper. She needed him to cooperate. 'I'm going to get something that belongs to me. Apparently, somebody has found something that belonged to my grandmother, and I feel it's only right that I look into it. I mean, it could be something important, you know? A way to find out what happened to her. And I feel I owe her memory that much, to check it out at least.'

'They can't just post it?'

She felt her frustration building. He didn't have the right to question her decisions any more.

'I'm going, James, so, I need your help,' she responded bluntly.

'So, what are you saying here?'

Of course, he was going to make her work for it. It was ridiculous for her to expect him to offer.

'I was wondering if you could take the boys.' She drew in a breath before she added, 'For four or five days.'

He gasped, incredulously. 'But it's not even my weekend.'

'I know it's asking a lot,' she hurriedly added. 'But they're off school and you don't have them very often. Surely you could do that for me.'

'I don't know, Esther, that is a lot to ask. I've got that golf tournament coming up, and need to practise.'

She swallowed down her frustration, as she wished she had time for things like a golf tournament.

'Maybe you could take them with you. They'd love watching you,' she added, hating how desperate she sounded.

He exhaled. 'Well, if I do this, you'll owe me big time.'

She knew what that meant. He was going to ask her something harsh. She lost all her steam as she waited.

'I want them at Christmas. Angela was just saying how lovely it would be to have the kids for Christmas Day. We could make it really special for them.' That stung as he continued, 'And you know, I thought that would be nice.' Her stomach cramped with the pain. He'd never asked for the kids at Christmas. He always had them on Christmas Eve or Boxing Day, but she always insisted she had them on Christmas Day.

She attempted not to plead. 'You know, that would be really hard on me.'

'Well, if you want to go away to Paris with whoever.'

'There is no whoever.'

'Well, whatever. Then I want the kids at Christmas.'

She felt the anger brimming up inside of her again, but she held it down. This was a fight for another day. 'Okay,' she agreed, reluctantly. 'But you've got to have them for the entire week. And no getting out of it. No leaving them with anybody else.'

'Of course I'll take care of them,' he responded defensively. 'They'll enjoy the golf. I'll have them caddy.'

She tried not to think about what that would be like, the two of them fighting over a golf bag with metal clubs in swinging distance. She had to let this go. She had to do this. She owed it to her mother and grandmother to at least look into what all this was about.

4

THE LOUVRE MUSEUM, PARIS, SEPTEMBER
1939

Isabelle

Isabelle Valette's heart constricted as she desperately sought hope in the sweltering, cramped space. But dread clung to her body like a second skin, an oppressive fog of fear that thickened the air. As she continued to peer through the blue haze of cigarette trails that snaked towards the ever-diminishing ceiling like a quiver of writhing cobras, every face was etched with the gravity of this moment in history, the feeling in the air as oppressive as the fog that then descended to choke them.

Finally, looking at his watch, one man in a dark grey suit rose and moved swiftly towards a desk at the front as a fearfully expectant silence descended on the room. All eyes watched intently as the Louvre Museum's director, Jacques Jaujard, adjusted the wireless setting as the polished mahogany box burst into life with the familiar hum, the dial illuminated with a warm, buttery glow. The French news service crackled onto the airways. As the newscaster began in a sombre tone to describe the news of the day, the entire room of people inadvertently drew in a collective breath. The waiting had been as excruciating as the news they were expecting.

Backing up, the director perched on the edge of his desk, as the words came, then the words they'd all expected, but would never be ready to hear. England had confirmed its support of Poland. The British would not back down from Hitler's evil regime. And this would mean only one thing: the declaration of another war. In the room, someone behind her groaned, and Jaujard's secretary stifled a sob. With his clipped, professional air, the French announcer laid out all the facts, and Isabelle's stomach tightened as she grappled with this new reality.

The broadcaster droned on, but after the first few minutes, Jaujard snapped off the radio and crushed the remains of his cigarette into an ashtray before casting a glance around the room. The look in his eyes shifted from fearful anticipation to calm determination, confirming that any glimmer of hope was now dashed.

'All right, we begin. You all know what you need to do.' His quiet but intense tone left no doubt as to the gravity of the situation.

In response the room erupted into life, with the scrape of chairs and the quickening of moving feet on the parquet floor. The cacophony of sound was almost deafening after being sat cramped together in the quiet for over an hour, but now a hum of determination invigorated them as they moved out of Jaujard's office into the museum.

As Isabelle strode out of the hot, dark room, she sucked in a lungful of fresh air, taking a moment for her eyes to adjust to the gloom in the corridor.

It was odd to see this beautiful building with its magnificent, tall stone-pillared walls and elegant curved windows in darkness. But the gallery's main lighting had already been turned off as a preventative measure against a potential air raid. She opened the lantern she already had in her hand, given to every worker to navigate the now darkened hallways and rooms of the Louvre. Even before the war had been formally announced, Jaujard had called for this precaution, not wanting to risk the possibility of illuminating the museum, as it would likely be a target for those aiming to strike Paris. There was always the risk of bombs being dropped without warning, and the fear of fire ran like ice through all of their veins. Especially for Isabelle.

As the news of the war travelled through the halls of the museum, a collective chorus of whispers rose to a nervous hum, the pitch vibrating like a swarm of ascending bees as the information was passed from one person to the next. Then the Louvre's vast hallways erupted into life as the long-waiting workers in their black cloth caps and worn beige overalls transformed into living marionettes, like a perfectly executed puppet show. Caps bobbed up and down and overalls rustled. They began an exquisite choreography that filled the galleries of France's most famous museum.

Isabelle moved quickly to the room where the *Mona Lisa* was being handled, the most experienced staff working on her. The hush in the room as she entered struck her as a sort of devotion. In the lower gallery, the rooms were alive with activity. In this room, where their most precious painting hung, the work was as quiet and meticulous as if the team were tackling a precarious medical procedure. The ambient light with the haunting glow of the many lamps created an atmosphere that was church-like in its reverence.

Jaujard was already there, giving his own instructions as the workers began to remove the portrait from the wall. As this historic beauty was lowered carefully to the ground, she was gently fitted into a velvet box, where she would remain for the rest of the war. Leonardo da Vinci's most treasured portrait at the Louvre would be given a prime place out in the safety of the Loire Valley to live out her life during the battles ahead. In the mysterious glow of their lamplight, the Mona Lisa looked so serene, her inscrutable smile willing them playfully to join her on her adventure. Isabelle knelt next to the picture to get one last look at her before the box was secured. She had never been this close to this precious painting before, and it was exhilarating and excruciating in the same moment, causing tears to prick her eyes. A question surfaced as she watched the workers gently pack her in: would she ever look upon that face again?

Behind her, Jaujard was also feeling wistful. His voice was barely audible but they all heard him whisper, 'Safe journey, dear girl, till we meet again.' And then he nodded to the workers to close up the crate as Isabelle placed on it the three red stickers that marked the painting's importance.

With the most complex job out of the way, Jaujard joined her as they continued to move swiftly to the next hall to supervise other workers.

'Did all the fibre arrive as planned?' he asked, his intense, worn-out expression hinting at all that he was holding right now.

Even though it was pitch-black outside the windows and thirty-foot-high stacks of sandbags already filled the space, she instinctively turned to look towards them as she answered him.

'Yes, this afternoon, I supervised the unloading myself.'

He nodded as she pictured the Tuileries Garden adjacent to the museum. Huge mounds of black dirt had been dug over in the elegant surroundings to create trenches to accommodate the many outdoor sculptures that would be buried deep underground for the length of the war. The bags of fibre would cushion them all before they were covered with soil.

'And the cataloguing?' he asked, the pressure he was under tightening his voice. 'Everything is in place,' she assured him.

All at once, a shuddering wave of sound erupted, wracking the city with a chilling wail. The terrifying notes of the air-raid sirens reverberated through the streets, their relentless screams commanding the attention of everyone in the museum. Captured in the glow of dismal green lamplight, all eyes were drawn to the darkened sand-bagged windows to listen to a stark reminder of their new, sorrowful reality.

As if frightened by the noise, Isabelle's lamplight snuffed itself out, and her hands shook as she struck a match to relight it. All at once the memory from her childhood slammed into her and Isabelle's heart raced, this new fear igniting her old one. She had become so accustomed to pushing it away, and yet here it was, bigger and more terrifying than ever. As she attempted to hold the flame steady in her trembling hand, her heart hammered with a force that she hadn't felt since that night. Isabelle squeezed her eyes shut, trying to block out the heart-wrenching sounds that she'd heard so long ago, even above the roar of the flames. Then out of the heavy shadows of her past came the voice that haunted her every day of her life since that fateful night, the desperate cry of her brother's tiny voice ringing out into the night: 'Isa!'

Esther

Esther stared at the chaotic mess of her bedroom. Her suitcase gaped open on the bed, piles of her clothes strewn everywhere, her shoes in a heap on the floor. She knew she had to pack for her trip but felt overwhelmed by the enormity of it all.

As she dragged even more clothes from her wardrobe, she again felt that twinge of loneliness she'd been purposely trying to avoid since she'd got home. But the truth was, it had been heartbreaking leaving the boys with their father. They had been with her nearly every day of their lives from the day they'd been born. And here she was, off on some cloak-and-dagger trip to Paris to meet with a stranger about some nefarious item that may or may not have belonged to her grandmother.

On one hand, she wanted to unravel the mystery behind her grandmother's story. On the other hand, it pained her to think of leaving her children behind.

As she attempted to place clothes into ordered piles, she relived the sting of dropping them off.

The boys had fought like cat and dog on the way to their

father's house, but as soon as they had entered Angela's semi-detached home, with its scent of potpourri from Marks & Spencer and plush cream wool carpet, they had suddenly morphed into these perfect little angels.

They'd raced into the house, leaving Esther like a disgruntled packhorse to waddle in behind them with all their belongings, both of them totally oblivious to her cries for help as they jumped out of the car and raced in to see their dad.

Esther made her way inside, juggling coats and bags. Stumbling into the house, she dumped the bags in the hallway before noticing Angela was there at the door to greet them with one of those fake smiles, like a hostess from a game show, a tray of freshly baked biscuits in one hand.

'Come on in, Esther,' she cooed, her smile not quivering for an instant. 'Biscuit?' She waved the tray under her nose. 'The boys arrived at the perfect time. I just pulled them from the oven.'

Esther politely declined, struggling not to show her resentment. She knew Angela was just trying to be kind, but she didn't have to deal with everything Esther had to.

Daniel ran up to his mother to show her what he was holding. 'Look! Dad got me the latest Pokémon game I've been wanting for ages. You know, the one you said we couldn't afford?'

'That's nice,' she squeezed out, the frustration contracting her voice. This was so like her ex-husband, always feeling the need to play one-up on her. He had known Esther had wanted to get Daniel this game, and she'd just saved up enough to get him it for Christmas.

Angela seemed to sense the tension. 'Why don't you get yourself off home?' she said, scooping the bundle of coats from Esther's arm with her free hand. 'Have a nice bath or something, ready for your trip.'

Angela raised her eyebrows, confirming that, no matter how

many ways Esther denied it, they both believed she was off on some illicit rendezvous with a man. *If only*. She barely had the time or energy to read a romance novel, let alone have a passionate affair.

As she hugged and kissed her children goodbye, Henry clung to her neck, and Esther felt the fear radiating from his little body.

'Everything's going to be all right, Hen,' she whispered into his ear. 'Mummy's going to call you every night, okay? I need you to be a big boy for me and not feel sad.'

With a stiff nod, tears glistening in his eyes as his jaw tightened, he swallowed down a stifled sob.

When she had finally got home, the silence of the house pressed in on her like a heavy blanket. She took a deep breath and, desperate to quell her unease, put on some music and went to the attic in search of her mother's old suitcase. It was emerald green and had rusted silver buckles, something from the sixties. She hadn't even had a chance to buy herself new luggage. After they'd got divorced, her honeymoon luggage had mysteriously disappeared. James must have removed her cases when he had left, leaving her with what was in the attic.

Esther sifted through the pile of clothing in the middle of the bed. She hadn't worn many of these clothes since before James left. Most of them didn't fit how they used to, or were from decades ago. With a heavy sigh, she tried them on, made a list of what she would need for her journey away from home, and began folding them into the suitcase.

Then suddenly it dawned on her. She was going to Paris, the city of lights. It didn't really matter what she wore; this trip could change her life.

Brigitte

Brigitte switched off the wireless, and the room plunged into an uneasy stillness. Looking across at her husband, her gaze met Samuel's; his face was etched with worry. Still, he managed a faint smile, his eyes reflecting a mixture of determination and apprehension.

'And so, we begin,' he murmured, his voice carrying a weight of solemnity. 'An adventure none of us wanted, yet one we must face.'

'Maybe we should leave,' she suggested, her words tinged with anxiety. 'Get away from here and find somewhere safer.'

Samuel's arms enveloped her in a reassuring embrace. 'And go where, my love?' he asked, his voice gentle but edged with resignation. 'Jewish people are facing hatred across Europe. It won't be long before Hitler's grip extends further than Germany and Poland. For now, Sophie is safe here, in a place she knows. I don't want to put her in danger by venturing into the unknown. She's too young to bear so much upheaval.'

He walked to the kitchen, and Brigitte followed him, her

eyes filled with concern. There was something unspoken between them, a weight that lingered beneath his words. Drawing a glass of water, he took a couple of sips before his gaze again locked with hers.

'Alexander approached me,' he revealed, his voice carrying a mixture of determination and purpose. 'They are forming and organizing a resistance; there is even talk of an underground newspaper. There's so much we can do if I join their efforts.'

Brigitte's eyes searched his face with a combination of worry and uncertainty. 'Samuel, are you sure you want to do that?' she asked, her voice trembling. 'Shouldn't we attempt to remain inconspicuous?'

His voice continued with unwavering resolve. 'As Jewish people, we're already a target, my love. Hiding in the shadows won't protect us. We can't let fear dictate our lives. We need to stand up for what's right, for justice.'

Her arms found their way around his waist, seeking comfort in his embrace; as she did so, her eyes drifted out of the kitchen window, where the darkness of the night concealed the Eiffel Tower, a dark mass against the moonlit sky. Paris beyond the window all of a sudden seemed both beautiful and foreboding. 'You're right, of course,' she admitted, her voice soft and also resolute. 'And, there is my father to think about.'

The words caught in Brigitte's throat as she pictured her lovely, kind-hearted father, who was in the lingering days of a terminal illness. He would be lucky if he outlived the year; he could not travel anywhere, and she could never leave her mother alone to care for him and also take care of her parents' gallery.

Samuel's grip tightened, his voice a whisper against her ear. 'We have people who care about us and we have each other, darling; that is all we really need.'

As their conversation hung in the air, they were interrupted by a soft presence. Brigitte turned to find Sophie, clad in her nightdress, standing barefoot in the doorway. Her voice trembled with concern. 'Why do you both look so sad? Did something happen on the wireless?'

Samuel knelt, enfolding their daughter in his arms, his voice tender yet burdened. 'My sweet Sophie. Unfortunately, the war you heard about has started.'

Tears welled in Sophie's eyes. 'Will that bad man come here and hurt us? Or take us away?'

The room seemed to close in around Brigitte as her thoughts spiralled in the wake of Sophie's innocent questions, the weight of impending darkness settling heavily on her shoulders. She gazed at her daughter's vulnerable expression, the reality of the world they inhabited bearing down on her heart.

Samuel's hands cradled the little girl's face, his gaze unwavering. 'No, darling. We won't let anything harm you or take you away. We'll live our lives bravely, painting, going to school, looking after each other. No fear will ever take away our love, which will be our strength.'

Brigitte watched, a mix of emotions surging within her. She wished she could fully believe in their ability to shield Sophie from the horrors that were unfolding. Now the war had been declared, and with it had come a chilling uncertainty.

As Samuel continued to comfort Sophie, Brigitte's mind raced with all this could mean for her and her family. The newspaper headlines of the last weeks had been so frightening; the early preparation for a potential war and the hushed conversations in the streets all painted a grim picture of the future. Their world, with just one wireless address, was transformed into a place of fear and unease. She yearned for even yesterday and the freedom they had once known, for the vibrant streets of Paris that now seemed to be tainted with shadows and sadness.

Brigitte crossed the room with a deep breath, kneeling beside Samuel and Sophie. She brushed a gentle hand over Sophie's hair, her touch a mixture of comfort and sadness. 'You need to get your sleep, darling; there is nothing we can do tonight,' she whispered, her voice barely audible. As Samuel and Brigitte gently guided Sophie back to her bed, the room seemed to hold its breath as if anticipating the tender exchange about to unfold. With her tiny hands wrapped around Samuel's fingers, Sophie settled back under her covers, her eyes fixed on her father's face, searching for a glimmer of hope.

'I don't think I can sleep, Papa; I'm too scared and wide awake.'

Samuel tucked the soft pink bedding around his daughter and snuggled her favourite bear beside her.

'Well, let's see if I can do something about that. This isn't the first time someone has faced a situation like this. I happened to know another little girl who also had her battles to win, and she was just your age.'

Sophie's eyes shone with expectancy, anticipating the beginning of one of her father's stories; still holding his hand, she nestled into the cocoon of blankets, awaiting what was coming.

Samuel's voice was a soothing melody in the hushed room. 'Once upon a time, in a faraway land,' he began, his voice carrying a warmth that captured Sophie's attention, 'there lived a brave young girl named Sophia.' A spark danced in their daughter's eyes as she recognized how similar the name was to her own.

'She had a heart full of courage and a spirit that shone like a star.'

Sophie settled back, listening intently; her imagination whisked away to the world her father was weaving.

'Every day, Sophia would wake up before the sun rose, smile at herself in the mirror, and don her favourite tunic dress; then she was off to explore her kingdom,' Samuel continued.

'But one day, an ogre stormed into the land with anger and words that threatened to weaken even the bravest hearts. A creature who believed that only those who looked and acted like him were important, and was cruel to people who were different. Citizens of the kingdom became scared of what he would do and they cowered in their homes behind their locked doors and closed curtains. But Sophia had a secret, a power that even the mighty ogre didn't understand.'

Brigitte watched from the doorway, her heart swelling with pride and love. She saw the way Samuel's eyes met Sophie's, filled with a deep affection that transcended the story he was telling.

'The mighty ogre tried to scare people with his bluster but Sophia, with her unwavering bravery, knew she would never let the ogre's anger make her feel less than she was.'

'What did she do, Papa?' Sophie asked, her voice a mix of curiosity and hope.

'Sophia rallied her friends and her family, just like the ones who love you,' Samuel said, his gaze drifting toward Brigitte with a gentle smile. 'They stood side by side, ready to face the ogre's narrow-mindedness together. You see, the secret the ogre couldn't fathom was that love – pure love – is a force more powerful than any weapon, any word, or any action. No matter the ogre's wicked deeds, they remained strong as long as they held love in their hearts. And together with Sophia's courage, love ignited a beacon of hope, a light that pierced the blackest night.'

Brigitte wiped away a tear that escaped down her cheek, moved by the sweet allegory Samuel was crafting. The parallels between their own reality and the story were poignant, a testament to their determination to shield their daughter from fear.

Sophie's eyes sparkled, as she clung to every word, obviously finding strength in the unfolding tale. 'And did they win, Papa?'

Samuel's voice carried a note of conviction. 'Yes, my darling,' he said, his eyes holding Sophie's with unwavering assurance. 'Through their courage and love, the ogre could not stay because without his ability to make them scared, he had no power over them, and even though he ranted and raved, and stomped and screamed and shook his fists at them, he eventually gave up because the love they all shared was stronger than anything he could fight them with. Then one day, he fled the land, and they never saw him again, and once again the land was bathed in the light of peace and love.'

As Samuel finished his tale, he brought his lips to Sophie's forehead in a gentle kiss before saying softly: 'You see, my precious Sophie, you are just like the brave girl in this story. You have a heart full of courage and are so loved by everyone around you. No matter what the world may say, remember that you are worthy, special, and loved just as you are. And whenever you are scared, close your eyes, put your hand on your heart, and think of all the love you have and that surrounds you, and no ogre or bad man will ever be able to rob you of that love.'

Sophie closed her eyes, her little hand moving to her chest as she pictured her father's words.

'It's working, Papa. I feel stronger thinking of all the love I have here in my heart.'

Brigitte's own heart swelled, her eyes locked onto her husband. At that moment, she saw the strength of their family bond, that transcended the confines of their small apartment.

Sophie beamed, her eyes shining with a newfound sense of courage. She nestled down under her covers, her heart lightened by the story of bravery and love.

Samuel and Brigitte shared a knowing glance as she yawned and her eyes began to close. Samuel stayed a while longer, gently running his fingers through his daughter's hair to soothe her until her little hand fell away from his and the ease of sleep consumed her.

As they turned off the bedside lamp and retreated from Sophie's room, Brigitte turned to her husband and whispered.

'Do you have a story to reassure me?'

He turned her to him and brushed her with a gentle kiss, his eyes glistening with mischief.

'Oh, I have something better that you would enjoy a little more. Why don't I show you?'

And as he guided her to the bedroom, unbuttoning his shirt, she mused at how this man she loved with all her heart could transport the world around her from bleakness to light just with his words and his tender heart.

7

Isabelle

After the terrifying citywide air-raid test the day war was declared, the museum staff continued to work through the night, only stopping briefly to grab something to eat and drink. Isabelle returned to her office at 4.00 a.m. Dropping into her chair, she slipped off her heeled shoes and stretched her sore toes before laying her head on her desk to close her eyes for a short time.

Jaujard discovered her there as the dawn was breaking, though in the cocooned darkness of the Louvre, only a faint glimmer of blue filtered through the gaps in the sandbags.

She was woken by his urgent voice breaking into her turbulent dreams.

'How are we doing with the trucks?'

She lifted her head abruptly from her desk, her heart pounding with the raw awakening. Jaujard's expression softened, a look of apology on his face.

'I'm sorry, I didn't realize you were trying to sleep.'

Isabelle blinked slowly in the dim light, her vision gradually coming into focus. Her eyes felt like they had been scratched by sandpaper and her throat was parched. She heard his voice but couldn't make sense of it. Then she remembered, with a tightening of her stomach, the radio announcement the day before. Still in her stockinged feet, the chill of the floor struck her to the core as, standing up, she rolled her shoulders, trying to work out the kinks in her neck. She attempted to uncurl her aching body as she shuffled over to the bulletin board on her wall, the board that updated her staff on all that needed to be achieved during the entire art evacuation. Isabelle squinted at the papers pinned to it.

'The trucks?' she croaked, finally understanding what was being asked of her.

Moving the artwork had been just as hard to organize as packing the art itself. Arranging the large convoy of trucks that would move the six thousand pieces of artwork from Paris had been her daily job for weeks.

They had had trouble finding trucks available, as they were constantly being commandeered for other important pre-war work. She had only finalized the thirty vehicles they would need the day before.

Under the watchful eyes of the police, a trail of trucks would transport the Louvre's valuable contents away from danger. She had made doubly sure that everyone was ready for this clandestine mission – the hastily acquired vehicles silently standing guard outside the Louvre waiting for their precious cargo.

She slipped her feet into her shoes, grabbed her coat off the hook, and followed the director of the museum outside. A fine mist hung in midair. The sun was just beginning to peek out from behind the horizon, and a cool, blue morning breeze brushed across her face, instantly waking her up. Jaujard scanned the line of vehicles, tapping a finger against his chin as he allocated art to trucks. They were an odd assortment, including a prestigious department store delivery truck, a well-used home removal truck, and a greengrocer's van. Jotting notes on a clipboard, Isabelle recorded each one's intended cargo.

She was double-checking the convoy's route in the afternoon when one of her younger sisters, Charlotte, appeared at her office door unexpectedly. Charlotte carried a basket of gifts beneath her arm, and a soft smile was spread across her sun-kissed face. 'I can't believe you are still here,' she said, her voice tinged with motherly scolding. 'You haven't left this building since the war announcement.'

Isabelle didn't bother to argue as her sister continued: 'I went into your room, even though I know you tell me not to and grabbed some fresh clothes and toiletries in case you need them.'

Tears welled up in Isabelle's eyes at her sister's sweet gesture. Of all the five Valette siblings, Charlotte was the one with the biggest heart. Except for Isabelle and Charlotte, all their other sisters had left home at a young age to pursue their artistic dreams, but Isabelle was hardly ever there and Charlotte had been content to stay home and look after their parents, with no real inclination to fulfil any great legacy except to love and care for them all.

'Now,' commanded Charlotte, 'you go and get changed while I set out some lunch for you. I have made my special potato fritters I know you love.'

Isabelle knew better than to argue with Charlotte, who could be quite persuasive when she had her mind set. And hugging her sister tightly, she thanked her profusely before shuffling to the bathroom to change into fresh clothes.

Charlotte had thought of everything, even slipping in some comfortable shoes that Isabelle was really grateful for.

As she sat at her desk in her clean clothes, devouring delectable lemon chicken and listening to Charlotte's chatter about their parents' comings and goings, various pets, and houseplants, she suddenly felt a million times better. Her sister always had the ability to anchor her to what was important in any storm. She even seemed untouched by the concerns that lay ahead with this fear of war. Her simple way of seeing the world was a balm on the troubled waters Isabelle had been living through for months.

That second night, Isabelle's body ached and she felt a jumbled range of emotions. From a sense of pride and camaraderie as they all worked together to save the museum's priceless artefacts, coupled with a sense of the enormity of their mission, the looming threat of enemy airstrikes, and her own crushing fatigue from hours of labour with little sleep.

In the waning hours of another sleepless night, she stood by Jaujard's side, watching the wrapping of *The Raft of the Medusa*, which was a huge painting, twenty-two feet wide by sixteen feet tall.

As they supervised the removal of this huge work of art, she gazed sadly at the figures brought to life in the painting. Every figure depicted in the image seemed to reflect her own inner turmoil and hopelessness. The picture captured a small, battered raft rocking on a turbulent sea, with its crew trying desperately to hang on, some of them being dragged below the billowing waves.

In the middle of the chaos, a lone sailor stood at the helm waving a tiny red scarf, his only hope that he could draw attention from a distant ship.

As Isabelle stared, a chill ran down her spine at how closely the painting's hues of deep amber and murky green mimicked her sense of dread and hopelessness. In the eerie light of the museum lanterns, every line and brushstroke seemed to capture her desperation, every character's face distorted with her own fear.

As Isabelle held her breath, the workers managed to successfully detach it from the wall. Géricault's masterpiece was a feat of painting genius – but also a logistical nightmare. The artist had employed bitumen, usually used for making asphalt, in broad swathes of his painting to achieve a deep black hue. Unfortunately, because of its sticky nature, it never fully dried, so moving it posed its own distinct set of difficulties, as rolling the artwork was impossible, requiring the utmost care.

Not to mention that its massive height made it a challenge to transport, since the convoy would have to pass under bridges and utility wires. The route had been carefully studied between her and Jaujard, and the route arrangements were made with workers of the French post office and telecommunications agency to temporarily disconnect telephones and telegraph wires to allow the convoy to pass safely.

Isabelle felt her exhaustion settling into her bones as the sun rose again in a pink explosion of joy, and she watched the first convoy of trucks trundle away from the Louvre's loading area, their precious cargo carefully secured. Jaujard came later to her office to check on her, his brown eyes warm and concerned.

'You need to get some sleep,' he said. 'And not here at your desk.'

She agreed to take a break after ensuring that the statues too fragile to move were in the safest corners. Her gaze lingered on the sculptures, their elegant lines and intricate details magnified by piles of sandbags that surrounded them. The fragile beauty of these centuries-old treasures made her heart ache as she realized how easily it could all be destroyed by a single bomb.

As Isabelle left for home later that morning, she glanced back at the loading area and saw crates that had yet to be taken to safety. Where would they end up? she thought. Would they all be returned? It was too much to hope. Jaujard's insistence that the art be moved had saved it for now, but she couldn't

suppress her sadness for the Louvre's loss, and the looming
danger that threatened them all.

As she moved through Paris, she hoped the walk home
would be the fresh perspective she so desperately needed, but
the streets of France were eerily silent. Parisians of all ages shel-
tered at local cafés, nursing their cups of espresso and even the
occasional shot of absinthe, the conversations among them
hushed and serious. Startling newspaper headlines were everywhere, the atmosphere thick with unease, and it was as if the
birds had forgotten their songs. The cobblestone streets near the
River Seine were devoid of life. Even the elderly woman with
the apple-red cheeks who fed the pigeons daily was missing
from the water's edge. Instead, she sat huddled alone on a park
bench under an ornate wrought-iron lamppost, frowning as she
stared at the newspaper in her hands. Everywhere Isabelle
looked, fear and uncertainty were palpable, and it seemed as if
the entire city was bracing itself with a growing sense of dread
of what was to come next.

8

Esther

Esther peered into the mirror as she tried to tame her unruly hair. She'd had a hurried appointment at the hairdresser's the day prior to leaving home. It had looked amazing when she'd left the salon, but now it was flattened on one side and she had no time to wash it again.

Since she had arrived the day before, everyone in Paris seemed to look sophisticated and chic, and it only made her feel awkward and frumpy, with her pale skin, red cheeks, and unruly curls.

'Oh, sod it,' she groaned in frustration before yanking her brush through it, attempting to create soft waves that matched the style from yesterday. She thought about the appointment with Monsieur Dupont, whom she had researched before leaving England and found was an esteemed art dealer, and as she dressed, she tried to imagine what this was all about.

Grabbing her jacket, she exited the rental and started down the street. Her destination was just a short walk away, on the other side of the world-famous Seine river. She admired the ancient buildings that lined the streets, but mostly she admired the beautiful people who walked alongside her as she passed bakeries and galleries.

Her stomach growled with hunger, and as she was early for her appointment, she considered stopping for breakfast. An inviting bakery with a shiny front counter, which displayed pies and sweet rolls, tempted her to step inside, the delicious scent of warm bread wafting out through the open door calling to her. She gazed longingly at all the delicious pastries in the counter's glassed front before finally deciding on the flaky croissants. Clutching the warm paper bag against her chest for comfort, she strolled outside to sit on a bench overlooking the river.

Esther watched the flow of the Seine as it meandered through the city of Paris, parting around stone embankments of bridges beneath a hazy morning sky. Hypnotized by the slow progression of boats that bobbed along the water, she opened the bag of croissants and pulled apart the fluffy, buttery strands. Taking a bite, she felt as if all of Paris rushed into her with its sounds and smells as she closed her eyes to enjoy the early morning sunshine.

Finishing her breakfast, she made her way through the city.

Music drifted from the nearby bank, and a solo violinist serenaded a painter capturing a watercolour of the Notre-Dame cathedral, the violinist's bow swaying in time with the painter's brush. They both nodded a good morning to her as she passed them. People filled the outdoor cafés, sipping tiny cups of strong black coffee. Laughter and conversation filled the air. Esther felt as though she had been transported to another world, and her spirits lifted with each step she took. Janine had been right in urging her to take some time away. Esther was so myopic in her own world, she sometimes forgot that people had other lives so very different from hers. So she might not look the most glamorous, but she was in Paris. She felt positively balmy as she walked, her melancholy dissolving like mist.

As Esther drew closer to her destination, her curiosity grew. She wanted to know more about her Jewish grandmother and was eager for anything that might provide insight into that part of her family's history. She had wished numerous times in the last few years that she had pushed for more details, because now, with her mother's dementia, there was little hope of finding out the whole story. Esther had presumed everything of her grandmother's had been ransacked or stolen, but now this tiny light in the darkness, a glimmer of knowing, excited her. Somehow, something from her grandmother's life had found its way through time and space to this present moment, and the possibilities of what that meant were endless.

When she finally turned into the street and glimpsed the magnificent apartment building in Montmartre, Esther let out a gasp, checking the address one more time to make sure that this was the right place.

Surely this couldn't be it? This was enormous. The pristine, cream-coloured building with the striking black-accented gables shimmered under the morning light. When he had spoken to her on the phone, Monsieur Dupont had implied her grandmother had lived here. Esther tried to imagine her humble Jewish mother arriving here on her way home from school. It seemed unfathomable.

As she stepped into the foyer, along the walls were pictures of the extensive renovations that had been done to create spacious apartments from what seemed like rabbit-hole dwellings. She studied them as she waited for the lift to descend.

She slipped into the lift and an older man wearing a navy beret, chinos and crisp polo neck stepped in beside her. Esther couldn't help but smile – the whole scene was so French, something she would have thought only existed in Hollywood movies.

The lift glided to a stop on the third floor, and Esther

walked down the hallway until she reached the door with the address she had been given. When it opened, a young woman with short bobbed blonde hair and a fringe, who was wearing a white flowing outfit cinched at the waist with a beautiful leather belt, greeted her. Her face lit up when she saw Esther standing there.

'Ah, you must be Esther. I'm Yvette,' said the young woman in fluent English, although with a heavy French accent. 'Come in.'

Esther walked inside the most beautiful room she had ever seen, and the first word she thought of to describe it was 'white'. Everything seemed to be that colour: carpets, sofas, walls. It was gorgeous but so impractical, like a magazine spread.

As Esther's feet sank into the white carpet, it felt like a cloud beneath her. She had never been inside so luxurious a place before. Without being asked, she removed her shoes as she followed her host into the front room, and with a sweep of her hand, the woman offered her a seat on a white leather couch.

On the table, three magazines were stacked for effect and at the far end of the room, silk curtains billowed out from an open window, ruffled by the morning breeze, revealing a breathtaking view of the Eiffel Tower. It was gorgeous.

The woman asked if she wanted something to drink and Esther nodded politely, opting for tea.

'Milk or lemon?' Yvette asked.

'Milk would be lovely,' Esther replied.

The woman left to prepare the tea and Esther studied her surroundings.

As the woman swished out to the kitchen, Esther looked around the room and felt the peace of this place. It was beautiful. Could her grandmother have lived somewhere like this? She had always imagined her life to be somewhat humbler, more in style with her mother's and her own life. It must have been so different during the war years.

As if reading her mind, the woman returned with her tea and began to explain the history of the building – how it had originally been comprised of smaller apartments before it was renovated.

'But, of course, we have wanted to renovate it ourselves, as many people have. So, it was quite a surprise when we opened up our wall to find your treasure inside it.'

Her treasure? Esther reflected on her choice of words. Was it hers?

Esther was brimming with curiosity but didn't want to rush this graceful woman, who floated around the room as elegant as a swan on her sea of white. But she was desperate to see whatever it was they had discovered.

'My husband and the dealer we called will be here soon. In the meantime, why don't you tell me all about yourself?'

Esther froze. What on earth could she say that this woman could even understand about her life? Where did she start?

'I have two children,' she stuttered.

'Ah, magnificent,' Yvette responded. 'That's so sweet. I have a lovely niece and nephew who sometimes visit me. They love Paris.'

Esther shuddered at the thought of children running around the pristine room with their sticky fingers marking their trail. This wasn't a place where kids could live. She was so glad she hadn't brought the boys.

But before the young woman could elaborate further on the thought, the door opened to reveal two men – a tall man with a whisky-coloured beard and sparkling blue eyes, followed by a shorter one in a dark suit with dark hair and curious green eyes – both talking in hushed tones.

Her hostess spoke hurriedly to her husband, Jean, in French and then introduced Esther. He stepped forward and shook her hand.

He was also wearing a crisp, white shirt and white trousers, disappearing into the surrounding walls. They talked quickly among themselves. He introduced the man behind him.

'Ms Walker,' the dealer said, offering her his hand, his voice low and comforting, 'it is I who called you. My name is Édouard Dupont; I'm so glad you could come. And please forgive me for being so vague over the phone when we spoke. In a delicate situation such as this, it is important to keep things quiet until all the facts have been established.'

Esther nervously nodded in understanding, suddenly worried they had come across a body in the walls of the house, her grandmother's skeleton perhaps lying in wait somewhere in the back of a cupboard.

'Shall we?' he suggested, sweeping his hand towards the bedroom.

She placed her tea on a coaster before following him into the bedroom, where Jean and Yvette had been knocking down a wardrobe to make a walk-in closet.

One of the walls had a hole in it. The sight of jagged red brick and dust looked out of place with the rest of the house, which was so white and clean and crisp, but there was a hole in the wall and there in the midst of it was a beautiful picture, the most beautiful, vivid picture she had ever seen.

Esther could feel her jaw drop in awe.

'We left the picture as we found it, wrapped in cloths, so that we wouldn't accidentally damage it. Then, after seeing a letter with your mother's name and birth date on it, we conducted research and were able to locate you. We knew many children had been taken to the UK during the war.'

Then he gestured to the letter that was propped up against the picture.

'And that is how we knew to get in contact with you. We also arranged for Monsieur Dupont to look it over as well.'

Esther was speechless. She hadn't anticipated anything like this. They all returned to the front room, and after seating herself again on the white sofa, Esther nervously turned over the yellowing letter in her shaky hand as a brim of emotion seared her chest. She read the words on the envelope:

Please give this to my daughter, Sophie Joselyn Goldstein.
Born in the Beaujon Hospital in Paris on the 18th of May,
1933.

As she finished reading, Esther was overwhelmed by emotion. Was this her grandmother's last letter before her untimely death? Were these her final written words? The only letter she would ever receive from her?

Yvette interrupted Esther's thoughts, kindly offering Esther a chair to finish her tea while she read. Staring at the elegant looped handwriting and then back at the group, she gulped down air as Yvette rested her delicate white fingers on her arm.

'Take your time, Esther, there is no rush.'

Esther nodded and, slipping her finger under the flap, she slowly opened the envelope.

9

PARIS, JUNE 1940

Isabelle

Isabelle strode at a clip through Paris, heading towards home. It was a striking day; the trees held the lush green of summer's wealth, and her shoes crunched over the new growth that pushed up through cracks in the cobblestone pavements, foreshadowing the abundance of the rest of the season to come. The sun was warm, with just the hint of a cool breeze that could be felt in the shady alcoves of the street. The perfect beauty of the day made it all the more bittersweet, with the Nazis on the outskirts of their city. She passed by a newsagent's, outside were papers filled with startling headlines and crisp, white broadsheets detailing the ongoing German advance. A French troop truck loaded with soldiers rushed past, acrid fumes belching out from the exhaust as the army continued to leave the city. It still sickened her that the French local authorities had decided to just hand Paris to the Germans without a fight. The reasoning was that they didn't want their precious city bombed. But it still felt cowardly to Isabelle.

At the Louvre, the enormous task of removing the valuable

pieces had been done the year before. Still other pieces not deemed so important, and those too fragile to be moved, continued to wait in half-empty halls, huddled behind their walls of sandbags for over a year now. The Germans were still mercilessly storming through Europe, and now France, and the news was very grave. With the aggressive way that Hitler was commanding his armies, it was no surprise that their own fair city would soon be occupied by the invading forces. The prospect of that was evident from the many families that had already left the city for the south. However, Isabelle had already decided long before that she would not leave the art that had been placed in her charge.

Pulling her attention from all the heaviness of her thoughts, Isabelle refocused on more pleasant things. It was her mother's birthday, and she had a lovely present tucked away in her bag: a picture of sunflowers – her mother's favourites – created by a local artist.

When she arrived home, she felt welcomed by the splendid rose garden her mother had cultivated all spring, and, opening the door, was greeted by laughter in a distant room.

Isabelle breezed into the kitchen. The scent of cooking spices and her mother's flowers clung to the air. Her youngest sister, Giselle, was entertaining her other sisters with a dramatic retelling of her performance from the night before. From what Isabelle could tell, a male dancer had nearly dropped her during the show. Two of her other sisters, Antoinette and Madeline, seemed utterly entertained by their sister's antics as she acted it out, and Charlotte, the practical sister, bustled around the kitchen preparing food, shaking her head.

'I don't know how you do it, Gigi. I'd be terrified to be on show like that.'

On spotting Isabelle, Madeline and Antoinette squealed with delight and formed their usual group hug, a giggling swarm of female energy, pulling Charlotte from her work, a plate still in her hand, into a familiar mingling of flowing hair, perfume, and warm bodies.

As they broke apart, Isabelle noticed their father, Bernard, in the doorway, with his usual half-smile and twinkle in his eye.

'*Mon Dieu!* I will die with all this bonhomie!' he said with mock exasperation.

Isabelle rushed over and kissed his smooth cheeks, enjoying the familiar scent of his shaving cream and the fragrant sandalwood oil that he always wore in his hair. In his hand, as always, was a book.

Their mother, Delphine, entered the kitchen in her favourite sunflower dress, cinched tightly at the waist, emphasizing her petite, slender figure. Her red hair was loose, long, and beautiful, with just a soft silk scarf keeping it back from her face.

'All my girls together,' she said in her usual singsong fashion, her slim freckled arms stretched towards them. 'Where is my hug? After all, it is *my* birthday.'

The girls all giggled and rushed to their mother and pulled her into their hug too.

'It is so good to be all together,' Charlotte announced enthusiastically.

'And this is all the good we will know at this moment,' her father said, his voice heavy with despair. 'I'm still in shock that even though France has the largest army in Europe, the Nazis are overrunning us. It won't be long before the Germans come here and destroy everything we have.'

'They will not destroy our love,' Antoinette reassured him, squeezing his cheek. 'We will always be a family, no matter what happens.'

The girls continued helping their mother with preparation activities as they talked about their lives.

Madeline, the eldest and tallest of the Valettes, spoke of her worries regarding the future: she owned a little bookshop in town and she had heard a lot in the news and from the book world.

'I am still devastated about the book-burning in Berlin,' she shared with her father, her emerald eyes filled with concern. 'Those books were a treasure we will never get back.'

Bernard shook his head, gazing out the window in disbelief. 'It is sacrilege what this man is doing. He is nothing but an animal.'

As they talked, Delphine and Isabelle crafted vegetable flowers to decorate the platters Charlotte was assembling. Antoinette as always looked immaculate with her heart-shaped face and long blonde curly hair; she picked at the food and was already a little tipsy, having had two glasses of wine, and Giselle was always so much energy in the kitchen, juggling lemons to make them laugh and keep their minds from the impending occupation.

The weather was so perfect they laid a table in the leafy walled courtyard at the back of the house. It wasn't large, but Delphine had worked her magic even there. Colourful ancient homemade pottery of all sizes brimmed with all manner of summer flowers including an abundance of pink and white geraniums, purple and coral-pink fuchsias and a large swath of wild flowers. From the back greening wall an ancient stone lion-mouthed waterfall rimmed with peagreen moss cascaded a gentle stream of water to add a peaceful ambience and for their feathered friends to drink from. The only part that brought a sense of sadness was the area where Delphine's art studio had once stood. Now an informal memorial garden to their late brother, a tree had been planted in the studio's stead and a lovely bench placed beneath it with a carving of Pierre's laughing face crafted by their father's own hand into the ageing wood.

Bringing out the platters of food, they scated themselves around the large wooden table in the same seats they had occupied since their childhood: Bernard and Delphine at the head and the foot, Isabelle and Madeline on one side and on the other, Gigi, Charlotte and Antoinette.

The aroma from the table laden with all their favourite food was intoxicating. A trout almondine decorated with lush slices of lemon, parsley and tiny slivers of almonds took centre stage. To its side, a jug of thick, creamy garlic aioli. An array of several colourful salads sprinkled with Delphine's edible flowers and including Gigi's favourite Niçoise was peppered with fresh green olives. In front of Bernard, a platter of his favourite sliced meats. And scattered around the table a whole slew of cheeses including a rich, smooth Camembert and baskets of crusty baguettes still warm from the bakery.

'How on earth did you manage to get so much food?' Madeline asked with surprise. 'Charlotte. You have worked a true miracle. I thought we already had shortages.'

'Charlotte is a miracle worker,' Delphine assured her, grasping the hand of her second-youngest daughter. You have no idea how much queuing she has been doing.'

Charlotte brushed it off. 'I was lucky Monsieur Feldman from the delicatessen on the corner of the rue des Rosiers has closed up shop and taken his family to the south. He has always been very kind to me and gave me the pick of his best meats and produce before he left, telling me he would rather give it to the dogs than have the Germans fatten themselves when they arrived.'

Bernard drew in a deep breath. 'Of course, like many in that district he is Jewish, and has a lot to fear from the invasion.'

Isabelle looked over at Antoinette, seeing her blue eyes flash up as she flinched at her father's words. She felt great sadness for her sister who was facing this war with a Jewish husband and young son.

As they started to eat, the sweet aroma of Charlotte's

THE LAST DAY IN PARIS

'How are you doing, Isabelle? I feel as if you are never home,' her mother asked as she tore off the heel of a baguette. 'Are you coping at the gallery?'

'It has been hectic,' Isabelle replied. 'We have so much more work to do protecting the paintings and sculptures we have left here in Paris, and the fear of the Germans arriving and taking over the museum looms over us all.'

'I don't understand why everyone is so anxious about the Nazis. They won't stay long,' said Gigi with confidence as she took a bite out of a soft, yellow pear. 'We've had enemies before and Paris has the most enormous army in the world. I'm sure eventually they'll take care of the problem.'

Despite Gigi's optimism, the mood around the table was less than positive.

Madeline frowned and shook her head at her youngest sister. 'No, Giselle,' she said firmly. 'Things are going to be different for us now.'

'But there's always a way to get what we want,' Antoinette responded breezily as she raised her third flute of wine.

'You always get what you want, anyway,' Gigi commented and a ripple of laughter filled the space, as it was well known that Antoinette was the most indulged of the siblings but also the most loved. Her exemplary violin-playing had resulted in a lot of attention being showered on her. Though Giselle was just as talented with her dancing, it was Antoinette who garnered the attention.

Charlotte rose to clear the table, but her mother grabbed her hand.

'Charlotte, sit down. We are all right. You don't have to rush to clean up.'

Charlotte sat back down, hovering on the edge of the seat, really wanting to get back to the kitchen.

'Where is your son, Antoinette?' she asked.

'And your husband?' said her father with a swig of his wine. 'I need some male company.'

'René has Benjamin. I have been so busy this week, he felt it would be good for me to have some time to myself. So, he went to see his own mother today and took Benjamin with him. Also, she is very fearful of what is coming, so René wanted to go and comfort her.'

'I miss seeing him; you should bring Benjamin more often,' Charlotte mused, as one of the many fat wild tabbies that she took care of jumped up and began to knead her lap.

'You are the sweetest sister ever,' stated Antoinette, taking hold of her sister's hand and kissing it.

'And you're the most incorrigible,' joked Gigi.

'Well, it's not easy being the most talented,' Antoinette laughed, running her fingers through her blonde hair, as an uproar erupted around the table, 'but I bear it well. Do you not think?'

After they had finished their lunch, they moved indoors to the cozy front room where Charlotte brought out a luscious raspberry pavlova, Delphine's favourite, with one candle alight in the top.

'How kind of you, darling,' gushed their mother, 'to not embarrass me with my full age in candles on your dessert.'

'Mama, you never look any older,' Gigi retorted. 'I hope I have all your genes.'

'Unfortunately, my dear, you also have some of mine,' their father joked, running a hand over his thinning hair as Gigi responded by jumping up and kissing him on the top of his head.

'You will always be handsome, Papa.'

As the afternoon waned, the conversation turned again to talk of the war.

'What do you think it will mean for Paris, Papa?' asked Isabelle thoughtfully.

'I think it will mean very hard times,' he said, 'from what I read of what he has done in other countries. He strips them of who they are, what they are.'

'What do you mean?' asked Antoinette, lifting a forkful of the pavlova that Charlotte had served up to them all along with coffee.

'I think France will be a very different country after he's been here.'

'Well then, it's our job to protect it,' said Madeline as she sipped her wine and plucked at a grape from the fruit bowl on the sideboard.

'What do you mean by that?' Delphine asked.

'The spirit and soul of our country. We might recover from this dreadful war. But what about our art and our other treasures? Look at what's happening. They're burning books. They're destroying art. What will be left of our heritage here?'

'I agree. I am not only scared for my family,' interjected Antoinette, 'but for all the creative works of René and the many Jewish composers at the conservatoire, and what if they take my husband away?'

The lively room became silent as they all contemplated Antoinette's situation, married young to a brilliant pianist. Her family was in real danger.

Isabelle glanced over at Madeline and noticed a single tear rolling down her cheek. It had only been a year since Madeline had lost her own husband to cancer; he had also been Jewish.

'We must do our best,' Giselle stated, trying to revive their spirits. 'All of us. We should make a promise that we'll do whatever we can.'

'Like what?' said Madeline with discouragement. 'No one will let us fight.'

Antoinette stood up, her hands firmly planted on her hips.

A determined glint had returned to her eye. 'Of course there's something we can do! Since we can't fight in the army, we have to fight for what it means to be Parisian. We must protect our heritage, our very soul.'

Their father smiled at the bravery of his middle daughter. 'Hear, hear!' he cheered.

'Madeline, couldn't you protect our literature in some way? I will do my best to save the music. Isabelle can save our art.'

'And I can help save our theatre works.' Giselle raised her glass.

'And what about me?' Charlotte asked with a chuckle. 'Have I nothing I can save?'

Her father's blue eyes twinkled as he pointed his fork in her direction. 'You,' he said, emphasizing his words, 'can save all the cats.'

The whole room erupted into peals of laughter.

Charlotte jumped up and began collecting the plates. 'All right, before that, I'll start by rescuing all you brave Parisian warriors from having to do the dishes.'

Madeline grabbed her sister's arm before she could flee the room.

'Antoinette is right.'

'I am?' giggled Antoinette, her eyes sparkling with her sister's confession, accepting readily the fact she was the most rebellious of all the sisters and was rarely right.

'Every one of us is important. Especially you, Charlotte. Let's make a vow, all of us. Let's make a vow that we will fight for the heart of Paris.'

Their mother held high her glass of wine and saluted them all. 'To saving the heart of Paris.'

'Yes.' her father added. 'Hitler doesn't stand a chance with all the Valette siblings on the case.'

All the girls raised their glasses too with a cheer and then downed their wine.

10

PARIS, JULY 1940

Brigitte

Brigitte looked carefully over her shoulder, her senses heightened with caution, before she swiftly stepped into the abandoned warehouse. The eerie silence enveloped her as she closed the creaking door behind her, shutting out the morning sunshine, the outside world and the prying eyes of the enemy.

Dimly lit by a few flickering lamps, inside the air hung heavy with the scent of dust and ink. As her eyes adjusted to the dark, Brigitte's footsteps echoed through the empty space as she cautiously navigated her way through the maze of discarded crates and stacks of paper that created a labyrinthine passage. As she ventured into the secret rooms in the warehouse, Brigitte noticed the remnants of a broken printing press, its skeletal frame a stark reminder of the challenges they faced. The walls now bore the marks of struggle, with faded slogans and symbols etched into the cracked plaster.

Brigitte's heart pounded in her chest as she finally reached the printing room. Inside, it was a hive of activity; the air was filled with cigarette smoke and the steady rhythm of machines, the clatter of typewriters, and the whispered conversations of determined voices. An ink-stained apron adorned one of the workers, who waved to her, his sleeves rolled up as he meticulously set each letter and adjusted the printing plates. This was a sanctuary of secrets and the Resistance, nestled in a hidden corner of Paris. As Brigitte nodded to the people she knew, the air hung heavy with the scent of ink, an earthy aroma that mingled with the tangible determination permeating the space. A symphony of mechanical prowess, as the ancient press groaned and spat out the Resistance's lifeblood: *Libération*.

Racks of freshly printed newspapers adorned the walls, their stark black headlines proclaiming defiance and demanding justice. The bold words leaped from the page, electrifying the atmosphere with a sense of purpose.

Amid the organized chaos, Samuel, her husband, stood at a press, his broad shoulders hunched over the machine. His eyes, a deep shade of hazel, were focused and determined, his brow furrowed with concentration as he scanned a sheet of paper, the ink still appearing wet from printing. His presence reassured her, but she couldn't shake the nagging worry that lingered in her mind. The risks they took, the sacrifices they made, were a constant weight upon her shoulders. Brigitte approached and their eyes locked for a brief moment and the intense, tired expression that she had seen on his face on entering changed to joy in seeing her.

'How was your night?' she said, her voiced raised to be heard above the noise in the room.

He smiled as he patted the pile of newly printed papers.

'Busy,' he said, his tired eyes glistening with the achievement.

I have brought you some breakfast,' she said, pulling out a paper bag of warm pastries from the basket she carried.

He reached an ink-stained hand to take her offering as he

brushed his wife's lips with a kiss of gratitude, a curtain of his thick black hair tickling her nose.

'And you haven't forgotten about our picnic this afternoon, have you? Sophie is so excited.'

Samuel's eyes lit up with remembrance, removing the weariness etched into his face.

'Of course not, I have been looking forward to it.'

'Extra! Extra! Read all about it!' a fellow Resistance fighter called out, waving a copy of *Libération* in front of her nose. Brigitte couldn't help but laugh at the man's zeal, as she took a copy to read, knowing that this little group were a flickering flame of resistance in a city drowning in darkness.

Outside the printing room, they all knew Paris stood under the iron fist of Nazi rule. Swastikas adorned every corner, mocking the memory of a once vibrant and free city.

'I will see you later,' Brigitte informed her husband, tucking the newspapers carefully underneath the fabric of her basket and kissing her husband goodbye as Samuel adjusted the ink-stained apron around his waist, and continued his work.

Hours later, at the corner of their street, Brigitte anxiously waited for Samuel. The worries and fears that had plagued her earlier threatened to consume her once more, but she fought to maintain her composure. And then, as if a weight had been lifted, Samuel's long, angular frame and beaming face with his shock of black hair emerged from the bustling crowd.

Brigitte's heart skipped a beat as her eyes met his, searching for any signs of distress or fatigue. But instead, what she found was a spark of resilience in his gaze. Despite the weariness etched into his features, there was a determined glint that spoke volumes about his unwavering dedication to their cause.

Sophie sprang up from the bench, her excitement palpable in the air. 'Papa! You're back!' she exclaimed, her voice filled with uncontainable delight.

'Yes, my darling explorer, time for more adventures together,' he said as he swept her up into his arms.

Brigitte's heart swelled with love as she witnessed the embrace between father and daughter. The bond they shared was unbreakable, a testament to their steadfastness amid the chaos that surrounded them. Brigitte joined them, her steps quickening with anticipation, and wrapped her arms around Samuel, feeling the strength of his presence anchoring her. Tears of relief welled up in her eyes as she held him close.

The sun shone brightly in the park as the family laid out the checked blanket, their small picnic spread enticingly displayed. Sophie giggled with delight as she danced among the flowers, her hands reaching out to touch the butterflies that fluttered around her.

Samuel's eyes glistened with a mixture of love and inspiration as he observed his daughter's joyous play. As Brigitte lay back on the blanket, soaking in the sun, Samuel carefully set up the little portable easel he carried with him always, selecting his brushes and tubes of paint with precision. The vibrant hues reflected the colours of the blooming flowers, and Samuel's skilled hand held the promise of creating a work of art that would forever capture the innocence and spirit of Sophie.

Brigitte watched in awe as her husband prepared his canvas, his face a mask of concentration and creativity.

Lying on her back, her gaze following their daughter, Brigitte noticed the way the sun illuminated Sophie's tiny figure, creating a halo of light around her. She felt herself fill with warmth and satisfaction as she watched Sophie attempting to catch a butterfly.

'Samuel,' Brigitte said softly, 'I'm so glad you want to capture these everyday moments on your canvas.'

Samuel smiled at the scene before him, his eyes never leaving Sophie. 'It's moments like these that remind me why I paint, why I continue to create despite the challenges we face.

This scene represents the purity and beauty that we strive to protect.'

He began to sketch the outline of Sophie's figure, his strokes both deliberate and gentle as he captured her grace and spontaneity. With each careful application, his brush breathed life into the canvas, weaving a tapestry of colour and emotion.

'The way Sophie interacts with nature is so pure and untainted,' Samuel continued, his voice soft but filled with reverence. 'Through my painting, I hope to convey the message that even in dark times there can still be solace and inspiration.'

Brigitte watched as Samuel mixed his paints, carefully layering them until they perfectly replicated the delicate petals of the flowers and fluttering wings of the butterflies.

'Is everything ready for the gallery showing?' Samuel asked, pausing as he shifted his head from side to side to gain more perspective.

'It is,' Brigitte replied with a smile. 'My mother is beside herself – she stopped by twice today already, unable to contain her excitement. She says all the tickets are sold out and your picture will be the jewel of the exhibition.'

Samuel stopped and his eyes found hers. 'I'm so glad it will be in the show. There is something about that picture that I have always loved. I think it is the piece that most reflected my heart.'

'I know what you mean,' Brigitte agreed, thinking of the beauty of his finest work, *The Hayfields of Summer*.

Brigitte rolled onto her stomach and rested her head on her hands so she could continue watching their daughter.

As the afternoon sun cast a warm glow over the park, Samuel continued to paint, his hand guided by a deep sense of purpose. The image on the canvas began to take shape, the vibrant colours dancing harmoniously. Brigitte had been dozing, when all at once she forced open her eyes and shuddered as her attention was drawn to the entrance of the park. A group of men, some dressed in grey uniforms with SS insignia pinned to their lapels, others in long civilian trenchcoats, walked purposefully towards them. Her heart skipped a beat as recognition dawned on her – it was the Gestapo. Had they found out about the paper?

'Samuel, something's not right,' she whispered urgently. 'We need to leave. Now.'

But Samuel, lost in his artistic trance, seemed oblivious to the danger lurking just beyond the flower-laden borders of their picnic.

Panic surged through Brigitte's veins, and she frantically grabbed Samuel's arm, pulling him away from his easel. 'Samuel, we have to go! They're coming for you!'

Samuel's hazel eyes widened with realization, and Brigitte's pulse shifted to a frantic gallop. His unfinished painting sat abandoned on the easel, its brushstrokes still alive with his dreams and visions for the future as he gripped Brigitte's hand tightly. They frantically scanned the park for an escape route, but the Gestapo agents had already closed in around them.

The leader of the group, a tall and imposing figure with black beady eyes, stepped forward in a sinister manner. 'Samuel Goldstein, you are under arrest for your involvement with the Resistance and your subversive activities against the Reich,' he declared in a low, ominous voice.

Sensing something wrong in the altercation, little Sophie raced forward and clung desperately to her father's leg. One of the Gestapo agents knocked down the picture and tore the little girl away from him, hurling her forcefully to the ground. Infuriated by this act of cruelty, Samuel lunged towards the agent in an effort to protect his daughter. And in the split second that Brigitte dashed forward to gather up her daughter, a deafening crack, the sound of gunfire, tore through the air. Brigitte gasped in horror and buried Sophie into her shoulder as she watched the bullets rip through Samuel's body mercilessly. Time seemed to stand still as Brigitte watched the love of her life crumple to the ground, his vibrant spirit extinguished in an instant. A scream tore from her throat, a primal cry of anguish that echoed across the park, cutting through the shocked silence.

The agents coldly surveyed their handiwork, their expressions devoid of remorse. One of them, the leader, smirked cruelly and turned to his comrades. 'Another rebel silenced.' Then raising his voice to be heard by the people who stood looking on in horror, he said: 'Let this be a lesson to anyone who dares defy us.'

With Sophie clinging to her side, Brigitte's world shattered into a million jagged pieces. She collapsed to her knees beside Samuel's lifeless body, clutching at him as if trying to will him back to life. Tears streamed down her face, as blood mingled with the vibrant colours of the abandoned painting, a cruel reminder of the beauty and hope that had been stolen from her.

11

Esther

Esther gingerly picked up the envelope with trembling hands. It felt tissue-paper thin and was discoloured by age, her mother's maiden name scrawled on the front. Her heart raced as she opened it, revealing a hastily written letter.

My beloved Sophie, you know what this is; we spoke of it. Do you remember our conversation before you departed on the train to southern France? Do you remember the secret I shared with you that must be kept at all costs? I hope so.

As Esther read on, tears began to well up in her eyes, blurring her vision. She paused to think of the grandmother she would never know and to take a breath. Glancing up to see all eyes in the room fixed upon her, she wiped away an errant tear before continuing.

If for some reason we should be separated, I want you to know that I love you and always will. However, there are tasks I must take care of, important tasks that only I can complete. If something should happen to me, Sophie, I want you to live an incredible life with no regrets. The fact that you returned when you did was a blessing, despite not being what I wanted. But I was happy to have been able to spend that short time with you. So please take care of yourself, my love. You are always in my thoughts, and know soon we'll all be together again.

Much love,

Maman xxx

As Esther reread the letter, she examined the handwriting, comparing it to her own, which displayed such similar strokes and curves. In that moment, she was filled with a deep feeling of admiration as she comprehended that the paper she held had once been touched by her grandmother – a woman she had known hardly anything about until now.

She glanced around the room and saw that Monsieur Dupont was watching her with concern as tears streamed down her cheeks.

Laying the letter aside, Esther moved back to the bedroom and ran the tips of her fingers along the ornate frame and studied the brushstrokes on the canvas. She felt an affinity with the painting, as if it held some kind of greater meaning, something that was connected to her family.

As the others followed and hovered in the doorway, she turned to them.

'This painting was obviously very significant to my grandmother,' Esther said softly.

'All antiques come with their own stories,' Dupont responded. 'This particular piece has an extraordinary one. We think it may be a forgery. We are still doing a few tests. We believe that the original, your grandfather's painting, was destroyed on a train bound for Berlin during the war. The Germans kept meticulous records, so we know that is the case. So the fact it's here is a surprise. Do you think your grandmother or someone she knew would have commissioned a copy for any reason?'

Esther shook her head. 'I can't really tell you much about my grandmother, as I never knew her and my mother's memory is failing, but I will ask her what I can.'

'You know nothing more?' he asked tentatively.

She shook her head sadly, trying to remember what fragments of stories she had heard from her mother, but they were all just too abstract.

What did all of this mean?

After she had regained her composure from reading the letter, Monsieur Dupont walked her through assessing the value of the painting. There seemed to be a lot that needed to be established to figure out its authenticity, and her head spun as he relayed it all to her.

Finally, they bid farewell to their hosts. The art dealer escorted her out of the apartment and they strolled along the sunny street.

'I'm going to do some more research on it today. Can you meet with me tomorrow, when I may have more information for you?' he enquired.

'Of course,' she replied.

'Wonderful,' he said. 'Well, it's lunchtime, and in France, lunch is taken rather seriously. Would you like to join me?'

'Oh, no need to worry. I'll just get a sandwich.'

His face registered horror at her suggestion. 'A sandwich? Please, it's no trouble. I'd be offended if you didn't come and have a proper lunch, my treat.'

Feeling self-conscious, she gazed into his sincere green eyes before responding. Convincing herself that it was perfectly normal for an adult to go out for lunch, she agreed and they ambled in to the centre of Paris.

He took her to a sunny café with lemon-and-white awnings, and they sat down at a table near the front next to a man playing 'Autumn Leaves' on a piano in the corner. She ordered a glass of white wine, which was crisp and light, and basked in the peace and civility of it all. Insisting he called her Édouard, the art dealer was easy to talk to, and they conversed nonstop as they waited for their food to arrive. Halfway through the incredible pasta dish she had ordered, her phone rang. It was Daniel. He had entered the text '999' – their code word for a problem.

'Excuse me a moment, please,' she said, her heart pounding, as Édouard was about to order dessert, and, stepping away from the table, she quickly dialled the number.

'Mum?'

'Yes, Daniel? What is it?'

'It's Henry. He tumbled from a tree and we had to bring him to the hospital, and now he's getting stitches.'

'What?' she exclaimed. 'What was he doing in a tree?'

'I caused this, Mum. I was climbing, and he wanted to climb. I told him not to, but you know what he's like. He did it anyway and fell.'

Her heart wrenched as she listened to her son's anguish, sounding so much younger than his nine years.

'Stop, take a breath. Where was your dad?'

'He was playing in his golf tournament.'

She paused and drew in a long, slow breath: she was starting to feel dizzy.

'Okay, don't worry. I'll call your dad in a minute. How is Henry, apart from the stitches?'

'He's okay, I think. But I'm really scared, Mum.'

'It's going to be all right, Daniel,' she reassured. 'Don't be afraid. Lots of people have stitches. Henry will be fine. You need to take care of yourself and I'll talk to you again in a little while after I've spoken to your dad.'

A wave of guilt swept over her as she hung up the phone and dialled her ex-husband's number, which went straight to voicemail.

Taking a deep breath, Esther hung up as she berated herself. She should never have left them. What was she thinking?

She stepped back into the restaurant and sat down.

Édouard gazed over at her with sympathy in his eyes. 'Was there a problem?'

'My son fell from a tree. He was following his older brother, and you know...'

'I'm so sorry,' responded Édouard.

'He was hurt badly enough to require stitches.'

'I can sympathize. My daughter, Camille, had a bike accident this week. She scraped both of her knees. That needed stitching up too. It's pretty common, I think.'

'I know, but he needed stitches and I wasn't there. I should've been there...' Her voice trailed off as she choked back tears.

He gently covered her hand as she continued.

'They are with my ex-husband; I'm divorced,' she whispered.

'So, you're alone?'

She thought of those words. She never really felt alone, not with two young children, but she supposed she was.

'Yes,' she answered quietly.

'I am too,' responded Édouard.

'Are you divorced?' Esther asked.

'No, my wife passed away from breast cancer two years ago. So it's been hard for Camille and me.'

He took a sip of wine, his eyes full of a sadness she knew too well, and she could feel the pain radiating from him, like an invisible wave.

'I'm sorry. That must be really difficult.'

He managed a tight smile. 'It is, but I had seven wonderful years with her.'

She hesitated before she asked her next question, not wanting to pry too much, but knew because he lived in Paris he couldn't take it the wrong way.

'Are you seeing anyone else?'

He shook his head sadly and said, 'No, I'm not. It would feel strange to be with somebody else after so many years with the person you love, your soulmate, and I'm not really interested in casual dating.'

Esther nodded in understanding. Even though her marriage had failed, she had a picture of what true love could be like, and she could empathize with him. 'I don't date either. But that's not because I wouldn't want to. It's because between working and taking care of two boys, I just don't have the time.'

They paid their bill, and he walked her back to the hotel, their conversation lingering in the air between them. They agreed a time to meet at his office the following day and parted.

As Esther stepped into the lift and the doors closed behind her, she felt a strange sense of contentment. It had been a delightful afternoon spent with someone who understood what it was like to live with the pain of loss.

12

PARIS, JULY 1940

Marina

Marina Belleveau sat poised in her red velvet café chair, her delicate fingers wrapped around the porcelain cup as she savoured the rich aroma of her drink. As she sipped, her eyes discreetly scanned the elegant surroundings for a target.

As she searched about her, the aroma of freshly brewed coffee wafted through the air, mingling with the murmur of animated conversation and the clinking of teaspoons against saucers. Soft, golden light cascaded through the café windows, casting a warm glow on the polished wooden floors and the ornate chandeliers that adorned the ceiling. This was her favourite spot, a haven of sophistication and refinement, attracting wealthy men who sought solace in its tranquil ambiance. Though the war had taken so many of the younger men to fight, it didn't worry Marina; the man she was happy to set her sights on was of an age when fighting was no longer an option.

From her earliest years Marina had harboured dreams of a life far removed from the poverty and struggles that had plagued her upbringing. She was determined to break free from the cycle her mother had perpetuated – a life of scarcity and endless children. Instead, Marina had devised a plan, a path to ascend to a world of wealth, comfort, and indulgence.

Every aspect of her life was meticulously crafted to manifest that. She carefully selected her wardrobe, choosing garments that exuded elegance without being overtly provocative. Each piece was chosen to accentuate her curves in just the right way, captivating the attention of potential suitors. She honed her skills through classes, refining the art of captivating men by saying the right things, laughing at their jokes, and employing seductive eyelash-lowering techniques. She devoured books on the art of pleasing men, becoming an expert in the delicate balance of demure and seductive allure. Marina knew precisely how to work a room, commanding attention effortlessly as she glided through social gatherings.

A young man nervously approached her. 'Excuse me, mademoiselle, would you by chance have a light?' She glanced at the man who stood beside her as she reached into her bag. He wore a nice suit and a nice gold bracelet but his hair was obviously cut by a cheaply priced barber and as his fingers grasped the lighter she proffered, she saw that his nails were ragged. Glancing down at his shoes, she saw they were cheap and scuffed. He wanted to give the appearance that he had money but he was not wealthy. The shoes always gave them away. She could tell by the look in his eyes he was steeling himself to ask her out. She would have to make her own move. Rising from her seat with grace, she adjusted her skirt, a subtle gesture to draw attention to her desirable silhouette.

'Are you leaving?' he asked despondently as he handed back her lighter.

'I have to meet my husband,' she lied with ease. He offered his assistance with her jacket. Marina, perfectly capable of donning it herself, smiled demurely and accepted his chivalrous gesture, effusively thanking him as though he had performed a great favour.

As she glided through the restaurant, she relished the hushed silence that followed in her wake, savouring the attention that seemed to naturally gravitate towards her.

Stepping outside into the golden sunlight that bathed the streets of Paris, Marina shielded her flawless complexion from the sun's rays, adding sunglasses and a large-brimmed hat that added an air of mystery to her persona. Yet, despite her polished appearance, her heart sank as she confronted the stark reality of her day. Without the support of a wealthy boyfriend to fund her lifestyle right now, she had been forced to secure a job. After careful consideration, she had obtained a position at a prestigious art gallery, recognizing it as an ideal environment to encounter potential suitors who saw art as both an expression of culture and a lucrative investment. Determined to impress with her knowledge and charm, Marina had devoted her evenings to studying the art, ensuring she would be well-versed in the subject when engaging in conversation with the gallery's esteemed patrons.

As she strolled through the vibrant streets of Paris, her designer handbag slung gracefully over her arm, Marina meticulously examined the captivating displays showcased in the shop windows. She absorbed every detail, always wanting to stay ahead of the latest fashion trends.

All at once a smell accosted her. She turned around sharply to see a dishevelled woman with a ragged child folded in one arm, another clinging to her hip.

'Do you have a little change you can spare?' she rasped, flashing gaping holes where there should be teeth. Repulsed, Marina moved away.

'No! Go away,' she snapped, holding one hand to her nose as she swiped at the woman with the other.

The woman shuffled away, leaving Marina shaken to her

core, as terrifying memories of her childhood assaulted her. Screwing up her eyes and catching her breath, she moved into the first store she found. She would buy herself something beautiful to recover from the ordeal. Memories of her mother's mistakes stung her – three failed marriages and seven children. Thank goodness Marina had escaped that life, leveraging her charms to secure an opportunity for higher education with an older, influential man who had taken an interest in her.

Ten minutes later, and with a newly wrapped bundle in her hands, she walked with effortless grace along the illustrious Champs-Élysées, Marina practised the fictional past she had carefully crafted for herself. If ever questioned, she hailed from a life of abundance and luxury in the sun-kissed south, drawn to the enchanting allure of Paris to experience the wonders of the City of Lights. Her fabricated identity, which even included a brand-new name, had become more familiar to her than her own true origins, a narrative she had honed and refined. No one would ever know the roots she had left behind, nor the hardships she had endured in her relentless pursuit of a brighter future.

As she approached the grand doors of the museum, Marina took a moment to compose herself, feeling the weight of her aspirations and the strain of engaging with people, particularly other women who could perceive her as a threat. Yet, she reminded herself of her purpose and the future she was crafting. She steeled herself, fully aware that the opportune moment was just around the corner, waiting for her to seize it.

13

PARIS, JULY 1940

Isabelle

Isabelle heard the lockstep thuds of hobnail boots hitting the ancient wooden floor before she saw them. The rhythmic sounds of marching steps echoed throughout the halls with machine-gun precision, imposing their collective, forced authority on every room as they claimed their territory. The sound reverberated through the whole building.

Isabelle stood motionless as she felt the chill of the stone wall at her back. Even though she had been expecting their arrival, her heart pounded in time with their marching feet, as if sensing her need to prepare for something even more sinister than she was expecting. The forcefulness of the intrusion was what shook her. Their apparent disregard for the hallowedness of this place. No one ever entered the Louvre in this way. Just the presence of beauty around you slowed you to a pace of appreciation. Even if you arrived harried, the graceful rooms and windows, or a Monet or Picasso, had the power to capture your attention and slow you to a stroll. And even though their masters had long since gone, been secured away to safer homes, there were still so many pieces of art and sculpture too fragile to move to capture attention.

She had feared this confrontation ever since the Nazis had marched into Paris the month before, commanding everyone to stay inside along with their clipped propaganda that was blared out of loudspeakers.

Isabelle rose from her seat to await her enemy, her mouth becoming dry, and she could feel her knees trembling beneath her skirt. She desperately wanted to run, but she forced herself to stand her ground.

The steps grew louder and her enemy rounded the corner, smearing the beauty of the elegant space with the angry grey that bled into every corner.

The leader of the small troop had an Aryan look to him, with white-blond hair and icy blue eyes. He loomed head and shoulders above the rest. In a different time and place, with his high cheekbones and strong, angular jaw, he would have been very attractive – but in the Nazi uniform with a swastika armband, he was nothing but repulsive to her. Nevertheless, his presence commanded respect. As they drew to a halt, the man stepped forward, his boots clipped and measured on the ancient wooden floor as he approached the desk. He removed his hat and tucked it under his arm. Beside him were two other men: one short and squat, the other dark and brooding.

'Fräulein Valette, I take it?'

Isabelle wanted to speak, but her mouth was too dry. So she just nodded her head. To be so close to the grey uniform, to be so close to her enemy, was daunting. Her eyes were instantly drawn to the gun at his side.

'I am Commander Richt. I oversee the art in Paris. Let me introduce you to the men who will be overseeing the Louvre and its works.'

He indicated the two men. The short, squat man wore the dreaded grey uniform. Beside him, the taller man of angular build, dark eyes, and a swath of brown hair wore a dark suit with the Nazi swastika armband.

The first stepped forward.

'This is Oberführer von Behr,' Commander Richt said. 'He is the commander of the Einsatzstab Reichsleiter Rosenberg, known as the ERR, and he is overseeing the Parisian art collections. And with him here is Hauptsturmführer Lohse, who is an expert in matters of art and to whom you will directly report. I have spoken to Monsieur Jaujard and I believe you were expecting us.'

She nodded. What was wrong with her? Why could she not speak?

Curiosity crossed his face before, apparently, he quickly dismissed her as he started to survey the room.

'As I'm sure you've been told,' he said, 'today we are here to evaluate the existing artwork at the Louvre. Our job going forward is to assess any pieces that come in from across the country. You will aid us in cataloguing and preparing these works.'

A chill ran down Isabelle's spine as he spoke; his casual tone seemed to be an attempt to conceal their threatening intent. She suspected they were plotting something far worse than what they let on.

She proceeded to show them around while being informed that she'd need to hire more people for the anticipated influx of artworks headed to Paris.

Isabelle nodded obediently, her mind racing with anxiety. She knew that the shipments they were expecting were likely stolen artwork, taken from the countries they already occupied. She couldn't believe she was being forced to assist the Nazis in their looting of Europe's cultural treasures.

The officer continued, 'I assure you, Fräulein, that your cooperation will be duly rewarded. The Reich will take good care of its loyal servants.'

Isabelle felt a surge of revulsion, stepping back from him. 'Excuse me, I have work to do,' she said, quickly making her way out of the gallery.

But she knew that she couldn't escape. Nazis were everywhere, and they had all the power. All she could do was pray for the safety of the artwork and the people of Paris, and hope that one day, justice would be served.

14

Esther

The following day, Esther anxiously awaited a call from Édouard, and when it came, his enthusiasm was contagious.

'Our craftsmen have removed the painting out of the wall and done some gentle cleaning on it, so it's ready if you want to come and view it at my office.'

Esther felt her heart beating faster in anticipation of seeing both him and the artwork again. The first thought took her a little by surprise, but she surmised it was probably to do with the fact she felt cared for in his company, especially about their shared loss.

She rummaged through her suitcase for something suitable to wear – pulling out a black skirt and a cream satin blouse that was a little snug around her chest. She strategically draped a scarf around her neck to mask the slightly gaping front, hoping it would suffice.

Before leaving, she called the boys to check in. Henry appeared quieter than usual but was recovering from his stitches, and Daniel was elated. Apparently, Angela had gifted him with two new games for his Game Boy. As she listened, a wave of annoyance washed over her; it seemed like a competition between them, as if Angela and her ex were trying to outdo Esther with money and gifts, and she didn't want that kind of dynamic with her children. She pushed the thought of James's girlfriend away from her mind and began to focus on her day.

Stepping into Édouard's office, Esther was embraced with a warm smile from his secretary, and she accepted the offer of coffee while she waited. On the walls were pictures of Édouard at various art galleries and openings. By the looks of the dignitaries he was pictured with, it was obvious he was well thought of. Moments later, he appeared at an office door, an elderly man at his side. They joked with one another with ease before he bid his visitor goodbye with a slap on the shoulder and greeted her with a warm handshake.

'I'm thrilled you're here,' he said to her. 'Come and see your treasure.'

Inside the office, his desk was a finely polished mahogany, and on it were pictures of his wife and daughter set within photo frames. A bookcase full of books stood along one wall, and several exquisite art pieces hung throughout the room. Above his desk, a small antique clock chimed every fifteen minutes.

On an easel by the side of his desk was placed the picture that had been covered in sacking the day before; the transformation was stunning. The dusty, greying picture had been transformed. The painting's evocative power was so profound that it transported Esther to the very essence of summer's enchantment. Through her misted eyes, she took it all in once more, immersing herself in the magical world the artist had crafted. Vivid hues of flaming oranges, passionate reds, and radiant golds danced joyously together in the painting. It was a masterpiece of creativity that stirred her emotions, evoking sensations as if she could feel the warmth of the orange-blazoned sun on her skin, catch the delightful scent of freshly piled hay, and hear the echoes of children's laughter as they frolicked through the grassy fields.

'My goodness,' she gasped. 'I had no idea this would look so different.'

'We're quite pleased with how well it has survived,' he remarked. 'If it is indeed copied, as we think it is, then it must have been worked on diligently. Is there anything else you can tell me about your family that might help?' he queried.

Esther shook her head sadly. 'I don't know much about my mother's past since she won't talk about it, and now she has dementia. The only thing I know is that she lived here with her mother and father before he got killed during the war.'

He nodded thoughtfully. 'As I told you yesterday, we feel this is commissioned art. People do that sometimes, so they can enjoy a beautiful painting in their home without needing to take the original from the gallery.'

Her fingers caressed the frame affectionately before her eyes misted over with emotion. 'It's so beautiful,' she whispered.

All at once, Édouard's eyes twinkled with excitement. 'How would you like to visit the place where this was painted? It's a renowned spot just outside Paris – a sprawling field full of wild-flowers during springtime and hay cutters during summertime. I'm quite familiar with it; my parents used to take me there on special occasions.'

'I would love that!' exclaimed Esther, unsure if she was more excited to spend more time with him or to see more of what the painting depicted.

'Excellent!' he replied. 'Give me an hour to finish my work, and you could get changed if you wish. We can take a picnic. I'm happy to provide some food.'

Esther couldn't contain her enthusiasm. When was the last time she'd had a picnic that wasn't squashed ham and tomato sandwiches on a beach with sand inside them?

'That would be lovely,' she replied, gushing more than she had intended, and she noted a smiled tugged at the corners of his mouth as she exited the office and made her way back to her room. There she changed into her jeans and a soft T-shirt so much more comfortable for her. The sun was shining high in the sky, and it was a perfect day to enjoy the outdoors.

A little over an hour later, she returned to the office to find that Édouard was already waiting for her. He had also changed into more casual clothes: a pair of light beige linen trousers and a well-fitted, short-sleeved denim-blue linen shirt – a comfortable yet elegant look that complemented his lean physique, making him appear effortlessly sophisticated.

A picnic basket sat on the secretary's desk. She acknowledged Esther with a warm grin, saying, 'It was packed for you from a lovely delicatessen here in Paris. I think you will enjoy it.'

Édouard gave his secretary some last-minute instructions before walking Esther to the car and opening the door for her. She slipped inside. It had a beautiful leather interior with the scent of a lemon wax polish. Everything was clean and tidy and air-conditioned. In comparison, she thought of her own run-down car at home – full of sticky sweet wrappers and old toys and books scattered on the floor. It was like another world.

As they drove out of Paris, Esther rolled down the window and let the soft breeze caress her skin while the sun warmed her face. Even though this wasn't a date, she had never been on such a romantic adventure before, and it made her heart flutter.

On the way, they made small talk about the weather and his business; he told her how he worked mainly as an art assessor valuing paintings but occasionally worked at auctions selling and buying art for clients.

'I know it's too early to probably think about this,' she asked nervously, 'but do you think this painting is worth anything?'

She looked across at him with hopeful eyes. Did she see a hint of disappointment? If she did, it disappeared quickly.

'Of course, there is always a market, particularly for a piece with such an interesting story,' he replied smoothly. 'I did some research before you arrived. This particular picture – its original – was destroyed during the war. Are you sure selling it is what you think you will do?' he asked gently, without judgement. 'I thought you might want to keep it for yourself because it may be part of your family's heritage.'

Esther felt a pang of guilt as they drove through the gorgeous French countryside, and she considered his words.

As she and Édouard pulled up to the spot where the original painting was created, she couldn't help but feel overwhelmed by its beauty. It seemed surreal that the artist could have stood here over half a century ago and brought this picture to life with their brushstrokes.

As she looked out at the spectacular views, she had second thoughts about keeping it, but what would she do with something so beautiful? There was no room in her home for it. And even though she had been an artist in her younger days, and had even worked in an art gallery after leaving school, her dream job, she didn't have anywhere she could show it. It seemed wrong that other people wouldn't be able to see it. And she was forced to admit that she needed the money.

Édouard spread out a picnic blanket amid tall grasses kissed by a gentle summer breeze that blew past them, ruffling their hair, carrying the scent of wildflowers. He pulled a bottle of chilled white wine from the picnic basket and spread out an array of French delicacies on a pretty periwinkle-blue tablecloth. As he uncorked the bottle with a satisfying 'pop', Esther took a soft, warm baguette from the fare. It was filled with crisp green salad and a creamy Camembert.

As they talked, she was conflicted, wondering if there was any way she could keep the picture. Was this what her grandmother had meant when she concealed it in the wall? That she wanted it to be preserved? Hoping to help with her decision, she asked Édouard to tell her more about what he had learned about the picture.

As he began to talk about his research, he became alive, and she could see he truly enjoyed his work.

'During World War Two, the Germans looted thousands of pictures from Europe and relocated them to Germany for their own collections.' Esther was shocked as he continued. 'The original picture we believe was painted by your grandfather, who, as you know, was Jewish. Though we are not sure of its whereabouts during most of the occupation, at some point, it must have turned up at the Jeu de Paume, a holding gallery for much of the stolen art. We know this because the Nazis kept meticulous records and this painting was placed on a train leaving Paris the year before the end of the war. We believe, though it was never clear, that the train was attacked by Resistance fighters and the original burned in a fire with many others.'

'How can you be sure it didn't escape the fire?' she asked.

'Because there were photographs taken not long after the event that documented the carriage that was destroyed. According to the German records, this piece of artwork was in there. I have a photo here I printed off earlier for you.' He handed her a black and white photo of a train carriage on fire. Off to the side was an image of four people hurrying from the scene. A man, and two women and a child – all of the people had their backs to the camera. Except one. The little girl being carried in the arms of a blonde woman looked back over her shoulder with terrified eyes.

'So, you can see why this piece of art is not only special to your family, but to the art world in general.'

Esther agreed, but felt like she needed to find out more about this family she had never known. Suddenly she felt angry at her mother for not sharing more about her parents. What had been so terrible that it had shut her mother down so completely? As they continued to eat and enjoy the view, she knew one thing: she needed to know the truth of what had happened, who painted this picture, and what really happened to her grandparents before she could decide.

15

PARIS, AUGUST 1940

Brigitte

When Brigitte received the call from her mother, Odette, a rush of intense grief slammed into her, taking her breath away and her feet from under her as she collapsed onto a chair. The memories of that terrible day in the park a month before were as real and vivid as always. She held her breath as she listened to her mother's distraught voice, every moment from the heinous day Samuel had been killed by the Gestapo as fresh in her mind as if it were only yesterday.

She closed her eyes, catapulting back to when Sophie had clutched desperately at her as they walked home. The utter devastation Brigitte had felt that had racked her body, only to return to the emptiness of a house that would never again hold his presence.

She remembered as though she was watching a dream that after the Gestapo had left, people Brigitte didn't even know had stepped out of the shadows to provide comfort and help, organizing the removal of Samuel's body and gathering her belongings so they could leave. But for Brigitte, this had only been the

start of her nightmare; she was to live through moments when
she would reach for his comfort a hundred times a day only to
remember what had happened and feel the pain crack her open
repeatedly.

Now as she listened to her mother's desperate cries, there
was more devastation to deal with. Hanging up the phone, she
made her way across Paris. The pain was so acute in her body
that it hurt her to move. The only thing that kept her going now
was Sophie and the knowledge that Samuel's courage and love
had become a guiding light in her life, and the memory of his
sacrifice lived on in her heart, fuelling her own fight for justice
and liberation.

When she arrived, Brigitte stood in disbelief, surveying the
wreckage of her mother's tiny gallery in Montmartre. Everywhere pictures were smashed or missing. Paintings that had
been carefully curated and hung with loving hands were now
strewn across the floor. Shattered frames lay like jigsaw pieces
among the broken glass. Brigitte felt a tight knot in her stomach,
her throat constricting as tears began to form in her eyes. She
looked around the gallery, trying to make sense of what had
happened. Who had done this? And why? She thought back to
the last time she had been here and all the dreams Odette had
had for the gallery – the potential, the promise of a bright
future, the way it had been her safe haven and refuge from the
chaos of the outside world. Now, those dreams lay broken and
battered.

Brigitte took a deep breath and quickly wiped away the
tears that were ever present since Samuel had been shot dead
the month before. Now was not the time for sorrow. She had to
find out who had done this. She raced upstairs to find her
mother.

'Maman!' she shouted, hurrying through the shop, glass
crunching underneath her shoes as she made her way through
the remnants of what had been a building filled with art and

life, that now was nothing but ruins. Someone must have robbed them.

She flew up the stairs towards the gallery apartment. She could hear sobbing. As she reached the top of the stairs, she heard Odette's sobs growing louder. Without even knocking, she flung open the door. Her mother was sitting at the kitchen table, surrounded by shards of shattered china and glass. Brigitte ran to her side and hugged her tightly.

'What happened?' she asked.

Odette just shook her head, apparently unable to speak, and Brigitte quickly went to get her some water. Placing a filled glass in her mother's shaking hand, she helped her gently lift it to her lips.

Through her sobs, her mother spluttered over and over again, 'My life is ruined, ruined.'

'Who did this?' Brigitte asked, but deep down, she already knew.

'Nazis,' Odette confirmed. 'They came early this morning and didn't even wait for me to open the door. They smashed it down, taking everything and breaking everything that was left.'

Brigitte felt heartsick. Her father had once been one of the most celebrated artists of the Parisian art scene. She still remembered their glittering receptions before he died.

But now, with the Nazis in power, and the fact they were Jewish everything had changed. Brigitte clenched her fists, feeling anger boil inside of her.

Suddenly she remembered her beloved husband's painting that had been displayed downstairs. In all the shock, she hadn't given it any thought until now.

'Samuel's painting?' she asked hesitantly, a sob catching in her throat.

Odette met her gaze, a sorrowful expression in her eyes. She was aware of how significant that painting was to her daughter. She slowly shook her head.

'It's gone, darling,' she whispered, also choked with emotion. 'I'm so sorry.'

The realization of her mother's words hit Brigitte like a tidal wave. Her chest tightened as a sharp pain spread throughout her body that made her feel as if she had been ripped apart, and she collapsed into the chair next to her mother. It was one of the last pieces of tangible evidence of her husband that she had left, the one piece of art that had captured his spirit so beautifully. The picture he was most proud of, with its memory of their love. She tried to hold back the tears, but they flowed uncontrollably down her face. If only she'd kept it at home, safe. She had only lent it to the gallery for a short time for an art showing her mother had been hosting.

Her mother attempted to comfort her as she wept. 'I'm so sorry, Brigitte. I'm so, so sorry.'

Brigitte shook her head. She took a deep breath and tried to compose herself, wiping away the tears with her sleeve. She couldn't let the painting go that easily. She stood up, determination in her eyes, and turned to her mother.

'I have to find it,' she said firmly. 'I won't let them take everything from us. I won't let them take him from me, again.'

Odette nodded, understanding the pain that Brigitte was going through. 'But how will you find it?' she asked.

'I'm not sure, but I will.'

Brigitte put on the kettle for tea as she tried to come to terms with so much loss. Her gaze moved from the worn sofa to the crooked bookshelves before restlessly stopping on the clock above the mantelpiece. It was ticking away minutes, seconds – how long until her picture could be found and returned to her? She knew she had to act fast but she had no idea where to start, and she couldn't sit around and do nothing. She was glad her father had died the year before and wasn't here to see the destruction of his precious gallery.

She stayed and helped with the aftermath as much as she

could, and packing a bag for her mother, persuaded her to come and live with her and Sophie.

Brigitte was determined to find the picture no matter what it took. First, she went to see an old friend.

Brigitte arrived at Philippe's gallery, a haven of artistic expression nestled in a narrow street of Paris. The quaint façade exuded a timeless charm, its weathered bricks bearing the marks of history. She gently pushed open the ornate wooden door, its hinges creaking in protest, and stepped into the cool, dimly lit space. Sunlight streamed through tall windows, casting a soft glow on the gallery's interior. The air was tinged with the scent of aged canvases and linseed oil, a scent that had always brought her comfort. Rows of paintings lined the walls, their vibrant colours and intricate brushstrokes capturing emotions and stories that danced across the canvases.

Brigitte's eyes settled on Philippe, the proprietor of this sanctuary of art, behind the counter. Her heart weighed heavy with the burden of her recent loss as she approached him. She longed for solace and understanding in this troubled time, and Philippe, who was another Jewish gallery owner, brought her comfort.

'Philippe,' Brigitte began, her voice tinged with vulnerability. 'I'm in desperate need of your help. Our gallery was ransacked by the Nazis, and my husband's painting, *The Hayfields of Summer*, that has immense sentimental value for me, has been stolen.'

Philippe's expression mirrored her concern as he straightened himself, the gallery's warm ambiance contrasting with the gravity of their conversation. She felt a sense of kinship with him, their shared understanding of the tumultuous times they were living in.

'I'm so sorry about Samuel's death, and so sad to hear about his picture, Brigitte; it is a beautiful piece,' Philippe said, his voice gentle yet resolute. 'The Nazis seek to eradicate everything that represents us. Our art, our history, our very existence is all at stake. It's a dark time for us, indeed.'

'Do have you any idea where it would have been taken?' she asked hopefully.

He shook his head. 'I don't, but I will ask around and if it comes up for sale in any of the other galleries, I will be sure to let you know.'

She contacted other old friends in the art world, hoping that someone might know something. Days turned into weeks, and she was no closer to finding the painting. She had hit a dead end, and she was feeling discouraged and ready to give up hope when she received a mysterious letter in the post. The sender was unknown, but the contents of the letter were intriguing enough to make her pursue it. It requested that she meet someone at a café in town on a certain day and time with some money if she wanted answers about the painting's whereabouts.

She arrived at the café on the appointed day. It was a dismal place, with tired brown tables and stains on the patterned carpet. The smell of stale tobacco and spirits seemed to linger in the air, clinging to the faded furnishings. She moved slowly inside, allowing her eyes to adapt to the darkness, anxiety coursing through her veins.

As she surveyed the smoky room, her gaze fell upon a red-faced man with an ample girth seated alone at a corner table. He gave her a small nod of recognition and motioned for her to come and sit with him.

Brigitte sat down across from him tentatively. He began speaking in a hushed tone, his voice rough, yet authoritative.

'I know where your painting is,' he said gruffly.

He waited, and, understanding, she slid an envelope of the money he had asked for across the table. He peered inside, nodded and tucked it into a pocket.

'It's being stolen along with other works of art to be taken out of France by the Nazis. I have friends who have trucks that have been commandeered to do this work for the enemy.'

He continued speaking, telling Brigitte that all of the artwork was being taken to the Louvre before it was shipped off to Germany or sold elsewhere.

'What can I do?' she asked with a heavy heart, knowing that, as a Jewish person, all sorts of restrictions had been put in place already.

'If I were you,' he said, 'I would get a job at the Louvre. They need people now to sort through that artwork.'

She thanked him before slowly walking home. Yes, she was Jewish, but maybe there was something she could do about that. As she walked, a plan started to form in her mind.

16

Isabelle

The early August sun blazed in through the windows of Isabelle's office, turning it into a sauna as she sat hunched over a pathetic fan, trying to document an art inventory in her perspiration-drenched blouse. Commander Bruno Lohse barged into her office without a knock, his tie askew and his forehead glistening with sweat.

'I have new orders for you,' he stated, brusquely.

'Orders? How interesting,' Isabelle responded coldly, not looking up from her books. 'I didn't realize I had joined the army.'

He bristled at her response.

Her new assistant, Marina, sashayed over from her desk and offered a seductive smile. She had only been working at the Louvre with Isabelle for a week but was already showing signs of being very friendly towards the invading army, which sickened Isabelle.

'Anything I can do to help?' she drawled, drawing closer to him as she perched herself on the edge of Isabelle's desk and gracefully crossed one long leg over the other, allowing her dress to ride up slightly to reveal smooth, sun-kissed legs.

Lohse continued, his eyes lingering lustfully on Marina's calves. 'Fräulein Valette, you need to come with me,' he ordered, then added to Marina in a softer tone, 'And you can come too.'

Isabelle's assistant beamed before jumping down from the desk as Isabelle blew out exasperated air and, placing a mark in her ledger, swept a hand across her glistening neck.

Lohse strode through the Louvre as the two young women followed him at a clip through the majestic halls of the former palace. A chill ran down Isabelle's spine as she noticed the changes that had taken place since the German occupation the month before. In place of the classical works of art hung on every wall were now grey banners with red swastikas, symbolizing Nazi authority. Security guards stood vigilantly at all entrances and exits, ensuring that everyone followed the strict regulations in place. Even the air seemed heavy with dread and anticipation for whatever purpose this elegant building was to be used for.

Isabelle was surprised when instead of veering off into one of the other galleries, Lohse headed for the main exit. Outside, the blazing sunshine blinded her, and she could feel the heat of the pavement even beneath her high heels.

'Oh, I love an adventure,' Marina burbled and Isabelle rolled her eyes.

Lohse pushed open a heavy wrought-iron gate to the Tuileries Garden that led down past a curving path edged with vibrant flowers and bordered by towering sycamores. The trees lining the sprawling parks looked listless in the heat, their fronds drooping like wilting flowers, and not even a whisper of a breeze stirred to give them all some relief as they walked the distance. Along the way, flowerbeds were in full bloom, and people lingered on benches to read or sat on worn stone steps to escape the sun's hammering intensity. Isabelle smiled to herself as she pictured the ancient statues hidden beneath the soil of these gardens that, as of yet, had not been discovered by the Nazi invaders who believed they were entitled to everything they saw. Otherwise she had no doubt they would have no misgivings in digging up these pieces of history to present to their beloved Führer.

'Is it much farther?' Marina whined, sounding like a petulant child.

'Not far,' Lohse responded.

As they passed the beautiful circular pond situated in the centre of the gardens, Isabelle's attention was drawn towards a young boy sailing a small boat and splashing his mother with glee. Isabelle felt an intense desire for a moment of respite from this oppressive weather herself – and wished she could splash cold water on her skin to bring her some relief.

They finally arrived at their destination, the Jeu de Paume Museum. Lohse unlocked the door and gestured for Marina to enter first. This private gallery, located at the north corner of the gardens, had been owned by the Louvre since 1922. It usually showcased international avant-garde art pieces, and it had already been stripped of many of its works before the war. As they stepped inside, their echoes reverberated down the long rectangular building that had once contained one of the first indoor tennis courts in Paris. The air was musty, like the inside of a library, but the shade was a pleasant relief from the heat outside.

As her eyes adjusted to the darkness, Isabelle noticed it was practically empty, a hollow ache settling into her bones. The crisp scent of wood polish and dust greeted her, along with a familiar pang of nostalgia for happier days. She remembered coming here as a child, hand in hand with her mother, gazing in wide-eyed wonder at the Impressionist masterpieces. And then a few years ago working here herself, curating exhibitions.

She feared that now the halls would echo with the stomp of Nazi boots and the barked orders of German officers and where once beauty and light had reigned, there would be now only darkness.

'In addition to your duties at the Louvre, you'll also be working here,' Lohse informed them.

Marina aimed a flirtatious smile in his direction. 'Will you be joining us?' Now out of the heat, her tone had returned to its original seductive tenor.

'I will,' he said quietly, his eyes drawn to Marina's full, red-painted lips.

Isabelle felt a wave of nausea as she watched them. 'And what exactly will we be doing here?' she enquired, staring around the main hall, trying to hide her exasperation. She loved working alongside Jaujard in the beautiful Louvre Museum and couldn't imagine what use they could be to a practically empty building.

He stiffened as he turned and met her gaze. 'What you have always done, take care and catalogue art.'

She glanced around the empty room sceptically.

'What art?'

He sighed impatiently before continuing, 'It will arrive soon,' seemingly annoyed at her lack of respect. 'You should prepare and equip your offices for whatever you will need.'

'And what should we do with this art?' she persisted.

'It will all become clear,' he answered tersely.

Moving away to put on the lights in the office, he left them alone in the main room.

Two days later, Isabelle was in the middle of scrubbing an old filing cabinet and sifting through a pile of dusty paperwork with her sleeves rolled up to the elbow at the Jeu de Paume when she heard the deep grumble of a van engine coming to a stop outside. Stepping out onto the loading dock, she saw Lohse getting out of the passenger side, clipboard in hand.

He barked orders at his men, their arms straining with the weight of large crates as they carried each one into the museum. As she got a glimpse of what brimmed inside, Isabelle's eyes widened at the sight of stunning oil paintings of sweeping vistas, intricate bronze sculptures, and glistening objets d'art glimmering in the dim light.

Isabelle noticed him avoid eye contact as she asked him suspiciously, 'Where did these come from?' Her mind raced with questions – even in wartime she knew a collector would be reluctant to part with such treasures – but before she could ask anything more, Marina sauntered into the room and flashed him a winning smile, saying, 'Hello, I have missed you. I'm glad you're back.'

He nodded at her, his eyes lingering over the curves of her body that were accentuated by the tight periwinkle-blue dress she wore with the sweetheart neckline that matched the colour of her eyes perfectly.

Ignoring Isabelle completely, he continued talking to Marina. 'I finally have some work for you. These items will be shown to potential buyers – some friends of mine and important people in the Reich who are interested in building their personal collections.'

As he spoke, one of the soldiers had just taken out a vibrant piece of modern art and was about to place it with the others lined up along one wall when Lohse stopped him.

'No modern art pieces. The Führer has been adamant in his disapproval of such work. Take it away and destroy it.'

Isabelle gasped and reached forward to grab the gorgeous picture with its spectacular mix of reds and yellows.

'Surely you can't mean it!'

'Let go.' His tone was low, yet firm.

'No,' she responded tersely. 'You can't destroy an artist's work.'

Lohse sighed heavily and crossed his arms over his chest. 'I do mean it, Fräulein Valette. This type of work is despised by Herr Hitler; he only approves of the classics that encourage family values and beauty.'

Isabelle tugged at the painting, refusing to comply as the bewildered soldier looked at Lohse for help.

'Let go, Fräulein Valette,' Lohse continued gravely. 'I do value your expertise, but if you make things difficult for me, I don't have any qualms about letting you go and having Fräulein Belleveau care for the private collections.'

Her assistant looked ecstatic at the prospect.

Isabelle held on to the painting, refusing to comply. And a cold chill ran through her as she inspected it, taking in the intricacy of each brushstroke and observing the rich colours that blended together. Her eyes widened when she noticed the distinctive signature at the bottom right corner; it belonged to a renowned Jewish artist whose work had been reported stolen. This painting wasn't just art, but a piece of history – a traumatizing reminder of the depravity of Nazi Germany.

Isabelle's hands trembled as she asked Lohse where the particular painting had come from. He peered at her unmoved.

Tears welled up in Isabelle's eyes as she realized how much pain and suffering this painting represented. She felt sickened by the thought of Nazis commandeering homes and taking away all the things inside, including these works of art that weren't theirs to take. With an overwhelming sense of sorrow, she released her grip on the picture and confronted her newfound mission: to restore justice and protect these pieces for history, because she had a feeling this was only the beginning.

17

Brigitte

Brigitte's stomach tightened as she hurried down the winding cobblestone street, feeling the chill in the air and the sense of dread with every step. Her destination was an address that she had memorized, deep in the heart of old Paris. The city's morning air swirled around her as she moved at a clip, and the old Parisian buildings seemed to loom down upon her, questioning her motives. When she stopped at Frank Renaud's dilapidated house, it had an eerie stillness about it, as if it were waiting for her arrival.

A retired butcher with heavy jowls and a grey complexion, Frank had been coordinating covert Resistance work even before the war had begun. She knew this because his wife, Cynthia, and her mother were such good friends and they trusted them. Mrs Renaud had even approached Brigitte's mother in the greengrocer's right when war broke out, her voice low and frantic. She had pleaded with her to get new papers, as Frank could help make it happen. But Odette was paralysed by fear, scared of the repercussions if she should be caught living a lie.

Brigitte, on the other hand, refused to give in to intimidation or hide in dark corners. And now she had no choice.

Making a determined decision, she pushed through the old wooden gate, and the hinges groaned their displeasure at being disturbed. Stealthily, she glanced behind her, feeling a sense of anticipation about what she was doing. Gripping the rusting door knocker with trembling fingers, she hesitated for only a moment before taking a deep breath and knocking.

Frank's wife, Cynthia, opened the door with its peeling green paint, her hands still wet from washing dishes as she wiped them on an old tea towel.

She welcomed Brigitte in as she stepped nervously through the door.

'Brigitte, what a pleasant surprise. It's been so long since I last saw you or your mother!'

Brigitte nodded, her heart thumping, her mouth dry as Mrs Renaud chattered away in an endless stream of conversation.

'Did you want a cup of tea? Tell me about Odette. I heard about the gallery being raided. So terrible. How is she doing? And little Sophie, is she well?'

Brigitte's mind was swimming with all that had happened with her family, and she didn't know where to start. Instead she changed the subject.

'Is your husband at home?' she finally enquired.

Taken aback by the intense way Brigitte asked, the woman arched her eyebrows with understanding. 'Yes, Frank is here. So, you and your mother have both reconsidered taking new identities?'

'No, she still does not want to take the risk. But I do. I have Sophie to think about and other things I need to do that I can't do because of who I am.'

'Yes, it's a tragedy for the Jewish community,' the woman

commiserated with her. 'I'm sorry you're going through this, Brigitte, but Frank will help you, don't worry.'

She ushered Brigitte into a sunlit living room where the furniture was low and unassuming, with small cushions in neutral shades to match the warm-coloured walls and shelves stacked two-deep with books that lined wooden bookcases. Pots of various sizes were scattered throughout the room, filled with plants and each placed so it could receive light from one of the open windows. Pressed between pots on a window sill curled Monsieur Pepe, a contented tabby, his nose twitching and its paws opening and closing as it dreamt of chasing birds.

At one end of the room, Frank was hunched over a small mahogany table. The warm yellow light from the reading lamp illuminated his weathered face as he carefully studied colourful stamps from around the world with a magnifying glass and tweezers. Brigitte was struck by the sight of him. He looked so unassuming, like someone's grandfather. Not a member of a French Resistance cell. But she guessed this was why he had not been caught. Because who would suspect this elderly stamp collector with a wife who loved plants of espionage?

'Brigitte needs your help,' his wife informed him.

Frank dropped the magnifying glass from his intense scrutiny, lifted his gaze to meet hers, and smiled warmly.

'Your mother has changed her mind?' he asked hopefully.

'No, no, she hasn't,' Brigitte replied sadly, 'but I have. Can you help *me*?'

He gestured for her to sit down beside him, pushing a pile of stamp books aside, as his wife diplomatically stepped away to make them tea while they talked.

'I can, my dear girl,' he reassured her in a calm voice. 'I have many contacts. Tell me what you want from me.'

She took a deep breath and paused for a moment before continuing slowly. 'I need a new identity. Could you do that for me?'

He nodded thoughtfully. 'I can do that. It will take a couple of weeks.'

'All right, and I can pay you as well. Anything you need.'

He waved his hand dismissively. 'No payment between us is necessary. We've known each other far too long. Odette was very good to Cynthia when she was struggling with all that sadness following the death of her mother. I will never forget her kindness.'

She handed him the required documents, and he carefully tucked them away in a secret drawer before patting her hand comfortingly.

'Leave it with me. It'll all be ready and waiting for you in two weeks' time. Now we should have tea,' he said nonchalantly.

As his wife arrived back with a laden tea tray, the warm, fattened tabby weaved around her legs for a treat.

Brigitte couldn't believe the relaxed way Frank was approaching all this. She felt incredibly relieved by his words, but also fearful – her life would be at risk every day once she changed her identity. Taking a deep breath, she reminded herself of why she was going through with this – she wanted to provide a better life for Sophie and help keep her husband's legacy alive. There was no turning back now. She had something to do, and she would not stop until it was done.

18

Esther

A week after she arrived back from Paris and after dropping the kids at school, Esther drove to the cream brick building that housed Sunlight Homes, where her mother had been living for a while due to her Alzheimer's.

Esther nodded at the woman who was always behind the reception desk – an older lady with an unmistakable air of vibrancy. One of those spunky seniors who never seemed to run out of energy, with clothes that reflected the 1970s. Behind her on the wall, a placard announced the day's activities. Like a holiday camp for seniors, residents could fill their time with exciting upcoming events such as chair yoga and origami for beginners.

The receptionist welcomed Esther with a smile, and her wrinkles betrayed her real age, as did the huskiness of her elderly voice. 'Esther, I hoped you'd be here today. Your mother is in a good place. She'll be overjoyed to see you. I even managed to get her to work on a jigsaw puzzle this morning.'

Feelings of relief flooded Esther. As much as she wanted to

be here for her mother, hard days were challenging when Sophie didn't remember who she was and looked at her with fearful eyes, asking her repeatedly if they knew each other. But if her mother was doing a puzzle, it might indicate some coherence.

She squeaked down the waxed grey hallway towards the room she knew so well. By this time, her mother would have been put in the day room with the other residents. Inside, it was light and airy and smelled faintly of lavender air freshener. In one corner, one of the elderly residents played a classical tune on the piano, his gnarled fingers gently gliding over the keys, while lined up around the room, hunched in beige leather chairs, residents sat listening. One woman knitted colourful wool mittens while another watched something on TV without sound. Her mother sat alone in one corner, staring out of the window, with an unfinished jigsaw puzzle laid out in front of her, a confetti of pieces scattered around her tiny table.

Esther crossed the room, her heart quickening. She still loved to see her mother, even though she had deteriorated so much. The older woman looked up upon seeing Esther and immediately recognized who she was. Thank God this would be one of the easier visits.

'Maman,' she greeted her mother cheerfully in French. She kissed her on both cheeks as she always did before sitting down across from her at her little table.

'Esther!' Sophie exclaimed, lifting a wrinkled hand to her cheek. 'What a pleasant surprise. Have you looked around here? I'm quite enjoying my stay. Everyone is so friendly.'

Her mother talked as if she was on holiday, not a full-time resident. At least she was in a good mood. Esther sat down next to her and told her about her day. In her bag, the photograph Édouard had given her burnt a hole in the lining. Would her mother be up to talking about it? Maybe it was wrong to do this when her mother was in such a good mood. Then Sophie said something surprising.

'When I was a little girl, I used to love to collect pinecones at this time of year,' she said, looking out of the window at an array of them scattered under a tree.

Her mother rarely talked of her childhood, and Esther wondered if this was a sign to ask her about the painting.

She drew in a deep breath. 'Maman, I just got back from a trip.'

'A trip?' her mother echoed with unusual interest.

'I have just been to Paris.'

Her mother's face fell a little, as though she remembered that place meant something to her, but wasn't sure what.

'Oh yes,' she said noncommittally. 'You went to Paris.'

She hadn't seen her mother this alert for so long. It might be the only chance she would get for a long time. But she was a little hesitant. Esther knew that asking questions about her mother's childhood could bring pain and confusion to her already fragile state. She paused, staring down at the children's jigsaw puzzle her mother had half-finished: a litter of golden retriever puppies in a basket. Then she decided to pursue it. She didn't want to make her mother feel distressed, but how long would her mother have the ability to talk to her and help with this mystery?

'I got a call from a Monsieur Dupont,' she continued slowly.

Her mother shook her head, not understanding.

'He is an art dealer. He found a painting in a wall of a building. Do you know anything about it?'

A shadow passed over her mother's face, as though past memories were crowding around her so tightly that she could hardly breathe. She closed her eyes briefly and then opened them wide and stared at the ceiling while taking a deep breath. A blue vein pulsed in her throat, her heart beating rapidly under the translucent skin. The room felt suddenly warm and

Esther hesitated, regretting bringing it up, when something in her mother's gaze shifted.

'A painting?' she asked in a soft voice, studying her daughter intently. 'My mother's painting?' she asked.

Esther's heart started to pound in her chest. 'I have a photograph of it here. Would you recognize it? If you saw it?'

'Of course,' she replied, though her voice faltered slightly with apprehension.

With a trembling hand, Esther pulled out the photo she had taken when she'd been in the apartment. Her mother took the image in her hand and studied it for a moment, tracing the picture with her finger, taking in the details of the painting that had been hidden in the wall of their old home – the beauty of the idyllic landscape of fields and children playing.

A wistful smile graced her mother's lips as she remembered. 'This was a copy of my father's painting,' she said in a barely audible whisper. 'My mother painted it to honour him. I remember, it was a secret between her and me. No one was to know about it.'

'Do you know how it got into the wall?' Esther asked gently, the excitement building at the thought of unravelling the mystery.

Sophie closed her eyes, overwhelmed by all the questions, and started to mutter to herself. 'So beautiful. My mother was such a beautiful woman.'

Oh no, Esther was losing her.

'Tell me more about the painting, Maman,' she coaxed her gently.

Sophie sighed deeply. 'The Germans destroyed it along with a lot of other art,' she replied, her voice filled with sadness.

'No, someone found it.'

'Found it?' Her mother's brow creased with confusion.

Not wanting to journey down this painful path of explanation with her mother any further than necessary, she decided not to elaborate.

'There's one more photograph, Maman. Do you think you would be up to looking at it?'

'Of course,' she answered, unaware of the gravity of the topic.

Esther knew it could be hard, but she had to try to at least find out more. She handed her the photograph of the young girl and the people hurrying from the train.

Sophie gasped, a fluttering hand moving to her chest. She suddenly spluttered out words in rapid French so fast Esther couldn't translate.

'In English, Maman, you have to speak in English,' Esther said softly. 'Do you know the photograph? Does it mean anything to you?'

'Where did you get this?' Sophie asked with that look on her face, the one Esther had seen before when she had talked about Paris, the one of terror.

Esther continued gently. 'I found it when I was doing some research about the painting that went missing. And this came up, and I couldn't help but notice the likeness of the little girl to my son Daniel, and I wondered...'

Her mother shook her head and closed her eyes.

'Is this you, Maman?' Esther gently coaxed. 'Is this you? In this photo?'

Sophie's face softened for just a moment, before fear seemed to take over as her brow knitted together and she stared down at the photo with tear-filled eyes. Her lip quivered slightly as she muttered something in French again. A single tear snaked down the elderly, creped cheek, and Esther felt she had gone too far. She would have to leave it for now. But before she could change the subject, Sophie spoke again in a whisper.

'That is me, and that is my grandmother.'

She paused to take a shaky breath before continuing.

'They put us on a train for our safety. But it is all my fault. My mother's death was all my fault.'

Esther was speechless at her mother's confession. Surely this couldn't be the case. Nazis killed her grandmother? Sophie was confused.

Sophie closed her eyes again and seemed to be quiet for so long. Esther thought she'd fallen asleep. But then her eyes sprang open with what seemed to be a desperate recollection.

'You have to find the children on the train. I know they will be able to help you.'

Then all of a sudden, it was like a veil descended, and the moment of clarity was gone. Her mother's gaze shifted to the window and became vacant. When she turned back to Esther, she enquired if she had been there long.

'Not long,' Esther responded, sadly, understanding there would be no more questions answered. She put the photographs back in her bag, took her mother's hand, and squeezed it.

'Would you like to help me with this jigsaw?' her mother asked as she caressed the large shiny pieces. 'I think I started it earlier. You could help.'

Esther wiped away a tear running down her cheek, then nodded. She moved closer to her mother, gathering pieces of the jigsaw while trying to remember every detail of their conversation – hoping that maybe somewhere within it was an answer to her questions. Her mother held her hand in hers lovingly, and together they worked on the picture. She had a little more of the story, but now there were more questions about children, children on a train. What did it all mean?

19

NOVEMBER 1940

Isabelle

Oberführer von Behr did not look impressed as he surveyed Isabelle's new cramped office at the Jeu de Paume. The air was still thick with a concoction of oil paints and varnish resulting from a spill that had happened before Isabelle's arrival, mingled with the dust that danced across creaky floors. One of the panes in the window was cracked, and rickety shelves were still overflowing with forgotten art books and catalogues, while piles of broken frames cluttered one of the corners.

Isabelle listened with a sense of dread as the heavyset, balding man in the Nazi uniform informed her of her duties and the protocol for dealing with dignitaries for the upcoming gallery showing.

'Do you understand the importance of this, Fräulein?' he demanded.

Soberly, she confirmed she'd heard him. Although, to be fair, she hadn't listened to much of what he'd said. She was still reeling from what all this meant. As she'd feared, they were going to strip them of their heritage. And worst of all, she would be helping them.

'Will you be ready in time?' he demanded, looking once again with disgust at the dishevelled room around him.

Lohse, who had accompanied the commander, interjected. 'We will be ready.'

Von Behr swivelled to address him. 'It is very important. Field Marshal Göring and his staff will be here to see what they want first. They will be arriving next week. And we want everything perfect for his viewing.'

He then proceeded to stride out of her office, demanding that she follow him. Isabelle felt a chill as she watched the commander inspect the gorgeous artwork that had just arrived at the museum. As he chose one painting after another for the showing, cold determination hardened inside her. Despair threatened to overwhelm her. She had no idea how to stop this; for now there was nothing else she could do but obediently follow him and hope against hope that something would change before it was too late.

As he left, she noted crates of new acquisitions had arrived and were now piled haphazardly, waiting to be unpacked and recorded. Isabelle approached the nearest crate and pried off the lid with trembling fingers. The first was a picture she knew. An 1890 pastel by Edgar Degas, *Portrait of Mlle. Gabrielle Diot*, gazed up at her. Tears pricked her eyes as she thought of the Jewish family it had been stolen from.

The day prior to Herr Göring's visit was a frenzied affair, as von Behr continued pushing for the Jeu de Paume museum to be cleaned and adorned in preparation for their esteemed guest. Isabelle hung pieces of art from wires on the picture rail, silently aware that each piece represented an individual life affected by Nazi persecution. In stark contrast, Marina seemed untouched by this reality; instead she flirted with Lohse while they made last-minute decisions on where best to place objets d'art.

There was a great deal of fanfare as the Nazis' honoured guest arrived the next morning. Extra soldiers buzzed about the gallery, their uniforms extra-pressed and buttons gleaming. Isabelle had been commanded, along with her staff, to meet the dignitaries at the front door. There was a chill in the air as she waited, and she shivered with the icy breeze that swept around the building stiffening the tiny hairs on her arm and with the fearful anticipation of meeting someone so well known within the Reich. Beside her, Marina indulged in flirtatious conversation with Lohse. As Isabelle watched her, she wondered if this girl realized just how dangerous it was to befriend their enemy in the way she was doing.

Isabelle was snapped from her deliberations by the deafening sound of a prowl of motorbikes flying Nazi flags roaring around the corner flanking a sleek, armoured, black Mercedes. But when Field Marshal Hermann Göring emerged from it with an air of superiority and was introduced to the Jeu de Paume staff, his odd stature surprised her, and she found it hard not to stare at his bulbous double chin that bobbed gracelessly as he surveyed her with scornful eyes. Oberführer von Behr explained that Isabelle had been tasked with documenting every request made by the field marshal, a fact which didn't seem to interest the loathsome man at all.

Following him and his entourage into the main gallery, Isabelle's heart pounded as she watched helplessly while this detestable figure greedily devoured each piece of art with his hungering gaze, and an uneasiness built within her, knowing he would soon take many of these precious works back to Germany.

After the field marshal had left, she sat looking at the order book in front of her, realizing for the first time that this would be ongoing. So many Germans would be coming through and taking their pick of the art. And she would be the person who was handing these Parisian treasures to each of them.

The next time Isabelle looked up from her desk, she was surprised to see her mother framed in the doorway. Her red hair was illuminated by the sun behind her, and she had a bemused look on her face.

'Isabelle, darling,' she said, coming forward and kissing her on both cheeks with the sweet scent of the perfume she always wore. Perfume and fresh air and flowers, that's how she thought of her mother. 'I had so much trouble finding you, I went to the Louvre and spoke to somebody over there, and they said they had you working down here in this little place.' She looked around at Isabelle's office, which looked tidier yet was still quite shabby. 'Did you get a demotion?' she said, quirking an eyebrow. 'Or did you upset a Nazi?'

Isabelle shook her head, pulled her mother into the office, and closed the door behind her. 'There's a lot I have to tell you, Maman.'

'Then I have come to take you to lunch. Though I nearly didn't get the chance. I had trouble getting in here. Thank goodness one of the secretaries came with me, as she needed to drop off something. There are guards everywhere. What on earth can be happening here that warrants so much security?'

'At lunch,' Isabelle continued in a hushed tone. 'I'll tell you everything.'

She picked up her bag and couldn't help but admit she was glad to see her mother. It would give her a break from this place. She walked through the hall, still set up for the showing, moving quickly with her mother by her side.

Fifteen minutes later, they were seated in their favourite café in Paris on the corner of the street. Beautiful pink awnings, a green façade, and flowers on every table brought back some joy to Isabelle's heart and some colour to her cheeks. They sipped a glass of cold white wine and nibbled on a basket of warm rustic bread as their favourite waiter, Anton, took their order. And as they made their way through a light, crisp salad, Delphine Valette looked across at her daughter.

'Are you all right? You look tired. There are circles under your eyes.'

'We're in the midst of a war, Maman. What do you expect?'

'You work in a gallery. Surely, there cannot be a lot of pressure. I know that you love your job, but they are just pictures. It's just art.'

'How could you say that, Maman? When you know how much art means to me and used to mean to you?'

She said the last thing before she meant to, and her mother looked down. She saw that she had wounded her with her words. She leaned across the table and took hold of her hand.

'I didn't mean it like that, Maman, I'm sorry.'

'No, no, you're right,' she said, pulling her hand free and taking hold of the glass. Isabelle noticed there was a slight tremor as she lifted it to her lips. 'I still feel that way about art. I just don't feel that way about my own art.'

Isabelle desperately wanted to talk about this. She tried to find a way to say it that was diplomatic and that wouldn't hurt her mother's feelings. 'Do you think there's any chance that you will paint again?'

The look on Delphine's face said no. Her eyes clouded with the sadness that she felt.

'Too horrible, what happened, Isabelle. You carry the burns and the scars too. I know.'

Isabelle suddenly heard the familiar voice in her head. Her little brother shouting to her through the flames as she desperately tried to get in to rescue him.

'But you didn't cause the fire, Maman, an oil heater did.'

'But your brother would still be here with us if I hadn't been a painter. I think this has also affected you profoundly. It's why you feel such a connection to the paintings. You feel like you want to save all the art, don't you?'

Isabelle looked away. She knew there was truth in those words but didn't like to admit it.

'Isabelle, art doesn't belong to any of us. We hold it like a bird for a short time in our hands. We get inspiration, and we make beautiful, passionate art, then we let it fly to live its life. If you try to hold it too long, it will die. Just like the bird in your hand. When I look at you, sweetheart, I wonder if you are holding on too hard. You never seem to have relationships or friendships. You seem so driven by what you do.'

'I am committed, Maman, that is all,' she said defensively. 'Yes, I feel passionate about the art, and if I could have also saved your paintings that day, as well as my brother, I would have done so. I hate what it has done to you and what it has done to our family.'

Delphine sat back on her chair and looked away. Isabelle could see tears in the corners of her eyes. 'We all have to live day by day. The best way we can.'

'I understand.'

Their main meal arrived, and they started to eat it in unbearable silence, each alone with their own regret.

'Tell me more about your work,' her mother said finally, trying to change the subject.

Isabelle felt that stone in her stomach as she thought about what she did now. She tried carefully explaining to her mother what was happening.

'Where is the art coming from?' her mother asked.

'I believe the Germans are ransacking Jewish homes. Some of the paintings I know are definitely those of Jewish artists, and from what I've been able to find out, I recognize many of the signatures. Many are from collections of Jewish and Masonic families that have left the city. So much art has been taken, and those who remained in Paris are forced to give up their work.

And then the art is going to be transported to Germany for Hitler and other Nazis.'

Delphine shook her head. 'There is so much this man has to answer for. But, Isabelle darling, promise me you will take some time for yourself. I understand your passion. I understand the pain, you know I do. But you also have to have a life. That is important, too. At least go out with friends or on a date. Try not to make it only about work.'

She squeezed her mother's hand and smiled. 'Of course, Maman,' she lied. She didn't even know how to go out on a date; she couldn't even imagine it. She wished somehow that she had more freedom in her life but felt so compelled to do what she did. Right now, this was her mission. And she would do everything she could to save the art she was in charge of. Even if it cost her her life, to her it was a worthwhile cause.

As she tucked herself back in her office after lunch, she unlocked her drawer and noticed the order book with a sinking heart. Then she suddenly had an idea. What if she was to keep her own records? What if she was to keep a record of everything, where everything had gone? And then, after this damn war was over, she could help get all the art back? Isabelle knew that the Nazi occupation wouldn't last forever, and she could take matters into her own hands.

She waited until the Nazi officers that patrolled the museum halls were at the other end of the room, then she slipped into a supply closet and chose an unobtrusive ledger smaller than the rest – one usually used for recording cash flow – in order to keep track of every stolen artwork item during this dangerous time, not just the destination, but also their place of origin, so they could return it when it was time for them all to come back. She would have to be covert. Her tracking of the art could not be discovered.

Isabelle's hands trembled as she prepared for the right opportunity to put her plan in place. When the room momentarily emptied at four o'clock, sinking into a silence only disturbed by her own pounding heart, she pulled out the small book she'd hidden in her sleeve and opened up the order book with Göring's desired acquisitions recorded inside. Looking quickly over her shoulder to make sure she was alone, she began to scribe, encoded with secret symbols unknown to anyone but herself and her sisters. She moved quickly, knowing that the staff would return soon enough, and she wouldn't trust Marina not to turn her in. She finished the list before slipping away unseen her book full of secrets into the pocket of her cream cotton dress just as Marina swaggered into the dark, empty office.

'You're here late,' Marina commented, also sounding annoyed.

'I was just finishing up a few things,' Isabelle said as she pressed the book in her pocket close to her body and hoped to God it didn't look obvious.

When she arrived home, she realized she had taken up a monumental task – she knew if this book was found, the repercussions would be severe. She would probably be sent to Germany to one of their many work camps she had heard of or, worse still, killed for her betrayal. Nevertheless, with the book open on the kitchen table before her, she steadfastly set out on an endeavour that could only result in something worthwhile: eventually returning important pieces of French culture for future generations to enjoy.

20

Brigitte

As Brigitte navigated her way through wartime Paris, she was met with a heartbreaking reminder of Nazi occupation at every turn. Swastikas hung from lampposts and adorned shop windows, military vehicles raced down the streets, and soldiers held a chilling presence, goose-stepping in long, intimidating rows in their stark grey uniforms. The hated red flag even flew from the Eiffel Tower, flapping in the wind like a warning to all who dared to oppose them.

Yet despite the dark clouds of war hanging heavy in the air, Paris seemed to be alive with energy. The cafés were still bustling, the parks were still filled with laughter, and the narrow cobblestone alleys still echoed with joyous conversations and music. Brigitte couldn't help but be impressed by the city's resilience, the way it refused to be cowed by the unwelcome invaders.

As she moved at a clip, the hem of her modest black skirt swished against her calves and her heart raced as she closed in on the museum. She braced herself for what she was about to attempt. She reminded herself that this was the only way to reclaim the most valuable thing left of her husband's legacy. All she'd ever wanted to do was be his wife and raise their daughter together. And here she was, like an undercover spy, going in to try and find the only real tangible thing she had left of him. She had his clothes and personal items, but this picture contained his heart – the essence of his very being, painted into every stroke on the canvas.

She crossed the street, straightened her skirt, and adjusted her hat, feeling the unfamiliar weight of high-heeled shoes. She was only five foot three but had thought the extra height would give her a feeling of courage. However, as she looked down at her feet, she wondered if she'd be able to stand in these shoes all day.

Finally, she arrived at the beautiful museum and, with fear and trepidation, noted the guards surrounding it. Her false identity papers were like hot coals in her pocket as she tried to look nonchalant when one stepped in front of her and asked her what business she had at the museum.

'I am starting a job here today,' she said, forcing herself to meet his icy gaze as a nervous hand fluttered to her pocket to check her false papers were still there for the hundredth time.

The tired-looking soldier held out his hand and she stared at it.

'Papers,' he responded sharply, annoyed at the fact she hadn't understood his action.

Drawing in a faltering breath, she pulled out the documents, and slowly he unfolded them. As he started reading, Brigitte couldn't look him in the eye. She was afraid her expression would betray her deceit, so she stared at the silver buttons of his uniform, counting silently in her head as she had done when she was a child. It seemed like an eternity before he finished reading, though in reality it had been only a few moments.

He thrust the papers back at her, and then, as if batting away a tiresome fly, he moved her on with an irritated wave of his hand. Her heart was beating so hard it felt as if it was pulsing out of her neck, and she prayed that he would not notice the rivulet of sweat that had snaked from under her hat down the side of her face and into her ear.

She began to move on when he called out a name sharply: 'Mrs Marceau.'

She kept walking, hoping whoever he meant would draw his attention away from her trembling legs.

He called the name again, more aggressively this time. When she turned around to see who he was talking to, she realized he was staring straight at her. It was her new name – and in all the panic she had forgotten it.

As she returned, Brigitte spluttered something about it being her first day and she was nervous.

He was uninterested in her apologies as he continued speaking. 'You'll have to get a pass at the desk if you're going to be working here every day, so we don't have to waste our time checking your documents.'

She nodded her understanding, but he merely turned away from her, straightened his back, and adjusted his rifle strap on his shoulder.

Brigitte walked into the cool, hushed rooms of the Louvre gallery and couldn't help but be in awe at its sheer majestic presence. Her heels clicked along the marble floor while she searched for the office where she had been instructed to arrive, clutching a little too tightly the papers she had been given in her trembling hand.

She rounded a corner and spotted a door tucked away from view with the same name that was on her letter. Taking a deep breath, Brigitte raised her fist and knocked on the wood-panelled door with two quick raps as she repeated her new name over and over in her mind.

Finally, the door opened to reveal a tall, striking dark-haired man in a grey suit; his face lit up with relief when he saw her.

'Ah, you must be Brigitte,' he announced, buoyantly.

She nodded as he invited her inside. The office was large, but still held on to the grandeur of its former glory. The walls were painted a creamy shade of yellow and lined with bookshelves stocked with leather-bound books. In the corner an antique globe sat beside an impressive mahogany desk.

He showed her to a chair and gestured for her to take a seat.

'We are so glad to have you. I am the museum's director, Jacques Jaujard. With this war in Europe, it has become quite challenging for us to get staff, so it's nice to have someone with your abilities available.'

He seated himself behind his desk, and she noted the window behind him was piled high with sandbags.

'Tell me more about yourself,' he asked as he reviewed her application.

Brigitte's stomach churned. What could she say that was of no consequence? She couldn't tell him anything to do with her husband.

'Well, there isn't much more than what was on my application,' she stammered. 'I have a daughter and just live here in Paris.' She knew she sounded pathetic, but she was so nervous.

He looked at her quizzically for a second and then encouraged her. 'That's good. And you have worked in an art gallery before?'

Her throat tightened as she remembered she had put that on her application, as she had spent many days working at her parents' gallery. But if she mentioned it now, he may know it and realize it was owned by a Jewish person. And honestly in this time and place, no one could be sure who might be a Nazi sympathizer.

'Yes,' she said. 'Here and there.'

'You were also an art student?'

'Yes,' she continued, feeling more relieved, 'I finished art school a few years ago.'

At least that was true, if nothing else. Her mind wandered back momentarily to her time at college, as her heart pounded. Her husband's laughing face, painting a portrait of her as an art project, her elbows propped on a stool. She wore her hair long back then, voluminous and dark, hanging in two thick braids down her back. That was the moment she knew she'd fallen in love. The pain she now lived through, had blotted out the memory and Brigitte tried not to let the sadness show on her face as she forced on a smile.

He glanced up from reading her application.

'Let me introduce you to some of our other employees and show you around. I'm sure you know already, but this museum operates under Nazi rule. Your job will mainly be at the Jeu de Paume, where you will help catalogue pieces of art coming from other collections...' His voice trailed off, and a look of revulsion crossed his face. Brigitte inhaled sharply; she knew all too well what he meant by 'other collections' – Jewish art, like her husband's painting. She sent up a silent prayer that she would see it again.

He got up and led her through the halls. At the end of the gallery, he knocked on a door and entered an office. A young woman was typing energetically at a desk inside.

'This is Isabelle Valette. She is an art historian and has worked here for several years and knows almost as much about the Parisian museums as I do. She is working between here and the Jeu de Paume. You will be helping her there.'

The young woman rose to her feet, towering above Brigitte. She had a graceful figure and golden blonde hair swept up in an immaculate chignon. Her eyes twinkled as they met Brigitte's own, and her lips spread into a wide smile when she grasped her hand. 'Welcome to our little family!' she said warmly. 'We are so lucky to have you here! I can tell you my hands have been full. It seems like there is always something that needs attending to.'

Jaujard departed with the words, 'So, I'll leave you in the competent hands of Isabelle.'

Brigitte glanced around the room, enjoying the endless pieces of artwork – sculptures, paintings, and sketches that were stacked against walls, strewn across tables, or hung up for admiration. As Isabelle briefed her about the job ahead, she couldn't help but be filled with gratitude at the opportunity to work among such beautiful creations. In all her nervousness about her plan and new identity, she had forgotten she would be in the midst of art, such beautiful art, and it would be very pleasant work until she put her ultimate plan in place and then disappeared.

21

Esther

It was about five o'clock in the evening when she got the call from the mortgage company.

'Ms Walker?' asked a gentle, yet hesitant voice on the other end of the line.

'Yes?' she answered as she gathered dried clothes into a basket and walked towards the stairs.

'It's home mortgages here. We were wondering about your latest mortgage payment. When could we expect it?'

Esther felt like she had been punched in the gut. She couldn't speak for a minute before she finally found words. 'I'm sorry, when could you expect it? What do you mean? Has it not been paid?' The cold reality of the situation slowly sank in with each word from the other end of the line.

'No, and this is the second month in a row that we haven't received a payment from you. And we are getting concerned.'

The shock of what she was hearing took her legs from under her, and she sat heavily on the bottom of the stairs, still clutching the basket. She wouldn't put anything past her ex-husband, but even so, this had caught her completely off-guard. 'I'm sorry, there must be some mistake here. My ex-husband pays the mortgage. He pays it every month. Are you saying that you didn't receive a payment last month?'

'That's correct. And, of course, we are in arrears for this month now too. And we wanted to check there was nothing we could do to help.'

Esther's stomach was clenching into an uncomfortable knot, and she was having difficulty breathing. The thought of potentially losing her home while failing to provide security for her children filled her mind and soul with terror.

This just couldn't be right. It had to be a mistake.

'Can I call you back? I need to speak to my ex-husband to see what's going on.'

'Of course. Let me give you my personal number.' The woman gave her a long number and a name and her confident assurance that when the payments were made, they could get her back on track.

As soon as she hung up, Esther noticed her hand was shaking as she dialled James's number. Her mind raced with possible solutions. Her husband had agreed right from the beginning of the divorce that he would pay the mortgage and keep a roof over his children's heads, and what she earned only just about covered everything else. The call went straight to voicemail. And it was as though his cocky, jokey message mocked her as she had a panic attack on the stairs. Taking deep breaths, she waited for the beep.

'James, this is Esther. I just got a call from the mortgage company. They said that you didn't make a payment last month and it's late again this month. Could you call me back and tell me what's going on?'

Two hours later, James finally called back, just before she was going to bed, and Esther braced herself. She'd already tried calling him back several more times and had just got the answering machine. Now she could tell he was angry, and his side of the conversation was terse and clipped.

'Esther, why do you keep calling? Is everything okay with the boys?'

'The boys are fine. I'm calling because my mortgage didn't get paid last month.'

He let out a long stream of air, and there was a long pause. She knew him so well. This wasn't good. If it had been a simple mistake or an oversight, he would have backtracked by saying he was busy or something. Not this time though. This felt calculated, almost rehearsed.

'The house is too big. It made sense when we were all living together, but now it's just not worth keeping. The housing market is doing well right now, and we could sell it for a lot of money.'

She couldn't believe what she was hearing. She closed her eyes and swallowed hard to fight back tears. Her mind raced as she tried to think clearly. 'But what about the kids' school and my job? There's nothing else in this area that's affordable.'

His voice showed no signs of sympathy or understanding; instead, it held an almost mocking tone as he continued to speak. 'That's ridiculous! Leave it with me. I'll find you another place. I can't keep paying outrageously high mortgage payments for a house I don't even live in anymore.'

'What do you mean you can't keep paying out for a mortgage? These are your children! You don't care if they have a roof over their heads?'

'Of course, it just doesn't have to be *that* roof, does it? Now look, stop bothering me. I'll look into this and get back to you in a couple of days. But I think it's time you moved out, Esther, and found somewhere else.'

He hung up. Esther was left standing there in the bedroom, looking into the mirror. She could see the pain etched on her face. She couldn't believe that he was doing this to her. How on earth had she fallen in love with this man when he was so manipulative and controlling of her and the boys?

That night, she tossed and turned in bed as her mind reeled with possible solutions to her problem. The following day, she decided to call Édouard and see how things were going with the picture.

'It's going well,' he replied while she prepared to leave for the day. 'We still need to run a few tests to determine its age and I'll let you know what we find out. I also have some other good news if you are open to it. The Louvre is having a special event over Christmas celebrating the work of what are called the lost artists of Paris. These were French artists who died during the Holocaust. And as your picture has such an amazing story, I wondered if you would be open to having it shown during that exhibition.'

'Oh,' said Esther, slightly taken back. She had forgotten the notoriety that her grandparents' story would bring. 'Of course, it would be an honour.'

There was a brief pause before she spoke again.

'About the picture...' She felt her heart sink as she prepared to ask him this question. 'I am seriously considering selling it now.'

He considered her words before answering.

'I would need to find the right buyer. But you said before you left that you wouldn't want to sell it. Did I get that correct?'

She felt conflicted. She didn't want to let go of the painting that had once belonged to her grandmother, which was her last connection with her. But she also needed to have a home for her kids to live in.

'Of course, I can start looking into potential buyers if you want,' he continued. 'Leave it with me. I take it that your circumstances have changed.'

She couldn't help it. She burst into tears. She hated it.

What was she doing to this poor man who had been so kind to her?

He listened as she sobbed, offering words of comfort. 'I'm sorry. I wish I could do more to help. Let me figure this out on my end and get back to you. I'll talk to a few people and make some enquiries.'

She nodded her head, even though he couldn't see it, and blew her nose. Tears streamed down her face as she whispered a barely audible, 'Okay,' into the phone.

Esther hated this. Why did James make her feel like this? She was a strong woman. She'd been so independent before she'd met him. But it was different now that she had children. She had to think of them, and she felt so trapped. She could go and get another job, maybe. But it was so hard. Everything about her present job worked for her and the kids. Esther finished work at three o'clock so she could pick them up at four. And her boss was good about giving her time off when one of the boys was ill.

She took in a deep breath and hung up the phone. She didn't know what she was going to do. This painting was her grandmother's work, and even though no one would remember it – not even her own mother – selling it felt wrong on so many levels.

22

CHRISTMAS 1941

Isabelle

Eighteen months after the Nazis marched into Paris, the Valettes prepared to gather on Christmas Eve for their family Christmas dinner. The atmosphere was sombre as Isabelle, Charlotte and Delphine prepared for the gathering – a far cry from the celebratory mood of years past. As she waited for her other sisters to arrive, Isabelle created decorations out of newspaper to hopefully bring some cheer. It was a meagre offering compared to the past, when she'd decorated their tree with long strands of crimson velvet satin ribbon or delicate intricate ornaments that glistened in the lights from shops there were now closed or boarded up with anti-Semitic slurs graffitied across them.

As she looped the paper strips, the smell of food cooking drifted in from the kitchen alongside the sounds of Charlotte and Delphine's conversation. From the other side of the house came the hum of her father's wireless, even though they were not permitted to have one, and he would be arrested if the Nazis found it. Bernard had been adamant he would not give it up, wanting to keep abreast of every new development. Isabelle was concerned at the effect the war was having on her gentle, mild-mannered father, who had become tight and anxious about the days ahead. As she listened to the drone of a sombre newscaster from her father's study, Isabelle's thoughts drifted between each one of her sisters. All of them so different but precious to her. The war had put a strain on all of them and the business of living through an occupation had scattered them, all consumed with the pursuit of surviving in this trying time. Madeline, who ran a bookshop in the centre of Paris, had been absent more often than usual. When asked about her mysterious travels, she brushed it off with a vague answer about buying books. But Isabelle was familiar enough with her sibling to know she was concealing something darker, heavier behind the mask she wore.

Isabelle understood this need more than anybody. She thought about the secret log book she always kept with her. If any of them knew of what she was doing, they would be worried for her, feeling she was risking her life for mere art, so she kept it her secret too. She also knew her sister was travelling to Frankfurt, which was very dangerous, although Madeline always played it down whenever she asked about it.

Meanwhile Gigi had gone from effervescent and playful to more thoughtful and reserved with each passing month. But most shocking of all was her sister Antoinette, who used to be so vibrant and full of charisma – now she appeared to be a mere shadow of her former self. She lived with the daily fear of her child being taken, as her husband had been near the beginning of the occupation. Isabelle had stopped asking about him whenever they got together now because the heartbreak in Antoinette's eyes was hard to deal with; she just had to hope that wherever René was, he would somehow come back to them alive.

As Bernard's wireless shifted from the news to a heart-stirring Christmas carol, there was a knock at the door. She pulled it open, and Gigi stood there with a huge bunch of mistletoe in her arms. Isabelle couldn't help but laugh at her youngest sister.

'Where are you planning on putting that?' she asked.

'Everywhere I can,' responded Gigi, 'with all the men away fighting the war, I will take kisses whenever I can get them.' Isabelle shook her head at her sister as she kissed her on both cheeks.

'Well, you won't find any men here,' she said, laughing. 'Trust me.'

Their father, who arrived behind them wide-eyed, scoffed. 'What am I, wallpaper?'

'Apart from Papa, of course,' said Isabelle, throwing her arms around her father and kissing him warmly.

'But he is already taken,' Gigi retorted.

'Yes, he is,' reiterated Delphine as she appeared behind them, hooking her arm into her husband's.

'My, my,' said Bernard with a broad smile, 'it has been a long time since I had women fighting over me. It must be this new aftershave you made me for Christmas, my dear,' he added, kissing his wife on the cheek.

'Gigi,' he said, pulling in his youngest for a hug. 'How lovely to see you, my darling. How are your shows going? Have they closed any more of them?'

'It is a constant battle, Papa, and I don't want to talk about it tonight. I just want to enjoy this dinner and be with my family.'

Madeline arrived right behind her sister. She had brought book gifts for all the family, wrapped in brown paper. She placed them under the tree as they joined Charlotte and Delphine in the kitchen, who were trying their best to make some sort of acceptable Christmas dinner.

'I don't care what you say,' Delphine exclaimed, looking at her daughters. 'It is hard to believe you can have a Christmas

Eve dinner without a turkey.' She nudged the small sliver of meat that they had been saving their ration coupons to acquire. 'It has been a challenging year, for sure.'

'I would rather have coal than turkey,' responded Gigi, 'I'm freezing all the time. The apartment that I am living in is like a fridge. I wear more clothes to bed than I wear out of it.' Her sisters chuckled at her words, understanding the effects of rationing far too well.

'However,' their mother continued, 'Charlotte is doing wonders, as always.'

Charlotte gave a hesitant smile; but Isabelle noticed there were lines around her sister's eyes and dark circles under them. In the past her fears were rarely seen; she was her most confident at home, taking care of them, where she could control her world. But the anxious nature she hid so well from the rest of her family by keeping busy was wearing thin, when her safety was just a knock at the door away, in a world where Nazis could drag a person away at a whim. But she had made the best of it, channelling herself into knitting socks for soldiers and every kind of volunteer work she could find. She'd even started working part-time at one of the hotels in town and occasionally brought food home for them all.

As the girls began to seat themselves around the table, their father looked nervously out of the window.

'Have any of you heard from Antoinette?'

The girls shook their heads, and the look they all exchanged conveyed the ongoing concern for their middle sister.

'Well, we have to eat,' Delphine said with a sigh. 'After all the ration coupons we have been hoarding for this meal, we are not going to let it go cold.'

They were about to serve dessert when Antoinette finally arrived, Benjamin asleep in her arms. It was evident from the wine on her breath as she kissed them all and her slurred speech that she'd been drinking before she'd even arrived.

'Darlings, sorry I'm late,' she said, laying Benjamin in a corner with a blanket that Charlotte hurried to get. Isabelle watched the little boy sleeping; at six, he had grown up way beyond his years since the beginning of the occupation. The impish little child they had known had become sallow and with-drawn when his father had been taken. They'd all attempted to bring him around. But he'd been very close to René and he grieved the loss of his father's presence greatly. He had even started wetting the bed, Antoinette had told Isabelle one day.

Once he woke that evening, they played with him, bringing him all his presents and trying to rally him. In return he tried to put on a brave face for them all. But Isabelle watched sadly, remembering how bubbly Benjamin had been before the war. His transformation was even more heartbreaking because of his age; she knew he shouldn't have to face such things so young.

After dinner the conversation, as always, returned to the war.

Papa raised a glass of homemade port to them all. 'To my wonderful family. One thing I know through all of this, it is important to love one another. Love is the most important thing we have right now. And to live every day is precious.'

Isabelle smiled, lifting her own glass as she looked around the room, taking in the love in her family despite their struggles. She felt a warmth spread through her chest as she realized their resilience in these trying times. She saw the tears in her other sisters' eyes but also the fiery determination that was so much a part of all their characters. They drank to each other's health, and even though they attempted to play some of their favourite Christmas games as they often did on Christmas Eve, Isabelle was grateful when it was over.

Antoinette left early a long time before the curfew, and no matter how many times Isabelle approached her, and asked her if she was all right, Antoinette just shook her head and remained secretive. It broke her heart and she felt like the sister she'd once known had disappeared. They'd all grown up so much through this war. And not in good ways. Isabelle felt unsettled as she went to bed that night, wondering where they would all be a year from now.

23

Marina

Marina turned around in front of the ornate mirror, her reflection shimmering in the soft glow of the vanity lights. The midnight-blue silk gown she had chosen clung to her curves, accentuating her slender figure. She ran her hands along the delicate lace-trimmed bodice, tracing intricate patterns across her décolletage and shoulders, dipping modestly to reveal a hint of her collarbones. Diamond earrings, a gift from Bruno, hung delicately from her ears, catching the light and casting shimmering reflections onto her creamy, flawless skin. She closed her eyes for a moment and took a deep breath, steadying herself for what lay ahead. It wasn't every night Marina was invited to an exclusive Nazi dinner party as a guest of honour; she would have to be on her game this evening. With a sweep of her hand, she dragged a shimmering curtain of golden hair over her shoulder, and, reaching for her clutch bag and fur wrap from the armchair, she crossed the room and opened the door.

The night was crisp, and stars glittered overhead like tiny silver pinpricks in an infinite black canvas as Marina stepped onto the pavement outside. From the kerb, Bruno got out of his sleek black Mercedes to greet her. As he strode toward her with an air of confidence Marina couldn't help but admire him in his pressed Nazi uniform. His grey-green SS jacket was perfectly tailored to fit his broad shoulders, the silver skull and crossbones on his cap shone in the moon's luminescence and the black insignia with the three silver stars on his lapel discerning his rank as Hauptsturmführer commanded attention. Tonight, he would impress ranking officers at the party in his formal attire.

'Good evening, Marina,' he said, with an easy smile. As he reached forward to kiss her on the cheek, the starched red armband with a black swastika symbol rubbed against her delicate exposed skin and she got a hint of his expensive French cologne with its sharp hint of lime.

As he stepped back to open the door for her, his presence exuded power, authority, and ambition – things both Marina and Bruno strived for – but it also reminded her of the tightrope they walked in pursuit of their ambitions: dating a Nazi was a dangerous gamble, but one that could provide valuable rewards for her.

Marina felt a mix of excitement and trepidation as she settled into the plush leather seat beside Bruno. The engine roared into life and Bruno's driver sped through the deserted streets of Paris under its curfew, weaving effortlessly through the light traffic. With the car's war-muted headlights cutting through the darkness as they travelled, the city's famed landmarks passed by in a blur of lights and shadows. The Eiffel Tower soaring over them, its majestic silhouette looming against the starlit sky. They passed the Louvre and the Champs-Élysées that stretched ahead, adorned with shop windows that whispered tales of luxury and extravagance.

Marina's heart raced with a heady mix of anticipation and anxiety as the car glided alongside the River Seine, its shimmering waters reflecting the silky white moonlight. Nervously,

Marina stole a glance at Lohse. His wavy hair was combed back, his chiselled jawline clean-shaven and she felt a strange mix of attraction and repulsion as her mind grappled with the complexities of their relationship. He was a good-looking man, but she didn't feel any attraction to him; she saw him as an opportunity to get what she wanted and then move on. There was no future for them; her only ambition was to secure a comfortable lifestyle for herself. She had no intention of ever getting married or worse still, having children. She would never put her body through something so grotesque. He noticed her watching him and smiled.

'You look stunning this evening,' he said, running his eyes down her body and squeezing her hand. 'I'm glad you made the effort. This is a very important dinner party for me. With the right impression, I can make great strides forward in my career within the Reich.'

Marina appreciated the compliment, but felt a sting of offence at being seen as nothing more than a pretty girl on his arm. Still, she returned him a smile, reminding herself that that would be his undoing, underestimating her, believing that a pretty package was all she was.

As they arrived at the party, Marina could feel something shift in the air. The venue was a palatial mansion nestled amid sprawling gardens in the outskirts of the city. As the car turned off the road, the grand entrance came into view, its imposing gates flanked by ornate statues and meticulously manicured hedges that framed the path leading to the entrance. The building stood out as a testament to wealth and power, its façade exuding an aura of timeless grandeur.

As they crossed the threshold, the well-dressed couple found themselves in a grand foyer, where a sweeping staircase spiralled elegantly toward the upper levels. Marina's gaze was drawn to the majestic chandeliers that hung from the ceiling, their cascading crystals casting prisms of light onto the marble floor below. The music of a live orchestra floated through the air, filling the space with a symphony of enchantment, while guests mingled amid the grandeur, their conversations a tapestry of voices and laughter.

As Lohse introduced Marina to the high-ranking Nazi officers, she skilfully navigated through the crowd, taking in everything. She could tell by the way their eyes travelled down her body that the officers she encountered were captivated by her presence. With a subtle smile, she amused them with witty conversation, effortlessly weaving through topics of art, politics, and the current state of the war.

Major Schmidt, a tall and stern figure, began to engage her in conversation. 'Fräulein, I must say, your knowledge of art is impressive. I have always admired the beauty and symbolism captured in the great masterpieces.'

Marina's emerald eyes sparkled as she responded, her voice carrying a playful yet knowledgeable tone. 'Thank you, Major Schmidt. Art holds a power that transcends time and boundaries. It has the ability to evoke emotions and shape our understanding of the world. In these troubled times, it is more important than ever to appreciate the beauty that art brings.'

Major von Stein, known for his sharp intellect and quick wit, joined the conversation. 'Ah, but art is but a reflection of the times, Fräulein. The chaos and uncertainty of war can birth equally compelling works of art. It captures the essence of human struggle and the indomitable spirit that emerges amid adversity.'

Marina met von Stein's gaze, a subtle challenge in her eyes. 'Indeed, Major von Stein, art can serve as a powerful commentary on the human condition. Yet, it is my hope that one day, once you have won the war, artists can express their creativity without the shadow of conflict and oppression looming over their canvases.'

The officers listened intently, appearing pleased with her

observations. As Marina continued her elegant dance of conversation she was also well-versed in the art of seduction and flattery, using her beauty and intellect as her weapons. Each officer was deceived into believing they had formed a deep connection with her, a sense of shared understanding that transcended the boundaries of rank and ideology.

As they were seated for dinner she was placed next to a particularly high-ranking officer, Colonel Müller, a rather round, short man with a balding head and red cheeks.

'Colonel Müller, it is an honour to be in your presence this evening,' Marina greeted him with a hint of flirtation in her voice. 'I must say, your reputation precedes you. I've heard of your strategic brilliance on the battlefield.' She took a sip of her wine, pleased with herself. She made it a point to know the officers that were well thought of. If they did win the war she wanted to make sure she was taken care of.

Colonel Müller reciprocated with a nod and a slight bow of his head. 'Thank you, Fräulein. Your words are most kind. But let us not speak of the war tonight. Instead, allow me to indulge in the pleasure of your company.'

He took her hand then and kissed it with a smile.

'Oh, Colonel, I couldn't agree more. Tonight, let us escape the harsh realities of war and embrace the beauty that surrounds us.'

Their conversation flowed smoothly, their words mingling with the clinking of glasses and the soft melodies of the orchestra. Marina skilfully guided the discussion towards art.

'So you work at the Jeu de Paume,' he said with some interest. 'I know little about art, but have acquired some pieces on arriving in Paris in the home I live in.'

Marina knew many wealthy Parisian residents had left for the south at the beginning of the war and Nazi officers had just taken over those grand houses without question.

Marina listened attentively as Colonel Müller began

describing the various artworks he had appropriated. Her heart skipped a beat when he mentioned a couple of valuable pieces by little-known artists she recognized, but she maintained a composed demeanour, masking her true enthusiasm.

With a casual smile, Marina responded, her voice tinged with a hint of nonchalance. 'Oh, Colonel, how fascinating. It seems you have stumbled upon some interesting works. However, you must understand that tastes in the art world have shifted since the war began. Many of the traditional styles and themes are considered out of vogue at the moment. Have you had them valued?'

He harrumphed, shrugging his shoulders. 'I am a man of battle; I have little time for such pursuits.'

She took another sip of her wine, her eyes dancing with calculated charm, her stomach tightening with the excitement of an opportunity. She adopted a casual tone. 'While these pieces may not be in high demand currently, there is still a market for them. Perhaps they could fetch you a little extra money.'

Colonel Müller's brow furrowed slightly, his curiosity piqued. 'Is that so? I must admit, Fräulein, I am intrigued. Could you elaborate on this market you speak of?'

Marina leaned in closer, her voice dropping to a confidential pitch. 'Colonel, there are art connoisseurs who appreciate the classics, even in these turbulent times. While the broader art world may be focusing on contemporary styles, there are still collectors who long for the nostalgia and elegance of past eras. These connoisseurs would value your pieces for their historical significance.'

She paused, her gaze meeting Colonel Müller's with a mixture of sincerity and persuasion. 'If you would permit me, Colonel, I have a contact in the art world, a trusted associate. He specializes in acquiring such pieces and has access to a network of discreet buyers who appreciate their true worth. I could arrange a meeting, and, together, we could explore the possibilities of selling these artworks at a fair price.'

Colonel Müller's eyes gleamed with a renewed sense of interest, his earlier disappointment fading.

From the other side of the colonel, Herr Schreiber, a man she had been introduced to earlier, gave her an intimidating glare.

'Fräulein Belleveau,' he began, his voice calm but laced with suspicion. 'I couldn't help but overhear your discussion on art. I must say, your insights are intriguing, but I can't help feeling we should be cautious. In these tumultuous times, one must be wary of those who seek to exploit the beauty of art for personal gain.'

Marina's eyes widened at his words as her composure was momentarily thrown off balance. Mustering all the charm she could, she flashed him a confident smile and spoke with a defensive edge to her voice. 'I understand your concerns, Herr Schreiber. All I hope to do is give collectors the chance to appreciate the history and beauty of works of art. Of course, if the colonel would rather take more time and pay extra for an official evaluation that could take months then that is also perfectly reasonable. But my services are available now and I'm willing to waive my fee as a courtesy to a new friend.'

At this, Colonel Müller crossed his arms over his chest and frowned, making it clear he wasn't pleased with Schreiber's scepticism towards Marina's offer. He cleared his throat before saying, 'Thank you for your insight, Herr Schreiber, but I feel very confident in Fräulein Belleveau's ability and do not have the time nor the inclination to go through an official evaluation.'

Marina shrugged her shoulders before offering another non-committal smile in response. As she watched Herr Schreiber turn away red-faced, she couldn't help but feel a sense of satisfaction.

Colonel Müller drew closer.

'So, you truly believe there is potential for a little profit in these artworks, Fräulein?' he asked.

Marina's gaze never wavered as she met his eyes and nodded, her voice laced with confidence. 'A little, Colonel.'

The colonel pondered her words for a moment before a smile played at the corners of his lips.

He leaned toward her and whispered conspiratorially: 'Very well, Fräulein. Arrange the meeting with your associate. Let us see if I can make a little money for my wine collection.'

Marina's heart raced with excitement, knowing that Lohse would be interested. And if this idiot couldn't be bothered to take the time to find the value of the art he himself was stealing, she wasn't going to feel any guilt. She continued to engage the colonel in conversation, skilfully weaving a web of intrigue and persuasion. With each passing moment, her conviction grew stronger, fuelled by the anticipation of the lucrative profits that awaited her.

24

SUMMER 1942

Brigitte

Brigitte had been working at the Jeu de Paume for almost two years and was so absorbed in her work that the deep, thunderous rumble of a truck backing up escaped her notice until a pungent cloud of diesel fumes infiltrated her office. She laid aside what she was doing and moved out onto the deck to receive the usual cargo of artworks to the Jeu de Paume. Outside, the smoky stench was intensified by the stillness of the summer heat that beat down on scorched concrete from an unforgiving sun. And as the driver handed her the work order, the acridity of the idling engine mingled with the sharp sourness of his briny skin and the faintest whiff of summer roses and jasmine that drifted from the Tuileries Garden.

'Some of these got left in one of the other warehouses by mistake. This collection is from various galleries,' the gaptoothed driver rasped with his usual disinterest. Another Parisian strong-armed into helping the Nazis, his distaste for his work was obvious.

As a team of Nazi ants unloaded them, Isabelle came out to look them over and allocated Brigitte and Marina the job of unpacking, cataloguing, and readying them to put up on display.

She and Marina began opening the crates, and there was the usual peculiar tension between them. Though she felt comfortable with Isabelle, there always seemed to be something dark lingering in the air whenever Marina was around – as though her gaze sought out secrets, or plotted sinister ideas. And Brigitte hated the way she flirted with the Nazi art dealers.

Marina eased off the lid of the first crate as an aromatic blend of oil paint mixed with subtle notes of warmed wood from the frames and packing fibre wafted out from between the wooden slats, and Brigitte's stomach tightened with the anticipation. It had been two years since she had last seen her husband's picture, and since then she had handled thousands of works of art. She had started to give up hope she would ever see his painting again. But still, every time a new crate arrived, she felt the same tingle of anticipation.

As she unpacked and carefully arranged the series of beautiful pictures against the walls, the vivid colours, shapes and hues transported her to scenes from times long past, works that may once have hung in someone's home or an esteemed gallery like her parents' before being cruelly taken by Nazi forces. She almost couldn't bear to look at them. Each artwork testified not just to artistic endeavour, but also to human suffering untold.

They levered off the lid of the last crate, and, pulling out a large frame, Marina carelessly peeled away the brown paper. The painting emerged from its protective cocoon. Brigitte had to stop herself from crying out as she drew in breath. In her hands Marina held her husband's masterpiece. A breathtaking tribute to summer's brilliance. Her eyes filled with tears as once again she looked upon *The Hayfields of Summer*, with its flaming oranges, reds, and golds brightly burning against one another in joyous celebration. The creativity was so evocative, it was as if she could feel the heat from the orange-blazoned sun, smell the bales of hay being piled into their neat stacks, and hear the echo of the children's laughter as they raced among fields of wind-whipped grasses. As she took it all in once again through her misted eyes, she realized that the strokes of his brush were as familiar to her as the contours of his face.

As she studied it, her whole body started to tremble, and she attempted to swallow down the dryness in her throat, unable to believe that Samuel's painting was right in front of her. Her heart tightened as she remembered the time he painted it, when they had still been a family together. Now her husband was dead and her daughter a shadow of the happy child she had been. And it stung.

Unaware of this picture's impact on her colleague, Marina placed it against the wall and continued unwrapping the next. Brigitte felt like she was going to faint as, one after another, Marina pulled out paintings that she recognized had been stolen from her parents' gallery.

'I'm going to go and get some water. I'll be back in a moment,' she informed Marina, her throat still tight from the shock.

Her colleague shrugged, nonplussed, as Brigitte left the gallery.

Brigitte raced and stumbled through the door, barely making it to the bathroom before her legs gave way. With a trembling hand, she held herself steady against the sink. Her face was ashen, and the dark brown eyes that stared back at her from the mirror were wild and animalistic as she tried desperately to suck in air.

'Oh my God, my love,' she whispered to the empty room, 'oh my God. I have found it.'

As she splashed cold water on her face, a new fear taunted her. As happy as she was to see it here, it would be on display. Göring or any one of his cronies, even Hitler himself, could steal it and take it back to Germany, where she knew she would never see it again. Yet stealing it herself wasn't an option – Lohse had been meticulous about documenting everything and would surely notice if anything went amiss from the ledger entries. She had to come up with a plan, but what?

After drinking a glass of water with a shaking hand, she returned to the museum gallery, her heart thudding again when she saw the picture.

'They're all out,' said Marina. 'I'm going to take a break.' She swished towards the loading deck, pulling a silver cigarette case from her pocket, and all at once Brigitte was alone with Samuel's picture. She walked over to it, and tears started brimming up in her eyes. She ran her fingers gently down the painting. It was just as she remembered it. Every inch of it made her heart swell with pride. With bittersweet memory, she recalled the many days she had watched her husband working on it, the trips out to the countryside where they had taken a picnic and baked in the sun on their red plaid picnic blanket while Sophie played and he painted, whistling one of his tuneless melodies.

Suddenly there was a voice from behind her. Brigitte turned quickly, snatching her hand from the picture.

Isabelle looked at her quizzically.

'Are you all right?'

'Yes, I'm fine,' Brigitte responded, her voice a little too fast. Her tone too tight. 'More pictures are here,' she continued, feeling the heat creep into her cheeks.

'I see,' replied Isabelle, not taking her eyes from Brigitte.

'Yes, we have unpacked them. They're all out.'

Isabelle looked at *The Hayfields of Summer* and then back at Brigitte.

'Beautiful, isn't it?' Isabelle commented.

'Yes,' came Brigitte's tight response, as she swallowed down her fear of being found out. Did Isabelle suspect anything? Could Brigitte trust her? She hadn't been expecting such an overwhelming response to seeing it again. But she felt as protective as if this were a child, and she had no idea how she was going to save it.

25

Marina

Marina tiptoed out of bed, a silvery path of moonlight guiding her through the bedroom. With slow and careful movements, she reached for a small blue velvet box on the dressing table that Lohse had given her. As she quietly opened its smooth lid, the elegant diamond earrings glistened. She had woken from a nightmare; she had been back in the family hovel. Her brothers and sisters crying with hunger, her mother drunk. Whenever she had these dreams she always reached for a touchstone, something to remind her that her life was now different. The earrings were her latest comfort. Reflected in the moon's soft glow, they shimmered like stars as she delicately placed them onto each lobe. 'They must be at least half-carat,' she mused, noticing the weight as she admired their beauty in the mirror.

Her body shuddered in disgust as she recalled the night before. Bruno Lohse was not a considerate lover, that was for sure. She remembered his rough, unshaven cheeks and his groping hands finding every part of her. But these diamond beauties were worth it. A good insurance against poverty and a nice goodbye present when he was called back to Germany.

All at once, his arms snaked around her waist without warning, stealing any chance of her lingering further, and she fought her desire to groan at the intrusion.

'What are you doing?' he whispered, his eyes heavy with desire as he nuzzled her neck and pulled her close, his breath laden with stale cigarette smoke and brandy.

Marina tensed at his proximity. 'I just wanted to see how they looked,' she whispered, attempting to keep the irritation from her tone, feeling caught, exposed.

'They look beautiful on you,' he slurred, 'especially when you are dressed like this.' His eyes moved to her naked body as he ran a finger down between her breasts.

'I think they'll look even better with my black dress,' she responded evenly, plastering on what she hoped was a convincing smile as she moved away from his side.

She didn't want to be manhandled any more. Besides, she had the next part of her plan she wanted to put into action. But how to approach it in a way that made it seem natural? Spur of the moment. She led him back to the bed. She needed to distract him while she placed the idea in his mind.

'Bruno, I was thinking,' she said as she gently caressed the soft hair on his chest, 'about what we were talking about the other day.'

He started to kiss her shoulder and she wished he would leave her alone.

'Mm-hmm,' he said, not really paying her comment any attention.

'About the art. You know what you were saying? About how much money it's worth?'

'Yes, one cannot forget that quickly,' he mumbled as he made his way to her ear.

'Well, I was wondering what would happen if, you know, one or two pieces went missing?'

'I was joking about that.'

'But what if they did?'

He stopped kissing her and sat up, running a hand through his dishevelled hair. His voice was stern as he clarified, 'No mercy would be shown to anyone who attempts to infringe on what belongs to the Reich. Thieves are sent off for hard labour in Germany.'

He suddenly sounded very Nazi, and she knew she needed to distract him again.

Pressing her bare breasts against his chest, she began kissing him passionately, and she felt the tension from his body release. She waited until he was a lot more relaxed, then she continued.

'But how would they know if something small was stolen? There is so much coming into the gallery right now. And dealers are starting to come in daily. It's hard to track everything. I can see how the odd thing could go missing and no one would know.'

He rolled her over onto her back and kissed her neck again.

'It would be impossible. Everything is recorded. There is a paper trail.'

She pressed her hand on his chest and eased him away so she looked him directly in the eyes.

'But what if the person recording everything missed a couple of items? With your contacts here in Paris, I'm sure you could find buyers on the black market.'

All at once he stiffened, his eyes widening as he realized what she was implying.

Marina attempted one of her most seductive smiles as he contemplated her words, the hunger stirring in his eyes. She had chosen her mark well. Finally, he shook his head.

'It would be too dangerous. Besides, once Hitler has conquered the world, we will be able to go anywhere. We won't need any money to do that. I will be well taken care of by the Führer.'

She didn't like to challenge his arrogance that they would win the war or that they were, in fact, a 'we'. So, she just smiled.

'Of course, yes, that I know. But just in case you wanted a little more, a little nest egg. Why would you not want to have a little security?'

He rolled away from her, his expression thoughtful. Grabbing his cigarettes from the side table, he absently lit up without even offering her one. As he pulled in a long draw, he held it for a second before blowing it out in a slow steady stream.

'What pieces of art are you thinking about?'

Her heart quickened. She knew he would be a pushover. The one thing that Marina was good at was reading men.

'There are a few pieces I know of that I've studied that are not so important right now but are set to become important in the future. So we should hide them somewhere until the time is right.'

He studied her face, thinking for a moment before he responded. 'You think it is possible?'

She could see the greed in his eyes growing now. She had him on the hook.

'Of course, I'm there all the time. It would not take much to hide them away as I unpack.'

He furrowed his brow. 'Could it be that easy?'

'Absolutely,' she encouraged him, dragging a delicate finger down the dip in his chest, drawing spirals on his stomach, making him shiver.

'You have been thinking about this?' he said, smiling at her.

'Yes, something for both of us.'

'I know the perfect buyer, and the kind of things he likes, but we would have to be very careful,' he warned.

'Of course,' she responded. Then in her most seductive tone added, 'I can be very discreet.'

He beamed, then, taking her chin in his hand, pulled her face so close she could smell the liquor on his breath once more.

'Yes, you can. But first, I want to make love to you again.'

'Of course, my darling,' she said, expertly masking her distaste, allowing him to lower his lips to hers as he kissed her again.

As he mapped her body with his insistent hands, she kept her eyes open and stared over his shoulder, thinking about how she could spend the money she would make out of the art she was going to steal and which pieces she would take. Marina had a plan and it didn't include anything long-term with Lohse, that was for sure.

26

Esther

Esther held her breath as she took the call from her ex-husband. He sounded positively cheerful as she answered the phone.

'I've got some good news.'

Surely his good news would be that they would work together to help keep her home! She had already contacted numerous banks and mortgage companies since their last call, trying to find out if she could get a mortgage herself, but she didn't earn enough, and it was looking more and more likely her bank would foreclose if he didn't pay the arrears. She bit her lip as she waited for him to elaborate.

'I found a great little flat not far from where I live, which would be perfect for you and the boys. I think you will love it,' he continued, either not caring or oblivious to her discomfort on the other end of the phone.

Her heart sank. In response, she found it difficult to even articulate words. She was exhausted, exhausted from the worry and the upset of this. And as she listened to him extol all the virtues of this 'lovely little place', her attention was drawn to the kitchen table where sat the three letters she'd had from the mortgage people warning her they would be foreclosing unless she paid her arrears soon.

'But what about the boys' school?' she eventually managed to splutter out. 'It's too far away.'

She heard him blow out air on the other end.

'Why are you always so obstinate?' he spat back. 'There are beautiful schools here. Angela's best friend's son goes to a great school around the corner. The boys could go there.'

'But they love their school,' she responded, hating the desperation in her tone. 'Henry loves his teacher. And you know how he struggled last year and she is amazing, and they are both doing so well now.'

'And they will do again,' said James defiantly. 'God, Esther, you sure know how to throw a downer on anything I do for you. I put a lot of time into this. The least you could do is go and look at the place. You can't just decide without seeing it. It will be a new start for you and the boys, and they would be closer to me so I could see them more often. You are always complaining about the fact I don't see them enough. You're always so negative about anything I want to do. Nothing ever changes with you.'

'Nothing ever changes with me?! All you think about is yourself and what you want.'

'I can't afford it, Esther, okay? I can't afford to keep you there any more. Don't make it more difficult for me than it already is.'

She suddenly recalled all the things she'd seen in his house, the nice new sofa, the bedroom set, his girlfriend's constant suntan from the holidays abroad, and the computer games he bought the boys. It didn't seem like he was short on cash. Angela's spending habits were obviously influencing him. She always looked immaculate, her nails and hair done, but surely he wouldn't allow some woman to dictate where his sons would live and his sons' happiness.

A sob caught in her chest and she swallowed it down past the acid bile collecting in her throat. 'Do you not care about what the boys want?'

'Of course I care about what the boys want. This is about the boys. They want to see their father more. Daniel told me that while you were off cavorting on your French holiday. Did you know that?'

Her head ached with the pressure. No matter what she did, she knew she could never make up for them not having a father around, and she hated that fact.

He continued and she could hear the anger in his tone. 'This conversation is over. Have you got a pen? Here's the estate agent's number. You can go and look at it or go homeless.'

'You would do that to your children?'

'Of course not. If it came down to that, we could always make other arrangements. Angela would love having the boys here full-time. All her friends have kids, and she often feels left out.'

Esther felt as if she had been gut-punched. That was where all this was coming from. He wanted to give Angela the kids she couldn't have, like a bracelet to flounce in front of her holiday set. This wasn't about what was best for the boys; this was about Angela getting what she thought she wanted. And Esther was standing in their way. Well, she wouldn't let her kids be used as pawns, not without a fight.

She got a pen and a piece of paper and could see her hands shaking as she picked up her phone again. Numbly, she took down the address he gave her, trying to absorb this new information. She had to have time to think. Work out what to do.

'You need to make an appointment with the estate agent, and don't ring back until you've seen it. I'm just not going to talk about this any more.'

She didn't even say goodbye, just hung up the phone, and swore, frustrated and angry.

Two days later, she made her way into the estate agent's, and a young man with acne, short-cropped hair, and an ill-fitting suit met her. He looked about fifteen.

'Hello, Ms Walker, delighted to meet you,' he said as he held out a dry, scaly hand. She gently shook it and drew in a breath; she had to give this at least a chance. She had promised herself that she would do that. Grabbing his keys, he walked her out to his car. He opened the door for her, telling her all about the flat and how it was in a lovely area near the good schools. James had obviously prepped him. 'It's nice and quiet and close to the park,' he enthused. She didn't even care as they drove along.

Finally, they arrived at the flat. She couldn't tell if it was just because it was a dull day, but it looked sad and unkempt as they walked towards it. As he unlocked the door, the first thing that hit her was a strange smell, a mixture of mildew and stale tobacco smoke. She knew that wasn't any way to judge a place, but it didn't make her feel very excited.

'The couple that used to live here were elderly,' he elaborated, 'so there is some work to do with the decor.'

He wasn't kidding. She walked from room to room. It looked like something out of a 1960s film set. She could probably sell this wallpaper on eBay.

'It needs updating, but it's got good strong bones and lots of lovely light,' he said, looking towards the windows. 'And here we have your two bedrooms.'

'Just two?' she said with alarm. She had three now; the boys had their own rooms.

'One is very large,' he countered quickly, revealing a

chipped front tooth as he gave her a crooked smile and swept forward to open the first bedroom door.

It was not a bad size and was quite well-lit, but the second bedroom was pokey. And she couldn't imagine both boys fitting in there. Which would mean she would have the small room and they would have the bigger room. She sucked in a breath, already feeling claustrophobic without a garden outside. She continued to look around the flat, listening to him blather on about all the good things about it, cheap bills and being close to the shops. But all she could think about was her beautiful Victorian semi-detached on the leafy, quiet cul-de-sac. All the work she'd done in it, refinishing the ornamental staircase, the floor she'd stripped in the hallway, her spacious kitchen diner, and the lovely three bedrooms she had decorated. It did not compare to this tiny box.

They finished the tour, and as they drove back, he talked to her about the next steps. The way he spoke made it sound like it was a done deal. 'Mr Harrington implied he would be putting in an offer quite soon,' he continued, oblivious to how this was making her feel. 'I would encourage him not to wait. A little gem in such a great neighbourhood won't stay on the market for long.'

Esther felt sick. She felt sick and manipulated and didn't know what to do.

She drove home from the estate agent's office in a blur of tears, trying not to think about it. Rubbing her eyes quickly in the mirror, she plastered on what was hopefully a convincing smile as she picked the boys up from school and decided she wouldn't tell them anything about what was going on as she listened to the recap of their day. She tried to keep it light as she drove them home and answered all their questions with the smile that ached for her to keep in place.

When she got home, she took herself off for a bath so she could cry quietly to herself.

Her phone rang as she got out of the bath and moved into the bedroom. She girded herself in case it was James. She wasn't quite sure what she was going to say to him. She was still reeling from the shock of what she'd been through that day. She picked up the phone.

'Hello, Esther,' said the voice on the other end and she realized with relief it wasn't James, but Édouard. Her heart gave a little flutter just hearing his voice. At least there was somebody out there who was friendly.

'We are still appraising your picture, but I have some good news. I have spoken to the Louvre, and they are excited to have your painting for the exhibition. It will open on Christmas Eve.'

She found it hard to speak.

'Esther?'

'I'm sorry. It's just been a hard day. Of course, I am honoured.'

'Is there anything I could do to help?'

His tone was so kind, as if he really cared.

'No, no, it's okay. Just family stuff.'

'It can be hard being alone, with children. I understand,' he reassured her.

She swallowed down her sadness. The last thing she wanted to do was taint this professional relationship with stories of her sad life. 'I really should go,' she insisted. 'Thank you for letting me know about the showing.'

'Of course,' he responded. 'And, Esther, you can call me any time.'

She hung up the phone and felt wretched. This was an awful decision. She felt as if she was betraying her mother and her grandmother for money. And as she looked again at the photograph she'd taken of the picture, she hated that she had so few choices.

27

SUMMER 1942

Brigitte

After a long day at work, Brigitte hastened home with an overwhelming sense of sadness. Although she was fairly confident that nobody suspected her ulterior motive for being at the museum, paranoid thoughts lingered with what it was she kept hidden, and she was still deeply moved about finding Samuel's painting.

As she waited for the tram, a flood of nostalgia swept over her. Seeing the picture the day before had opened up her heart in a new way and she felt vulnerable. Memories of them as a family. Flying a kite with Sophie that was still in a tree at the park. Him sitting on the floor teaching his daughter to paint and then watching him paint his own work with such determined fervour that it was as if every brushstroke bore his soul onto the canvas – each colour and perspective masterfully chosen to bring beauty into existence. She smiled as she remembered how the intensity of working on his craft caused an endearing crease to groove itself between his brows. Hurried meals that were eaten over the easel as he discussed with her all the techniques and choices in his latest work while she listened to him, in awe of his brilliance. Once finished, he would take her in his arms, the scent of fresh paint still clinging to his favourite baggy blue working shirt that, though it was washed endlessly, still held fragments of every past painting endeavour along with the memories entwined within its fibres. Then his passion would be for her alone, because he had loved his wife to the same depth as his work. Brigitte knew that she would never find a love like that again.

When she arrived home, she received a warm welcome from her daughter, who had been reading in her bedroom.

'Maman,' Sophie called out and ran to throw her arms around her. 'You look so beautiful.'

'Thank you, darling,' said Brigitte, wiping away the last few tears that had crept from her eyes on the way home as she held her daughter in her arms, kissing her flower-scented, curly hair and warm cheeks.

'Look, I've been painting,' her daughter announced, showing her the picture she had created.

'It's beautiful, my darling. How was school? Did you have fun?'

'I did, Maman. But more teachers left today to fight and some children are leaving the city altogether. It will be over soon, won't it?'

'We can hope,' Brigitte responded, hugging her daughter close, though she didn't feel very confident in that fact.

Brigitte strolled into the kitchen, where Odette was preparing food. Her mother had lived here with them since the raid on the family gallery.

'Brigitte,' said her mother, coming over to kiss her on both cheeks. 'You look wonderful. You must have had a good day?'

'I didn't have time to tell you yesterday because you were back checking on your gallery but I saw it, Maman. Samuel's picture.'

Her mother looked at her incredulously. 'After all this time? I can't believe it; that is a miracle.'

Fierce determination crept into Brigitte's eyes as she continued.

'Now I have to figure out what to do about it,' she added.

'Do?' Odette asked, stopping from washing the dishes as she looked over at her daughter with concern.

'I can't have the enemy take it from me, Maman, not when it was Germans who took his life.'

'What do you mean?' her mother asked, her voice pitched a little frantic.

'I'm going to find a way to steal it.'

Odette swore softly under her breath, as she moved to close the kitchen door so Sophie couldn't hear them. Then she grasped her daughter's hand. 'Please don't take any chances, Brigitte. If anyone found out about your papers...'

Brigitte lowered her voice. 'I will be careful, don't worry, but some things are worth fighting for.'

Odette shook her head, but now Brigitte had seen his painting, she was more determined than ever.

As she was clearing out some of her husband's things later that evening, she found his wedding ring, and a photograph returned to her after his death and it shook her to the core. Brigitte crumpled to the floor and sobbed. She tried to muffle her cries, but Sophie must have heard her, because soon she was there, staring at her from the door, her eyes wide with fear.

'Maman, what is it?' she asked.

She wanted to comfort her, but she was so distraught. She shook her head and held her hands out to her as Sophie moved cautiously towards her mother. Even before she got to her side, Brigitte pulled her in for a hug and held her tightly.

'I'm sorry, Maman,' Sophie sobbed, tears in her own eyes. 'Whatever I did, I'm so sorry.'

'You have done nothing wrong, Sophie,' Brigitte spluttered, 'nothing wrong.'

She held her like that until both their sobs subsided, and finally, Sophie pulled away, slowly, uncomfortable in her mother's tight grip. Studying Brigitte's face, her tiny thumb rubbed a tear away.

'Don't cry, Maman, please don't cry.'

Brigitte shook her head and planted a smile on her face, pushing through the pain. She knew it was a pathetic attempt.

'Go and play, darling,' she said, her voice hoarse and dry. 'I will be fine.'

Hesitantly, her daughter walked towards the door, looking over her shoulder tentatively as she slowly entered the hallway. Then Brigitte heard her tiny feet pattering down the hall and into her bedroom, escaping the fearful world of a sobbing adult.

Brigitte picked up the photograph again and studied it. It had been her husband's happiest moment. He was standing in the gallery in front of his painting *The Hayfields of Summer*, the one that was a masterpiece, or was going to be one day. Beside him in the photograph, her father was beaming. In both their hands glasses of champagne. Samuel's picture was huge and bright behind them. Even though the photograph was black and white, she could make out the painting's hues and its beauty so distinctly. Now that she knew where it was, her job was to protect it until she could figure out what to do.

She tucked the photograph into her bag. She had more pressing matters to attend to. With her mother now living with her, she needed to continue to work.

Walking Sophie to school the next day, Brigitte was obsessed with Samuel's memory. It clung to her like a shawl, wrapping itself around her, suffocating out all of the air. As she dropped off Sophie, she kissed her daughter on the cheek, and Sophie looked back at her tentatively, afraid to leave her mother alone.

She pulled her mother's face down to her own, then, 'Remember to feel the love in your heart, like Papa taught us. That's what makes us strong,' she said, sounding very grown-up. Brigitte's stomach tightened with the memory of the night when war was declared. Sophie placed her tiny hand over her mother's heart to remind her, and Brigitte wanted to drop to her knees and sob with the sweetness of that one act. But instead she bit back her grief.

'Thank you for reminding me, Sophie. Papa was always so wise. I'll be fine,' she said, stroking her cheek. 'You go and have a good day.'

Sophie nodded but still looked over her shoulder two or three times before entering the school building.

Brigitte held her breath as her daughter disappeared inside. Before this war, Sophie's school had always been a safe place, but now she hated her daughter being out of her sight, never sure whether, as a Jewish girl, she would be free from harm.

As soon as Sophie was inside, Brigitte started to make her way across town. Hurrying to arrive early, she thought about it all the way there. Could she stand in front of the picture again without breaking down? Flashing her pass at the guard, she checked the office. It was empty. She was thirty minutes early. The other girls weren't there yet. She had a moment to see it without anyone around. Brigitte moved swiftly through the museum until she arrived at the main room, where his picture was already being staged. Pausing momentarily at the door, she attempted to collect herself. She hadn't looked at this in depth since his death; she had been paralysed with the shock the day before and desperate to hide from Marina all her feelings. Today, this was going to be hard.

Tiptoeing across the polished wooden floor, she could see the corner of the canvas and caught her breath as she gently moved towards it. Once she reached it, she stood directly in front of it and looked deeply into her husband's work, tears stinging her eyes. What could he have been if this war hadn't happened? What kind of artist could he have become? What kind of sublime work could he have created? The colours were as vivid as ever, the beauty, the texture, the scope; she closed her eyes as she drifted back in time – a good memory.

The time they'd first met, at art school. She had been playing at it compared to him. Brigitte remembered seeing him, tall and thin, for the first time in the painting studio. His black hair dishevelled, a lock of it hanging heavily over one eye. He'd stood staring at his canvas, such intensity in his expression. She had been curious and had walked up behind him to look at it. Even from a distance and even in the early stage the picture was at, right at the beginning, she could see he had a skill that she could only ever hope to attain.

Yes, she knew the basics. She knew how to create paintings; she knew how to do scale. But he had this gift, and she could see it. Totally unaware of her presence, he had stepped backwards, right onto her foot. She had yelped with surprise, and he turned in shock, not expecting anybody else to be in the room.

Brigitte had looked up at him then, staring up into his warm hazel eyes looking down at her with a surprised expression on his face. She sidestepped him to get out of his way.

'It looks good,' she said, pointing towards the canvas and rubbing her toe.

He looked back at it with disgust, as if that was the last thing he was thinking. 'It is terrible,' he said; then, he snarled, 'I just can't get the proportions right. See how these trees are all wrong?'

She couldn't see anything of the sort; it looked magnificent to her.

He then proceeded with a lengthy retelling of what he'd been trying to achieve and what he'd been doing. But she heard very little of it as she looked up into this man's face. Something about being next to him felt familiar, as though she'd known him before.

And after that first meeting, it hadn't taken them long to fall in love. It had been a whirlwind romance, and she'd been nothing but happy to support him. And when they'd married, she got pregnant straight away with Sophie and they were over-joyed. Their happiness was complete when he got the news that one of his pictures was to hang in the gallery. She remembered the day like it was yesterday. The excitement, the anticipation, watching the unveiling, the appreciation from everyone around them. She had been so proud of him that day. So proud of what he had achieved.

'This is all for you,' he'd said to her later as they drank their bottle of champagne. 'This is just the beginning, my darling,' he had said, kissing her lips.

She'd never realized, she thought with bitterness, there would be no more beginnings for him.

She looked around surreptitiously, walked closer, and brushed her finger down the painting with the thrill of what she intended to do in honour of his memory.

28

Isabelle

Isabelle stood motionless in her office, her eyes fixed on the heavy logbook she held in both hands. A wave of fear rolled over her as she slowly ran her finger again down the list of items that had arrived at the museum the day before and realized with dread that three of the items had gone missing. She knew all too well what the consequences of such a discovery could be. She wouldn't be able to explain it away, and her job, let alone her life, could be in jeopardy.

She narrowed her gaze and re-entered the gallery, peering again at the other prepared pieces, wrapped in canvas and ready for transport. She was confident that the three items had been among those, yet now the corner they had stood in was empty.

Isabelle glanced up from the logbook to see Brigitte standing in the doorway with a stack of papers clutched in her hands. She had asked her to assemble the descriptions of each art piece and put them together into a catalogue as Lohse had demanded. Brigitte laid them down on the top of her desk with a sigh and looked over at Isabelle. She must have sensed the apprehension in her expression.

'Is everything all right, Isabelle?'

Isabelle turned to Brigitte, her anxiety palpable. 'Did you see the three pieces that were against the wall? In the gallery yesterday?'

Brigitte shook her head and followed Isabelle into the gallery, intrigued.

Isabelle pointed to an empty corner. 'There were three pieces that I left here last night. And they're no longer here. Did you move them anywhere?'

Brigitte shook her head again, horrified. 'I would never move any pieces without first talking to you.'

The two women scoured the room, with Isabelle growing increasingly more agitated as they failed to find any trace of the missing artwork. 'I have them catalogued, but now they don't seem to be here any more,' she muttered under her breath, frustration and fear evident in her voice as they moved back to the office.

Brigitte nodded and as she focused on organizing the descriptions into an easy-to-read format for buyers, Isabelle continued searching through the logbook until she found something that made her pause: there was no record of where the missing works had come from originally, something which should have definitely been noted down by whoever had unpacked the boxes. At that moment, Isabelle realized with dread that this might not be an accident but rather, something deliberate.

Marina breezed into the gallery, her strong perfume mingling with the smell of wood and canvas that always lingered in the building. She wore a cream-coloured knee-length dress and very high heels that clicked against the hardwood floors as she walked. Her long blonde hair flowed in curls down her back, a look of disinterest on her face. She was over half an hour late, but Isabelle dared not chastise her, not with her now being involved with Lohse.

Isabelle turned to her. 'Marina, did you see three pieces of art we had in the gallery here? They were stacked against this wall.'

Avoiding Isabelle's gaze, she inspected her nails and shook her head. 'I didn't see any art. You must have made a mistake.' She sounded very unconvincing, then continued, 'I was in here all day yesterday and I don't remember them.'

Was Isabelle losing her mind? There had been so many pieces passing through the building. Maybe she was thinking of a different day. But when she looked back at Marina, her face was flushed red and Isabelle knew she wasn't telling her the truth.

'It's such a beautiful day today,' Marina said, changing the subject, her voice far too upbeat for the tension in the room. 'Are you girls going out this evening?'

Isabelle and Brigitte exchanged knowing glances. 'No, we can't go anywhere,' Isabelle said, her voice laden with sarcasm. 'There is a curfew.'

'I could always get you dates with some of the Nazi officers I've been meeting lately. Then you wouldn't have to stay at home,' she mused.

Brigitte, disgusted, mumbled something about taking care of her daughter and hurried away, saying over her shoulder, 'I need to get on with cataloguing for the buyers.'

Isabelle watched her go and then turned back to Marina. 'Let's keep looking for those missing pieces before anyone else arrives.' She began to search every possible nook and cranny in the gallery but found nothing.

Lohse strode into the room an hour later and took in the general disarray in the office. 'Is there a problem?' he asked Marina.

'Isabelle has misplaced some of the art,' she quickly answered without missing a beat.

Isabelle shot her assistant an icy look, but remained silent. That wasn't true. She hadn't misplaced anything; it had gone missing.

Lohse furrowed his eyebrows, and his eyes narrowed as he assessed the situation. 'What do you mean, misplaced?'

Marina pushed past Isabelle, picked the book up from the desk, and handed it to him. He studied it.

She expected him to be furious, though he just became quiet. All she saw was a bead of sweat roll down one cheek, though his face otherwise conveyed no emotion as he checked the records.

'Records have to be correct. We can't make the same mistake again. From now on, Marina will be responsible for logging the art pieces in the book and coming with me to inspect new acquisitions. You' – he held out his hand for the key to the drawer holding the logbook – 'will do something else.'

Reluctantly, Isabelle handed him the key, aware of Marina's excitement at getting this honour.

'Isabelle, I believe there's some dusting to do,' she suggested as she pursed her lips.

Isabelle glanced at Marina, who then smiled triumphantly. How could she be so accommodating to the Nazis? What did she think she was accomplishing?

Marina moved closer to Isabelle and opened the book. The smell of her expensive perfume filled the air, almost making Isabelle's eyes water. 'It looks rather simple,' she said languidly, not taking her gaze off the commander. 'Do I just log the name and number of each piece, then record where it's going?' Her words were directed towards Isabelle, but she sought reassurance from Lohse.

'That is correct,' Isabelle replied.

'Well, that seems very easy.'

Isabelle gritted her teeth, feeling a surge of anger at Marina's condescending tone.

'I suppose we should get started. I wouldn't want to keep the commander waiting.'

She flashed him a seductive smile as they headed off to inspect the new acquisitions. Isabelle couldn't shake off the feeling that something wasn't right. She kept a close eye on Marina, watching as she fawned over the commander's words, throwing back her golden head of hair in a gentle laugh as he joked with her.

As soon as she could, Isabelle went to the bathroom. When she got there, she slipped her secret logbook out of her pocket. And there they were, all three pieces of work. She couldn't have made a mistake twice. There was a real problem here. Somebody had stolen three pieces of art from the museum. And it had to be someone she was working with. There was no way that anything could get out of the museum any other way without them being able to track it.

Suddenly, with a shiver, she knew without a shadow of a doubt it was Marina and there was nothing she could do about it.

As Isabelle moved back to her office and watched her assistant stride around the room with her German, making new orders for the Nazis, her heart sank. How would she record where everything was going now? Things would become much more difficult for her if she couldn't have access to the logbook. Everything seemed to be slipping away from her again, and she was terrified. How would she get the art back after the war if she didn't know where it was going?

She suddenly had a vision of all these works disappearing into the world, never to be found again, and her heart ached for it. She knew people were dying on battlefields and she was just working in a gallery. But they were already being stripped of so much – food, safety, freedom – it just seemed so important to find a way to hold on to their humanity. Their culture. She pictured the empty walls of the gallery. What if nothing ever came back? What if this was it? Every artist's legacy, their genius, the beauty they brought into the world gone forever. The thought was more than she could bear.

29

Esther

The rain was relentless on the day Esther moved into the flat in November, and the three of them were soaked to the skin by the time they reached the front door. As icy rain slipped down the back of her collar, she fumbled with the key, her frozen fingers struggling to hold on to it with the paper tag handed to her by the estate agents with their new address emblazoned on it with a black marker.

The key predictably slipped to the ground and bounced on the cement step as Henry rushed to pick it up for her. As he looked up again, she saw the fear and vulnerability in his young brown eyes, and she knew it was her job to set the tone. She couldn't allow them to see any of her true feelings. As she turned the key in the lock and pressed her weight against the stiff door she commented jauntily, 'A new adventure, eh, boys?'

The boys had been hard work all through the move, as devastated as she had been, only acting out instead of getting upset. So, when she showed them their room, she tried to be upbeat.

'It's going to be fun to share together. You'll love being with your brother.'

The two of them looked at her as though she had two heads.

'But he's really messy,' retorted Daniel, 'and I want to keep my room tidy.'

'I'm not messy,' responded Henry, punching him on the arm.

'Okay, enough,' she said, 'let's have something to eat.' She had bought them fish and chips for the move, and they sat there like a sad ensemble, quietly eating, listening to the pouring rain hammering down the kitchen window, trying not to notice the 1970s avocado-green kitchen units. She hoped to be able to sell her grandmother's painting in the new year, once the appraisal was finished, and hopefully it could help them into a new place. She was determined to have her independence back, no matter what happened.

As she was clearing away the dinner and the boys were in their room deciding on their beds, her phone rang. She picked it up and moved out to her bedroom.

'Hi, I just thought I would check in. How did the move go?' James sounded cheerful and chipper, as though it was something they'd all wanted. She bit back her anger.

'We're in,' she said quietly. 'There's a lot to do, obviously.'

'I'm sure there is, but you'll make it homely like you always do, Esther.'

He was trying to be friendly. He felt guilty; she could tell.

'Well, you know it's hard on the boys. Such a move, and we'll have to see how it works out.'

'That's partly why I was calling. I have some really good news.'

Esther's stomach clenched. Whenever he had good news, it was always good news for him. Not for them.

'Yeah?' she said.

'The boys are going to be really excited about this. Can I talk to them?'

'What's this about, James? I don't want you to get them all riled up. It's hard enough, what we're going through today.'

'I promise you this is really good news. Get the boys. I've got something to tell them.'

Against her better judgement, she called the boys from their bedroom, where they were arguing over who was going to have which bed.

'Your father wants to speak to you,' she called out.

They came running in, with that innocence of youth that didn't see all the manipulation that was going on behind the scenes. Daniel grabbed the receiver first.

'Hi, Dad,' he said, so upbeat that she felt her heart wrench. Even though they'd been through so much, they still loved their father. Daniel's eyes shone with excitement. 'We're in our new house. I've got to share with Henry. It's not going to be very much fun.'

'I don't like sharing with Daniel, either,' Henry chirped in, trying to pull down the phone to his level. 'He's got too much stuff.'

They bickered for a while before their father stopped them. 'Well, I've got something to tell you that should make you happy. Now you know you're coming to me for Christmas, don't you?'

'Yes,' said Daniel as his eyes grew with anticipation.

Esther felt her heart sink. In all of the moving, she had forgotten this. She had forgotten that not only would she be in this horrible place, but she wouldn't even have the boys for Christmas. She listened closely as she quietly put away glasses in the cupboard from the box she had dropped off the day before.

'Well, I've got some great news. We're all going to go to Spain for Christmas. Angela and I made the decision last week.

It's too cold here in December. And we'd love to get some sun. So, we're going to treat you and Henry to a holiday.'

The boys started a shout with excitement, bouncing up and down.

'Yay, going on holiday for Christmas.'

Esther felt as if her blood ran cold. They hadn't agreed to anything like that. He was just supposed to be having them for Christmas Day. She allowed the commotion to calm down before telling the boys to go and unpack their boxes.

'I'm going to look for my bucket and spade, and where are my sunglasses, Mum?'

She promised to help Daniel find them as he raced off to his room to look for them. Esther grabbed the phone and walked to the farthest part of the house, where she slammed the bathroom door and hissed into the receiver, 'What the hell was that?'

'What do you mean?' responded James, defensively.

'You just promised to take the kids to Spain for Christmas.'

'God! I thought you'd be happy. There's never any pleasing you, is there? First you complain when I don't see them. Then when I want to take them away on holiday, give them a bit of a break from the English weather, you're complaining. What would you have to complain about this time?'

'You have no idea, do you?' said Esther. 'How long are you planning to take them on this holiday?'

'We booked it for six days,' he said sheepishly. He knew what he was doing.

'Six days. So, I won't see the boys at all over Christmas. And when do you leave?'

'We have tickets for Christmas Eve. We'll be back before New Year. You can have the boys for New Year.'

'Well, thanks very much. That's really kind of you. Our agreement was that I'd have them Christmas Eve.'

'And you *will* have them Christmas Eve.'

'What, for the two hours before they fly? All excited to go on holiday.'

'Esther, I'm not speaking to you any more. You have to make everything so difficult. This is why I couldn't stay married to you.'

'As I recall, it was me that divorced you,' she shouted into the phone.

He matched her level of anger. 'Look, get the kids' passports sorted out; we've already bought their tickets. I'll talk to the boys next week.' And with that he slammed the phone down.

Just over a month later, she stood at the airport with the boys, one in either hand. It had been a hard month of readjustment for them. Fortunately, the boys had actually liked their school, but everything else had been awful. It'd been more challenging for her to get to work. It took her another half an hour, and the flat was just so small and unfriendly and the boys were always on top of each other. She had tried her best to make it habitable. The sooner she could move from this situation, the better, though with the housing prices in the area where she wanted to live, she wasn't even sure how that would happen.

As James and Angela arrived, she hugged both the boys. They'd opened their Christmas presents from her that morning. Henry was hugging his new toys, and Daniel got the little hand-held game she had bought him and was going to enjoy it on the plane. Henry looked so small as she looked down at him. She brushed some hair from his forehead and kissed him.

'Now, you're going to be good, aren't you, Henry? You're going to have a lovely time on holiday.'

His little lip started to tremble.

'Can you not come with us, Mummy?'

Her heart broke.

'You know I can't come with you. You'll have a lovely time with Angela and your dad. And you'll be playing on the beach and having fun.'

'But I'm going to miss you, Mummy, and what if Santa brings presents to our house and we're not there?'

'I already told Santa where you would be this Christmas, and your presents will be waiting for you, as he knows all about it,' she said, trying not to allow the quiver to be heard in her own voice.

James and Angela greeted her as though they were all old friends.

'Are you looking forward to getting on the plane, boys?' he said, riling them up.

'Yes, Daddy,' they responded, though it wasn't very enthusiastic. Both boys looked exhausted from all that was going on, and even Daniel seemed to be sad. She hugged them both tightly as she said goodbye.

'All right then,' James responded, 'let's go.' And hoisting Henry up into his arms, he marched off towards the gate, Henry looking over his shoulder, offering a tiny, sad wave to his mother as they moved at a clip.

'See you next week,' said Angela, waving in turn with a broad smile. 'I'm sure they'll have a lovely time.'

Esther watched James walk her children away, and she couldn't stand the thought of returning to that flat without them. Suddenly she had a wild idea.

An hour later she was standing in front of the British Airways desk. 'How much would it cost to get a flight to Paris?' she asked. The guy smiled at her and gave her the price.

'How soon can I go?'

'We have a flight going later this evening.'

'I'll take it,' she said, handing over her credit card and praying it didn't exceed the limit. She knew this was a rash thing to do. But she couldn't stand the thought of being alone.

She would find somewhere to stay when she got there. Her thoughts drifted to the last time in Paris. In all of the difficulty of her life right now, only Édouard's friendliness seemed a beacon of light. Maybe he would have some good news about the painting, so she could sell it and move on.

30

SUMMER 1942

Isabelle

Isabelle rushed through the darkened streets, her footsteps echoing in the still night air. Streetlamps cast a dismal glow over the silent city, and the curfew warning bells tolled ominously in the distance. Her heart pounded as she tried not to think about the danger that awaited her if she was caught. But no matter how much fear coursed through her veins, she could not make herself turn away from the priceless pieces of art in need of protection at the museum, the ones she had left unlocked. Right from the beginning of the war, Lohse had made her keep the most expensive pieces in a locked room at the museum. She thought of those pieces now. Three Picassos were among them, one a beautiful sketch of a child. With all the worry of the missing art pieces, she had been preoccupied and forgotten to lock the room before she'd left and she had no guarantee that the museum would remain unscathed during the night. With all the riots, uprisings, and looting happening in Nazi-occupied France, anything was possible and she couldn't believe she had been so careless.

Isabelle moved stealthily through the gardens of the Tuileries, careful not to make a sound. At night, the magnificent sculptures that usually filled the grounds with life cast eerie shadows, looming over her as if watching her every move. Fear crawled up her spine like a spider as she advanced, her arms wrapped around herself for warmth, ever alert to any hint of danger lurking in the night.

She made her way around the edges of the path, keeping close to the shadows so that no one would see her. As she approached the building, she thought for a minute she saw lights flickering from within the museum but knew she had to be mistaken. No one would be there at this time of night. She froze for a moment to be sure, her heart beating wildly in her chest as she debated what to do next. Far off, a night bird called out, and at her feet an unseen creature scurried into the undergrowth. But something inside of her urged her forward, telling her that she had to protect what she had left exposed.

At the museum she crept past the two tired-looking Nazis taking a break, smoking a cigarette, and joking with one another. At the door, taking a deep breath, she reached her hand into a pocket and quietly lifted out the keys, noticing her hand was shaking. She slipped into the Jeu de Paume, wondering what she'd say if someone caught her here at this late hour.

Closing the door behind her, she felt an immense sense of relief settle over her. The museum was dark yet still managed to be breathtaking. On each wall, paintings glowed with a soft luminescence and gardens of flowers seemed to reach out and embrace her in their beauty. She always felt at home among them – as if each portrait were a beloved family member, offering solace and comfort. But there wasn't time to linger; even though she felt grateful for their presence, Isabelle had a job to do.

She sped swiftly through the hall on a hastened tiptoe to the private room she had left unlocked and, as she turned the corner, breathed a sigh of relief. It appeared nothing had been disturbed. After the problem with the logbook, the last thing she needed was anything else to go missing.

Isabelle checked twice. All the paintings for the afternoon were still there. She quickly went to her desk drawer, pulled out the keys, and crept towards the room. Locking it, she placed her keys back in her desk and locked the drawer. She took a moment to gather herself. She still had to make it back, still had to make it home without being seen by the Nazis. But at least she'd protected the art that was so important to her.

She was just about to move from her desk when she heard something far off in the museum. She stopped for a second. Was it a voice? Impossible. No one would be in the museum this late at night. She started to move again, and then she heard a laugh. She was sure of it. Muffled but close by. Her heart began to pound again. She should run – that would be the sensible thing to do – but she had to find out who it was. Maybe it would be a clue to the missing art.

She crept towards the room she could hear the muffled voices coming from. As she approached, she could now quite clearly hear two people talking in hushed voices.

The door was slightly ajar at the far end of the corridor, and light spilled out onto the wood floor. She moved towards it slowly. She didn't want to be spotted, but she had to see who it was. She crept into the shadows to look inside as the smell of smoke drifted towards her. Someone was smoking around the art, and that was very dangerous. So, this was not a burglar, who would surely not take the time to have a cigarette. Peering into the room through the crack of the door, she was shocked by what she saw, and she had to control herself from gasping out loud and alerting them to her presence.

Marina was draped across one of the desks, her blouse unbuttoned, her pink bra exposed, and sitting at the desk was Lohse. Isabelle felt sick. As she watched, Marina slipped down from the desk and started to button up her blouse. The commander took a moment to pull her towards him and kiss her neck savagely as she giggled.

'We do not have to leave yet, my darling,' he said.

'Oh, but we do,' she responded coyly. 'We have to get this done.' Her tone was playful and light. To Isabelle, this love affair looked as if it had been going on for a while.

They moved from the desk and to the back of the room, where Marina and the Nazi began gathering pieces of artwork into a crate he had set aside.

'Is the truck ready?'

'Do not worry, my love. I have it all in hand, both the truck and warehouse are ready.' She brushed his lips with a kiss.

'Cover the artwork to protect it from the sides of the crates,' he encouraged.

She tapped his face playfully. 'Leave it all with me.'

After packing the crate, they moved it out of the door at the end of the room towards the loading dock.

Isabelle had to follow them. Creeping outside, she kept out of sight as they loaded the crate into a truck. Frantically, she looked around, trying to figure out what to do. Then she saw her solution. Propped up against one of the walls was an old bicycle one of the delivery lads used to take messages back to the Louvre.

She would have to be careful, but without a second thought, she mounted the bike and followed behind the van, keeping her distance so they couldn't see her.

What the hell was Marina doing? And what warehouse was she talking about? So many questions and no answers. But as she pedalled with all her might, she was determined to get to the bottom of it all.

31

Isabelle

Isabelle broke into a sweat as she rode her bicycle through the shadowy streets of Paris. It was well past curfew and a risk to be out at such a late hour. But what else could she do?

She'd acted on instinct, grabbing a bicycle and pursuing Marina, but now an unfamiliar fear shot through her. Was she being brave, or foolish?

As Isabelle kept to the shadows, hiding from the Nazi patrol cars, her mind raced. What would she do now that her worst suspicions had been confirmed? What else had Marina stolen? To whom was she delivering the stolen artwork? Isabelle felt a knot form in her stomach as she cycled through the night, desperately seeking answers.

As Lohse turned down a side street, Isabelle pulled her bike to a stop, gasping for air. Peering out from the shadows, she watched in horror as Lohse and Marina unloaded the crate of valuable art into another warehouse. She felt a pang of sadness and anger as she thought of all the hard work she had put in to protecting these pieces of art and now this. She knew that she had to do something before they could get away with what they were doing.

She quickly ran towards the entrance of the warehouse. Fortunately, the door was not locked, so Isabelle easily slipped through it without being detected. Once inside, she slowly made her way through the darkness towards Marina and Lohse, who were preoccupied with their task. She knew she couldn't just take the art back. She would need a plan. Isabelle strained to hear their conversation.

'What will you do to offload the art?' Marina questioned.

'There's always someone in the black market interested,' Lohse replied. 'We'll keep it here for a while to make sure nobody notices its absence from the gallery, then I'll get in touch with some of my contacts in Paris and sell it on.'

'And how will we be paid?' Marina queried, her tone hinting at suspicion.

Lohse moved towards her and lightly kissed her lips. 'Leave that to me; I'll take care of everything and get what we deserve.' He gave her a smirk as he finished speaking.

Isabelle was not convinced by his words and nor was Marina, who seemed just as doubtful, judging from the expression on her face.

Hearing enough, Isabelle quickly slipped out of the warehouse and retrieved the bicycle. She pedalled as fast as she could through the cold, dark streets, eerily quiet because of the curfew.

She was not too far from home when she heard the sound of some activity in front of her down the street. Raised voices and people screaming. Isabelle recognized the sound of a Nazi raid.

She pedalled desperately, pushing her bike to its limits. But the sound of Nazi patrol cars seemed to get ever closer. As the road curved back into town, there was an alleyway that cut through to the other side. As the headlight of a Nazi patrol swung around the corner, she darted into the blackness between two buildings, jumping off her bike and holding her breath as a group of armed men marched by in lockstep. Just then, her bicycle dropped to the ground with a loud clatter and the soldiers halted and turned, shouting out in broken French for whomever it was to show themselves.

With no way out, she sprinted down the dark path, her lungs burning from fear and exertion, praying that what felt like eternity would end soon. Fear coursed through her veins; every second could mean capture or death. As the shadows engulfed her, Isabelle felt an iron grip clamp down on her shoulder, and before she could react, she was pulled into a dark house, the door slamming shut behind her. Adrenaline raced through her veins as the unknown assailant clamped his hand over her mouth, muffling her cries as she tried to scream.

The still air inside was heavy with a musky concoction of cigarettes and alcohol, and even in the darkness, Isabelle felt the penetrating heat from a man's gaze. His dark brown eyes were the only thing visible in the room as he hissed, 'Stop! Do you want to alert the entire city to your presence?'

Isabelle trembled with fear, but when he asked if she would promise not to scream when he removed his hand from her mouth, she nodded meekly. Better to take her chances inside than face certain death from the two Nazi soldiers outside.

As soon as he released his grip, Isabelle sucked in a lungful of air. It burned her throat as she attempted to catch her breath and steeled herself for whatever might come next. As her vision grew accustomed to the dark, her eyes frantically darted around the room, looking for any form of escape or something that could be used as a weapon should he prove to be dangerous.

The room was small and cramped, with only a single flickering candle in the kitchen casting eerie shadows on the walls. Isabelle could feel the man's eyes on her, and the intensity of his gaze made her heart race. She couldn't see his face clearly, but she could sense that he was tall and muscular, with an air of danger about him.

'Who are you?' he demanded, his question cutting through the air like a razor-sharp blade.

But Isabelle wasn't about to back down easily. Her defiant spirit took over as she countered, 'How dare you! And who are you?'

A knowing smile tugged at the corner of his mouth, acknowledging her bravery. 'You're very bold,' he remarked, his words laced with intrigue. 'A woman on her own in the house with a man she doesn't know.'

Her heart pounded in her chest like a drum, but she refused to show fear. 'I asked you a question,' she asserted, her voice trembling slightly.

'My name is Jules,' he revealed, but Isabelle remained cautious, unsure of his intentions.

'Why did you pull me inside?' she pressed, suspicion etched across her features.

'The Nazis are everywhere tonight,' he spat back. 'There has been a big raid. If you had stayed out there, they would have arrested you.'

He stepped away from her and eyed her quizzically. She was starting to make out his features in the dark, which weren't that unpleasant. He was tall, about six foot two, with dark hair, and wearing a cream vest. His broad shoulders were visible just beneath that, his arms well defined. And she could work out that he was a bit older than herself. Maybe mid- to late-twenties.

'What are you doing out at this time of night on your own?' he said, letting her go and offering her a chair. She still felt unsure and decided she would make pleasant talk for a while but not tell him anything important.

'I work at the Jeu de Paume.'

'For the Nazis? Then why were you running away from them?'

'I don't want to work for them. I have to work for them,' she said, clarifying.

'No one has to work for them if they don't want to.'

He offered her a cigarette, and she shook her head. He then offered her a glass of what looked like whisky. She shook her head again.

'So, you work at the museum. I hear they are moving many of the art pieces out from Jewish homes to take away to Germany. Is that correct?'

She nodded, and he must have seen the pain on her face.

'I take it you disapprove.'

'Of course I disapprove. No French person should approve. This is our art, not theirs.'

'So, what are you going to do about it?' he asked as he pulled a chair from the table and straddled it. 'Are you going to help them or stop them?'

'What do you mean stop them? I can't do anything.'

'Well, I just thought you seemed quite bold out here in the streets on your own. Maybe you had a plan.'

She felt the flush on her cheeks, and he must have caught it.

'You do have a plan, don't you?'

'Look, I don't know who you are. And I need to get home. So, if they're gone, I'm going to go.'

'All right,' he said, pulling back from his chair. 'Of course, you're free to go.' He stood up and followed her to the door, where they both listened quietly to the footsteps now echoing far away.

'Hide out down this alley and it'll take you back out to the Jeu de Paume or wherever your home is.'

She nodded and moved towards the door. She looked back at him.

'Thank you,' she said.

'You're welcome.'

She opened the door a crack, and the alley was clear, then looked back at her captor with a bob of her head. She was gone, arriving home safely. She used the back gate, not wanting to alert her mother to the late hour she was arriving home; with any luck Delphine had gone to bed early.

Closing the back door on the quiet house, she laid her back against it as she thought about all that had happened that evening, and felt the weight of what she had learned. Also about the stranger who had saved her, those dark, intense eyes upon hers challenging her to do more. She was determined to do just that and now, she had a clear idea of what that could be.

32

Brigitte

Brigitte nervously stirred her tea, the spoon clinking against the china cup as she tried to hold back the tears as she remembered her conversation with her daughter earlier that day. They had been browsing at the local market when a well-dressed man from the art gallery remembered Brigitte. After some polite conversation, he left, and it was then that Sophie, in a hushed whisper, asked, 'Why didn't that man call you by mine and Papa's last name? Do you not like it?' The simple question caused tears to prick Brigitte's eyes and sent a pang of emptiness through her chest. She quickly spun a tale about how during the occupation she had to assume an alias, but still, it hurt.

Later, her daughter had dissolved into tears. Brigitte's heart had ached as she cradled Sophie in her arms, her gentle touch stroking the young girl's hair. The pain etched on Sophie's face, the weight of her grief, truly weighed heavily on Brigitte's shoulders. Quietly rocking her, feeling the young girl's body trembling, her muffled sobs echoing through the room, Brigitte had whispered soft words of comfort into the stillness.

'It's all right, Sophie. I'm here.'

Sophie sniffed. It's just... I miss him so much, I'm frightened I will forget him.'

Brigitte tightened her embrace. 'You will never forget him and you always have your memories. Losing someone we love is incredibly difficult. Your father was wonderful, and his absence leaves an immense void in our lives.'

Sophie's chin quivered as she continued. 'I found this today. It had fallen behind my dresser.'

Brigitte drew in a breath as she looked down at the photo her daughter handed to her: Sophie, on her fifth birthday. The three of them surrounding her cake and Samuel smiling proudly as he looked down at his daughter. Sophie, dressed in her favourite fairy dress, was caught giggling with joy.

Brigitte swallowed down her own grief. She couldn't indulge in her own pain right now; her daughter needed her.

Even so, her voice was tight as she responded. 'Oh, my darling. Memories can be so bittersweet, but they also remind us of the love we shared. Your father cherished you deeply, and I'm certain he would want us to remember him with joy and love, even through the pain.'

Burying her face in her daughter's sweet-smelling hair, Brigitte continued in a whisper. 'Remember, you will never have to face this alone, Sophie. We will navigate this journey together, one step at a time. And your father's love will always surround us, guiding us through the darkness.'

Even after Sophie had cried herself to sleep, the anguish of loss had still weighted their home in a blanket of sadness that refused to leave. Brigitte was deeply sorrowful for her daughter and the toll this was taking on both of them. But she had so many other things to worry about ahead of them. Being Jewish was dangerous enough without false identities and secret plans. When Brigitte looked out at the world around her, she saw so much suffering. She knew it would be easy to give up hope and succumb to the darkness of despair, but instead, she held on to the plan she had crafted to keep them safe from harm. She refused to let fear win.

She waited until the moon had slipped away, leaving the night sky dark, and until the stars had blinked out one by one. Only under the cover of heavy darkness did she feel she had a chance of safety and protection. As she waited, her mother's gentle snoring drifted in from the spare room, a comforting reminder of the safety that existed in their home.

And only when she was certain that all was quiet did she dare to look in at her daughter. Sophie lay tucked up in her bed, her face now finally relaxed in peaceful sleep. Smiling to herself, she brushed a hand across Sophie's forehead, feeling the warmth of the little girl's skin, and the tension in Brigitte's body began to melt away. She closed her eyes and breathed a sigh of relief. Knowing that her daughter was now finally asleep, she could begin her new nightly task.

Brigitte tiptoed back into her bedroom and checked her blackout curtains were firmly drawn so she would be safe from prying eyes. She didn't want to alert the enemy. Her heart raced as she pulled her old dresser a few inches from the wall. A dull scratching and rattle accompanied each movement as it was shifted. Carefully she unscrewed the boards one by one, revealing the secret compartment she had created within. Gently, she reached inside and drew forth a large piece of canvas.

Brigitte unfolded it and placed it on its easel in the centre of the room. She lit a single candle against the darkness, the warm flame casting a gentle light over the painting. Stepping back, she searched the picture – a peaceful landscape starting to come to life. She felt proud to be copying Samuel's amazing master-piece, a reminder of the beauty of life in times of darkness. She pulled out stiff brushes from beneath her bed and began tracing strokes onto the canvas. Slowly, she studied the part she was going to paint next, the corner she'd been memorizing all day every time she passed it at the museum. Locking in her memory every proportion, brushstroke, shade of paint, and hint of light, she would emulate it just as he had made it. It was her only hope of her plan being executed.

'I may be able to work the strokes, my love, but I will never be able to light it with your passion,' she whispered out into the darkness. Sometimes she would pretend he was there with her as she painted, watching her work from a corner, guiding her hand. Tonight, she could feel his presence more strongly than ever before. It was as if the air was thick with the scent of his cologne, a familiar blend of musk and sandalwood that had always sent shivers down her spine. She could almost hear his voice in her ear, telling her how beautiful her art was and how much he loved her.

As she dipped her brush into the paint, she closed her eyes for a second and let herself sink into the moment. Then, supporting her hand to keep it steady, she moved it towards the canvas. She always hesitated for a second, fearful she would destroy all the work that she had done so far. And then she would dive in, gently stroking the brush back and forth, adding the colour, checking the light, making sure it was exactly as she remembered it. Then she could feel the canvas coming to life beneath her fingertips, the colours blending together in a way that was magical. It was like a dance, one that only she, her art and the presence of her husband could perform together.

She lost track of time as she painted, caught up in the flow of the moment. When she finally became so tired her eyes were closing, she yawned and stretched. Stepping back, she looked over her work with a critical eye, and satisfaction washed over her. Taking a shaky breath, she put down her brush, carefully hid the picture away, and blew out the candle, letting the darkness take over once again.

33

Esther

Esther stood in the plaza, her breath fogging from the cold winter air as she gazed up at the Louvre, its glistening windows shimmering under the abundance of golden Christmas lights. She stepped inside the Louvre building and marvelled at the beauty of its illuminated displays, pyramid windows aglow with the colourful lights and Christmas tree that lit up the foyer and reflected off the glass. Inside she noticed the sign for the evening reception Édouard had mentioned to her. People mingled around the show, drinking glasses of wine and eating delicate canapés off silver trays. Her heart quickened. She yearned to see her grandmother's picture once more.

She paid her admission and moved through the museum to peruse the beautiful art. When she had been younger, Esther had studied art herself. But it was so long since she had even had time to consider painting. Now she knew more about her grandfather's painting she wondered if she might start again. She had a lovely mentor who had helped her in her younger life, who had lived close to her in Chipping Campden. She was pulled from her reverie by someone tapping her shoulder, and turned around to see Édouard.

'Esther, what are you doing here?' he asked with curiosity. 'Let me get you a glass of wine and you can tell me what is going on.'

She complied, and soon they were perched in a corner, chatting while sipping on their drinks. Esther recounted how her children had gone on holiday with their father and without thinking twice she'd got on a plane.

'The pull of fate can be so powerful,' he said, wistfully, as he gently touched her arm. 'You needed to rediscover your roots. Your mother is ill and your children have gone, making your world seem so uncertain. But then you could rely on the solid platform of your ancestry. I've done some research and apparently your grandmother was very brave before she died, risking everything to try to save this artwork – which is remarkable.' He then relayed the events of her grandmother's dramatic death as in one last desperate attempt she had tried to save her grandfather's art from being stolen and taken to Germany by the Nazis.

Tears welled up in Esther's eyes as she listened to a story she had never heard before. 'I wish I had her strength,' she whispered when he had finished.

Édouard scoffed at the suggestion. 'What do you mean? You certainly have your own courage and bravery. Being there for your mother, raising two boys on your own, making the choice to leave a bad marriage. Many people could never find that kind of strength.'

Esther looked into his hypnotic green eyes and suddenly had the most irrational thought. She wasn't sure if it was the mood lighting combined with the glass of wine in her hand or the fact it was Christmas, but all of a sudden, she had this overwhelming longing to kiss him, right here in the middle of the Louvre. She could feel her heart racing as she resisted the urge to reach out and run her fingers through his dark, thick hair.

He seemed to sense her shifting emotions, as he paused mid-sentence, looking at her quizzically.

Emboldened by the wine, she was about to blurt out something stupid to the tune of, 'You're lovely.' But before she could act on her impulse, she was saved by the interruption of a slender man wearing an expensive suit who drew Édouard away to talk about a painting.

Minutes later he returned. 'We should go and see the picture that brought you here,' he encouraged.

They strolled towards it together, and Esther was in awe of its beauty even from a distance. The painting was set aside, on a high plinth with a red velvet base, its golden tones and bright reds lit brilliantly in the dark room. Mesmerized, she moved closer, feeling drawn to the vivid landscape depicted in *The Hayfields of Summer*.

She smiled. Édouard had been right. She had needed this physical representation of family courage right at this moment, to help her feel strong enough to move ahead in her own life. As she stared at the faces depicted on the canvas, it was as if she had been transported to a distant time and place, a world filled with limitless possibilities. For a moment, Esther felt surrounded by the same joy and hope she had felt as a child.

She read the short description by the picture. It told a brief history of it being found in a wall and how the original had been lost during the looting of the art from Paris. On a single line below were the words 'artist unknown'. She mused to herself about how many women of the past, like her grandmother, were known as artist unknown.

Édouard was pulled away to talk to someone and she continued to look around the gallery alone, sipping her wine and feeling more connected than she had in a long time. She thought of the photo of her grandmother at home in the box in her wardrobe. It had always been something passive, irrelevant, just a memory of a time gone by, but now she realized that there was so much more to it. Her grandmother had been brave and involved. Painting a picture probably under the cover of darkness to preserve a memory so important to her, and those genes were in Esther's own DNA. She wondered what her grandmother would tell her if she were still alive.

All at once she stopped and caught sight of something out of the corner of her eye. Rapidly she moved closer to a display of photographs illuminated on a board. It depicted Parisian heroes that were non-Jewish. People who had fought, and some who even had died, to keep the work of these lost Jewish artists alive. Esther couldn't help but gasp, as in the centre of the board was a picture of a young woman whom she recognized immediately as the woman in the picture with her grandmother. Quickly she read about her and how she'd managed to save tens of thousands of pieces of art with her bravery. She looked back at the photo and noticed she was standing under the same stone pillars from Esther's own picture at home.

Édouard startled her as he returned to her side.

'Do you know much about this woman?' she asked him breathlessly.

'Of course.' He smiled. 'This is Isabelle Valette. We in the art world are forever in her debt for her bravery.' He went on to tell Esther her story. After the war she had even gone to the Nuremberg Trials to uncover the Nazis who had been involved in the looting of their treasure.

'And would you know where this is?' asked Esther, pointing to the pillared building set behind Isabelle in the picture.

'Ah, yes, this is the Jeu de Paume, a small gallery not far from here. It was the place the Nazis stored the art before it was transported to Germany.'

'Would it be possible to visit it, do you think?' Esther asked. 'I think my grandmother worked there.'

'Yes, it should be open the day after Christmas. Will you still be here?'

Esther thought for a second, trying to calculate how much money she had on her credit card.

'I think so,' she said, warming to the idea of staying.

'Then I would be honoured to take you there. If you would like.'

'Yes, I think I would like that,' she said. Her face reddened as she felt that pull of attraction to him again. But she covered up her embarrassment by turning away, saying, 'I have this over-whelming need to know all of my grandmother's story.'

'Of course,' he said, then seemed to be grappling with saying something. Finally, he asked in a quiet tone, 'Esther, where are you staying tonight?'

She shrugged. She hadn't even had time to book a room yet. 'I suppose I will just go and get a room in a hotel,' she said offhandedly.

He began to chuckle. 'On Christmas Eve, in Paris?'

'You think I might have difficulty?' Suddenly, she felt pretty silly. She hadn't even factored in the holidays.

'Impossible,' he added.

He must have seen the panic in her expression as she had visions of sleeping on a park bench. He covered his hand with hers.

'If it is not too uncomfortable for you, you are welcome to stay with me and Camille. She would be very excited to meet an English lady. She practises having tea parties all the time.'

'Oh no, I couldn't impose...' she began to say, before he shook his head.

'I insist. You would be my guest and doing me a great favour. It's very hard to be alone for Christmas. I know it is still hard for me with my daughter ever since my wife died. The loneliness, the traditions that you've established with another person.' His voice drifted away as he contemplated his own words.

'I understand,' Esther reassured him.

There was a slight pause while he seemed to be contemplating asking her something.

She smiled to encourage him as he drew in breath and asked his question.

'What are you doing tomorrow?'

Esther shook her head. 'I really don't know. I didn't think much past getting on that plane and just coming here. It was as though I was driven...'

'Or pulled,' he added. 'My daughter and I would be pleased to have you. It would be delightful.'

She suddenly felt panicked. Had she thrust herself upon this poor man and his family?

'No, that is so kind of you. But I'll just get a flight back tomorrow.'

'On Christmas Day!? No, that would be terrible,' he said. 'You will stay and have Christmas dinner with us tomorrow, and there'll be no more about it. Do not think anything of it. It's just two friends enjoying Christmas together, and both are alone at this time. So it's not a big deal. We'll be excited to have you.'

34

SUMMER 1942

Isabelle

Isabelle stood outside the Jeu de Paume and frantically patted her pockets again as a bead of warm sweat trickled down the back of her neck. The keys definitely weren't there. She searched her bag for the third time, her mind reeling with the consequences. She heard footsteps and, glancing over her shoulder, saw Brigitte hurrying up the path to the museum. Her breath was coming in short, jagged gasps, signifying she had been running. She was grateful it wasn't Marina. The last thing she had wanted was to alert her to the situation, especially after what had happened with the logbook.

'I seem to have misplaced my keys somewhere,' she said hurriedly. 'I must have left them on the kitchen table.'

'Don't worry,' responded Brigitte. 'I have mine with me.' She dived into her bag and pulled out the keys, unlocking the door. They both walked inside.

Isabelle couldn't believe that the keys were gone. She hadn't left them at home; that had been a lie. Charlotte had cleared the table before she'd left, and she always kept them in one place in her bag. The last time she had remembered seeing them was when she'd unlocked the door of the museum the night before.

She removed her hat, smoothed her blonde curls into place nervously and hung her coat on the hat stand. Pressing a hand to her stomach, she sighed, feeling it tighten with fear. Her gaze landed on the desk in front of her. She searched every corner, as if hoping the keys would appear by magic. Even though she knew it was hopeless, she opened each drawer slowly, rifling through its contents until they were all laid bare. Nothing. The lost keys were nowhere to be found.

Worrying was pointless, but still, she couldn't help but feel a chill run down her spine, not only with what might happen if they got into the wrong hands, but because of the consequences of her actions in such politically charged times. Everyone was under suspicion, and no one could be trusted.

It was around midday when Brigitte came into her office. Isabelle had her head down, checking the brochures for accuracy for the next scheduled event.

'Mademoiselle Valette, someone's here to see you,' Brigitte called from the doorway.

Isabelle sighed. 'Can you handle it, Brigitte? I'm up to my eyes.'

Brigitte's eyes widened. 'He insists on speaking with only you, and he doesn't look like our usual clientele.'

'What do you mean?' Isabelle asked, looking back down at the page she was reading.

'You should come and see,' Brigitte answered with the hint of a smile.

Despondently, Isabelle put down the catalogue and walked towards the counter. To her surprise and horror, she saw the man from the night before. Before she could say anything, he offered his hand.

'Miss Valette, we met a few years ago. I am a friend of your family,' he said with a broad smile and unwavering conviction. She was taken aback. The night before he had seemed nice-looking in the darkened room, but in the full light of day he was very striking. Gone was the day-old stubble and instead of a vest he wore a nice-fitting suit. As he held out his hand for her to shake it, the smell of a sultry aftershave wafted towards her, and she could feel heat rising in her cheeks, not only with how his warm, brown eyes drew her in this morning, but also because of his outrageous lie.

Yet she also understood why he would cover up their meeting from the previous night. How else would they explain what had happened?

'Ah yes, give me your name again?' she asked softly, trying to keep her tone steady.

'Jules.' His eyes twinkled mischievously. 'Would you have time for coffee with me? I would love to catch up with you and your family news. You may be interested in something I have to share with you.'

He raised his eyebrows slightly as he emphasized the last word and instantly she understood he had her keys. She flicked her eyes sideward. Marina was right next to her at the desk, eyeing him up and down, lustfully. But she didn't seem to suspect anything.

'Ah, yes, that would be wonderful,' Isabelle responded. 'I am pretty busy, but in an hour's time, if you could come by, we could go for lunch.'

'Excellent,' he said. 'I look forward to hearing all about what your family has been up to. See you in an hour.'

He turned to leave the gallery, and she tried not to show her relief at him moving away from the desk.

Marina looked up. 'Who was that?' she asked, her eyes following him all the way out of the door.

'An old friend of my family,' said Isabelle flatly, not prepared to elaborate or lie any more. She wasn't as good at it as he was.

She spent the next hour in knots, not only because she was worried about her keys, but also because she would now have to have lunch with this man. Not that he was unpleasant. But she suspected he was in the Resistance and she was still thinking about the way he had challenged her to get more involved in saving the art; that felt dangerous. And now she would spend time with him.

At one o'clock sharp, he arrived, and she smiled as she gathered her bag and coat.

Marina couldn't bear it. She stepped out from behind the desk to greet him. 'My name is Marina Belleveau. If you have any need of anything in the gallery, I can also help you. I know you are friends with Isabelle, but there are other things that I might know that she doesn't.'

A curious look crossed his face before he took her hand and shook it gently.

'Thank you, Miss Belleveau. Very nice to meet you. Isabelle, shall we go?' he said, catching her eye.

She nodded, hoping no one could hear her heart thudding in her chest or see her shaky knees below her skirt. Then, outside the museum, she turned to him. 'You have my—'

He signalled at her to be quiet.

'Not yet,' he said, 'we're not far enough away yet. There are too many people about.'

They walked together down a winding street that led to a tiny bistro. The pavement was lined with old trees whose roots formed small ridges along the edges, and their branches drooped over the two as they walked just below them. The leaves rustled in a light breeze and cast dappled shadow along the path. The café was a little ramshackle hole in the wall, empty except for a grey, fluffy cat stretched out in the sun on one of the tables. Jules gestured towards the table sitting under an umbrella near the door. A tired-looking waiter with a day's worth of stubble greeted them with two menus and they ordered their lunch before settling into conversation.

'We meet again, Isabelle.'

She couldn't wait any longer. 'You have my keys?' she hissed.

He put his hand in his pocket and slid them across the table to her.

'You must have dropped them in my house, though it did intrigue me what a woman working at the museum would be doing out in the middle of the night with her keys to the gallery. No good, for sure!'

She sat back in the chair and blew out a sigh of relief and frowned with curiosity.

'How did you find out my name?'

'I know a few people,' he said covertly.

His answer confirmed to her he was working for the underground. She wondered whether because of that, she could trust this man with her secret. She desperately needed to confide in someone, and she didn't know who else to talk to.

'You said last night you wanted to protect this country.'

He glanced around and then nodded.

'These people that you know, can they make things happen? Things to stop what is going on here?'

The waiter came with their drinks and Jules waited until they were alone again.

'Maybe. Why do you ask?'

She sucked in breath. 'I need help.'

He sat back in his chair, a curious look on his face. He seemed to be weighing up if he could trust her too. No one could really be sure of anyone's loyalty during this time.

'What kind of problem?' he asked, taking a sip of the wine the waiter had just placed on the table.

She decided to take a chance.

'As you may already know, the Nazis are using the Jeu de Paume to house many of their "finds", as they call them, from Jewish homes. Beautiful art, paintings and portraits. They are all being shipped to Germany for the Führer and his group. But last night, I found something out. The girl you met at the museum, Marina – she's stealing some of the art for herself. I need someone who can help me come up with a plan to figure out a way that we can trap her. If Göring or his men find out, the consequences could be very serious.'

He narrowed his eyes, as if assessing her, before saying, 'You seem to care a lot about art.'

Isabelle felt annoyed. 'Of course I care about art. It's the most important thing in the world. If all of our treasures leave this country, what will we have? Where is the heart and soul of this nation?'

'I've always seen the heart and soul as the people,' he said quietly.

She felt reproached.

'Of course,' she said, 'that goes without saying.'

'It does?' he said. 'I just wondered for a minute. I might be able to help you. But there's a cost.'

'What cost?' she asked.

'Dinner this evening with me.'

She felt her cheeks glow pink. It wasn't that he wasn't handsome, but she had so much on her mind right now.

'If I decide to have dinner with you, you will organize somebody to help me?'

'I will decide after dinner. You might be working for the enemy,' he responded with mock seriousness. A smile spread across his face, assuring her he was actually joking. 'You also might enjoy it.'

She became defensive. 'This is for the art,' she said.

'We will see,' he said, scanning her face. 'Because maybe I can convince you differently by the end of the evening.'

'Don't be so sure,' responded Isabelle.

Though her interest was indeed piqued. And she actually looked forward to the evening when she would see him again.

35

Brigitte

As soon as Brigitte arrived home from the gallery that night, she knew something was wrong. Her mother was at the doorstep of the apartment, wringing her hands and pacing anxiously. When Brigitte caught sight of her expression, she knew that whatever it was, it couldn't be good. Odette gave her a polite smile, but the tension in her grip as she pulled her inside told her otherwise.

Fear overwhelmed Brigitte. All she could think about was her daughter.

'Is Sophie all right?'

'Sophie is fine,' came the swift assurance from her mother as she whisked her past the living room, signalling to where Sophie was quietly engrossed in painting.

Before Brigitte had the time to even say hello to her daughter, she was already being dragged into the kitchen.

Once they were alone and she'd closed the door, Odette lowered her voice before speaking again. 'The Nazis have arrested Frank Renaud.'

Brigitte felt all the air rush out of her chest and sat down heavily in a chair at the kitchen table as her mother continued.

'I just found out this morning. I went to the bakery as usual and stood in line, as we all have to do. We were discussing rationing and swapping recipes, talking about the weather and how nice it had been. And then somebody told us all about Mr Renaud. Apparently, the Germans went to his house yesterday and raided it, taking him and his wife away. And no one has seen him since.'

Brigitte let out a long, slow breath she had been holding and thought about the ramshackle house and the sweet man who had provided her with her false identity. He was the man whose safety her family depended on.

'Do you have any idea where they've taken him?'

Her mother shook her head. 'But it can't be good. Brigitte,' she said solemnly, 'you've got to think about yourself. You've also got Sophie to think about. So maybe you should get away. Now. Perhaps not stay in Paris but get away from here.'

Brigitte's skin grew cold. She couldn't leave. She couldn't leave without finishing what she was doing for her husband.

'I can't, Maman. I have something important I need to do.'

Her mother stared at her in disbelief, grief lining the wrinkles around her eyes. 'What do you have to do? What's more important than your life? Or your daughter's? They could come and march you away tomorrow if he's been exposed – it won't be long before they round up everyone he's helped.'

Brigitte was filled with dread of the danger she was living under, but she didn't want to give up all the work she'd been doing, and leaving would mean leaving behind her last memories of Samuel.

'Maman, I just need some more time,' she said softly.

· · ·

Two days later, her mother's face looked even grimmer than before.

'What's going on?' Brigitte asked in a hiss as she followed her mother into the kitchen again.

'Do you remember Hannah and her sister?'

A memory of two sweet older Jewish women they knew flashed into her mind.

'Well, they were taken away today,' her mother said, her voice trembling.

Fear permeated every corner of the room as Brigitte grasped for a plan that would make things right.

Her mother interrupted her thoughts with an urgent suggestion. 'You have to think about this – I want you to start planning to leave.'

Brigitte felt overwhelmed by events. Even if it was a coincidence about Hannah and her sister, her mother implored her, 'I don't want this to happen to you. It may only be a matter of time before they trace you too.'

Sophie rushed into the kitchen.

'Maman, look what I did.' She placed a picture in front of her mother on the kitchen table, a beautiful picture she had drawn.

'It's lovely, darling. You did a wonderful job. How was school?'

Sophie went into an extended rendition of her day as Brigitte tried to think, with her mother peering at her with that worried expression knotting her eyebrows.

After everyone went to bed, Brigitte went straight to the picture and started working. She would work tirelessly now, through the night if she had to, to finish the work. As soon as it was finished, she and Sophie could get out of town, and they would be safe. She would still have to travel under the assumed name. But maybe, maybe, if she were lucky, they would not be found out, and she would get away. But what about her mother?

Her mother wore the yellow star. It could be any time they would take her away. Brigitte couldn't deal with everything. But she knew she felt compelled to finish what she had started. She felt compelled to finish this picture if it was the last thing she did.

36

Esther

It was late when they left the Louvre, and the winter air was cold and crisp, stinging Esther's cheeks as she and Édouard strode through the streets of Paris. It was late, but the spirit of Christmas was everywhere in the air. The festive cheer seemed to be welcoming them at every turn, with carols being sung in French, the peal of church bells calling people to midnight mass, and the scent of spiced wine wafting from nearby bistros.

They crossed a bridge over the Seine, where holiday music echoed from party boats. and the Eiffel Tower was twinkling brightly, its white lights dancing in the night sky like a beacon. Esther smiled, marvelling at the beauty of the scene before her. As they made their way closer, the lights seemed to envelop them, as if in a warm embrace.

She suddenly felt giddy and as she drank in all the beauty around her and the pleasant company of this kind man, she suddenly felt as hopeful as a schoolgirl.

On the way home, they walked through the Jardin du Luxembourg, which had been transformed for the night. The elegant gardens were lit with colourful Christmas lights and decorated with fragrant fir trees, giving the grounds a magical ambiance. As they passed the Fontaine de l'Observatoire, they paused to listen to a solo violinist playing a haunting rendition of 'Silent Night'. The music filled the air with a peaceful, reverent atmosphere, and as she stood there, the cold breath of the night fogging the air, Esther looked up into the night sky at all the stars twinkling above and she breathed deeply.

As the final notes of the carol echoed around them, she felt an incredible assurance that everything was going to be all right in her life.

Her thoughts were interrupted as Édouard leaned in to whisper to her, 'This is a famous wishing fountain.'

She looked down into the still, black water and caught sight of the flash of silver and copper coins lying among the stones.

Édouard pulled out two bright silver coins, his fingers soft and warm as he handed one to Esther, urging her to make a wish. Taking the coin from his hand, she held it close to her heart and closed her eyes.

Please, let me be able to find the right place to live for me and the boys, a place my ex-husband cannot take away from us and somehow still be able to keep my grandmother's painting, too, she wished quietly to herself.

Without another word, she tossed her coin into the fountain and watched as it disappeared beneath the rippling water.

Édouard did the same and they smiled wistfully at each other as they continued to make their way through the gardens.

When they arrived at his lovely apartment, his daughter came rushing to the door to greet him, a harassed babysitter on her heels.

There was a hurried conversation in French, which even Esther understood from the gestures implied, though the babysitter had tried to get his daughter to bed, she had been waiting for her father to come home.

Introductions were made but Esther took herself hastily off to bed to let Édouard get his daughter to sleep. But once she was under the soft covers in his spare bedroom, she didn't find herself thinking about her children as she normally did. She found herself dwelling on Édouard, the beautiful evening and her growing feelings for him. It seemed impossible because they lived such different lives, but she couldn't deny the fact she felt something more for him than just friendship, and the fact they lived so far away from each other saddened her.

37

SUMMER 1942

Isabelle

Isabelle stared at her reflection in the mirror, her stomach fluttering with nerves. She had never been on a real date before; not for lack of desire, but she struggled with the idea of being emotionally vulnerable with another person outside of her family.

She nervously fixed her necklace, a gift to her from Madeline some years ago, and brushed her hair thinking about the night ahead. As much as she wanted to impress Jules, she felt a strange pang of concern. Could she trust him with all of her secrets?

She forced herself to take a deep breath. If he was in fact a freedom fighter, as she suspected, he was someone she could trust; but how could she be sure?

As she walked down the stairs her father noticed her from his study and came out to look at her.

'My goodness, is this Isabelle? You look amazing,' he retorted incredulously, drawing the book he was reading to his chest in a gesture of surprise. Hearing his comment, Delphine joined him in the hallway, drying her hands on a tea towel, as Isabelle's cheeks glowed crimson.

'It is an old dress, Papa. You know how hard it is to get new clothes now.'

'But it looks perfect on you,' he continued, as he nodded his head with pride.

'Are you going out?' her mother asked with excited anticipation.

'Only with a friend,' she said, playing it down, knowing that that wasn't quite true, but she didn't want them to worry if she revealed the truth, besides which she wasn't enjoying this display of attention she was garnering.

'What friend?' her father asked quizzically.

'A new one,' she said, a little too hurriedly for it to sound casual.

And though her father still seemed suspicious, he just nodded his head.

'Well, I am glad to see you doing anything that isn't work,' her mother said, hugging her daughter. 'You look beautiful. You should wear your hair down more often,' she added, smoothing down her daughter's blonde curls.

Isabelle nervously touched her hair. She liked having it up for work and had forgotten how different she looked with it down.

'Well, have a lovely time,' her mother enthused. 'And don't forget to be back before the curfew at nine o'clock.'

'Of course, Maman,' Isabelle responded, kissing both her parents on their cheeks before leaving.

The Parisian night sky was full of stars, and Isabelle felt a sense of calm wash over her as she walked the quiet streets. She was still nervous, but her determination to learn more about Jules and the underground network spurred her on.

As she made her way to the bistro he had suggested they meet at, Isabelle felt a sense of trepidation wash over her. Her hands were clammy, and she could feel her heart pounding against her ribcage.

As she entered the restaurant, she had never felt more uncomfortable or uncertain in her life. But as soon as she laid eyes on Jules, she felt her breath catch in her throat, and all of her worries suddenly faded away. He was already waiting for her at a corner table, dressed smartly in a dark jacket and trousers, and he stood out among the other patrons who were laughing and talking noisily around him. He seemed apart, yet immensely confident at the same time. He joked with the waiter as she watched him, admiring his effortless charm from a distance before she made herself known.

Jules finally spotted Isabelle standing shyly by the door, and his face lit up with a smile, which only made her heart flutter even more. He approached her with an easy grace, and she felt a flush rise to her cheeks as he smiled at her.

She could hardly believe that the night before she had felt so much animosity towards this gorgeous-looking man.

'Isabelle, you look beautiful,' he said, taking her hand and kissing it lightly.

For a moment, she forgot everything. They sat down, and Isabelle ordered a glass of red wine to calm her nerves.

Over dinner, Jules regaled her with tales of his exploits with the Resistance, and finally, over his glass of wine, he lowered his voice as he looked at her. 'So, you wanted my help for something?'

'That was the arrangement, yes,' she stammered, glancing nervously around her. She had held her secret so close to her heart for so long, it felt strange to share it with someone she hardly even knew. 'I have a problem.'

He sat back in his seat and scanned her face, listening intently as she continued.

'As I told you over lunch, one of the girls I work with at the museum is stealing art. What I didn't tell you is that she is working with a Nazi art dealer stealing the works that come in to the museum.'

'Why would you care,' he said nonchalantly, 'if the Nazis want to steal from themselves?'

She felt hot with anger. He seemed to have no regard for what this meant.

'First, if it is found out by the Nazi commanders, we will all be in trouble, and secondly, I want you to help me steal it back and hide it.'

Jules raised an eyebrow, his interest obviously piqued.

'Steal it back?' he said, leaning forward with a smirk.

He took another sip of his wine as he considered her proposal. A look of mischief played across his face.

'Isabelle, this is dangerous. If you're caught, it could mean your life.'

Isabelle nodded, her heart pounding in her chest. She knew the risks, but the thought of the art being lost forever was just too much to bear. 'I understand, but I have to do something. This art belongs to the people, not the Nazis. Besides, if we steal it back, who are they going to report it to? They would have to admit they'd stolen it in the first place.'

He considered her words as he scanned her face, his gaze drifting to her lips.

'Do you have any information on where the stolen art is being kept?'

'Last night, that's what I was doing. Following them on my bicycle.'

A look of amusement played on Jules's lips as he repeated, 'On your bicycle? I didn't realize we had a bicycle brigade of Resistance fighters.'

Isabelle couldn't help but smile at his teasing. 'Well, it's the only mode of transportation I had at the time,' she said ruefully.

Jules finished his drink and then leaned in closer to her. So close she could feel the whisper of his breath on her lips and a surprising shiver ran down her back. 'All right, Isabelle. I'm in. But we need to be careful and we'll need a plan. Are you up for this?'

Isabelle nodded, feeling a surge of adrenaline at the prospect of taking action. 'Yes, I am,' she said with determination.

He leant forward even closer and for a minute she thought he might kiss her but then her attention was drawn to someone passing the table. He was a shorter, older man, balding, and with intense dark eyes. He wore beige linen pants and a blue shirt buttoned to the neck. She recognized him instantly and jumped to her feet.

'Señor Picasso!' she gasped.

The man stopped short, peered at her for an instant, before his eyes lit up with recognition.

'Miss Valette, from the museum,' he responded, crushing out the cigarette he was holding into a nearby ashtray before taking her hands and politely kissing her on both cheeks.

'I heard you had left Paris for the south,' she said.

He lifted his arms as he shrugged his shoulders. 'There is no peace anywhere to be had right now and besides, my studio is here and I missed the buzz of the city.'

She introduced Jules. 'I love your work,' Jules said enthusiastically, as he shook the painter's hand.

Picasso shrugged again. 'It is not so popular with our visitors. Not that I mind; I have no wish to have my work hanging in Hitler's front room.'

They all smiled at his comment as he bid them goodnight and left the restaurant.

After Picasso was gone, Jules insisted on walking her home, and as they strolled down the street together, Isabelle felt a continued unexpected sense of ease and comfort in his presence that was new to her.

When they reached her house, she led him to the gate to the

back terrace. The last thing she needed was her family seeing her with this handsome stranger and all the questions that would provoke. They paused outside the gate; the air was scented with Delphine's flowers just beyond the wall and the sound of the waterfall was all that could be heard.

In this darkened space, it felt somewhat intimate and as their eyes met, she saw something warm and inviting in his gaze. He then leaned forward and she braced herself, realizing for the first time she wanted a man to kiss her and that shocked her. He seemed to contemplate that very action as he stared down at her lips, but then, thinking better of it, kissed her gently and slowly on the cheek. Even so, Isabelle felt herself blushing as he drew away from her.

'I'll see you tomorrow,' he said in a whisper, before heading back down the path and disappearing into the darkness of the night.

The next day, Isabelle wasn't working and found herself eagerly making her way to Jules's house to discuss their plan for stealing back the art from Lohse and Marina. When she arrived around noon, she was pleased to find him studying several maps of the city, and she showed him where the stolen art pieces were being held.

Jules looked up from the maps, his eyes gleaming with determination. 'Are you ready to become a fully-fledged Resistance fighter?'

Isabelle smiled. 'I have been doing that since the beginning of the war, just not outside of the museum.'

He laughed, highlighting points on the map. 'First, let's go over the details of what to do if there is a problem. There are established safe houses at strategic locations all through the city. If we're compromised, we can quickly retreat to one of these safe houses, so memorize these addresses.' He indicated three points on the map closest to Marina's warehouse. 'There we'll have provisions, alternative clothing, and resources to blend in.'

'Having multiple escape routes and temporary hiding places, making it difficult for the Nazis to track us down,' Jules continued, 'we should also have prearranged signals and codes to communicate with our fellow Resistance members. I will teach you those; that way, if we get separated or need assistance, we can send discreet messages to coordinate our escape and regrouping efforts.'

Isabelle nodded, feeling a certain thrill.

'We will move under the cover of darkness, utilizing the shadows and reduced visibility to our advantage. It will make our movements less conspicuous and increase our chances of evading detection. Taking full advantage of back alleys, hidden passages, and any other discreet paths that can provide us with an advantage. We can walk these paths in the daytime, so you know them so well you can navigate them with ease once it is dark.'

They spent several hours discussing tactics, possible routes that could be taken, and options for escaping if they were spotted or followed by enemy forces during their mission. By dusk they had formed a detailed plan.

As she left his house that evening, he paused at the door again and looked into her eyes deeply before leaning in and giving her another gentle kiss on both cheeks. But as he did so, this time his lips grazed her own, sending a thrill through her body. But she quickly pulled away. As attractive as this man was, they had to stay focused on their mission, and she wasn't going to let her heart become caught up in anything that would distract her from that.

'Goodnight, Isabelle,' he said. 'Tomorrow I will take you to the Resistance meeting, where we can get people to help us.'

38

Esther

On Christmas morning the peal of church bells woke her up and she couldn't believe that it was already ten o'clock. She stepped onto the little black wrought-iron balcony of Édouard's apartment to see all the morning festivities unfold before her. The cold winter air made her shiver as she wrapped her dressing gown around her, but the sight before her warmed her heart. Below her, on the streets of Paris, people were bustling about, spreading joy and cheer. Children were running around with sparkling presents, their laughter echoing through the streets. The smell of freshly baked croissants and hot chocolate wafted up to her nose from a nearby apartment.

But as she looked around, she saw something that drew her in. A dark-haired, handsome man was walking towards her building. He wore a long camel-coloured coat that swayed with each step, and his eyes sparkled in the sunlight that was peeking through the clouds. She realized with a jolt it was Édouard, a small package tucked under his arm.

As he neared the building, she couldn't help but feel a little nervous. But as he looked up and saw her standing on the balcony, she felt her heart skip a beat.

'*Bonjour, Esther, joyeux Noël,*' he called up with a wave.

Esther felt her cheeks flush as she waved back, her heart beating faster.

'Happy Christmas, Édouard,' she called back, a smile spreading across her lips. 'Where have you been, so early?'

Édouard looked up at her with a mischievous glint in his eye. 'I have a little present for you,' he said, holding up the small package in his hand.

She moved back inside to anticipate his arrival and noticed herself in the mirror. She looked rested. The lines across her forehead seem to have softened.

'Happy Christmas, Esther,' she whispered into the mirror. 'Look what you've got yourself into now.'

As she made her way to the bathroom, she passed a bedroom where a little girl with Édouard's green eyes looked timidly toward her. Esther moved inside and smiled, getting down to the little girl's height.

'Good morning, Camille.'

Camille smiled back shyly. 'Hello,' she said in English in a soft voice.

Esther smiled at the little girl, trying to put her at ease. 'Well, your father is a new friend of mine, and I thought I'd come and spend some time with you both on Christmas.' She spoke slowly, hoping the girl understood some English. She couldn't help but feel a pang of sadness as she looked down at her. She couldn't imagine how difficult it must be for her to grow up without her mother.

Camille's face lit up at the mention of Christmas. 'Do you want to see my presents?' she said in French, though Esther got the gist of what she was saying. Jumping off the bed, she ran to a pile of unwrapped gifts in the corner of the front room.

Esther followed Camille, smiling at the child's energy and

enthusiasm. As they looked through the presents, she swallowed down the pain of not being with her own sons.

Camille's eyes lit up with excitement as Édouard arrived home. Esther couldn't help but feel a twinge of envy as she watched the way Édouard looked at Camille. She could tell that he was a wonderful father and that he loved his daughter deeply.

'Édouard, you're awake so early,' Esther said as she turned to face him.

He nodded, his eyes never leaving his daughter. 'Yes, I just had to run a few errands before we ate. We have already been up for hours,' he said, shooting a playful rebuking glance towards Camille.

Esther smiled at him, the package he had brought still tucked safely under his arm.

'And what's in the package?'

Édouard grinned, holding it out to her. 'Open it and see.'

As Esther unwrapped it, she couldn't help but feel a flutter of excitement in her chest. Inside was a beautiful miniature of the same hayfields as her grandfather had painted.

'I had this at my office. This artist does not have the flair or passion of your grandfather's work. But I thought you might like it.'

Esther smiled broadly and ran her fingers over the intricate details of the painting. 'It's perfect,' she said, her voice soft and full of emotion.

'I'm glad you like it,' Édouard said, his eyes warm as he watched her.

'I have nothing for either of you,' she said despairingly.

Camille shook her head. 'Papa Noël brought me so many gifts. I am fine,' she said quickly in French as her father translated for Esther.

He added with a whisper, 'She understands some English but doesn't like to speak it.'

The little girl looked up and blushed a little.

'Come, Esther,' she said in broken English. 'You can play with some of mine.'

Esther laughed. She was quickly swept up in this family's love and fun. Camille was delightful. Édouard cooked a beautiful brunch, and as they sat at the table, he raised his glass.

'To new friends and family.'

'And to Maman in heaven,' his adorable daughter added.

'And your amazing mother.' He smiled, the sadness etched on his face for a moment.

Hours later, the two of them sat on his balcony with a cheese plate and a glass of wine.

'You really saved me today, Esther. I was not looking forward to it. But, you know, when you have children, you have to do the best you can.'

'I understand,' she said, taking a sip of her wine. 'And Camille is such a wonderful child, she made the day so much brighter.'

Édouard smiled, his eyes softening as he looked out over the Parisian skyline. 'She's my everything, you know. I never knew I could feel so protective until I had her. It was so hard when we lost her mother.'

Esther felt a pang of jealousy, wishing she could have a man who loved her boys like this. But she pushed the feeling aside, not wanting to ruin the moment.

'I'm sure you'll find someone,' she said, trying to sound optimistic.

Édouard chuckled, shaking his head. 'I don't know, Esther.'

Esther understood the complications of dating in her own life.

'But don't give up hope,' she said, placing a comforting hand on his arm. 'Love has a funny way of finding us when we least expect it.'

Édouard smiled at her, his eyes softening as he looked at her. 'Perhaps you're right,' he said, his voice low and husky.

39

SUMMER 1942

Isabelle

A few days later, Isabelle met Jules at his house one evening. They barely spoke as she followed him down narrow alleys and they wound their way through the silent streets of Paris to the Resistance meeting. He was cautious as they travelled, looking carefully down streets for Nazi checkpoints and making sure that she was always with him.

Finally, he led her down a dimly lit alley with the overwhelming stench of rotten fish and decaying vegetables. She thrust a hand to her nose. He noticed her grimace and smiled, whispering, 'The Nazis don't like the smell either. A good deterrent, don't you think?'

Eventually, a blue door with peeling paint came into view, and Jules knocked three times with a special rhythm. A stooped man with drooping red eyes and a heavily lined forehead opened it, peered up at him, and nodded, indicating that he could come in.

They traipsed past him into a hallway crowded with dusty furniture and old framed photographs that were hung crookedly on the walls. The air was stale and heavy with the musky scent of wet fur, likely from an ageing pet somewhere in the house. Anxious anticipation bubbled in her chest as she ventured farther into the building. At the end of the hall she glimpsed a dimly lit room which was filled with thick, grey smoke and the pungent odour of tobacco mingled with the stale smell of alcohol. Inside the room she could sense the buzz of serious conversation that permeated the atmosphere like a thick fog.

She looked around, taking it all in. There were perhaps twelve to fifteen people inside, older men, women, and young boys in their late teens, all sitting on chairs or on the floor, drinking, smoking and talking in hushed tones.

They all turned to look at her and Jules as they entered, but quickly returned to their conversations. It was very crowded and there was just a single wooden stool available near an overflowing ashtray. She sat down, feeling out of place and vulnerable. She had never been in a room full of Resistance fighters before, and she wasn't sure how to act.

A man with a thick moustache and a scar over one eye stood up and walked over to Jules. They exchanged a few words, and he introduced her using a false name. 'This is Emilie.' He nodded towards her. And the man nodded back as he viewed her cautiously.

In the centre of the room, there was a group of men huddled around a table illuminated by a single light bulb. A hush fell over them as one man looked up and noticed the newcomer.

'Who is this?' asked one who seemed to be the leader.

Jules quickly explained why he had brought her in, and the men nodded in understanding. They returned to their map and continued their whispered discussion about cutting important German communication cables.

As Isabelle's eyes continued to adjust to the dim, smoky room, they finally turned their attention to Jules, who explained her mission – to protect Parisian art from the Nazis' grasp – but they seemed unconvinced. The leader of the group shrugged his shoulders and said, 'People's lives are of greater importance. Why fight for paintings?'

Isabelle paused, feeling the weight of the whole room's questioning gazes upon her. She cleared her throat and spoke up for the first time.

'If Hitler is allowed to take away these works, or worse, destroy them, what will the people who are fighting have to come home to? We must protect what makes us Parisians – our past and accomplishments belong to us. What right have the Nazis to take that from us?'

She made a good argument.

Slowly the leader nodded his head, considering her plight.

'I can give you two people,' he said, signalling towards two of the men to his side. 'They will liaise with you, and you can work together on the details.'

Isabelle nodded. That would have to be enough.

After the Resistance meeting, Jules invited her back to his home. Entering the house, he didn't turn on a light but lit a candle. It rendered a soft, yellow hue to the otherwise plain room. Furnished sparsely, there was only a sofa and a couple of armchairs. But a bookshelf stood in the corner, filled to over-flowing with books of various genres.

'Would you like something to drink?' he asked, gesturing towards the small kitchen. 'I have some wine if you'd like.'

She agreed to a drink. He poured them both a glass of red wine, and they sat down at the small wooden table in the corner of the room. She took a sip of her wine and savoured the rich, bold flavour.

She felt coy as he looked at her over the rim of the glass. They had spent a lot of time together over the last two days, eating together and planning their mission, but being alone with him like this was something entirely different. As they sat there in the candlelight, they talked and laughed and drank more wine. The conversation flowed effortlessly, and she felt a deep connection with him. He was serious about his Resistance work, but there was also something playful about the way he saw the world. He lived for the moment and seemed to drink deeply of every second.

All at once, he sat back and stared at her.

'What?' she asked, feeling uneasy with his intense gaze.

'I was just wondering who the real Isabelle was.'

She felt her cheeks flush as she looked down and stammered, 'What do you mean?'

'You are just very careful, as if you are frightened of revealing the real you.'

Isabelle took another sip of wine, feeling exposed under his piercing gaze. Turning towards him, she stared back at him. The wine was having an effect, loosening her tongue. 'I guess I just haven't had a lot of people in my life that I can be myself around.'

'And why is that?' he asked pointedly. 'A beautiful woman like you should have a thousand men vying for your attention.'

'I am very busy with the gallery. I don't have time for—'

He cut her off. 'I don't believe you. I think you use your job as an excuse not to get close to people, and what I want to know is why?'

Isabelle shifted uncomfortably in her seat. He seemed to be able to see right through her façade, but she didn't know how to reveal the truth. She took a deep breath and let it out slowly before speaking.

'It's just... I'm scared to let anyone get too close again.' She glanced up at him, her stomach cramping as she took in the look of confusion on his face. 'Something tragic happened to me when I was younger. I lost someone precious to me, and I'm afraid that could happen again if I don't stay on my guard, always be careful.'

'That must be exhausting,' he responded, gently touching her arm.

'I'm used to it now,' she said, the bitterness in her tone obvious.

'How sad,' he muttered as he pierced her with his look.

She felt anger rising. She didn't need his pity. She had a good life.

'I probably should go,' she said coldly, pulling her arm from under his hand.

He quirked an eyebrow, as if he knew she was avoiding him. 'What happened, Isabelle? What happened to you?'

She swallowed down the bile that rose in her throat; this conversation was getting a little too real for her. She started to stand, but he reached out and placed his hand on top of hers, sending a shiver through her body.

'You don't have to be scared,' he whispered. 'I'm here now, and whatever it is I won't let anyone hurt you again.'

'It's not like that,' she protested, shifting, feeling like a cornered animal. She had said too much. No one outside of her family knew anything about this.

'I'm not going to let you leave like this,' he said gently.

She pulled away from him and grabbed for her coat, but when she turned around, he was right behind her. In the depths of the darkness, he pleaded with her, 'Isabelle, please allow me in.'

As she fought against his grasp, tears flowing down her face, Isabelle found herself caught between the urge to resist and the weight of her weariness. She yearned for someone to share her struggles, someone who would wholeheartedly offer their care.

Recognizing her internal battle, Jules whispered tenderly, his words infused with affection and unwavering resolve, 'Have faith in me, Isabelle. I am here for you; tell me who did this to you?'

'Me! I did this... I killed someone!'

The look of shock on his face was palpable. And in that split second, she pulled against his chest to free herself, taking him off guard with her confession, allowing her enough time to bolt towards the door, but he caught up with her and pulled her towards him. She wanted to fight, but she was also exhausted with everything. She so wanted to share all this weight with someone else. Someone who cared.

As if sensing her thoughts, he whispered through the darkness. 'Let me help, Isabelle. You don't have to do this all alone.'

40

Esther

On the day after Christmas, a gentle white snow started falling from the sky in a silent, graceful descent, and Édouard and Esther made their way through Paris on their way to the Jeu de Paume, a building now used as a museum of modern art.

The snow added a special touch to everything around them, imbuing everyday scenes with an almost magical quality that made her feel far removed from reality. And as she walked, Esther was aware of something. That though she missed her boys more than she could imagine, this trip had changed her. Softened her somehow. Given her hope that life could be beautiful.

When they reached the Jeu de Paume, the ancient building seemed to be filled with secrets, its windows peering out over centuries of art and culture like mysterious sentinels. Entering the museum's grand hall felt like stepping into a whole new world, one full of priceless treasures and rare artefacts. For a few moments they simply stood still, captivated by all they saw as Édouard explained to her the history of the building in a reverent whisper. How it had been used during the war as a storage space for stolen artworks from across Europe before eventually being transformed into a museum of modern art in the decades that followed.

'It is home to many treasures,' he said, his voice tinged with admiration.

Inside the white pillared building, Esther wanted desperately to find anything pertaining to her grandmother, and her heart began to race with anticipation. She couldn't imagine what it must have been like for her to work in this very building during such a dark and tumultuous time in history.

As she looked around the room, Esther felt overwhelmed by the sheer number of paintings on display. She wondered if her grandmother would have had to keep track of so many of them. As she looked around the long room, she tried to imagine what it would have been like filled with Nazis and also the fear her grandmother would have gone through being Jewish. In the far corner there was a small tribute to World War Two, and she eagerly went over to it to see if there was any clue to confirm her grandmother had worked here.

As Esther approached the display, her heart beat faster with each step she took. She saw a few photographs but none were of her grandmother. She was just about to turn away when something caught her eye. In the background of one of the pictures, slightly out of focus, was a painting of a hayfield and she recognized it straight away as her grandfather's art hanging on the wall behind a group of Nazis, including Herr Göring. This must have been before it had been destroyed on the train leaving Paris toward the end of the war.

Esther couldn't believe her eyes. She sucked in breath as she stared at the photo, trying to imagine her grandfather's work hanging on the wall behind such evil men.

As she studied the photo, Esther noticed something else. In the background next to the picture was a woman. She had her head slightly turned from the camera, as if she was afraid to be captured by it. But Esther recognized her grandmother's figure and hair immediately. Her heart skipped a beat as she realized that this was proof that she had indeed worked in this very building during the war.

Esther felt a mix of emotions. Part of her was relieved to have confirmation that her grandmother Brigitte had been here, but another part of her was filled with a deep sadness. She couldn't help but wonder what she had gone through during those years of war, working in a place where she must have been constantly reminded of the danger surrounding her.

She looked at the photo once more, focusing on her profile. Even though her grandmother was blurry, Esther felt as if she could see the fear and sadness etched into her face. It was a stark reminder of the horrors of war and the impact it had on so many lives.

As she stood there, lost in thought, Édouard approached her. 'What have you found?' he asked softly, his eyes filled with curiosity.

Esther turned to him and pointed at the photo. 'This,' she said, her voice filled with pride and emotion. 'This is my proof. My grandmother worked here during the war.'

Édouard studied it. 'And yes, here is your grandfather's picture. Do you think this is why she worked here?' he asked thoughtfully. 'To watch over his work?'

Esther shook her head, her eyes fixed on the photo of her grandmother. 'I don't know,' she said slowly. 'I think she was just trying to survive. Maybe she didn't have a choice.'

Édouard nodded, his expression thoughtful. 'Yes, I can understand that,' he said softly. 'So many people did what they had to do to survive during those years.'

Esther took a photo of the framed picture and sighed as she checked it. 'I just wish I could have known her,' she said quietly.

'I wish I could have heard her stories, understood what she went through.'

Édouard placed a hand on her shoulder. 'I know,' he said gently. 'But you have her art. And it must have meant a lot to her if she desperately wanted your mother to have it, and that is a gift.'

Esther nodded, grateful for Édouard's kindness. She knew that she had a lot to process, a lot of emotions and thoughts to sort through. The longer she was here, though, the less she wanted to sell the picture. She now connected with it in such a deeper way. But what if the money in selling it was the only hope for her to have some control over her own life? She felt so conflicted.

They made their way back to Édouard's apartment, the air filled with a sombre silence as they walked through the snowy streets. Esther couldn't help but feel a deep sense of gratitude for his companionship during this trip. Without him, she would have been lost. He had been her guide, her support, her friend. And she knew this trip had changed her.

Also, as she'd uncovered all the truth, just how brave her grandmother had been, it was as if she had not only given her the gift of beautiful art, but also of courage. This tiny woman with the intense dark eyes had reminded her to stand up for what she believed in. Protect what was hers. And in Esther's case that was her children, and she made her mind up that when she got home, things were going to be different. She wasn't sure how yet. But she was no longer going to put up with James calling all the shots. Esther was going to find a way to take away the power he had over her and her family.

41

Isabelle

Slowly, as if approaching a fearful animal, Jules closed the distance between them as Isabelle lifted her chin to face him, the hardwood floor creaking beneath his weight. And even though she was tall, he towered above her. As he reached up to cup the nape of her neck, his fingers brushed against strands of her hair that had loosened from her chignon. It was barely a whisper of a touch, but still it sent a ripple of delight down her spine, and for a moment, she forgot how to breathe.

He leaned in closer. Was he going to kiss her? He appeared to consider it for a moment, but instead he tenderly brushed his thumb across her lips before resting his palm lightly on her breastbone. The warmth of his touch flooded through her, calming her nerves.

His fingertips felt like they were burning her skin, it was so sensitive, and his gaze held her in place. She parted her lips, trying to find words to break the spell he had cast over her. Running her tongue along their dryness, which still tingled gently from where he'd touched them, Isabelle forced past her parched throat as she spoke again.

'You don't understand,' she whispered, trying to suppress the longing he'd awoken inside of her. 'You don't know anything about me.' She heard her own pain in her words. 'You don't know... what I have done.'

'Whatever you have done doesn't change how I feel about you.'

'But my brother is dead... because of me. How would you feel being with someone who has that on their conscience?'

He slowly reached out and his fingers entwined with hers and he gazed earnestly into her eyes. His voice was soft yet encouraging as he said, 'I'm so sorry that happened to you. It's a terrible loss. But you need to move forward from the pain, trust yourself and your inner strength. Your heart is more than capable of handling whatever comes its way. You have no idea how much energy it takes to hold on like that. Keeping your feelings locked behind this wall will not protect you from your past. Nothing can. Believe me, I know.'

His eyes found hers and she saw exquisite pain behind them as he continued.

'I have also killed someone I care about, my childhood best friend, and even though it was an accident there isn't a day goes by that I don't have regrets. But I still have life in my body. And not living fully would make his death in vain. I live for him every day. If you can't find the will to live for yourself, you should find the will to live for your brother.'

Tears pricked her eyes with the profound truth of his words. Her mind reeled at this new revelation. It was as if a heavy veil had been drawn away, and she could feel his sorrow mixing with her own. She drew in a sharp breath, the weight of their shared pain palpable.

'How do you do that?'

'If you truly want to live,' he whispered, 'you'll have to learn to let go. Life's richest treasures are always waiting for those courageous enough to accept fear's invitation.'

Then, as if her hand belonged to someone else, she lifted it and cupped his cheek. The heat of his skin rose up to her palm and sent a ripple of electricity through her body. She could feel the shape of his face beneath her fingertips and the coarse stubble that grazed her hand. His breath faltered, and she tilted her head to the side in anticipation, their lips barely an inch apart.

Before he could say any more, she pulled him down towards her, until his lips touched hers. It was so gentle she wasn't even sure they were kissing at first. Then, closing her eyes, she felt the warmth of their connection as he sighed gently and his grip around her waist tightened, the kiss deepening – her fingers finding and tangling in his hair.

Emboldened by her surging feelings, she wrapped her other arm around his back and pulled him closer till his hard chest pressed against hers as he intensified their kiss. Even with the strong feeling of passion she sensed from him, he was so careful, so tender that it made her body throb, her stomach ache, and her legs want to melt from under her.

Isabelle stopped fighting her reeling mind and began to give way, giving in to her desire, and it surprised her when tears of relief sprang to her eyes.

His hands moved slowly along her body, tracing lines down her sides, across her back, and over her arms. She gasped softly, as every caress seemed to awaken something new inside her, a burning desire that she had kept buttoned down for so long. This new sensation coursed through her veins, and despite the hesitation she still felt, Isabelle found herself gripping his arm tightly, trying to keep him close.

She wasn't sure how long they stood in the dark, the haunting candlelight dancing between them, their lips lost in their kiss, their bodies entwined, endlessly. She just knew that when he gently pulled away from her, the world had changed somehow, tilted to a new degree, and everything felt different.

'You should go,' he whispered as he gently rested his forehead against hers. 'If you stay, I'm not sure what I will do. And I don't think that's what you want.'

She nodded, swallowing down all that she wanted to experience with this man, and quickly, before she could second-guess herself too, Isabelle opened the door and walked out into the cool night air.

42

DECEMBER 1942

Brigitte

Just before Christmas, Brigitte finally made it over to the Renauds' house. She just needed to see it for herself to believe it; she had held out hope these past months they would return. She hurried along the path, looking surreptitiously behind her as she made her way down the familiar street. She thought back to the day she had first been here to get her false papers so long before. When she arrived at the ramshackle gate, her stomach twisted uncomfortably as she approached the house. At first, nothing looked amiss. But then she noticed the door was slightly ajar and the wood around the door was splintered, as if the Germans had smashed it with their rifles. She slowly tiptoed up the path and pushed open the front door. The hinges creaked, the only sound to be heard as it echoed out into the darkness.

'Hello?' she said hesitantly, hoping more than anything that somebody would call back to her. Maybe the Germans had taken and released them... at least his wife. She had nothing to do with the forgery work. But a dark, cold hollowness greeted her.

With a quick look over her shoulder, she stepped inside. The warmth that she'd always felt from this little home was gone. Inside, it was dark and cold, and it chilled her to the bone. Her eyes slowly adjusted to the dim light. Debris cluttered the floor, and with each step, her shoes crunched on broken glass and china.

Tears filled her eyes as she thought of this kind couple who'd risked their lives to help her. She made her way through the piles of broken furniture that was turned over and drawers frantically searched through; even though in her heart she knew it was in vain, still she called out their names, but there was no answer.

The Renauds were gone.

She continued to stumble through the house. Somewhere a tap was dripping and she was aware of an earthy smell, but it wasn't until she stood in the front room that she understood. Every one of Mrs Renaud's plants had been smashed onto the floor, trampled, and stamped on. It was so awful to see, Brigitte gasped at the senseless destruction. She walked into the centre of the room and looked around, trying to remember it as it had been. The table that Mr Renaud always sat at had been wrenched open, the drawers on the floor. No doubt some of his papers had been found there. Every picture of their family he had proudly taken with his new camera was thrown down and broken.

She wanted desperately to clear the room, ready for their return, but she had that awful fear. That might never be the case.

She turned back and was on her way towards the front door when she heard something. Someone else was in the house. Stepping back into the front room, she hid out of view. She could hear a person moving about, rustling through the broken china. What if it was a Nazi? She suddenly feared they would question her. It was stupid that she'd come here. Or was it someone ransacking the place, who would find her and maybe hurt her?

Brigitte held her breath, listening to the quiet steps that seemed to pad softly throughout the hallway. She flattened herself against the wall. And then she saw who it was. Monsieur Pepe, the Renauds' tabby cat. When he saw her, he looked up at her with frightened eyes. The happy, contented cat she had seen so long ago looked half the size, even in the short time since they had been taken. Rationing was affecting everybody, but this was heartbreaking; this poor tabby. She dropped to her knees and held her hand out to him. He jumped up into her arms as if he sensed she'd come to save him.

'It's all right, Monsieur Pepe,' she whispered, stroking his head. 'I've got you now.'

He looked straight at her and let out a mournful meow, and she could see how much he missed his mistress. But what could she tell him?

She left the house with Monsieur Pepe in her arms. She couldn't take him home. Sophie was allergic to cats. And that would give her mother something else to worry about. So she made her way to the gallery, wondering if someone there might take the cat.

When she arrived at the building, Isabelle was already in her office, her head bent over her desk. She smiled up at the sight of Brigitte with the cat in her arms, putting her pen down on her ledger.

Brigitte shut the door to Isabelle's office because she needed to trust someone. All the way to work, she had been thinking about Sophie and how she was risking her daughter's life with what she was doing. But she had a good feeling about Isabelle. She seemed trustworthy.

Isabelle listened intently with great surprise as Brigitte admitted she needed to get her daughter away from Paris.

'I might be able to help you,' Isabelle responded. 'I know of a train leaving the city, taking children to safety. You could put your daughter on that train.'

Brigitte was so relieved. Just until she finished the painting. Then she could join her daughter.

'What about this fella?' Isabelle asked, stroking the cat's soft, furry head as he padded around her desk.

'I don't know what will become of him,' Brigitte said sadly.

'Unfortunately, I can't take him,' responded Isabelle, shaking her head. 'I'm so rarely home. I'm always so busy. But I know someone that will have him. My sister Charlotte is a great lover of cats. So, I will take him home to my family.'

Brigitte handed the cat to Isabelle, and he purred contentedly as he kneaded in her lap.

She left the gallery feeling a sense of peace for the first time in weeks. Knowing that her daughter was going to be put on that train gave her hope that they might both make it through this war alive. She thought about Monsieur Pepe and hoped that he would find a happy home with Isabelle's family. She knew that it was a small comfort, but it was better than the alternative.

As she walked through the streets, her mind wandered to the Renauds. She made a silent promise to herself that she could never let that happen to her family.

When she arrived back at their apartment, Sophie was waiting for her and waved to her at the door. Her heart sank. Though she knew it was for the best, it would be so hard to put her daughter on a train without knowing what would become of either of them. But to stay in Paris was just too dangerous. She walked into the building to tell her daughter that her life was about to change and, the hardest thing of all, she couldn't give her any guarantees that it would ever be the same again.

Inside the apartment, Brigitte closed the door behind her, taking a deep breath to steady her nerves. Sophie stood in the living room, her face beaming with anticipation. Brigitte couldn't bear to see that innocent smile fade away, but she had to be strong. She had to protect her daughter at all costs.

'Sophie,' Brigitte began, her voice trembling slightly. 'I have something important to discuss with you, my darling.'

Sophie's eyes widened, sensing the gravity of her mother's tone. 'What is it, Maman?' she asked, a hint of worry creeping into her voice.

Brigitte moved closer to her daughter, taking her small hands into her own. 'You... need to leave Paris, Sophie,' she said, her voice barely above a whisper. 'It's not safe for you here any more.'

Her daughter looked at her with confusion, and Brigitte felt a fresh wave of guilt overwhelm her; how could she explain to her young daughter the horrors of war and the relentless pursuit of their enemies?

'But why, Maman?' Sophie's voice trembled, her eyes beginning to fill with tears. 'I can't leave our home! You promised when Papa died that we would stay together no matter what!'

Brigitte grasped her daughter's hands tighter, steeling herself against the sorrow threatening to consume her. 'I know, my sweet girl, but it is not safe here any more. The Nazis... they want to hurt us. They want to hurt our family.'

Sophie clung to her mother fiercely, sobbing uncontrollably as fear and confusion overwhelmed her tiny frame.

Brigitte fought through her own tears, struggling to find the right words to soothe her daughter's anguish.

'It's going to be all right,' she whispered, wrapping her arms around her tightly. 'You are everything in this world to me, and I will do whatever it takes to protect you.'

Sophie looked up into Brigitte's eyes, still trembling in terror. Brigitte's heart broke at the sight of her daughter in such distress. 'You are going away on a train,' she said softly, wiping Sophie's tears away from her cheeks. 'The sister of the lady I work with is taking a group of children to the South of France where it is safer. She will keep you safe until we can be together again.'

The young girl clung on to her mother for dear life, too afraid to let go. Brigitte held Sophie close.

Sophie's eyes were red and swollen from tears as she stared up at her mother, struggling to hold back choking sobs. 'But when will we see each other again, Maman?' she pleaded desperately, the fear in her voice almost tangible.

Brigitte took a deep breath before speaking, her own heart aching with sadness. 'I don't know for sure, my love,' she whispered sorrowfully. 'But soon, I promise, in the next few weeks, and in the meantime, you can take a little holiday with some other children.'

They clung to each other, mother and daughter, seeking solace in their shared embrace. In that moment, Brigitte knew that the path ahead would be treacherous and uncertain, but she would do anything to protect her daughter. The decision was made, and now they would face the unknown together, their love and resilience guiding them through this darkest of times.

43

JANUARY 1943

Brigitte

Isabelle, Brigitte and Sophie hurried along the street. The weather was so cold, and a thick mist had descended upon the city, leaching up from the ground and swirling about their feet, cutting their visibility down to just in front of them.

The pale morning sun had not yet risen, but the darkness was already fading, the sky beginning to glow in a halo of light through the mist with the promise of a new day. The air had taken on the chill of the impending dawn, and the young girl with her hand clasped in her mother's shivered. All their breath was visible in the icy morning air.

Brigitte looked down at her young charge. Her daughter looked so vulnerable, so much younger than her nine years. Her dark eyes were fearful yet resilient, her hair in two shiny braids. A dark, felt cloche hat, a gift from her grandmother, was thrust low onto her head to just below her ears, and a thick scarf was wrapped twice around her neck. In her hand, a little brown suit-case, a label with her name and address dangling from the handle.

Sophie sensed her mother looking down at her and smiled nervously up at her.

Isabelle also sensed the fear between them and squeezed Sophie's shoulders as she spoke. 'It's going to be okay, Sophie,' she said softly. 'You're going to be safe. You're going to be travelling with someone very special: my sister Charlotte. She is very kind.'

As they arrived at the Gare de Lyon for the train to Montpellier, the station bustled with activity. Everywhere Brigitte looked, she saw red flags with their black swastikas hanging limp in the damp air and Nazis in grey uniforms, their guns slung over their shoulders, intimidating eyes searching from one person to the next, looking for anything out of the ordinary. Isabelle lowered her gaze and Brigitte felt her stomach clench in fear as they hurried forward with Sophie tightly tucked against them. She glanced down at her little girl again, who seemed lost in a world of her own, her chin quivering with the cold.

Compared to the station, the platform was oddly deserted, save for a few travellers here and there, huddled in their coats, barely visible in the hazy light of morning. The dense fog flattened the air to an echoing silence so that every sound seemed amplified – the rustle of coats; the clatter of heels on pavement; the occasional cough or sneeze.

Brigitte noticed Isabelle seemed to be searching desperately from one passenger to the other, trying to find her sisters. She spotted someone far off down the platform first.

'There's Antoinette,' she said somewhat thoughtfully.

Brigitte looked across at the young woman shivering on the platform. She had a heart-shaped face, blonde hair, and long blonde ringlets.

As they hurried towards her, Isabelle seemed concerned. 'I hope everything is all right. Lately she has seemed so withdrawn. I'm sure it is her concerns about her own son, Benjamin.'

To ease her own worries, she gave Brigitte a half smile and reached out and gripped Sophie's hand tightly.

Brigitte drew to a stop.

'Before we go over, I need to speak to Sophie for a second.'

Isabelle nodded and made her way over to greet her sister. Brigitte drew her daughter aside.

There was one thing left she had to do. And she was debating whether Sophie was up to the thing she needed to task her with. But if she didn't tell her this and something happened to her, there would be no way of anyone finding what she had hidden.

'Sophie,' she whispered, a quiver in her voice, 'there is something very important I need to tell you. Are you able to keep a very special secret?'

Her daughter's eyes grew wide as she looked up at her mother. Slowly, she nodded her head as Brigitte drew in a breath. She had been debating all the way to the station, but now she was sure she needed her to know this. She needed somebody else to know this. Somebody who was leaving Paris. She took her aside and told her all the secrets about the picture.

'Whatever you do, Sophie, I need you to keep it a secret.'

'How long for?' responded Sophie quietly.

Brigitte didn't like to say, 'This is just in case I don't survive,' so she said, 'When we feel safe again, Sophie, that's when you can tell.'

Sophie nodded.

As they both approached the group of Isabelle's sisters that had gathered, a wave of conflicting emotions washed over Brigitte. On the one hand, she held tight to the need to protect Sophie; on the other, the thought of letting go of Samuel's daughter seemed like a betrayal of her beloved husband's memory.

Sophie clung desperately to her mother's side, her small fingers trembling with fear.

The station seemed strangely still in contrast to its usual bustle of activity, as if time itself had stopped to hold its breath, wondering if she had the courage to do this, too. Isabelle approached them, compassion radiating from her. 'Sophie, it's time,' she said softly. 'My sister Charlotte is here.'

Brigitte met Sophie's gaze and saw confusion and longing swirling within her daughter's eyes. Tears welled up, silently pleading for them to stay together. It felt like someone was tearing Brigitte's heart out of her chest as she knelt down, cradling Sophie's face in her trembling hands.

'My precious Sophie,' she whispered, her voice choked with grief and sorrow. 'How I wish we could stay together, that I could shield you from all harm. But you must understand this is our only chance to keep you safe from what is going on in our world.'

Sophie's lip quivered, her hands trembling, her eyes filled with a mix of pure fear and entreating desperation. 'Maman, please,' she begged, her voice shaking. 'I can't leave you. I'm scared.'

Brigitte's heart broke further at the sound of Sophie's plea and every impulse in her screamed to keep her close and never let go. But at the same time, she knew that this was the only way.

She held her daughter close then, love and pain merging into one within her chest. She choked back tears as she attempted to explain the reasoning behind her decision, yet words failed her. All she could do was kiss Sophie's forehead.

As people started to board the train, Sophie cried out again.

'Maman, please,' she begged, 'I want to stay. Papa wouldn't have wanted us to be apart.'

Brigitte's heart shattered, torn between the desire to protect her child and the overwhelming ache of letting her go.

'You have to, darling; *this* is what your papa would have wanted. A chance for you to have a wonderful life, and I can't be sure of that if you stay here. Sophie, this is my last chance to get you to safety; you have to go with Charlotte. I have no idea how else I could get you out of the city; you are too young for identity papers and your grandmother wears the yellow star, and it makes it hard for her to travel with you. Please, my darling, be brave for me.'

Reluctantly, Brigitte peeled Sophie's trembling fingers from her hand, and gave her tiny hand to Charlotte, a profound ache pulsating within her. Sophie resisted, clinging to her mother with all her strength, her cries echoing through the desolate station.

Brigitte rose to her feet, tears streaming down her face, her voice cracking with agony. 'I love you, my darling. Take care of yourself.'

The porter announced the final boarding for the departure of the 7.47 to Montpellier, the train that would take her beloved daughter away from her.

And as Charlotte began to lead Sophie away the little girl reached out her other hand, her tiny fingers grasping for Brigitte. She got a handful of her coat and once again Brigitte removed them as the train's horn blared, its deafening sound drowning out Sophie's anguished cries.

Then she watched in despair as her distraught daughter boarded the train, until the train slowly pulled out of the station, taking her precious Sophie away.

It was only then that she allowed the full weight of their separation to settle upon her shoulders and it felt like an insurmountable burden, her heart shattering with each fading cry of her child. She knew without a shadow of a doubt this marked an end for her; without her husband and daughter, she would never experience completeness again. The last day Paris would truly be home. Tears streamed down her face as she collapsed into Isabelle's arms, her grief consuming her.

'You did the right thing,' Isabelle assured her as the station grew quieter, the mist casting a sombre pall over the scene. Brigitte remained on the platform with Isabelle for a long time, unable to move, her cries blending with the echoes of the departing train, her heart fractured into a million pieces.

44

Esther

After the visit to the Jeu de Paume, Esther followed Édouard back to his home, taking in the sights of Paris as they walked. When they arrived, he began preparing dinner: a hearty roast lamb with rosemary and roasted vegetables. She offered to help, but he waved her off, insisting that she be his guest instead. As they ate, he told her all about the research he had done on her grandmother's picture and grandfather's artistry.

'Of course,' he said, 'if your grandfather's painting had survived the train bombing, it would be worth much more than your grandmother's. He was a brilliant artist who was just starting to rise in popularity at the time – his work is very collectable.'

Later, as they drank coffee in his comfortable front room, he pulled up an image of a man standing in front of *The Hayfields of Summer*, holding a glass of champagne at a gallery opening. And Édouard told her about his work with the Resistance.

'This is my grandfather?' Esther choked back tears,

expanding the picture on the screen so she could see him clearly.

Édouard looked shocked. 'You don't have any other pictures of him?'

She shook her head slowly, smiling through her tears at the likeness of her own features echoed in the man in the picture.

'I'm so sorry, Esther, I had no idea. I assumed...'

'My mother was very traumatized during the war. She would never talk about her parents, and my great-grandmother died not long after she arrived in England after the war. My mother was then adopted, and they were not kind to her.'

The sadness of her mother's life hit Esther in a new way. Being here in Paris, knowing this had been her mother's home for the first years of her life, finding out her grandparents' story was helping her feel more connected to her mother and her past. Her mother's history had always been so vague to her it was as if it wasn't real. But now she was looking at people who shared her features, her sense of determination. And that feeling of being connected to them felt so good.

After Camille had gone to sleep, they wandered out onto the little black wrought-iron balcony and Édouard draped a thick woollen sweater around Esther's shoulders before fetching two glasses of wine. As they sipped in silence, watching fireworks exploding against a black sky far across the river, they talked and shared the bottle of wine, and he opened up about his late wife's death and how he had nursed her to the end himself.

Esther could feel the pain in his tone, and her heart went out to him. As she listened, she realized how much she liked the way she felt around him.

'Esther, I know it is very early for us, and we've only really just met, but I want you to know that I haven't felt like this around any other woman since my wife. There is a comfort and an ease that I feel with you that I don't feel around people very often.'

She felt her stomach constrict then as he spoke.

'I know what you mean,' she said softly. 'I feel the same way. It's been a long time since I've felt this comfortable around a man. Over the last few years, I've become rather cynical about relationships, and my whole life has been about raising my children.'

He nodded his head. 'I understand that. Camille is my world too, but it's hard being both mother and father.'

As they leaned on the balcony and continued to watch the fireworks, he gently took her hand; she felt a sudden, over-whelming warmth rush through her at his touch. She drew in a faltering breath, and he looked across at her with an affectionate smile.

'Are you afraid of me?' he chuckled, playfully.

'No, not afraid – just out of practice,' she said teasingly, slowly exhaling and trying to hide the fact that she was utterly terrified.

Even in the dark, she could make out the silhouette of his face as he studied her expression intently. Slowly, he started leaning forward, as if to kiss her.

Oh God... was he really going to kiss her? Before she had time to think, she placed a gentle hand over his chest.

'I can't do this. I just can't do it. I have a life, and I have a job, and I have children. And you're French, and you live here, and I live there, and I can't do this.'

'Okay,' he said gently, starting to pull back, and she felt horrendous. She wanted to be close to this man so badly.

Then, making a rash decision, she pulled him to her and initiated the kiss they both wanted. He laughed softly against her lips as the sensation of his body against hers filled her with such warmth. One hand found her waist and pulled her closer. He was gentle but sincere in the way he sought her.

His fingertips brushed tenderly against her cheek. They were warm and soft against the coldness of the frigid night air and she shivered. His other hand slid up towards the little roll of fat just below her bra strap, and she tried with no avail to suck it in. But he didn't seem to notice, let alone be repulsed. She could feel his tenderness, and she'd forgotten what that felt like, unconditional acceptance.

His lips were so sensual, hers seemed stiff and cold. It was as if they had forgotten how to do this. She felt a twinge of panic in the back of her mind: *Oh God*, she was a wet fish, an English wet fish. He didn't seem to notice as he continued to kiss her, and slowly she forced herself to relax and then finally to unbutton – that was the only word for it. She let herself go. She had been so uptight, holding everything in her life together, and she hadn't even known it.

As a loud firework crackled in the background, her mind began to swim, and then she started to become weak. What was she, fifteen? She knew how to do this, she reminded herself. She slipped her arms around his waist and pulled him towards her. It felt good to have him in her arms, a man, a real man. But what did this mean?

Stop overthinking it, Esther, she said inwardly, rebuking herself, and tried to relax. She'd just pretend she was in a movie in Paris. It would be a story for Janine when she got back.

When he pulled away, they locked eyes, and she felt a wave of vulnerability pass between them: he too was a little scared by what this meant.

'That wasn't so complicated, was it?' he said.

She shook her head and smiled, not wanting to admit to all the thoughts that had gone through her mind. As he squeezed her hand again, she wanted nothing more than to stay there in his arms, in the warmth of Paris, but she had responsibilities at home in England that could not be ignored. Sighing deeply, Esther forced down the sadness of that truth and stepped back.

'I haven't wanted to kiss anyone for so long. It's a little nerve-racking for me too. Though I need to be honest with you, as lovely as this is, and it really is lovely, honestly, my life is in England. I have two children to raise and a life to sort out, and living in his awful flat. I just can't see a way forward for us right now.'

He looked out towards the fireworks in silence, and she caught a glimpse of what appeared to be tears glimmering in his eyes. She imagined kissing someone after his wife's passing was stirring up emotions for him too. And she felt something tugging at her heart as he slowly nodded.

'I know it seems impossible, but I just want you to know that this is special to me. I don't bring people to my home to meet my daughter ever,' he said softly.

'I understand,' she whispered, as she gazed into his eyes with admiration and appreciation. 'Maybe fate will find a way for us.'

As they both looked back into the night sky, the romantic lights of the fireworks danced around them, illuminating their faces with an ethereal glow. But as much as she desperately wanted it to be true, she couldn't imagine any way for them to be together, and her heart felt both heavy and full all at once.

45

Isabelle

She had been working at the Jeu de Paume in the stifling July heat. The kind of heat that seemed to penetrate every inch of her skin, leaving her feeling sticky and exhausted and she was about to take a break for lunch when, suddenly, one of the French drivers burst into the room. He was sweating, his face pale with fear.

'Nazis,' he gasped, trying to catch his rasping breath. 'Dozens of them over at the Louvre. They are destroying all the art.'

Isabelle didn't even wait to hear more; she sprinted across the Tuileries Garden towards the Louvre, her heart pounding with dread.

Racing into the building, she looked around in a state of terror and disbelief as she laid eyes on the unspeakable crime von Behr and his men were committing. They careened up and down the floors, leaving behind nothing but heaps of ruin in their wake. Using their battle knives, they brutally slashed and stabbed painting after painting. The halls echoed with their destruction, the sounds of frames being wrenched from the walls, splintering and being thrown to the ground, canvas ripping and tearing; each gash echoed through her own body as though her own heart was being wrenched out too.

She rushed through the museum, her chest pounding with each crushing blow of glass and shrieking rip of canvas as irreplaceable pieces of art were recklessly decimated.

Jaujard, the museum's director, stood rooted in shock in the middle of one of the grand halls in disbelief, his face twisted in anguish while he witnessed the utter devastation all around him. The rest of the staff surrounded him, also frozen in terror, eyes wide with fright at the rampant anarchy that had been unleashed.

'What is happening?' Isabelle gasped breathlessly as she fought to regain her composure from running.

Jaujard's gaze met hers, his expression vacant. 'An ultimatum from the Führer – anything not deemed art in his eyes must be destroyed, anything he calls degenerate,' he answered flatly, the shock and horror obvious on his face.

Isabelle felt as if her heart was going to shatter. The sheer heartlessness of this act sickened her to the very core.

All at once the thunderous roar of trucks rumbled through the Louvre, then they screeched to a stop. Isabelle watched in horror as the German soldiers began tearing down masterpieces they hadn't already destroyed, ripping them cruelly from their frames and carrying them away. Her heart raced and her hopes of salvaging any of these works seemed to diminish with every second that passed. Jaujard looked grief-stricken beside her, his hands clenched tightly into fists.

'What are they doing with the art?' she asked in a frightened voice, but he had no answer, just shook his head in disbelief.

Von Behr shouted orders to take them to the Tuileries Garden, and Isabelle knew then that this was not going to end well. She spun around and raced back to the gardens, desperate to beat the stolen artwork there. Her mind was whirling with ideas on how she could possibly restore and preserve these beloved pieces.

As the Nazi truck lumbered and screeched to a stop in the middle of the gardens, Isabelle felt her heart quake. Her mouth was suddenly devoid of words as she watched the Nazis begin unloading crate after crate. When the first one was pried open, it revealed a canvas slashed almost beyond recognition. She felt her stomach drop in dread—it was her beloved painting, *Hope*, her one touchstone of light amid these dark times.

A feeling of rage swelled in her as she watched the Nazis with horror. She saw pictures by Miró, Klee and Picasso being carelessly cast onto a pile in the middle of the gardens. There had to be at least five hundred of them. Lohse emerged from the gardens, Marina trailing behind him. She felt a red-hot rage rising within her, tears starting to sting her eyes. Without thinking, she rushed toward them and screamed, 'What is wrong with you? What the hell are you doing?!'

Lohse spun around to face her, and his face twisted into a snarl. 'This is none of your business.'

Isabelle felt her temper flare even more as she shouted back, 'This *is* my business! You're stealing and destroying priceless artworks. How can you do this?!'

Lohse's voice rose to a menacing growl. 'It's not stealing if it belongs to Germany. We can do what we want with it. And I think you should control yourself unless you want to be arrested.'

Brigitte was suddenly at her side, dragging her away from the scene.

As she turned Isabelle smelt the burning paint and wood before she saw flames, as thick, acrid smoke filled her nose and stung her eyes. She was overwhelmed with the horror of watching this beautiful art burned before her eyes. The flames bit into the wood as hundreds of Impressionists' paintings started to melt down together, creating a grotesque merging of colours and distorted shadowy shapes that ghosted in and out of the flames.

She was suddenly overcome by a wave of terror, catapulted back to the depths of her childhood nightmare. It was as real as if it had happened yesterday. All at once she could smell the same pungent smell of burning paint and wood from so long ago, the heat searing her young nostrils and throat, causing her to gag and cough. The taste of ash and smoke on her tongue, acrid and bitter like bile. Her vision blurred with tears as she watched red-hot flames lapping and hissing from every corner of the building from her past, engulfing all in its path with tongues of fire sending up thick plumes of smoke that billowed out of the sides of her mother's studio. She remembered the heat emanating from the door as intense, blistering the blue paint and sending waves of hot air against her face as she screamed for help. And then how she had tried over and over to enter again and save her brother, but the flames had been too fierce, the inferno surging forward, spreading in all directions as it bellowed with an earsplitting roar. A window had shattered with the heat and she had run to it, calling Pierre's name over and over again as she looked in at the terrifying sight. Her mother's easel alight, the last canvas she worked on half-finished as paint dripped from it in a waterfall of mixed muddy colour, and then that lone voice calling out to her through it all. 'Isa!'

And suddenly thrust back into the present, the world was spinning around her. The last thing she saw as she slipped to the ground was Brigitte's concerned face, and then everything went black.

46

Esther

The next morning, she got a phone call from her son.

'Mum, it's me.'

She could tell something was wrong. 'Daniel, are you okay?'

'We're getting on a plane tomorrow.'

'What? I thought your dad wasn't coming back for another two days. I'm still in Paris.'

'Yeah, he's sending us back early. He doesn't want to have us here any more. Him and Angela want to do grown-up things and they said we would be happier at home with you.'

She could sense sadness and rejection in her son's voice and her heart broke for him.

'Well, you still have time off school. We could still have fun,' she responded, trying to jolly him along. But Esther was furious after she hung up; her hands shook as she dialled her ex-husband's number. Her rage was all-consuming, but she had to handle this right. She couldn't afford to cause a problem between them. After all, she was living in his dismal flat. He could make things worse for her by making her live elsewhere or allowing her to be homeless and taking the boys from her. She thought about the new sense of courage she had started to feel after learning her grandmother's story. The phone rang out three times and then clicked to voicemail.

'Hello. It's James here,' said a rather drunk voice, then both he and what sounded like his girlfriend laughed and then there was a splash of water. They had obviously been sitting somewhere drinking by a pool when they decided to re-record his message. 'We're not here right now because we're in Spain having a really good time.'

'And we don't want to talk to you anyway,' added Angela in the background, and they both started laughing.

'Leave a message after the beep if you want,' he said, 'and I might get back to you.'

'But I won't!' said Angela at the end as they both laughed again.

Esther waited patiently for the beep and then spoke in a calculated way.

'James, this is Esther, call me as soon as you get this.'

And she hung up the phone.

She turned away from the desk and looked out of the window. There was a beautiful view of Paris from Édouard's office. It was an icy day, but the view was gorgeous. The sun was shining behind the Eiffel Tower, and she could smell food cooking in the other room. Her host was preparing lunch early so they could eat together. *Édouard*. She thought about him for a second and closed her eyes. Last night had been interesting; she had found it hard to sleep after their kiss, her thoughts turning over and over in her mind, common sense battling with her desire to give in to her surging feelings.

She thought about the phone call she had just made to her ex-husband. And now she would be leaving before she could at least explore these newly awakened feelings.

Édouard called from the kitchen that the food was ready

and she pulled herself back from the memories of the night before. As she stepped out of the office, she noted he was whistling a song. A happy French tune that she didn't know.

'I hope you're hungry,' he sing-songed as she arrived in the kitchen and he turned to greet her with a smile. But as soon as he saw her face, the joy in his expression evaporated. 'Is everything okay?' he asked cautiously.

'My ex-husband has decided he's had enough playing father and is putting my children on the plane home tomorrow.'

Édouard swore in French under his breath. 'Oh, your poor children. How are they coping with that?'

'Daniel is being very brave, as always. I'm sure Henry is beside himself. I hate what he's doing to them.'

'It is wrong and I'm so sorry.'

'Me too,' she sighed. 'It means I must get a flight back as soon as possible.'

'Of course. Would you like me to call someone?'

'No, it's okay. I can do it.'

They ate lunch together quietly. Both felt the sadness that they would be parting so abruptly.

After that, she called the airline and managed to get a flight out the next day, which would get her back in time before the boys arrived. After she hung up, the phone rang. It was James. She took two deep breaths before she answered it.

'James,' she said curtly.

'Hello, Esther,' he said, sounding as if he had been drinking. 'Did Daniel get hold of you?'

'Yes, he did. So what exactly is going on?'

'We want to go up the coast with some friends that we've made here. There'll be a lot of wine and drinking, and I don't think the kids would enjoy it very much.'

She ground her teeth together. 'No, they wouldn't. Sometimes, you must make sacrifices when you have children.'

'Look, are you going to be a downer? If so, I'll hang up. Can you never be happy for me? I'm having a great holiday, a great time. But I don't want the kids to be doing something they won't enjoy. So I'm sending them home.'

'And how do you think that makes the kids feel?' she said, snapping back at him.

'They had a great holiday,' he said defensively. 'Father Christmas spent loads of money on them. They've been swimming in the pool every day. So I don't think they have anything to complain about.'

'No, you wouldn't, would you? You wouldn't understand what's needed here. They just wanted to be with you, James. They didn't want all of that. All they want is time with their father. And you can't even do that. You can't even take care of them in the easiest place in the world to do that.'

'Okay, that's enough of your attitude. You're spoiling my holiday. Look, they'll be on the plane at three o'clock tomorrow afternoon. Be at the airport to pick them up.' And then he hung up.

She threw her phone onto the bed with anger. This made her so mad. They just wanted to play happy families when it suited them. He had no understanding of commitment. God knew how the boys would feel when she picked them up the following day. She packed her bag slowly, with the weight of sadness, the thought of returning to that horrible flat gut-wrenching. Then, picking up her phone, she came across the photo she had taken of the painting at the Jeu de Paume; and she remembered her grandmother and she suddenly felt braver. She could do this. Her grandmother Brigitte had faced much worse, and Esther had that same spirit inside her.

47

Isabelle

After the fire, Brigitte insisted on helping Isabelle home, even though Isabelle didn't want to trouble her friend. Delphine had been working in the garden when the two women had arrived, and instantly knew something was wrong.

'What happened?' she asked, rushing to her daughter's side.

'Inside, Maman,' Isabelle whispered, as she looked around hesitantly for the Nazi soldiers she had often seen patrolling up and down their street.

Once inside the kitchen, her mother drew her a glass of water as Brigitte explained what had happened.

'You look so pale,' her mother commented as she laid her freckled hand on her daughter's forehead.

'I will be all right, Mamam, I just need to catch my breath.'

After Brigitte left, her mother busied herself making her daughter some soup to strengthen her, and Isabelle walked out into the garden to take some air. It was as she sat down on her brother's bench that she could let fall the tears that so dearly wanted to flow.

'Oh, Pierre,' she whispered into the warm, smooth wood, 'I miss you so much.'

Her mother found her sobbing there a while later, and, sitting beside her daughter under the comforting leaves of their tree, she pulled Isabelle to her.

'It was as if I was right here again, Maman,' she said, her words tight, her throat sore from crying. 'As if it was all happening again. What has kept me going since that night was my desire to somehow put the world right. I knew I couldn't bring back my brother, but I thought if I saved the art, it was the next best thing. And I have even failed to protect what I have been given. It was all burned, Maman, all gone.'

Her mother rocked her, holding her close. 'My dear, sweet daughter, why do you feel it is your job to keep the whole world together? You did not start this war; you are not responsible for everything that is happening. I know we have talked about this many times. But it is also not your fault your brother is dead. I too have regrets. Why did I leave the heater on? Why was I not watching you both better? But Pierre's death was an accident, that's all, an accident. I wish I knew how to take this burden of guilt from you. We all bear the scars but you for some reason think it is your job to carry all the pain. You can't; there will always be things out of your control and you have to come to terms with that. But more than that, you have to find a way to forgive yourself, so you can open up again. I remember the amazing little girl you were before, and imprisoning yourself in that one horrible moment has taken everything that is good from your life. Please, Isabelle, let life in again.'

She took her daughter's face in her hands and stared deep into her eyes. 'Isabelle, it wasn't your fault.' Isabelle nodded slowly, as her mother became more adamant. 'No, look at me! It wasn't your fault! Please, I want you to leave the past here at this bench; because you do not honour his memory with your guilt. He would not want you to live like this.'

Her mother's words struck her deep in her core and she knew, as hard as it was, she had to try to let go of the pain she had been holding on to in order to let love in again. In order to let Jules in.

After the conversation with her mother, she made a decision; she had to talk to Jules again, take the risk he had challenged her to take. If she didn't, she would be stuck on this bench for the rest of her life. She needed to be courageous enough to take this invitation that fear was handing her. And it would start with her story, so he understood.

She arrived at his door, her stomach in knots as she knocked softly. He opened it looking crestfallen.

'Oh my God, Isabelle,' he said. 'I heard what happened.'

Isabelle nodded, bleakly, as he pulled her inside, guiding her to a seat in his front room. He took two glasses from the kitchen and poured them each some wine.

'I am so sorry about the fire; those bastards will pay for what they have done, trust me,' he said, taking her hand as he sat beside her.

She nodded her head. 'I hope so, but that is not why I am here.' He studied her closely; she was going to be brave. 'There's something I want to share with you, about what we were talking about the other day, about my past,' she said, taking a long, stuttering breath. 'I think it'll help you understand me better – why I'm so closed off, why I'm afraid to love.'

His eyes met hers as he waited.

'When I was a little girl, just five years old, I had a brother, Pierre. He was a year younger than me. We were the best of friends. We did everything together. They used to call us the twins, because wherever I was, Pierre was. We even slept in the same bed. Even though they separated us at night, we'd find our way into one bedroom by the morning. My mother is an incredible artist. You may have heard of her.'

She told him her name, and his eyes grew wide.

'Of course, Delphine Valette is well known, but she has not created art for many years.'

'No, she hasn't because of something I did, something that stopped her from ever painting again.' Isabelle took a deep breath and swig of her wine, ready to tell him her story, the story that was so hard.

'My mother had the most amazing artist's studio in the corner of our garden. The sunlit sea-green building was a wonderland for me. Inside canvases sprawled on the floor and leaning in stacks; paint stains on the walls; brushes nestled in jars; exquisite colour everywhere. The light inside was magical; morning sunlight would hit the crystals my mother dangled in the tiny shuttered windows creating rainbows that leaped around the walls and the studio was my favourite spot to make daisy chains while listening to my mother's humming as she painted vibrant florals onto canvases, or to play hide-and-seek with Pierre. In the corner the paraffin heater that my mother kept on to warm it just added to the enchanting atmosphere.

'But one day while playing I couldn't find Pierre no matter how hard I searched. As I dragged my feet around the room looking for him, the mesmerizing blue and yellow flame from the paraffin heater beckoned me, and as I drew closer to it I could see fairies captured in the flames dancing inside it. I stood there transfixed, watching them for a moment, realizing all of a sudden that I wanted to release the fairies, to set them free.

'I took a small piece of paper from the floor and impulsively pressed it behind the glass. To my delight it burst into flames, sparkling like a dancing ember in my hands. Little fire fairies of yellow and orange dancing in my palm.

'When I felt the searing pain touch my tender, young skin, I automatically dropped it. The paper landed on something that ignited immediately. A flammable paint stripper, we believe. And I still cannot believe how quickly the room ignited.

'I ran screaming from the studio before I remembered about Pierre, still hiding inside. I tried to go back in, but the smoke was overwhelming, black and thick and it smelt of tar, and the worst of all...' Isabelle closed her eyes, a sob catching in her throat. 'I could hear him calling to me from inside.'

Jules brought her hand to hold against his cheek as she continued with a trembling voice.

'The place went up like an inferno. The studio was literally burned to the ground within a few minutes. And even though my father got in there quickly and managed to pull my brother out, it was too late. Pierre had died because of the smoke. I still remember that same black smoke marring Papa's tear-stained face as he held in his arms the tiny limp body of his only son. The sound that came from my father that day I will never forget. It was inhuman, pain and sorrow, regret and deep loss, and I was responsible.

'I know my mother and family have forgiven me for what I did because I was just a child. But something in my heart snapped then. A fiery rage connected to the art, a reminder of my brother's death and his life slipping away from me. When I see art being destroyed, that moment comes flooding back like a fireball, destroying everything in its path. I'm consumed with this inner turmoil, and yet I'm powerless to push it away.'

He gently kissed her fingers. 'It is no wonder you feel the way that you do. Of course you would.'

He pulled her close into a hug and held her gently, kissing her damp cheeks, as she began to cry, the tears welling up and rolling down her face in a long, warm stream.

She hadn't intended to let him make love to her. She had just intended to hold him, but as their bodies pressed together, an overwhelming urge to be closer to him overtook her. Electricity running through her veins, she couldn't seem to stop.

Slowly she started to unbutton his shirt.

He tenderly placed his hand on hers, gently stilling her movements. His voice was rich and warm as he asked, 'Do you really want this?'

'Yes, I want this, more than anything, I want to experience all that love has to offer on the other side of fear,' she responded, adamantly. And then added in a whisper, 'And I want to experience this with you.'

Gently, he lifted her into his arms and carried her into the bedroom, where he lowered her onto his cold, white sheets. Not taking his eyes from hers, he slowly undressed her, with such tenderness it made her ache for him in a way she had never known. As he removed her dress, Isabelle caught her breath as the chilliness of the air around her naked flesh aroused her.

Shivering, she snaked one hand into his thick, dark hair, causing him to moan with pleasure as she slid the other up under his open shirt, luxuriating in his smooth, warm skin which was now a field of goosebumps.

As his lips found hers, he tasted of wine and something minty, his skin of a spicy aftershave, and as their naked chests melded together she felt his heart hammering in rhythm with her own.

Through his open window a conversation drifted in, two women talking about their washing and Isabelle wanted to laugh with sheer delight. As they were talking of the mundane, she was in the midst of the extraordinary.

Their hands brushed against one another as their clothes gradually peeled away completely and Isabelle caught her breath at the sight of his toned physique and the sheer vulnerability of being so exposed to him herself. For weeks now, she had wondered about the body below the layers, and all at once it was hers to have. And even though they were completely naked, vulnerable, exposed, she was surprised how natural it felt to be this close to someone in this way.

He lifted his head from kissing her neck, panting slightly, the air heavy and electric with expectancy.

'Isabelle, are you sure you want me to do this, have you done this before?' She shook her head and seeing his dejected response, clarified with a laugh. 'No, I have not done this before, and yes I want to do this with you.'

As their bodies entwined into the act of lovemaking, surrendering themselves to each other, she felt the pain slipping away with each new height of pleasure and for the first time in her life a deep, soulful connection, a feeling of being one, and in that oneness, she felt safe and loved. Slowly the years of being separate, alone, different, were gone in an instant and replaced with the feeling of finally coming home, coming home to herself. The tears came again, but this time there was no sadness; this time, there was only the subtle unwinding of a tightened spring, gradually uncoiling with relief.

48

Marina

Marina crept closer to the inner door, her ear pressed against its cool wood. Von Behr's voice boomed through the thin barrier, unmistakable and powerful. She could feel her heart beating in her chest as he spoke. His words chilled her to the core:

'The thing is, Lohse,' he said, 'they know too much. There has been concern from higher ranks of the Reich. We need to deal with them.'

Lohse sounded surprised. 'Is that necessary?'

Von Behr's pacing feet echoed through the office as he talked. Marina could feel his nervousness even behind the closed door. 'They've seen and known too much. If our enemy were to gain a foothold here in Paris and speak to them, it could be dangerous. We want nothing to be traced back to us.'

Lohse exhaled heavily. 'What are you planning on doing?'

Von Behr stopped pacing, and Marina could feel his hesitation.

'Well, they would be dealt with of course. But, what is it to you?' he said gruffly.

She strained to listen. Did he mean sending them away to Germany? And 'dealing with them': the reality of those words was too awful for her to consider.

'Nothing,' Lohse sighed, 'I just think it's unnecessary. They have worked hard and can be trusted. Why don't you let me speak to them? Make it clear they have to keep this work a secret.'

Von Behr seemed to relent. 'Ultimately, the decision is yours. I just want you to know there has been concern, and things have been said higher up in the Reich.'

Marina felt regret. Had she made a mistake befriending the Nazis? She had hoped that this friendship would save her. Von Behr's ominous words and their implications echoed in her head. She could feel her skin prickle with apprehension, and she clenched her fists tightly at her sides, trying to remain composed.

When von Behr finally left, Marina cautiously crept away from the inner door so that Lohse wouldn't catch her eavesdropping.

Waiting till she heard von Behr's footsteps echo away, she walked quietly down the corridor. When she reached Lohse's office, she forced herself to act casually and knocked on his door, going in and asking him to sign some paperwork relating to the shipment they were sending out the next day. Lohse looked up from his desk and Marina could see the worry clearly etched into his face. She wondered if he too felt regret over what they were doing.

After he finished, she picked up the signed document and slowly walked towards the door, the air around her heavy with anticipation. She paused for a moment before turning back around to face him.

'I thought it would be nice to eat together, maybe this evening. Will you be free?' she asked, searching his expression for a hint of what he was thinking. He looked tired, and she wondered if it was from working too hard or from the pressure of conversations like the one she had just overheard.

'I have a lot to do, Marina,' he said without meeting her gaze.

'Oh, come on.' She smiled encouragingly at him, moving towards him and perching on the edge of his desk, allowing her skirt to rise, hoping her smooth long legs would do the trick. 'One dinner is not going to kill you. You have to be satisfied.'

His eyes quickly ran down her body, understanding her implication, and the desire was obvious.

'All right,' he said after a beat of silence. 'Why don't you come to my place at seven?'

'I'll bring the food,' she responded enthusiastically, flashing him one of her most seductive smiles.

Marina left the office feeling more uneasy than ever before. She left with her heart pounding in her chest, unsure as to what might happen once they were alone together.

Later that evening, she arrived early at his apartment and nervously paced outside the door, the sound of her heels clicking ominously on the pathway like a ticking clock. Her fingers gripped a cigarette between them, the smoke rising up and stinging her eyes with its acrid presence. Grinding it out with the toe of her shoe, she took a deep breath, trying desperately to keep herself calm before knocking on his door with a smile gracing her lips and wearing her best perfume and fresh make-up.

Carrying in the food that she had purchased with her ration card, she went in.

'I see my cook is here,' he joked as she entered the room. The kitchen obviously belonged to a bachelor, stark and unwelcoming, bare of any decorations or cooking appliances, except for a stovetop which had clearly scarcely been used since the original inhabitants of the apartment had left, and Lohse habitually dined out.

He offered her a glass of wine, which she took with shaking hands, trying not to let him see how much the earlier conversation had affected her.

As she chopped vegetables, she tried to speak nonchalantly. 'So, I noticed that von Behr was here today. I saw him in the corridor.'

His eyes flashed up to meet hers.

'Is there anything else we needed to work out for him, any treasures he was looking for this week?' she said, trying to sound vague.

He paused as he took a sip of his wine, appearing to decide if he wanted to tell her what had been discussed. Finally, blowing out air, he relented. 'He's concerned about you, Isabelle, and Brigitte, and all the information you know about the art.'

'Know?' she said, as if she had no idea. 'What do you mean? We're just working hard to support your needs.'

'There are concerns that you know too much.'

She faked a confident laugh. 'Not too much. I don't know anything,' she said, portraying a lack of concern. 'All I know is that we work hard. I have no memory of anything that goes in and out of that gallery. So why would we be of any worry to the Reich?'

'That's what I thought,' he said with a smile. 'You girls are not going to be a problem. But you need to watch yourselves. Don't be caught doing anything you shouldn't be. It also means we've got to be more careful.' He hinted at the art that they'd stolen.

She looked at him solemnly. 'They can't trace that, can they?' she asked quietly, her voice tight as she stopped preparing the food.

'As you didn't log it, I don't think so. But we need to be care-ful, just in case. So I think we should stop for a while.'

'Is there any news on a buyer for the art from last week?' she asked, trying not to reveal the urgency with her tone. Maybe she would cut her losses and run, get out of Paris. Take any money that they'd made up to now and be gone. This situation was getting too difficult for her, too uncomfortable.

He finished his drink, and put his arms around her waist.

'Don't worry about such things,' he said, nuzzling into her hair.

'I was just wondering if there had been any interest.'

'No, not yet,' he said a little too quickly, clarifying that he wanted to finish talking.

'You had said there was maybe a buyer, and...'

'Shhh,' he said, kissing her neck, and then turned her around and kissed her fully on the lips. She allowed it for a moment, then she slowly pushed him away with a hand on his chest.

'The food is going to burn.'

'I don't care about the food,' he said. 'Turn it off.'

'But we need to eat. Are you not hungry?'

'Oh yes, I'm hungry,' he said cryptically, 'but not for food.'

She smiled at him and allowed him to kiss her neck and throat as he wrapped his arms around her. She turned off the stove and he led her into the bedroom and made love to her.

Later, Marina watched him sleeping, the reassurance of his snores puncturing her rising anxiety. The excuses he made for the buyer echoed in her mind, and suddenly she had a crushing suspicion. Without making a sound, she carefully left the bed and tiptoed to where he kept his briefcase in the next room. Taking a deep breath, she opened it and sifted through its contents. At the bottom of the case was a bill of sale for one of the pictures she remembered stealing; it was for an exorbitant amount of money, a sum that he had never mentioned. Her heart sank. She had to find out what this was about.

Replacing the bill of sale, she silently closed up the case, then returned to the bedroom. She searched his pockets and found the warehouse keys – she would make a copy tomorrow – and then she placed them into her bag before slipping back into bed. An alternate plan would have to be put into action just in case it all went wrong. Everywhere felt unsafe now just like during her childhood; fear shrouded her from all directions – but instead of her estranged family it now came from the Reich, from her lover, and from her co-workers. There was nowhere that she felt safe.

49

Isabelle

Once their plan was in place, Isabelle and Jules worked tirelessly to recover the art that Lohse and Marina had stolen, ever vigilant in their clandestine mission. After careful planning and execution of their strategy, they set up another warehouse in a safe place on the outskirts of Paris. Then they would sneak out at night to reclaim the most critical pieces Marina had stolen. Isabelle remained ever aware as she accompanied Jules on their journey through the darkened streets of Paris, dodging Nazi patrols. As they moved swiftly together, Isabelle found herself feeling strangely alive in the presence of danger.

One night, they made their way down the backstreets until they arrived at the warehouse. There they met up with two other Resistance fighters who helped them remove the art each night. Earlier, the Resistance team had managed to pry open a window that they used each evening to get in and out, without disturbing the door or the locks, which may have alerted Lohse to their presence.

This evening, the rickety old warehouse seemed to creak

with every breath, as if it were alive and aware of the danger that lurked outside. The windows, grimy with dirt and dust, obscured any hint of what lay beyond the walls. Inside, though, it was cavernous, with the smell of dust and polish that hung heavy in the air, like a forgotten museum. An Aladdin's cave of every kind of art and stolen piece crammed inside. Glass cases glinted; gold gilded frames and the occasional green patina shimmered off silverware when caught in their torchlight. Marina and Lohse had so much art in there that it was easy for them to steal just a few pieces back each night.

They would always work the same way. Isabelle would look through the stolen works, removing the most at risk Jewish art that was irreplaceable or important to her country. Then the team of Resistance fighters would take them to their own warehouse.

The work was harrowing, but also rewarding. Not unlike her work at the Jeu de Paume. In her secret notebook she had already logged thousands of precious pieces of art from all over Europe, recording diligently exactly where it had come from, which was mainly private collections, and where it was being shipped to.

She climbed through the window and was digging in the back of the warehouse when her practised eye caught something she didn't expect – a breathtaking Renoir, one of the last paintings created by the artist. Shocked and awed, she gasped with surprise at this gorgeous painting.

With shaky hands, Isabelle lifted the stolen artwork and showed it to Jules, their breaths catching in their throats as they marvelled at it. 'It's beautiful,' he whispered as the beam of the torch danced across the canvas.

All at once one of the other men urgently hissed out a warning. 'Someone is outside.'

Isabelle glanced out of the murky windows. Nazi patrolmen

closed in on the warehouse. Hobnailed boots echoed on the pavement.

Jules swiftly pulled Isabelle down to the cold concrete floor, his grip firm yet gentle. Their bodies pressed together, their breaths mingling in the tense atmosphere.

Her voice barely a whisper, Isabelle murmured, 'Jules, what do we do?'

Jules tightened his hold on her, his voice filled with determination. 'We stay quiet and still. We don't make a sound. We'll wait for the right moment. You remember the escape routes and safe houses just in case we get separated?'

She nodded uneasily.

The room fell to an uncomfortable silence, broken only by the sound of their hushed breathing. Isabelle's heart pounded in her chest, her thoughts racing as they listened to the approaching danger. The seconds felt like an eternity, the weight of the stolen art clammy in her hands.

Across the room, the other Resistance fighters crouched against the wall, their faces etched with concern. Isabelle caught their eyes, a silent exchange of shared anxiety and resolve.

One of the fighters spoke, his voice barely audible. 'I'm not sure I can hold this much longer,' he said, straining under the weight of a bag he had lifted above his head, ready to hand out of the window.

They all eyed one another nervously as they waited in silence for the Nazis to move on. But instead of leaving, one of the soldiers lit a cigarette and the two of them began to talk. As they all waited with bated breath, overwhelmed by the weight, the fighter shifted his position, and the bag toppled from his hands, dropping to the ground with a clatter and alerting the guards, leaving Jules and Isabelle no choice but to run. He pulled her to her feet as the sound of Nazis ordering them to stop echoed out into the silence of the night. She had never been so glad that the windows were so dirty, hopefully making them hard to trace.

Jules bolted out of another exit, pulling her along with him. With adrenaline pumping through her veins, Isabelle felt Jules squeezing her hand tightly for assurance as they raced down dark alleyways at breakneck speed, never stopping until they were sure no one was pursuing them. Finally feeling safe, they stopped, pausing to catch their breath, and she turned to him with concern.

'We can't stop here,' Isabelle spluttered out in wrenching gasps. 'We have to go back for the Renoir. It's very valuable.'

Jules shook his head in amusement. 'Not tonight. It would be too dangerous.'

Regaining their equilibrium, they walked back down the dimly lit streets to her home, and Isabelle could feel the electricity between them, heightened by the escape. The smell of an earlier rainfall filled the air, while in the distance a sudden rattle of gunfire was a reminder that war was still going on around them.

They stopped at her doorstep, and he looked down at her with an intensity that brought butterflies to her stomach. He hadn't kissed her since they had made love, but now he moved closer. She could see the attraction he felt for her and it scared her a little. She desperately wanted to make love to him again; it was like an addiction, the memory of their time together filled her thoughts every day and taunted her nights, when her body ached to feel him close to her in that way again. But there had been no time. He seemed to sense her desire, but, hearing a Nazi patrol at the end of the street, grazed her lips with a gentle kiss. Which still made her shiver, just having him close to her.

He stepped back and gave a small bow of his head. 'Until tomorrow, my little magpie,' he whispered softly before disappearing stealthlike into the night.

An hour later, Isabelle lay staring at her bedroom ceiling unable to sleep with the mixture of conflicting emotions, when all at once, there was a rap at her bedroom window. It made her start: surely, he had not climbed a ladder to her window, and how did he know where she was? Gingerly she peeled back the blackout curtain and, instead of Jules, saw the pixie-esque face of her youngest sister, at the top of the ladder her father used to clean the windows.

'Gigi, what are you doing here?' she asked, unable to keep the exasperation from her tone.

'Open the window, quickly!' her sister hissed back.

Isabelle unlatched the window and her sister leapt in with a giggle.

'I got stuck on this side of town and there are patrols everywhere tonight,' she whispered, pulling the curtains closed behind her. 'I was at a party and I think they might be looking for me.'

'Who?' Isabelle asked.

'The enemy,' she responded, raising her eyes as if this was all a game to her.

'Why?'

'Well,' she said, swallowing down a gulp of water from a glass on Isabelle's sidetable. 'I might have taken this.' She pulled out a wad of francs from her pocket with a giggle.

Isabelle's eyes widened. 'Giselle!' she hissed incredulously. 'What were you thinking?'

Gigi continued to prowl the room, pulling out a spare nightdress from her sister's drawer as she started to unbutton her clothing while she resumed her story.

'Is it my fault that all those ridiculous young German foot soldiers want to all come to Paris on leave for a good time? They are always hanging around the dressing rooms, mooning after us. I just decided it might be time to get a little payment for all the time I have to spend with them.'

Gigi jumped into her sister's bed. 'So, I can't get back to the apartment tonight in case they are looking for me.'

Isabelle shook her head as she got into bed alongside her sister. 'Won't the girls you live with be worried about you?'

'No,' said Gigi, fluffing the pillow, 'I often don't come home.'

Isabelle looked at her sister in horror.

'Where are you?'

'You know,' she said with a mischievous grin. 'Having fun at parties, dancing and other things.'

'Gigi, you shock me. I thought being a ballerina, you had to be disciplined.'

'I do, at the theatre and in the day, which is why at night I like to let loose a little. Get my hair out of a bun, use my primed body in other ways.'

Isabelle felt her cheeks glow with her sister's confession. She turned off the light and lay down. Gigi wrapped her toned body around her sister, hugging her as she continued whispering into her neck.

'I was surprised you were still awake.'

'I only just got in,' Isabelle let slip before realizing it.

'What! Isabelle Valette out after curfew? What is the world coming to? What were you doing?'

Isabelle shook her head. 'I can't say.'

'Can't or won't? Come on, Issie, who is he?'

Isabelle turned and smiled; she desperately wanted to tell somebody and before long she was telling her youngest sister the whole story about Jules. Except she didn't tell her about the Resistance work; she didn't want her sister to know in case it all ended badly.

'I'm so happy for you,' Gigi sighed as she finished her story. 'Who knows if we will even survive this war, and Isabelle, you deserve to be loved. I never thought you would ever let anybody in.'

Isabelle turned over and thought about her sister's words:

she never thought she could either. But since she and Jules had made love, another concern had started to grow in her. She desperately didn't want to lose him. She felt the pain and pleasure of truly loving again and it made her feel so vulnerable.

With all the Resistance work he was doing for her, what if he was taken from her and arrested or worse? What she had been doing hadn't mattered when it had just been her life she was risking, but now she had a lot more to lose and that scared her.

50

Esther

Esther anxiously paced the arrivals terminal at the airport, her stomach in a knot with anger at the thought of her children alone on an aeroplane. What was James thinking? Daniel came across as mature, but he was still only nine. She spotted them as they walked through customs; their sunburned faces were drawn and their clothes dirty and dishevelled. She shook her head in disbelief, noting they were still in shorts, grubby T-shirts, and flip-flops. James hadn't even thought to dress them properly for the weather in England.

Seeing her, they waved excitedly. Racing up to her, they both threw their arms around their mum. Pushing away thoughts of James, Esther forced a great big smile and gave them a hug. God, she'd missed them, enjoying their little bodies clinging to her, a strange smell of coconut suntan lotion and sea salt in their hair. Pulling back from the hug, she looked at them more closely. Henry's hair was lighter than when he had left, and Daniel's nose was freckled and peeling.

They started talking without catching their breath about all the different things they had done, the places they had visited, and how it had been at the beach.

'We even saw a shark,' said Henry enthusiastically.

'No, it wasn't,' said Daniel, 'don't believe him.'

'It was a shark!' he argued persistently.

Esther retrieved their suitcase from the conveyor belt as they continued to bicker between them. She was glad to see them, even though they were arguing. She had missed them so much.

Before they left the terminal, Esther opened up their case and took out the warm jackets they'd been wearing when she'd seen them off on the outbound flight. Then once they got into the car, she handed them both a paper bag of their favourite chocolate and Henry shot her an exasperated look. 'We couldn't get any of my favourite sweets over there, Mum. I didn't like the food at all. It was weird.'

Daniel quickly cut in, 'It was the same as here. Dad ate at all the English bars.'

Henry shook his head and tore open one of the bars of chocolate. 'No, it wasn't. It tasted weird.'

The boys fought back and forth all the way home and as they pulled up outside the flat, Esther's heart sank as the usual reality set in that this was where she now lived. The boys bounced out of the car, eager to get inside and start enjoying their toys and video games after their time away from home. Henry, exhausted, immediately fell asleep on his bed, his paper bag of goodies still clutched in his tiny fist. And in the front room, the buzz of Daniel's Game Boy was comforting.

Esther sat at the kitchen table, trying to figure out what she needed to do to move forward. Should she see her lawyer? That seemed like so much effort and money. But surely it was wrong what James had done. She couldn't go on like this, and she knew it. She would have to sell the picture, get her own home, and make a life for her and the children. But selling the picture caused her heart to wrench. She had been so sure of that back when she had first discovered it. But now, after spending time in her grandmother's story, and knowing how important it had been to her to save, she was definitely having second thoughts.

Her ex-husband called the second week of January. She had heard nothing from him since Christmas and she braced herself as she answered his call, expecting the next drama.

'Esther,' he said, sharp and to the point as always.

'James,' she responded in the same tone, her voice level.

'We've got something to tell you.'

'Hi, Esther,' sing-songed Angela into the phone.

Esther groaned inwardly. Why did they always sound like teenagers?

'Hello, Angela,' said Esther patiently as she sucked the side of her cheek nervously, waiting for whatever this was going to be.

'Angela and I have decided to get married.'

It was so sudden, Esther was dumbstruck. Finally, she was able to splutter out, 'Congratulations,' trying to keep the irritation from her tone.

'And not just that!' Angela continued excitedly, apparently grabbing the phone as her voice got louder. 'We decided to move out to Spain. We just bought a bar!' she shrieked. 'We're going to be bar owners! We're going to own our own place!'

Esther was left momentarily speechless again.

'I'm sorry. I just need to understand what you just said. Did you say you're going to leave England and move to Spain?'

'That's right,' James affirmed, taking the receiver from his excited fiancée. 'We're going to start a new life over there. We're sick of the cold and the wet. We want to live in the sunshine.'

Esther closed her eyes, feeling overwhelmed. Part of her was relieved – it meant she wouldn't have the same hassle she had with them here – but now what? What did that mean for the boys and to her financially? And how were they able to afford to buy a bar? Hadn't he just told her he didn't have any money?

'And what about the boys?' she said, automatically thinking of her children.

There was an intake of breath on the other end of the phone and he must have moved away from Angela because he spoke to her in a tightened way.

'The boys will visit me during the holidays, as most kids do. They'll have a lovely time out there.'

Her voice rose with barely contained emotion. 'But what about other times of the year when they want to see their father, their birthdays, football matches? What about things they want you to come to?'

He sighed heavily down the line. 'Look, Esther, will you stop being so selfish? This is a chance of a lifetime for us, and we're going to take it and you are not going to make me feel bad about it. I'm a good father.'

She bit her lip hard so she couldn't say how she really felt about that as he continued.

'Anyway, I'm going to go now and celebrate, but we'll be making arrangements pretty soon. Once we have packed up the house, I want to see the boys before I leave, so make sure I can have them towards the end of the month.'

'What about the flat?' She knew she sounded desperate but couldn't help herself.

'The flat?' he responded cautiously.

'The flat that I'm living in?'

'What about it?' His voice had a slight edge of petulance.

'How can you afford that and the bar?' she replied equally tersely.

'You still want me to pay for it? I'll have to think about it, Esther. You know I've got a lot going on.'

The implication hung heavy in the air that she would be homeless once he left and her stomach tightened.

'We can figure this all out another time,' he said dismissively. 'You're such a wet blanket. Anyway, I've got to go. Angela's waiting to go out to karaoke.'

And with that he hung up.

She stared at the phone in her hands, mind swirling with conflicting emotions. James's insensitivity and lack of care would never fail to shock her. Her thoughts drifted to Édouard – how different he was. Why couldn't she have met him twelve years ago?

Though, through all this upset, she felt a glimmer of hope that if James was caught up in his own life, then there would be less back and forth here. She had to find a way to be financially independent of him if it killed her. That was what she needed to do. And the only thing she could think of was to sell the painting. It would be the only way to give her some power to start rebuilding her life.

She closed her eyes and thought of that picture of her grandmother, a small Jewish woman standing defiantly behind the Nazi officers in the Jeu de Paume. She admired her grandmother's resilience and sent up a silent prayer for her own strength. Now more than ever she needed to summon up her grandmother's courage to find the answers she needed.

51

SUMMER 1943

Brigitte

For days now there had been frantic activity in the museum, and Brigitte tried to remain quiet and not draw attention to herself. Her heart was still heavy with missing her daughter, who had written her sad letters about missing her home in Paris. Tension was high in the museum with the Germans. Many of their troops were being withdrawn to support the war on the Eastern Front, which was going badly with Russia. The soldiers that were left behind had started becoming more aggressive in their behaviour; they grabbed people roughly, pushed them to their limits without breaks, desperately getting the art moved quickly through the Jeu de Paume.

One morning, von Behr stormed into her office, ordering her to get more men to help with another shipment. She could feel her heart pounding as she found the group of French workers who had been recruited to assist. Shaking their heads at the exhausting demands, they shuffled back into the museum from where they had been taking a short break on the dock.

Von Behr marched around, pointing imperiously at various

pieces of art he wanted crated before stopping in front of the painting that belonged to Brigitte's husband. She held her breath as he studied it for a second. Brigitte had been surreptitiously moving it around the gallery, hiding it behind other pieces. But with the museum being emptied, it was now fully on display.

'And this one,' he said with a swish of his hand.

Brigitte's heart started to thunder in her ears.

'Excuse me, Herr von Behr, I believe that Herr Göring had stated he didn't want this piece on his last visit,' Brigitte lied.

'I am in charge,' he snapped back. 'You will do as I say.'

Brigitte's heart sank as she watched the men move methodically around the room, detaching art pieces from the walls. Fear and desperation welled up inside her; she had to prevent them from taking Samuel's painting – but how? She glanced around frantically, her mind racing to come up with a solution. As they approached the wall where his piece hung, she held her breath, sure that at any moment they'd be reaching for it.

But then Marina strode in. She looked anxious and upset. Lohse had not been around lately. Brigitte wondered if he was preparing to go back to Germany and Marina wouldn't be going with him as she'd expected.

'What is going on here?' Marina said sharply, her gaze sweeping over the scene.

'We're moving out more of the art pieces,' one of the men replied.

'I thought you weren't taking any of these,' she said, peering at him.

'We just do what we are told,' he said with an exhausted shrug.

Brigitte then watched in horror as two of the men grabbed her husband's picture and started to crate it. Just the tip of one of the golden-hued hay bales was showing as the lid came down.

They carried it out onto the deck and she followed, obviously trying to hold back her tears.

Then the driver called out, 'It's full! We can't get any more in tonight! We'll have to come back tomorrow!'

Brigitte teased out the breath she was holding, thinking she might faint.

The men shrugged, left that last crate containing her husband's picture on the dock, and carried on sorting the rest of the art that was already on the truck, then they shut the van doors and drove away.

As she listened to it rumble away, Brigitte's heart was thumping, her legs ready to melt from under her. She looked around the dock. She was alone. She slowly approached the canvas that had been Samuel's passion. Lifting it out of the crate, she carefully ran her fingers down it. Tears poured down her cheeks. So many memories of him painting it flooding back to her. The paint in his hair, the expression of concentration on his face as slowly it had started to take shape. Then the bottle of champagne that had cost them a week's wages to celebrate its completion.

And once again those same words. 'This will be the first of many, my darling,' he had whispered into her hair as they lay entwined in each other's arms that night, the taste of champagne still on his lips.

Wrapping her own arms around her body, she closed her eyes and tried desperately to feel his arms around her, holding her, loving her. But try as hard as she might, Brigitte couldn't recall the feeling of being held by him today. All she felt was an overwhelming sense of numbness that had taken hold of her body – an anxious fear that she'd somehow failed him by not making sure there would be more pictures like this one. There would never be many as he had envisioned. And she was its only hope.

Flashing open her eyes, Brigitte's heart raced as she realized she had to do something. Her own painting wasn't quite finished, it took such a long time because she could only memorize a small portion at a time of the picture in the gallery, but she would have to improvise because time was running out.

She raced into Isabelle's office. 'I have to go home. I'm not feeling well,' she said. Before Isabelle could even answer, she grabbed her bag and was gone.

Arriving home, she raced to the bedroom and moved her dressing table. Her own picture wasn't completed to her satisfaction, but surely it was close enough. She would have to wait until closer to curfew when the museum would be shut. But it was big and she was so tiny. How would she get it through the streets? She had no choice; she had to do it herself.

Just before she opened the panel there was a knock at the door. She stopped and held her breath. Who could it be? She crept out into the hallway, and, peering through a crack in the door, she recognized the figure of a woman. With a sigh of relief, she opened the door. 'Isabelle,' she said, 'oh my God, Isabelle.' She tugged her friend inside and into the kitchen.

'I was worried about you when you left. You were so pale. I just wanted to check on you. Also, I noticed you staring again at that picture of the hayfields in the crate. It is something personal to you, isn't it?'

Brigitte's voice was tight and emotional as she answered. 'My husband painted it. It was the only work he truly loved. He was shot in front of Sophie and me at the beginning of the war.' The anguish and hatred were obvious in her tone.

'Oh my God, Brigitte, no wonder you feel so deeply about it.'

Brigitte sank into an armchair with a heavy exhale before adding, 'I have been guarding it. Showing the Nazis other pieces when they have viewed it. Lying, saying that this kind of piece is out of style. And hard to resell. Anything to stop them taking it. And now they're going to take it away, at any rate.'

'What can I do to help?' Isabelle asked with concern.

Brigitte hesitantly regarded Isabelle, her gaze lingering on the woman's face as she tried to assess whether she could be trusted. After a moment, Brigitte realized that there was no other choice; she needed help and Isabelle was her only option. She motioned for her to follow her into the bedroom. Opening the panel, she pulled out the bundle wrapped in sacking. Unwrapping the canvas with trembling hands, she revealed the painting.

'You took it from the museum? How did you do that?' Isabelle asked, obviously confused.

Brigitte shook her head. 'I didn't take my husband's picture. I painted this.'

'What!' Isabelle responded incredulously. She was spellbound. 'This is so good. What a brilliant copy. You did this? You're so talented.'

'No, I am not. It has taken a very long time. But I know that picture like the back of my hand. And I had to do something.' Isabelle ran her fingers down the canvas, touching and studying it.

'It is a shame that you have to give this up. It is really beautiful.'

'Truly. It is worth it. It is worth it for what I have left of Samuel. Will you help me, Isabelle? I have to get it into the gallery before they come for my husband's picture tomorrow.'

After a moment of consideration, Isabelle nodded her agreement. 'I'll help you. I know someone.'

At twilight, Isabelle turned up with Jules in a truck and the three of them carried the picture between them draped in a cloth along with other furniture so it looked as if Brigitte was selling something. They just hoped no one would stop them.

The three of them got in the van and made their way back to the museum.

When they arrived, Isabelle's heart sank when she saw two guards on duty. One was always intrusive and enjoyed flirting with her. 'Let me do the talking,' she whispered sternly to her two companions. The guard's face lit up when he saw her, and she returned his smile as she stepped out of the van. Inside the vehicle, Brigitte held her breath.

'You're working late?' the guard said, running his eyes down Isabelle's body.

'We ran out of space in one of the vans earlier today and I managed to get another this evening,' she replied.

'I should check it, just to be sure you're not smuggling any people in for a party!' he joked, making his way to the back of the van.

Brigitte still could hardly breathe as Isabelle sidled up to him, running her hand through her hair.

'We're so behind. Oberführer von Behr is not happy. Surely you don't want to waste your time,' she said, looking up at him suggestively. 'Wouldn't you rather chat instead?'

He turned and smiled at her before pulling out a cigarette packet from his pocket and offering one to her. After lighting it, she looked up at him again, and Brigitte noticed Jules grip the steering wheel a little tighter as he watched them in the mirror.

'We can get to know each other while my assistant does the drop-off,' Isabelle said seductively. The German was putty in her hand and she discreetly signalled for them to go.

Jules drove them to the back of the museum, where they found it dark and deserted.

Rushing inside, Brigitte stood frozen in the dimly lit museum, her heart pounding with the weight of their daring act. The sound of approaching footsteps sent a shiver down her spine, as another soldier's voice resonated from outside on the dock.

Brigitte's eyes widened in panic, and she motioned urgently for Jules to follow her into the shadows. 'We can't risk leaving my picture on display after they thought it had been packed already,' Brigitte breathed, her voice tense with worry. 'We should place it in the crate concealing it with sacking, then it won't arouse suspicion.'

She and Jules lifted her husband's painting swiftly out of the packed crate, replacing it with her own work.

All at once, another soldier's voice could be heard at the end of the museum.

The two of them froze.

'The storage closet,' she hissed.

They struggled back through the museum with her husband's picture and into a dark closet at the end of the hall. They hid it behind mops and buckets at the back, wrapped up in a blanket. She would come back for it tomorrow. She would think of a way to get it home then.

Isabelle appeared in the hallway and Jules approached her. 'I have to leave and deal with the other matter we discussed.'

Isabelle nodded and, climbing back into the van, Jules left. Brigitte realized that there was a lot more going on here with the Resistance than just her painting. Isabelle put her arm around her friend and hugged her as Brigitte started to cry with relief, recalling everything that she had done for this one painting. And now she hoped more than anything that they wouldn't get caught, and she would get it home to where it belonged with her, where she could look at it and remember him for the rest of her life; then she could join her darling daughter and they could be together again.

52

Marina

Marina was tormented with conflicting emotions after she'd overheard Lohse and von Behr's conversation. Fear and panic rose inside her, as well as a deep sadness that she had to leave the city that she loved so much. She knew it was the only option in order to avoid being sent to Germany if Lohse changed his mind.

She started packing her belongings, deciding to leave for the South of France the next day, where she had an aunt. She had already made substantial money with Lohse, but there was one more important piece she had her eye on – the Renoir painting that she'd hidden far out of sight. She felt magnetically drawn to the painting. It was the one piece of art that she had stolen just for herself, and if she took it with her, it would ensure she would have no money worries for the rest of her life.

That evening she left her apartment under the cover of darkness, entering the warehouse through an unused side door, and was careful not to turn on any lights that might alert Nazi patrols to her presence. Obtaining the painting meant financial stability, but it also could bring great danger if she was caught in the act. It had been hard these past years having Lohse handle the sale of the art, but unfortunately, he had all the contacts and she always thought if their plan backfired that Lohse would have to take the blame. But now she wanted something for herself.

She crept through the warehouse tentatively, her heart thumping in her chest with every creak and groan of the building, when she heard a muffled sound coming from the corner of the room. In response she darted behind a wall. Peering around the corner, she was startled to see three men illuminated by a faint torchlight in hushed conversation at the far end of the building. She squatted behind the wall, not daring to breathe, and watched in horror as they loaded art into black bags and carried them out through a window they had levered open. Her mind raced with questions as she listened to a conversation between two of them.

'You brought us all the way back this evening for just one picture?'

'Ah, this is not just any picture, this is a Renoir, the last one he painted.'

Marina's stomach muscles tightened. They had been here before, and how did a band of what looked liked Resistance fighters know the worth of that picture?

Could Lohse be behind this? But that didn't make sense. Why would Lohse steal from himself? All at once, one of the men stepped forward, and his face was illuminated for a second in the torchlight of one of the other men. And then she recognized him! She had seen him at the gallery; he and Isabelle were friends. She never forgot someone that good-looking and she remembered he had arrived one day saying he was a family friend and had taken Isabelle out for lunch. Fear began to take over as she watched them lifting the bag one to another out of the window. Did this mean that Isabelle was behind this theft?

Did it mean she knew of her and Lohse's plan of selling art on the black market? Then with crushing sadness she saw the same man lift the Renoir from its hiding place and delicately place it in a bag.

As they all scrambled out of the window, fury bubbled up inside her. How dare someone steal from her, and the very picture she knew was her only way of getting out of Paris? But then an idea came to her – maybe this could work in her favour.

After the men left, she raced back into the warehouse, haphazardly pulling pieces into a bag. She had only been going to steal the Renoir, but now she had someone to point a finger at. She could blame Isabelle, then have her and this family friend arrested for the theft, leaving the way ahead for herself to get away with her own haul. After packing a substantial bag, she slowly and carefully made her way out of the warehouse, attempting to not make any noise or draw attention to herself. Once outside, Marina took a deep breath and began to walk quickly towards her apartment, grateful that no one had noticed her. Tomorrow she would go to Lohse and tell him what she had seen – ready to lay down her trap.

53

Esther

After James had told Esther his news about moving to Spain, she was in a state of shock and disbelief for days, but ultimately, she was relieved. With that kind of distance, it would be harder for him to manipulate her. The boys were a different matter. They were both heartbroken and dealt with it in different ways. Henry had meltdowns all the time, whereas Daniel had become very sombre and wouldn't talk to her about it.

She just wished they had something to look forward to, something to take their minds off it all. She was thinking about this as she drove over to her old house one morning. She had received a call from the new tenants that they had a box for her they had found in the attic that she had overlooked when she'd left.

As she pulled into the driveway of her old home, it glistened with a confetti of frosted ice crystals, shimmering in the early morning sunshine, and she sighed with the sadness of how lovely it all looked.

The new owners, a lively young couple brimming with lots

of ideas for changes in the house, greeted her at the door. She stepped inside, and the first thing she noticed was it smelled different – not bad, just different – and all around there was evidence of those changes in process. Life and the house had moved on, and she tried not to cry.

As the young man handed her the box, with a loving smile over at his wife, she wondered if he would finally finish the unpainted corner of the hallway that James had neglected.

In the car she blew her nose and wiped the smudges of mascara from under her eyes, prompted by the couple of stray tears that had escaped as she had walked back up the path. To cheer herself up, she decided to take a detour into Chipping Campden, a beautiful little Cotswold market town she loved that was not far out of her way home. It was an unusually lovely sunny day for January, and as she pulled into the main street, the creamy Cotswolds stone buildings glistened in the sun.

Esther took a deep breath and stepped out of the car and into the small town. As she strolled down the high street, she felt a pang of nostalgia. She had spent many days here in her childhood, shopping in the high street with her mother, browsing the tiny secondhand bookshops, and having afternoon tea in the quaint teashops dotted around.

Her gaze shifted to the far end of the street, and in the distance, she spotted the old, familiar gallery window. Memories of her mentor flooded back. He'd been a friend of her mother's, and Esther and he had formed a firm friendship during her childhood. Even though he was much older than her, he was very good-looking in the way only men of a different era could be, and as a teenager she'd had a huge crush on him. He always made her feel very important, even as a child.

As she reached his shop, she admired the antiquated, bevelled bow window showcasing one of the owner's breathtaking landscapes artistically lit with tiny spotlights. Scattered around the picture was a display of different-sized easels, canvases, and a rainbow array of art supplies.

As she walked inside, a carousel of his homemade cards and the smell of coffee and pipe tobacco greeted her. Around the walls she admired other gorgeous pictures, and on one side there were racks of brushes and paints.

He was as always dressed impeccably in a tweed suit and a blue-striped tie and was reading a book behind the counter. Looking up as she walked in, he broke into a wide smile.

'Esther, what a lovely surprise. Tell me, how is your mother?'

'She's doing as well as can be expected,' said Esther as she moved towards him and gave him a hug.

He nodded his understanding. 'Ageing is not for the weak of heart, trust me,' he joked.

'You're looking so well,' she complimented him.

'Oh, yes, I am, aren't I?' he joked. 'I'm not long back from a holiday, as you can see by my wonderful tan,' he chuckled.

He smelled wonderful. His usual spicy aftershave was familiar to her, and it brought back so many good memories.

They started to chat amicably as she told him about her adventure in Paris.

'My,' he said, in awe of all her experiences, 'I need to hear more. Let me close the shop. It's January and nobody comes in anyway. I'm mainly here just to keep the seat warm. Let's go into the back and make a cup of tea.'

She followed him to the back of the shop. The gallery had been created from two converted cottages. The front cottage held the shop and a studio above it, and the second, situated behind the first, included a kitchen, living area, three bedrooms, and a large cottage garden. Everything about it was warm and welcoming. She breathed a sigh of relief as he put the kettle on and then joined her at his scrubbed pine kitchen table.

As she sipped her tea, Esther told him about her discovery,

her visit to the Louvre, and the picture her grandmother painted and how finding it had changed her life. She didn't tell him about her new budding romance with Édouard; it was too new and she was still processing what that meant to her.

She then told him about her heart-wrenching decision about whether to keep the painting and he totally understood. 'I hate living in the horrible flat my ex-husband has forced me to live in, but I know eventually I will find the right home. Maybe if I can get a better job, I will be able to afford it.'

He leaned back in his chair and ran a hand through his thinning hair. His face softened in understanding, and he gave her a kindly smile. 'Life moves on and new opportunities unfold at the right time,' he commented wistfully. 'In fact, moving on is what I plan on doing.'

'What do you mean?' Esther asked, feeling a sense of sadness.

He shifted in his seat before continuing. 'Well, I've been here for forty years, and it's time for me to spend more time in the garden. I have a little place in Brighton that I like to go and visit; I want to spend more time there. I have a friend who I'd like to see a little bit more.'

The way he said 'friend' made her think it was a lady friend, though she didn't push him. He was a very private person.

'What will you do about the gallery?' she asked. She could feel her heart sink at the thought of it potentially closing, that precious touchstone of her youth.

'I was actually thinking of having somebody run the shop and maybe live here in the house. It's all paid off. I could afford to also pay them a wage for running the shop. It does very well in the summer. There are still lots of local artists that like to come in, and we do a couple of gallery shows a year which are very successful. But it's so hard finding the right person. Someone you can trust.' He looked at her quizzically, then, before appearing to make up his mind about something and touching her arm gently, he asked, 'Esther, I don't suppose this is something you might be interested in? I know you loved working here on Saturdays when you were at school.'

Esther paused for a moment, stunned by his suggestion. Her mind raced to think about the implications of this offer. 'What do you mean?' she asked, needing clarification that she had understood him correctly.

'Well, you've got your lovely boys, and it's a beautiful, roomy house. Don't they go to the school up the road here? And you've always loved this town. You've told me that before. I think it would be a perfect little place for you. You wouldn't have to pay any rent. The cottage would come with the job. I'd also pay you to run the gallery.'

Tears began to well up in her throat as she looked around the cottage, reminiscing on all of the memories she'd made here.

'You could get out of that flat and you could put up your grandmother's masterpiece right here in the gallery and make a fixture of it. I'm sure with its colourful history it would become quite a talking point. You could have gallery showings and get back to your own art. When was the last time you painted, Esther?'

She shook her head, her eyes misting over. 'I don't even remember.' She felt a wave of excitement wash over her as she began to consider the possibility – no rent, no more awful job.

He told her how much he could pay her, and it took her breath away – it was double what she earned now.

'Are you sure?' she asked, hardly believing the good fortune that was being bestowed upon her.

'Of course,' he said with a warm smile, his wrinkles deepening around his twinkling eyes. 'My shop does very well, and you'd be doing me a huge favour. We'd both be in excellent hands, and I know you would take care of it.'

Tears flowed down her cheeks as she took his aged hand in her own.

'This is a dream come true. You have no idea,' she said, barely able to contain her joy.

His face broke into a broad smile as he tapped her hand and pulled a crisp, white handkerchief out of his breast pocket and offered it to her. 'Well, it seems like it's a deal for both of us,' he said. 'I will get to spend my time in Brighton, where I want to be, and you will get to have a home for the boys and your own place. A piece of art is so important, particularly one that has the significance of the picture you've told me about. You need to keep it close to you; it's all you have of your grandparents. It would be worth preserving.'

She threw her arms around him and hugged him tightly as he laughed softly in response.

'Well, I'm glad I could make your day.'

'You have no idea,' she said, 'you have no idea what this means to me.' The boys would now be able to return to the school they loved, and she could live where she wanted to and be free of James, at last.

54

Brigitte

Brigitte was at work the next day when she heard a noise behind her. With a thumping heart, she spun around and saw her mother standing there with an expression of fear, her daughter, Sophie, clinging to her waist. Odette looked frantic and pale, sweat dripping down her forehead as she took deep, ragged breaths. Brigitte's stomach twisted with dread at the thought of what could happen if they were discovered by Nazi guards.

'Oh, my goodness, Sophie, what are you doing back here in Paris?' her mother gasped with exasperation.

'I missed you, Maman,' Sophie said softly, squeezing her tightly.

'But how did you even get here?' Brigitte whispered.

The little girl's lip trembled, even as her jaw grew firm. 'I ran away,' she replied. 'I was so homesick, it has been so long since I saw you. I left in the middle of the night and travelled to the train station, then used the money I had hidden in my shoe to buy a ticket. I kept myself hidden, just in case any Gestapo agents got on board and asked me where my parents were.

'I squeezed myself between two luggage carts, creating a narrow nook to hide me. It was uncomfortable to stay cramped there, but I was willing to bear it to get home to you. Once the train began moving, I listened carefully to the conversations around me to hear where I was and when I heard I was in Paris I came home to you and Grand-mère.'

Brigitte shook her head, amazed at her daughter's resourcefulness but also concerned about what to do next.

She hugged her daughter tightly. 'I can't believe you did that alone, even though I have to admit it is lovely to see you again.'

It was then Brigitte noticed the worry etched into Odette's face.

'What is it, Maman? Is something wrong?'

Odette raised her chin, flashing a look towards Sophie before saying, 'Sophie, get your grandmother a drink of water.'

Sophie nodded and Brigitte told her where to go as the little girl skipped away to another room.

Odette waited until the little girl was out of earshot then inhaled sharply. 'They came for us today, the Germans, they came for all of us,' she began with a tremble in her voice. 'We only just made it out in time... I was coming back from the shops, rounding the corner, and saw them – dozens of officers marching up the street towards our apartment building. Sophie hadn't seen them yet, and I panicked. Grabbing her arm, I tugged her away quickly, trying to think of what to do.'

Brigitte suddenly felt her legs give way beneath her and she collapsed onto a chair, struggling to catch her breath. Panic clouded her vision and she found herself unable to move.

'What shall we do, Maman? What should we do?'

Isabelle would know.

. . .

Brigitte rushed to Isabelle's office, her heart pounding in her chest.

'Isabelle, I need your help,' she said in a hushed tone as she frantically shut the door and quickly approached her friend's desk. The fear was evident in her voice. 'My mother and daughter are here, and the Gestapo have come for us.'

Isabelle's eyes widened in fear and confusion. 'Sophie has returned? And why would they come for you?' she asked, shock palpable in her voice.

Brigitte couldn't bring herself to say the words out loud, so she gestured towards the door instead. Peering outside, Isabelle saw a woman sitting in the gallery with a yellow star sewn onto her clothes.

'Is that your mother?' she asked. 'But she is wearing a yellow...'

Understanding dawned in Isabelle's eyes as she realized what this meant. She turned to her friend with sadness etched into her face. 'That means you're Jewish too,' she whispered.

Brigitte nodded soberly, her eyes filled with a mix of fear and determination.

Isabelle grabbed her arm, her voice filled with urgency. 'What do you need me to do?'

'Well, we have to get my *maman* out. And I thought that maybe they could go with the art.' Brigitte knew how risky it was, but what other option did they have? She glanced around at the crates of artwork that had been prepared for shipment that day.

'I have an idea,' Isabelle said. She walked outside and spoke to the truck drivers who had just returned from their route. Their tired faces told a story of exhaustion from being over-worked. Brigitte silently prayed she could trust these workers.

Isabelle took out some money from her bag. She handed it to one of them and said, 'I have a very precious cargo that you need to take with you today. But you can't tell anybody, do you understand?'

The man looked up from beneath his flat cap, and his brown eyes grew large as he looked from the money to her face. 'It is dangerous?' he asked cautiously.

Isabelle nodded solemnly. 'It is a little dangerous. But no one will know if you are really careful.'

He hesitated then finally nodded in agreement. 'What do you need me to do?' he said warily.

Isabelle and Brigitte walked inside and gestured for him to come in. Odette and Sophie stood huddled together. Pointing to them, Isabelle spoke clearly and distinctly. 'You must take this lady and her granddaughter and put them on the train with the art.'

Sophie's eyes were wide with fear as she grabbed her mother's arm. 'You too, Maman?'

'I cannot go,' Brigitte replied. Her lips were quivering as she got down to her little girl's height and clasped her shoulders.

'But you have to leave now,' her mother insisted.

Brigitte shook her head determinedly. 'No, I can't,' she said, biting the inside of her cheek. She had to make sure the art she had forged was packed correctly before it would be loaded onto the train later that afternoon, and there was still the crate to pack.

'But I will come tomorrow. The train always stops at Chelles-Gournay station. You can go to your sister in Brou-sur-Chantereine. Go to her and I will follow you both tomorrow.'

Her mother hesitated for a moment before nodding firmly, and Brigitte hustled Sophie and her mother onto the truck. She pulled out some canvas sacking from behind one of the crates and handed it to them.

'Hide yourselves beneath the sacking in case any of the trucks get stopped. At the moment, the Germans are far too busy fighting the Allies to care about a truck full of art. But you never know.'

Isabelle instructed the driver to make sure they stayed hidden among the crates of artwork being loaded onto the carriages.

Her mother's eyes found her, full of concern and worry. 'What about you, Brigitte? What can be more important than saving your life?'

Brigitte took a deep breath, brushing away the tears that threatened to fall. 'There is something very important I have to do. Please take care of Sophie.'

Sophie began to wail. 'No, Maman, I don't want to be away from you again!' she cried, throwing her arms tightly around her mother's neck. 'Is this my fault, because I came back?'

Brigitte's heart broke for her daughter, but she didn't have time to explain before someone might catch them.

'You have to go, Sophie, go now,' she said sharply. 'No more tears.'

Sophie looked heartbroken, but Brigitte knew she would join her soon and she could explain everything then.

She moved them to the truck, Sophie sobbing into her grandmother's skirts, and they checked the two of them were covered with the sacking as the older man stuffed a bundle of cash into his pocket, lit a cigarette, and nodded his head before driving off with the most precious cargo hidden behind the crates.

Isabelle placed a comforting arm around Brigitte's shoulders, as, once the truck was gone, she sobbed.

'Why didn't you go? What is so important?'

Brigitte shook her head. 'I have to make sure the picture is back hidden in the house.'

'I could have done that,' Isabelle insisted.

'No, there are Nazis there and you have done enough. I will join them tomorrow as soon as Samuel's picture is safe.'

Just then Bruno Lohse appeared, accompanied by Marina, and the air seemed to thicken with even more tension.

'We need to look at the latest shipment that arrived.' Marina stopped and stared at the two of them. 'What's wrong?' she asked brusquely.

'Nothing, I just had some bad news about a friend,' Brigitte said dismissively as she wiped at her eyes and cleared her throat.

Isabelle went back to her office and Brigitte finished packing up her copy of the painting for the next shipment. She looked at the picture one more time. It wasn't completely finished as she would have wanted. But hopefully it would do for what was needed. This would also go on the train and be transported to Germany.

'We need to look at these before they go,' Lohse said. 'I need to check what they are.'

'But they have already been documented,' persisted Brigitte.

'That is not your concern.' Lohse's tone was icy, and Brigitte felt a chill of fear run down her spine. She stepped back as they began to scrutinize each painting, glancing from one canvas to the next. Brigitte's heart thundered in her chest; she knew if they found out the last painting was a forgery, it could cause all kind of problems. Lohse removed each piece of artwork from the crate and held it up to the light before comparing it with the photographs in the shipping catalogue. When he reached the forgery, he paused and inspected it with intense scrutiny. Brigitte dared not watch, looking down and balling her fists as she awaited his verdict. Finally, after what felt like an eternity, he dropped the canvas into its rightful place and gave Marina a barely perceptible nod.

They quickly loaded the wooden crates, securely strapping them in place with thick rope. Brigitte let out a long slow breath as they left the room. With this forgery on the train, Samuel's work would be safely tucked away at her home for her and

Sophie to enjoy after the war. And no one would be any the wiser. Anxiety bubbled up inside her as she contemplated the possibility that someone might find out about what she had done. She closed her eyes and sent a silent prayer to the heavens, hoping her efforts weren't in vain.

Sitting down in a chair with relief, she spoke gently into thin air. 'My darling, soon your work will be safe.' She stood slowly, stomach still churning with apprehension, and made her way out of the room. As she left, her mind drifted back to her daughter and mother on a train to safety. She would join them both tomorrow, and they would find a way to be together until this terrible war was over.

55

Isabelle

After Sophie and her grandmother left, Isabelle and Brigitte continued working in a tense silence. The air felt oppressive under the weight of fear that their plan could go wrong and they would be caught.

Jules had pulled the Renoir out of his sack, and she had gasped again at its beauty. 'It's gorgeous,' she'd said in awe. Then suddenly reminded of their urgent mission, she added, 'Now remember we still need to get Brigitte's picture back to her home. Why don't you come to the museum when it's closing? That way there will be fewer soldiers around who might spot you.'

But Isabelle was now filled with dread; the museum had officially been closed for thirty minutes and still he hadn't arrived.

Finally, at six o'clock, Jules brought the van to a stop on the dock and Isabelle rushed out to greet him.

'Thank goodness you're here,' she said, her voice shaking.

'Were you worried about me?' he said with a half-smile.

'No, just the Renoir,' she said with a curl of her lip. 'Did you get it to our warehouse?'

'I did.'

'Brigitte is almost done preparing her husband's picture. And will need to take it back to her home. We have to be careful; apparently they have started raiding her apartment block.'

He followed her as they moved into the Jeu de Paume.

'I'm sorry I was late. I had a meeting with the Resistance. Some of them are preparing to blow up one of the trains leaving Paris this evening.'

Isabelle froze mid-step, her breath catching in her throat.

'What?!' she hissed, her heart pounding against her ribcage.

'We're blowing up a train this evening,' he repeated solemnly.

Isabelle felt sick to her stomach.

'Which train is it?' Her mind raced as she struggled to remember the train Sophie and her grandmother would be on.

'It leaves at 6.30 from the Gare de l'Est,' he muttered under his breath.

Fear seized her chest as realization flooded through her veins like ice water. She rushed to her office to check the outward-bound schedule.

He followed, bewildered.

She finally looked up, horror-struck.

'Not only is our artwork on there, but Brigitte's family is too. They've been smuggled out with the crates. We have to warn them.'

Jules grimaced as he contemplated their next move. His jaw clenched tightly with obvious apprehension of the danger they were about to face. With a determined glare, he announced, 'I know where they're planning to be.'

Isabelle nodded. 'Let me get Brigitte, just in case she needs to be there for Sophie. This has been distressing enough for that little girl.'

Isabelle bolted through the museum, finding Brigitte packing her husband's picture.

'Hurry!' Isabelle exclaimed with a tinge of panic in her voice. 'We have to go!'

'Where?' said Brigitte, looking panicked.

'The train that your mother and daughter are on – the Resistance is planning to blow that up today. We have to go and stop it. Jules is going to drive us to the station.'

They stepped out into the hallway, only to find one of the Nazi guards blocking their way.

'Why are you here? I thought all of you workers left at five thirty,' he grumbled. 'We have strict instructions from Commander Lohse to make sure the building is vacated by that time.'

Isabelle fumbled for an excuse as she glanced anxiously at the clock above his shoulder. If they didn't leave soon, the train would depart, and there was no telling what consequences that could bring.

56

Marina

Before she left her apartment, Marina dialled Lohse's number and nervously started to explain what she had witnessed the night before. He responded with a mixture of anger and shock, his voice taut with disbelief.

'What exactly were you doing at the warehouse alone? And where did you get a key?'

Marina had been so eager to tell him what she knew that she had forgotten about stealing his key and getting a copy. She swallowed hard, searching for an answer.

'I had to check on one of the pieces and I noticed your key on the table,' she said, ashamed of the lie, hurrying to finish. 'That's not the point, though; someone is stealing from us and I think I recognized one of the men as a friend of Isabelle's.'

He exhaled sharply. 'I don't remember leaving it on a table. We can talk about this later. First, meet me at the museum where I can question her.'

He paused for a moment before continuing sternly: 'But, Marina, I'm very unhappy about this. You should not have taken my keys and gone there without me. If the soldiers had seen you there alone as a French citizen – they would have asked questions. We will need to talk about this later.' He had slammed down the phone then.

She arrived at the museum fuming and had barely taken off her hat when she heard the low rumble of someone arriving at the loading dock.

As she rushed out to see if it was Lohse, she was met with a shock: there was the very man she had seen at their warehouse, sitting, waiting in a truck out on the dock.

He nodded at her without realizing she had seen him the night before, stealing from them.

As Lohse exited his vehicle, in a hushed whisper, she quickly filled him in on the situation, and he demanded she fetch some guards. As she arrived back with them, she watched Lohse yank open the cab door and drag Jules out.

'What are you doing?' Jules shouted indignantly, struggling against him.

'What have *you* been doing, is more appropriate,' spat back Lohse.

'I'm just here to take art crates to the train station,' he reeled back defiantly.

'No, you're not,' Marina countered venomously. 'I saw you last night in our warehouse.'

His face hardened and he narrowed his eyes at her before he spoke. 'What warehouse? I don't know what you're talking about, mademoiselle.'

'Don't lie to us!' shouted Lohse as he gestured towards the guards, who forcefully clamped their hands onto Jules. 'You will be held for interrogation by the Third Reich, and if we find out this is true, you will be executed.'

Marina stared incredulously at Lohse, a chill through her veins. He was getting away with himself. How was it possible to interrogate this prisoner without informing von Behr of what they had been hiding?

He must have sensed her concern, because he hissed at her, 'I want to talk with you in private,' before turning away and marching back into the gallery, slamming the door behind them as soon as they reached his office.

'What are you doing? Arresting him like that will draw attention to what we have been trying to hide here,' Marina confronted him.

'Will it?' he taunted, moving closer to her until her back was pressed against the wall. 'We've had a nice run, but now it's time to reveal the truth – and it looks like you'll be the one taking the blame.'

She could not believe what was happening. 'What?! What are you talking about? We're both implicated!'

Marina's heart pounded in her chest as she contemplated his chilling words. The room seemed to close in around her, suffocating her with a sense of impending doom. Her hands trembled uncontrollably, betraying her fear.

'Not according to my report,' he hissed, his voice dripping with malice. 'Apparently, I uncovered grave discrepancies in the logbooks, and I have undeniable evidence that only you had access to them and the hidden art. And what's more,' he sneered, 'I found you collaborating with this relentless Resistance fighter.'

A wave of terror washed over Marina, paralysing her. Her mind raced, desperately seeking an escape from this nightmarish situation, but she found none. The weight of the accusation pressed down on her, crushing her spirit.

'Besides,' he continued, his voice now colder than ever, 'who do you think they will trust more – a French citizen or a decorated Nazi officer?' The question hung in the air like a suffocating fog, intensifying her terror.

Marina's anger burned within her, threatening to consume

her, but it was overshadowed by a bone-chilling fear that gripped her soul. She knew she was trapped, trapped in a web of her own deceit and manipulation.

He pressed on mercilessly, relishing in her torment. 'And as for any black-market deals... well, there is no record of them, is there?' His triumphant grin twisted Marina's insides, robbing her of any hope. She felt her strength drain away as she slumped into a chair, defeated and broken, realizing the depths of her own naivety and vulnerability.

Isabelle

Isabelle's heart raced as she and Brigitte finally got away from the guards' interrogation at the front of the museum. But when they reached the loading dock, Jules was gone and the door of the truck was wrenched open.

'He was just here,' Isabelle cried desperately.

Without another thought, she ran back inside to look for him, only to find Lohse and Marina having a heated argument in the office.

Racing back out to the dock, she shouted, 'We must go without him – we haven't time to wait!'

'How?' Brigitte snapped, exasperated.

'I can drive,' Isabelle replied hastily. 'My father taught his girls how. He said one day it might be helpful. Now I'm glad he did.' She quickly searched the van for keys while Brigitte paced anxiously back and forth, but they were nowhere to be found.

Glancing around the dock, Isabelle spotted Lohse's Nazi truck parked in one corner. She rushed over to the door and tried it; it opened easily and the keys were already in the ignition.

'Come on!' she shouted to Brigitte, her voice rising with urgency. 'We'll use this one.'

'We can't take a Nazi truck!' Brigitte exclaimed, incredulously.

'Yes, we can! I don't know where the Resistance is blowing up that train, so we have to get there before it leaves the station!'

Isabelle and Brigitte jumped into the truck, a sense of urgency pressing down on them. The night air was cold, a chill that hung in their lungs like a lead weight as they flew down the winding roads.

They raced through the streets of Paris, each twist and turn adding more anxiety to Isabelle's already frantic state. Brigitte concentrated on the map, issuing orders to Isabelle. The look in her friend's eyes was frantic but determined. Isabelle noticed that her heart was pounding faster and faster with each passing minute. She glanced back at Brigitte and saw that she was feeling the same way as she anxiously gripped her seat.

'We'll get there,' Isabelle reassured her. 'Don't worry, we'll get there.'

Brigitte nodded in agreement as Isabelle pressed down on the accelerator and they flew down deserted streets, praying they would not meet any Nazi patrols.

Refocusing on the map, Brigitte pointed out a narrow alleyway coming up on their left. 'Turn here!' she screamed at Isabelle, who quickly swerved across the road, cutting off someone who blasted their horn at them. Isabelle held up her hand apologetically as they skidded around the corner at the rue du Faubourg Saint-Martin.

As they raced into the Gare de l'Est, they screeched to a stop, but it was too late. As if mocking them, the train belched black smoke, letting loose a long, mournful whistle. Biting at the rails with its steel wheels, the train rumbled thunderously away as it gained speed rapidly.

'No!' Isabelle cried, her heart sinking into her stomach. 'Quick.' She jumped back in the truck. 'I have an idea.'

Brigitte nodded and, pushing down hard on the accelerator, Isabelle screeched back out onto the road.

'We have to cut the train off farther up the road.'

'What do you mean, cut it off?' Brigitte asked.

'It's the only way; if we don't, the next train station is thirty miles away,' Isabelle responded.

Isabelle drove the truck with a reckless abandon, pushing it faster and faster. She careened it around each corner, pushed to its limits as they sped down the winding roads.

Brigitte clung to the seat in fear, looking terrified.

Finally, they spotted the train in the distance. It was moving at an incredible speed, but there was still a chance they could beat it to the Chelles-Gournay station – if only Isabelle pushed the vehicle even harder. The engine roared as she put her foot down flat on the accelerator.

But when they approached the next station, with a thunderous whistle, the train picked up speed and hurtled past the platform without stopping.

They followed, keeping the train in their sights. As it slowed for a signal they sped past it.

Suddenly, Isabelle's attention was snatched away by a flash of movement in the corner of her eye, a dark silhouette amid the rustling bushes, a glimmer of silver hinting at something more. Her heart stuttered, a moment of recognition hitting her like a lightning bolt – Resistance fighters, waiting in the shadows.

'Oh my God, Brigitte, look.' Her passenger followed her gaze and gasped with the realization of what it meant.

With instinct taking over, Isabelle wrenched the steering wheel to the right, the screeching of brakes filling the air. As the vehicle skidded to a halt, Isabelle and Brigitte leapt out, their breathless forms racing towards the concealed figures.

Their voices rang out in urgent calls, but the approaching train's piercing whistle swallowed their cries whole. It bore down on them like an inexorable force, its metal might hurtling towards them.

As if echoing the train's warning, another train roared by from the opposite direction, its own whistle shrieking in a cacophonous symphony. Suddenly, the night was rent apart by a colossal explosion, a cataclysmic blast that tore through the darkness with an intensity that left them reeling. Heat, fury, and the metallic screech of destruction filled the air as a fireball blossomed into the sky. Isabelle and Brigitte were thrown to the ground by the force of the explosion.

Through the haze, flames licked hungrily at the ground, racing towards the abandoned truck on a wave of relentless heat. As they lay there, disoriented and overwhelmed, beams from the other train swept over the scene like a spotlight, casting their chaotic tableau into sharp relief.

And then, as if conjured by the chaos itself, Isabelle's gaze fixed upon a face emerging from the back of the truck, a man with a mix of desperation and fear etched across his features. The sight was surreal, like a ghost in the shadows.

'Oh my God. Jules!'

Brigitte turned to follow her gaze, comprehension dawning as they both realized that Jules was trapped in the back of the Nazi truck, his wrists and hands bound by ropes, his face marred by streaks of blood.

As the voracious firestorm roared closer, Isabelle sprang into action. With a burst of strength fuelled by desperation, she rushed to the truck's tailgate, her fingers fumbling against the metal. With a final surge of determination, she yanked the door open, Jules's eyes filled with relief as he met her gaze.

Isabelle seized him by the collar of his shirt, and with a surge of strength that felt almost supernatural, she hauled him out, dragging him from the brink just moments before the inferno engulfed the vehicle and with it a second explosion tore through the night, bringing everything to a bone-rattling halt.

58

Isabelle

Isabelle frantically wrestled Jules away from the tracks as black smoke billowed into the dark sky, choking them all on the fumes, and an eerie silence descended on the night. Then suddenly, Isabelle heard Brigitte's desperate cries as she sprinted towards the burning carriage, screaming her daughter's name. German soldiers jumped from the train, guns held high and pointed menacingly at her, obviously believing they were under attack.

'Halt!' one shouted, his order echoing like thunder through the night, reverberating off the trees in the distance.

But it was as if Brigitte didn't even hear them, a mother's instinct propelling her forward. All at once the sound of gunfire rang out into the night, and Brigitte's body collapsed and crumpled to the ground.

Isabelle ran towards her friend with her hands held up in surrender. 'Please! Please don't shoot! She's just a museum worker!' Dropping to her knees in the dirt, she clasped tightly

on to Brigitte's hand. Her friend's eyes flickered open, her
ragged breath hot in the stagnant air.

Isabelle stared down at her, an overwhelming sense of shock
and disbelief washing over her. Brigitte's formerly pristine
blouse was now covered in a thick coat of blood oozing from a
wound in her chest.

Isabelle clutched Brigitte's hand tightly, her mind racing as
she tried to think of a way to save her friend. She looked up at
Jules.

'Do something, *please* do something!'

He attempted to stem the bleeding but his hands were still
bound and it was as if they both knew it was hopeless. A sob
caught in Isabelle's throat as she thought of this amazing woman
and all she had done for love. It seemed so wrong that just as she
was about to be free, she would be robbed of her daughter and
her life.

'My daughter,' she whispered in obvious pain. 'Save
Sophie.' Then Brigitte reached up and gripped her arm, her
claw-like grip desperate. 'And the painting,' she choked out.
'You must save them both, so Sophie has something left of her
father.'

Isabelle felt her feet moving of their own accord as she
raced towards the train, a rush of adrenaline and fear coursing
through her veins, her heart pounding in her chest with dread.
The acrid smell of smoke and fumes assaulted her senses, and
angry orange fingers of fire licked at the sky. Then she remembered that smell, a smell that made her skin crawl – burning
paint, coming back to haunt her from the past. Uncontrollable
memories swept through her mind, and without thinking, she
reached the train, entering a world of smoke, ash, fire and fear.
Just then she heard it, a voice that echoed through the chaos,
echoed through time. A voice she knew all too well.

59

Isabelle

From the carriage, a child's voice rang out again for help through the roar of the inferno.

'Help! Please, someone help me!' The child's voice was high-pitched and urgent with fear and desperation.

Disorientated by the smoke and memories, Isabelle called back.

'Pierre, I'm here! I'm here!'

As she did so, Isabelle choked on the thick haze of smoke, her vision blurring as she desperately searched for her brother. She stumbled towards the burning art, frantically yanking anything she could from the flaming crates and tossing it out of the carriage. Pierre was still hiding there somewhere and she had to find him. The searing heat scorched her skin as if branding her flesh; every movement seemed to bring another wave of unbearable pain as her hands blistered with the heat. Despite the pain radiating through her body, she brazenly pushed forward, the heat and smoke pressing in like a noose, cinched tightly around her chest.

Suddenly, an explosion threw her backwards with bone-shaking force, rocking the carriage, which groaned under the fatigue. As she slammed against a wall, she hit her head hard, seeing stars and nearly blacking out. Dazed and in agony, Isabelle struggled against unconsciousness. Pressing her finger to the sharp pain pulsing from her head, she felt something warm and sticky matting her hair. Blood. Her eyes began closing. She just wanted to give up. She wanted to let go. She wanted to die. This time she didn't want to be the one left behind.

Suddenly someone touched her arm – and a gentle, still voice whispered into her ear, 'It's okay, Isa. I am okay. You have to live. Please don't let go.' Her eyes snapped open in shock and she looked towards her arm. Nothing was there. Had she dreamt it? Her brother had spoken to her. She knew it was her brother.

Summoning all the strength left in her body, she lifted her head as it pounded and she pulled herself to her knees. The art was burning and she could save it this time. Through the roar of the flames Isabelle heard someone calling for help and Jules's words echoed through her mind: 'People are more important than art.'

Bleeding, trembling, and coughing, she crawled desperately across the floor, her lungs screaming for air as unbidden voices echoed from the adjoining carriage. Pulling herself up, she hurled her body at the door, but it refused to budge. Her weakened fists pounded against the thick wood, desperation and fear coursing through her veins. Suddenly, a figure appeared to the side of her, Jules's silhouette illuminated by the inferno behind them.

With his hands now free from their restraints, Jules threw himself against the stubborn door, his body slamming into it with a resounding thud. The lock protested, groaning under the pressure, until it finally gave way with a tortured creak. The screams inside grew louder, mingling with the crackling flames and the acrid smoke that filled the carriage. As the smoke billowed out, obscuring their vision, Isabelle's heart pounded with fear and determination. She strained her eyes, desperately searching for any sign of Brigitte's mother and Sophie amid the chaos. Within the swirling flames and the agonizing screams, Isabelle's gaze caught a glimpse of a frail figure stumbling through the smoke. It was Brigitte's mother, disoriented and coughing, her face etched with a mixture of fear and desperation. Isabelle's heart surged with a renewed sense of purpose as she propelled herself forward, racing towards the elderly woman.

Jules followed close behind, his determination mirroring Isabelle's. With every breath, the air grew thicker, making it harder to see and breathe. But she pressed on, her body stinging with the heat.

Finally, they reached Brigitte's mother, and she extended her arms to steady her fragile form. Isabelle's voice, strained and filled with determination, cut through the roar. 'We're here, we've got you. You're safe now.'

Brigitte's mother clung to them, her body trembling with exhaustion and relief. Tears streamed down her face, mingling with the soot and sweat, as she whispered words of gratitude amid gasps for air.

With Brigitte's mother supported by Jules, Isabelle turned her attention back to the burning carriage. Flames leapt higher, moving closer to her, threatening to consume everything in her path. But she had to find Sophie.

She braved the scorching heat, her eyes darting through the smoky haze, searching for a glimpse of the young girl's face.

And then, from below a pile of debris a small figure emerged from the smoke, coughing and sobbing. Sophie, her eyes wide with fear, stumbled towards Isabelle. Isabelle's heart swelled with a mixture of relief and anguish as she opened her arms, embracing the trembling girl.

Together, with Brigitte's mother and Sophie now in their care, Jules and Isabelle made their way back through the burning carriage.

'Thank God,' the older woman cried as they all scrambled out of the smoke-filled train.

Jules helped Brigitte's mother while Isabelle held Sophie tightly in her arms. The flames licked closer as they ran out into the warm night air. All the way Isabelle whispered desperately into the child's hair, 'It's okay, Pierre, you're safe this time, I've got you.'

But then she remembered this wasn't Pierre; it was Brigitte's daughter, Sophie. Looking down at the little girl whose face was streaked with tears and smudged with smoke, Isabelle felt an icy wave crash over her heart. Sophie clung tighter to her neck as if her life depended on it, whispering through sobs, 'I need to tell my *maman* that I'm so sorry I came back, I should never have come back, this is all my fault.'

With a crushing realization Isabelle remembered her friend lying in the grass, unable to ever hear her daughter's plea, and she felt grief-stricken for the little girl.

As the Nazis frantically attempted to extinguish the fire, Jules pulled them away from the train to a wooded area off to the side. His voice seemed loud in Isabelle's ear as he hissed urgently, 'We have to go now! We must get out of here right now before someone starts asking questions!'

Already someone was taking pictures of the scene and Isabelle knew it would only be a matter of time before what they had done was discovered.

Amid the frenzy, a pair of shadowy figures emerged from the haze and smoke. Isabelle's eyes locked with the scarred man, the same one she had seen at the Resistance meeting. Recognition flickered between them, and she realized they must have been part of the daring plan to blow up the train.

Jules rushed over to them and wasted no time in explaining their predicament. 'We need a way out of here.' His voice was laced with desperation.

'We both have transportation. We can get you to safety.'

She tried to hand the little girl over to her grandmother, but Sophie wasn't letting go – her fingers snapped around Isabelle's neck with an iron grip as she screamed, 'No! I want to go with you to my mother!'

Isabelle dropped the girl to the ground and knelt down to Sophie's level, her brows furrowed with sadness at what was to come next. She softly brushed the girl's hair aside and spoke in a gentle voice. 'Sophie, I have something important to tell you.'

Sophie looked up at Isabelle with wide eyes, silently nodding her head in response.

'I'm afraid your *maman* is no longer here with us.'

'I don't understand. What do you mean?'

'She has gone to be with the angels,' Isabelle said, her voice barely above a whisper.

Sophie burst into tears as her grandmother sobbed beside her.

Sophie, overwhelmed by grief, spluttered out, 'She is dead, isn't she, just like my papa and it's all my fault.'

Isabelle swept a tear-streaked strand of hair behind the little girl's ear before continuing, 'It's not your fault.'

'What will happen to me, now?' the little girl wailed.

Isabelle enveloped the little girl in her arms, feeling her quivering body, her sobs reverberating into her shoulder. The child had been Brigitte's only daughter, and now she was motherless and fatherless. 'It will be all right,' Isabelle whispered, rocking her gently.

She glanced at the little girl's grandmother, whose expression was adamant.

'I cannot stay in Paris. I cannot stay in this place one more day. I will find a way to take Sophie to England.'

Looking at the sobbing child, Isabelle nodded sympathetically and placed a comforting arm around the older woman's shoulder. She wished that Brigitte was there to hug her daughter and tell her everything would be all right.

After Sophie was safely in her grandmother's arms, Isabelle pulled Jules aside.

'We can't stay here; the Nazis will surely start questioning and investigating what happened.'

Jules nodded, his eyes scanning their surroundings.

Isabelle swallowed down her pain as she glanced back at the burning train. 'And we can't leave Brigitte here.'

Jules nodded, squeezing her hand to comfort her as he took a deep breath, his mind racing for a solution. 'I have a contact who can provide us with a safe house; Sophie and her grandmother can stay there. It's not far from here. We can take them there temporarily until we think of a long-term plan.'

'I know it; I can take them,' one of the freedom fighters said, nodding toward Brigitte's mother.

'Take care of them,' Jules said, clasping a hand on his shoulder as the group nodded and departed through the woods, the sound of Sophie's frantic sobbing echoing back towards them as they went.

Isabelle, Jules and the man with the scar made their own way back through the woods.

As they approached the scene she noted the soldiers were still fully occupied fighting the fire that was building in momentum, threatening to engulf the whole train. They had no time to deal with the death of an enemy. Isabelle's hands trembled, her grief mingling with determination.

Tears streamed down her face as she took Jules's hand.

He squeezed hers gently, offering her a comforting presence.

As they drew closer her footsteps faltered, and her heart pounded with a mixture of dread and sorrow. Her eyes welled up with tears, blurring her vision as once again she saw the lifeless body of her dear friend.

A gut-wrenching sob escaped Isabelle's lips, as if all the pain and anguish she had been holding back had finally found release. She reached out towards Brigitte's still form. The enormity of the loss crashed over her like a tidal wave, threatening to consume her with its overwhelming force.

'Brigitte,' Isabelle choked out, her voice a broken whisper. 'How could this happen? How could they take you from us?'

Her fingers smoothed back hair from her friend's face, every touch a bittersweet reminder of the vibrant spirit that had been snuffed out too soon. Memories flooded Isabelle's mind, of shared laughter and whispered pain, of a friendship forged in the crucible of war. It was almost unbearable to accept that Brigitte was gone, forever beyond her reach.

Tears streamed down Isabelle's face, mingling with the soot and ash that stained her skin. Lifting her towards her, she held Brigitte's lifeless body against her, as if by sheer willpower she could breathe life back into her, restore the warmth to her skin, and the light to her eyes.

'I'm so sorry, Brigitte,' Isabelle whispered into her hair, that still smelt of lavender soap.

She knew she had to find the strength to carry on, to fulfil the promise she had made to protect Sophie and the painting. But in that moment, all she could feel was the weight of her own helplessness and the unbearable ache of a friendship cut short.

Jules gently placed a hand on Isabelle's shoulder, offering a wordless comfort.

With a heavy heart and trembling hands, Isabelle kissed Brigitte's forehead one final time, whispering a heartfelt goodbye. As Jules lifted up Brigitte as if she was no weight at all, Isabelle forced herself to rise, her legs feeling weak and unsteady beneath her. Though her spirit felt shattered, she followed Jules as they moved through the night, her heart breaking with her grief.

60

Isabelle

On the outskirts of the city, concealed behind the decaying walls of an abandoned warehouse, a small group of mourners gathered in a dimly lit room. The air was heavy with a musty scent of frankincense. Partly to purify the spirit, partly to disguise the smell of the moulding wallpaper. Even though this was a place of worship, it was devoid of any religious symbols or distinct Jewish markings; yet it held the weight of centuries of tradition and resilience.

As the mourners gathered, Sophie clung tightly to her grandmother's hand, her small frame consumed by grief. Her once bright eyes, now clouded with sorrow, gazed upon her mother's lifeless form with a mix of confusion and anguish. Isabelle felt a wave of empathy at the loss that weighted her young shoulders, a burden no child should bear.

She knelt and took the little girl's hand as Sophie's eyes widened with sadness, her thin lips trembling as she spoke. 'But why did this have to happen? Why did Maman have to leave us?'

Isabelle drew in breath and attempted a reassuring smile. 'We may never fully understand why certain things happen, especially when they are so painful. But in these moments of sadness, you must remember the love that your mother left behind. You carry that love in your heart, always.'

Sophie nodded as two huge tears rocked on the brims of her lashes.

She looked up at Isabelle, her watery eyes searching for solace. 'Will it ever get better? Will the pain go away?'

Isabelle swallowed, wanting to be honest with the little girl, remembering her own childhood grief.

'Not completely, but it will lessen until one day all you will have left are the good memories, the ones you will want to keep with you always.'

In the absence of a proper *mikveh* for ritual purification, the sacred task of *tahara*, the washing and dressing of the deceased, had been performed discreetly and with utmost care by those entrusted with this sacred duty. Brigitte, adorned in simple white linen, lay before them, a symbol of the indomitable spirit that had defied the horrors of their time.

As the service started, Isabelle respectfully moved to the back, her voice barely above a whisper as she recited the ancient prayers, her trembling hands clutching a small prayer book. The words, laden with centuries of Jewish tradition, carried a weight that transcended the confines of the room.

Then, together, they carried Brigitte to her final resting place, a hidden corner of a secluded cemetery in the woods, where other souls, lost to the atrocities of war, lay in silent repose. The gravesite, unmarked and inconspicuous, would remain a testament to the resilience of a community forced to mourn in secrecy.

It was later, at the meal of consolation, that Isabelle finally got a chance to talk to Brigitte's mother, Odette. A heavy sense of sadness hung in the air of the neighbour's home as Odette sat down upon a worn-out sofa, her eyes brimming with sorrow, and Isabelle's heart broke for her.

Isabelle spoke softly, her voice laced with genuine empathy. 'I cannot even imagine the pain you and Sophie must be feeling. Brigitte was truly a beautiful soul. I miss her terribly.'

A heavy sigh escaped the older woman's lips as she nodded in agreement, her eyes turning towards the little girl, reflecting a grandmother's worry for her future. Sophie was sitting huddled in a corner of the room, her petite frame engulfed by overwhelming sadness.

'I fear that this shock, this loss will leave an indelible mark upon her tender soul,' Odette confessed, her voice filled with gentle concern. 'How does a child get over such a horror? How does she ever come to terms with the death of her mother after only just losing her father a few years ago?' She shook her head sadly as she let out a heavy breath.

Isabelle's heart sank under the weight of those words as guilt settled heavily upon her shoulders. 'I wish there was more I could have done, something to avert what happened,' she said regretfully.

Odette turned her gaze back towards Isabelle, the weight of their shared sorrow heavy in the air. Her voice was warm and full of understanding as a single tear spilled down Isabelle's cheek, followed by another as she stood motionless, her shoulders slumped forward.

'Do not blame yourself, Isabelle.' Her hand rested reassuringly on Isabelle's arm. 'You have been a cherished friend to us all, and Sophie has benefitted greatly from your help.'

Isabelle nodded slowly before raising her eyes to meet the older woman's gaze. Despite the tears brimming in them, they shone with an inner strength and resolution.

'You are right,' Isabelle whispered, determination hardening her voice. 'Sophie needs our unwavering support now more than ever. We need to get you both to safety as soon as possible. The soldiers that came for you before will come again. Jules will help us.'

61

Esther

When Esther opened the front door of her flat, she couldn't believe who was standing there.

'Édouard,' she said, in total surprise. Her hand went to her hair, which she knew needed washing. And she noticed the tomato ketchup stain on her top from where she had taken care of the boys at dinner. 'What are you doing here?'

He smiled broadly at her. 'I came to bring you this,' he said, and he held out a huge box he held in his arms.

'The picture?' she said, her heart leaping.

'Yes, the picture,' he said.

'I thought you'd send somebody. I didn't realize that you would come yourself. Please, come in, come in.'

She stood aside and allowed him to enter. It had been a few weeks since she had seen him and even though they had kept in touch by phone and email, it was just so thrilling to be with him again. And so strange to be with him in England, where she just wasn't used to him being around her sons.

The boys eyed him warily from the kitchen while eating their dinner.

'Come into the front room,' she said, 'and let's talk here. I'll put the kettle on. Do you want a cup of coffee?'

'That would be lovely,' he said as he looked around the room. 'I'm glad you decided to keep the picture.'

'Yes, it was the right thing,' she answered, thinking back to the conversation that had happened on the phone the week before. She had thought long and hard and realized that money would come and go, but she would never get the opportunity to own part of her history again. After thinking about what her grandmother had gone through to protect it, she just couldn't let it go to somebody who didn't know her family.

She brought him a cup of coffee, and the boys wandered into the front room and shyly and quietly watched him from the corner. Esther introduced the boys, who nodded at him. And then Henry pointed at the box.

'Is that a gift for us?'

Édouard chuckled.

'Yes,' Esther said, 'this is something very important, Henry. This is part of your history.'

They opened up the package together and looked at the gorgeous painting. It looked a little ostentatious for her tiny flat, but it was so beautiful. The colours vibrant as ever. The children playing in the fields, the hay bales glinting in the sun.

'Wow,' said Daniel, 'that's awesome.'

'Your grandmother painted this,' she said. 'Isn't it beautiful?'

Daniel walked towards it and went to touch it.

'Be careful,' Esther said. 'Go and wash your hands first.'

'Where are you going to put it, Mum?' said Henry, looking around the room.

'It will go in our new house when we move. The one attached to the gallery.'

They continued talking into the evening. Édouard had booked a hotel in the area.

'I would offer for you to stay here, but the place is so small,' she said with a sigh.

'No, no, of course not. I had no expectations. I just wanted to see your face when you opened the box and saw the painting again.'

'I have one more favour to ask you. How long will you be here?' she asked.

'I can be here a couple of days,' he said. 'I do not have to rush back; my sister has Camille.'

'I would love to take this to show my mother. She's in a home nearby, and she hasn't seen this since she was a little girl. She may have questions you can help answer, and honestly, I kind of need the support. I know that's a lot to ask.'

'No, of course not. I'm happy to help.'

As they parted he kissed her on both cheeks, and it felt awkward with the boys watching and so strange being here in England. Things had felt exotic in Paris, and now she was alone back in her known world, and it just didn't feel quite the same. She was worried about what Édouard thought about it all.

The next day she dropped the boys at school and went to pick Édouard up at his hotel. They drove to her mother's care home, and Esther explained about her mother's dementia.

'It comes and goes, but somehow her long-term memory tends to be much better than her short-term, and things can trigger her. So, she can be quite lucid in her long-term memory.'

'That is not unusual with dementia,' he responded as they travelled. 'My grandmother also suffered with it.'

They arrived at the home and were greeted by the usual woman, who smiled and looked across at Édouard with admiration. She didn't say anything, but her eyes implied she approved as she told them Sophie was in the day room.

'Your mother is in a good place today,' she said, smiling. 'I'm so glad you have come to visit her. I saw her this morning, and we had a nice chat.'

They walked through the endless halls and into the huge unfilled day room. Esther's mother sat at the table in her usual place, looking out of the window.

'Maman,' Esther called out.

Her mother turned quickly and stood to her feet. 'Oh, I'm so glad you're here. Esther, it's been beautiful today out there. I've been watching the squirrels running up and down the tree, and we have some new birds.' Then, noticing Édouard, she paused. 'Hello,' she said. 'I'm sorry. I was talking without realizing somebody else was here.'

'Mother, I'd like you to meet Édouard. He's a friend of mine.'

'Oh,' she said, reaching forward and gently taking his hand. 'It's a pleasure to meet you.'

'Your daughter has told me all about you,' he said with a smile.

Sophie nodded coyly. Esther could instantly see that her mother was concerned. With her memory issues, new people were always a little intimidating.

'We have brought something to show you, Maman,' Esther said, pulling out the picture and holding it up to her mother. 'Do you remember this?'

Sophie let out a little gasp and brought her hand to her mouth, sitting down heavily in the chair behind her.

'It's so beautiful,' she said, her eyes filling with tears.

'It's the painting that your mother painted.'

Sophie stared at it, shaking her head in disbelief. Then, she lifted herself out of the chair and moved closer to the painting, staring intently at it. Examining it closely, tears brimming in her eyes.

'I have not seen this for so long.' Then she looked down and smiled as she looked into one of the corners. 'But you're mistaken. This is not my mother's painting; this is my father's painting.'

Esther sighed. They had been doing so well.

'No,' she corrected her gently. 'Do you remember I told you your father's painting was destroyed in a train accident?'

'No, no, no,' she said adamantly, 'this is my father's painting.'

'How could you possibly know that?' Édouard asked, intrigued. 'The assessors cannot tell because it is of the same era and the same age as the original painting. However, they are sure that this is your mother's painting because the German records say the original was placed on a train out of Paris.'

'No,' she said. 'I remember before I got on a train earlier in the war, my mother told me a secret about how I would know the difference between the pictures.' She ran her hand down the painting to the bottom right corner and showed them an area there. 'This is how you can tell.'

Édouard looked at where she was indicating, pulling a looking glass from his pocket, then he looked up and smiled at her mother.

'That is craquelure,' he said. 'Older paintings have those cracks in the canvas from ageing. See, other areas have that too. There is nothing special about that, I'm afraid.'

'But there is,' she said, her eyes glistening. 'Look very closely at it.' Esther and Édouard looked very closely at the corner and then saw it. Some of the cracks had formed into what looked like letters.

'You see,' her mother said, running her fingers across the bottom of the painting. 'Do you see that? The B and the S are my parents' initials. My father painted them so that his love story would live on. He made it look like ageing because then he said that as the picture aged, so their love would, too, within the canvas.'

Tears brimmed in Esther's eyes.

'This is my grandfather's picture,' she said, looking at Édouard, who was shaking his head.

'Who would have known?' he said. 'But she is correct. There are two initials here.'

'The letter,' said Esther, remembering something. 'Do you remember in the letter where she spoke of the secret and how my mother would know?'

Édouard nodded his head. 'Of course.'

'It's so beautiful,' Sophie said, with tears in the corners of her eyes. 'I'm so glad you brought it back to me.'

They all sat and admired the painting for a while, and then, as they left, Édouard turned to Esther. 'This picture is now priceless. How do you feel now that we know this about it? This could buy you a house.'

But Esther shook her head.

'I loved it when it was my grandmother's picture. And I love it even more now it's my grandfather's. I can't think about the money, Édouard. I can't think about it. All I want to do is keep it.'

He nodded as he covered her hand, smiling. 'I'm so glad,' he said as they made their way to the car.

62

MARCH 2011

Esther

Esther surveyed the gallery, feeling a swell of pride unlike anything she had ever experienced. Her new assistant had already laid out the tables for the evening: china plates and napkins, glasses for the toast, tables dressed in elegant black tablecloths, hors d'oeuvres, wine, and champagne chilling in the fridge.

It was the first time she'd been alone all day and she moved towards the window, her steps accompanied by the soft notes of classic guitar music playing on her CD player. Taking in a deep, full breath, she watched as the sun began to set across the small town, allowing its rays to stretch across her face, filling her with joy.

Moving away from the window, Esther made final touches around the room before stopping at the painting that hung on the wall at the far end of the room, waiting behind a velvet curtain, ready for its unveiling.

She pulled on the little gold cord for a second to check her grandfather's art. The warm red and yellow hues were illuminated by the setting sun, making it come to life and dance before her eyes. She ran her fingers delicately down the canvas, careful not to mar it in any way, until she arrived at her grandparents' initials as tears seemed to follow her fingers, tracing their way down her cheeks. 'Thank you,' she said in a whisper. She thought about how her grandmother had been shot and killed by a Nazi, she thought about her grandfather dying because of his work with the Resistance, and she thought about how their lives had seemed so tragic.

And yet, out of this tragedy had come this gift for her, trapped in the walls of a French apartment for so many years.

She closed the curtains again and continued to prepare the gallery for the exhibition. It wasn't long before her assistant arrived back and the boys tumbled down the stairs dressed up in their shirts and ties. Janine was keeping them under wraps and looked exhausted.

'How do you do it?' she said under her breath as the boys continued to skip around the gallery. 'They nearly wore me out, and I've only had them for an hour.'

Esther smiled as she watched them. 'I remember I don't have them this age for that long. As hard as it is and as tired as I am, there'll be a day when I'll miss this.'

Janine nodded as they looked around. 'The cottage is beautiful. I'm so glad you made the move.'

'It was just right to be here for me and the kids, and the boys love being back at their old school.'

Not long later, Esther's nerves began to rise as people started to arrive and fill the gallery with the gentle hum of conversation and she was faced with giving a speech, something she wasn't accustomed to. As the crowd hushed eagerly, Esther stepped up to a podium and took a deep breath.

'I want to thank you all for coming to celebrate this special event with me,' she said, her voice a little breathy with her nerves. 'Over sixty years ago, my grandfather painted a beautiful picture. He put all of his heart and soul into it. And my grandmother loved it. And recently I have found out my grandfather was shot and killed by the Nazis for his involvement with an underground paper. His story is documented in the story of the Resistance paper *Libération*. We believe that my grandmother then worked to preserve this precious picture, to carefully recreate Samuel's painting from memory, despite her fear of discovery. When finished, she somehow managed to get it into the gallery and switched it for the original. Because we didn't know of her tenacity, we assumed that my grandfather's picture had been destroyed when a train carrying artworks was attacked by an underground group attempting to stop the Nazis' retreat. However, I now know that this work of art we admire is truly my grandfather's masterpiece that she saved and hid within the wall of her apartment. That was only discovered in the last year. It is indeed an unbelievable story and one that is amazing even to me. She paid with her life for what she did. But we have this beautiful work of art to live on in her and my grandfather's memory. So now I present to you, with great admiration and pride, *The Hayfields of Summer*.'

She pulled on the gold cord, and the velvet curtains swished open to reveal the masterpiece, humming with vibrancy under the warm yellow glow of the spotlights. Next to the picture on the wall was the story of her grandmother's bravery, along with the picture of Brigitte and Isabelle outside the Jeu de Paume. The audience clapped with admiration.

And as Esther looked out into the gathering of locals, she suddenly became transfixed by a familiar face in the crowd. It couldn't be him, could it? She held her breath as he disappeared into the throng of people. Then, he reappeared and began to move towards her. Her eyes lit up with recognition.

'Édouard, what are you doing here?' she said softly, her voice tender and full of wonder.

He moved closer and her heart started to quicken. 'I could

not have missed coming to see this beautiful art where it should be. I was so glad you never sold it. I always thought it should stay in your family. It is your heritage; your grandmother and people like her died saving French art. The least we can do is honour their memory.' His eyes drifted to the photograph of her grandmother on the wall. 'You are a lot like her, you know,' he said gently. 'And not only in your looks. That same fierce determination to do what is right and the unwavering love of your family.'

Tears sprang to her eyes as she spoke. 'Édouard?' she said quietly. 'I'm so glad you came, but where do we go from here?'

He smiled wistfully and then looked deep into her eyes. 'When my wife died, I could not have imagined ever being with another woman. It would have felt like a betrayal. But since meeting you, there was such an ease to our friendship right from the beginning, and I find myself thinking about you all the time.' His words filled the air between them with warmth and possibilities as he continued. 'I never imagined that would ever happen again. I see it all as a gift, a gift I want to keep experiencing, if you are open to that?' he asked questioningly.

She smiled. 'I'm not sure how it could work with us living so far apart, but I feel the same way too. I would like to take it slowly, but I am open to seeing what happens.'

'Paris is not so far away, and with the tunnel now...' he added as he covered her hand with his own.

All at once, Henry crashed into one of the tables, sending a glass smashing to the floor, and she moved away to deal with it. When she returned, Édouard had drifted into the shadows to talk to someone else, and it gave her a chance to admire him from a distance. Why couldn't she have love and everything else? She deserved it, didn't she?

They were coming to the end of the evening and Esther was gathering up abandoned drinks and stray napkins when an elderly woman appeared before her. She put a gnarled hand on

Esther's arm, and the way she gripped her made her blood run cold. She then pierced her with a resolute expression.

'I knew your grandmother,' she growled in a quiet voice that carried immense weight. Esther straightened in surprise. Who was this?

The old woman continued, 'Brigitte was a good woman. And I have many regrets about what I did during that time. If you want to know more about her, you need this.' She thrust a business card into her hand, and Esther noted it was an address for a bookshop in Paris.

Esther looked up to ask another question but the woman had vanished.

Édouard approached, seeing Esther's concern.

'Is everything okay?'

'There was a woman here,' she said, her eyes searching the gallery in vain. 'She said she knew my grandmother and she gave me this card.'

Édouard examined the business card and nodded his head.

'Yes, I know of this bookshop. In fact, her granddaughter is there now. From what I know, Madeline Valette is quite elderly but still very vital.'

'I wonder if she is related to Isabelle Valette, the one in the picture with my grandmother. She said she would have more to say about her. And then she just disappeared.'

He raised his eyebrows. 'How intriguing. We could go together and visit this place if you want, see what this is all about?'

She nodded, blowing out air. 'I thought I had unravelled all the secrets.'

'Maybe fate has other ideas for you,' he said with a smile.

Esther slipped the card back into her purse and had this strange feeling that this was not the end, but a beginning. Then she remembered the words her mother had said to her a while ago. 'Find the children on the train.' Could that also be part of what needed to be uncovered?

Then as Henry tore around the gallery pretending to be an aeroplane and Daniel sat slumped in the corner playing one of his games, she started to feel a sense of excitement about her future. Her life had felt so bleak just the year before, but since then so much had changed. Now, she glanced over at the picture and then Édouard. There seemed to be endless possibilities.

EPILOGUE

AUGUST 1944

Isabelle

The air in the museum was heavy with anticipation as Isabelle sat in her office, waiting for the news they were all hoping for. She had been back at the Louvre for a while now, as the activity at the Jeu de Paume had slowed to a stop. The last days of the occupation had been a frenzy as the Nazis frantically attempted to get as much art shipped out of Paris as they were being driven out.

She still missed Brigitte and still had nightmares about her friend's death. Marina, who had been arrested, had then disappeared when the jail was attacked by freedom fighters and as the Nazis had retreated. There was a rumour she had gone to England. Now the rooms of that museum were empty, a hollow shell. Nothing but dust and the memories of all the war had wrought.

In the weeks leading up to this day, she had been frantically trying to catalogue what pieces of art had been moved out of Paris and get the few that remained into hiding.

All at once a distant cheer went up outside and she sat back in her chair, feeling a mixture of relief and sadness wash over her. Standing up, she squinted out of her window through a gap in the sandbags. Draped in a tattered French flag, a group of young men were singing 'La Marseillaise' at the top of their voices as they danced down the street sharing and swigging from a wine bottle between them. As she watched the celebrations outside, her thoughts drifted back to Brigitte and the night she had been arrested at her apartment. Isabelle remembered how it had taken hours to convince the gun-toting Nazis that she wasn't Jewish before they'd finally let her go. It was just one of many horrific moments during this long and brutal war.

But she hadn't dared to venture back to Brigitte's apartment again, just in case she was seen and picked up. She would wait until Sophie returned to retrieve her picture. It would be safe in the wall for now. She had not seen Brigitte's family since her funeral, after which Jules had taken them to his contacts on the outskirts of the city. And from what he told her, it seemed that once the Allies had freed France, they had made their way to England.

Jacques Jaujard stepped through the door, and a sob of relief escaped Isabelle's throat. His face held a mix of exhaustion and exhilaration. 'It's over,' he declared. 'Paris is liberated.'

Isabelle leapt from her desk and rushed into his arms, tears flowing down her cheeks as they shared an awkward, yet exuberant embrace, both of them silently celebrating their newfound freedom. They both had experienced a lot of pain and loss during the war, so much suffering and the shared mutual pain of watching the destruction of many Parisian treasures that Isabelle would never forget.

She was in the midst of celebrating with her colleagues when a secretary called her away. Seeing the urgency in the woman's eyes, she swiftly made her way to the phone, her champagne glass still trembling in her grasp. Taking the receiver, she heard her mother's voice shaking with fear. Dread spread through Isabelle's body as she tried to brace herself for the news awaiting her. 'Maman,' Isabelle said softly, her own voice quivering.

'Oh, Isabelle,' her mother wept, 'Isabelle, you must come home. You must come immediately. One of your beloved sisters is dead.'

'What?' Isabelle said, her voice tight with the shock.

But before her mother could give her any more details, she burst into wracking sobs and hung up the phone.

In that moment Isabelle felt like time had stopped as a cry escaped her chest. Each of her sisters was too precious to lose. She tried to figure out which one it could possibly be. Madeline had been travelling back and forth to Frankfurt and she hadn't seen her for so long. Or Antoinette, who had disappeared without a trace? Giselle, always taking risks, or darling Charlotte – too kind and lovely to face such a cruel twist of fate. Tears streamed down her face as despair enveloped her. She wanted to scream, to rail against this tragedy that had stolen away one of her most precious sisters.

A wave of nausea hit her as she hung up. Trying to come to terms with the inevitable, she gathered what strength she could muster before making her heartbreaking journey home. It felt even more gut-wrenching as all around her the city celebrated.

She wished for Jules to be there beside her for whatever fate lay ahead, but he'd been on an underground mission outside of the city for months now and so she would have to confront this tragedy alone.

As Isabelle made her way sombrely through the lively streets, her heart heavy with grief, she couldn't help but reflect on the fragility of life amid the backdrop of a liberated Paris. The cheers and jubilation around her felt distant and muted, as a veil of deep sorrow descended upon her world. And as Isabelle gathered her strength to face the tragic news that awaited her she knew her life would never be the same.

A LETTER FROM SUZANNE

I want to say a huge thank you for choosing to read *The Last Day in Paris*. If you did enjoy it, and want to keep up to date with all my latest releases, just sign up at the following link. Your email address will never be shared and you can unsubscribe at any time.

www.bookouture.com/suzanne-kelman

Thank you so much for taking the time to read this story. It was in the midst of the chaos during the Covid lockdown, a powerful moment ignited the inspiration for this book. I can still vividly recall the tears streaming down my face as I watched a shaky video of an Italian neighbourhood on someone's phone. A single voice brought the community together, their voices rising in song, a defiant anthem against the darkness. It was at that moment that I realized how, in our darkest times, we find solace and refuge in the beauty of music, poetry, art, and storytelling. These expressions anchor us.

Driven by this realization, I set out on a quest to uncover how art triumphed amid the ravages of war. During my exploration, I stumbled upon the extraordinary tale of Rose Valland, an art historian from Paris. Her audacious mission involved documenting the fate of thousands of stolen artworks. Her story painted a vibrant picture of determination – a young woman who carved her own path through the realm of art and beauty, orchestrating her own silent revolution.

As I delved into Rose's story, I became captivated by every aspect of her life – from her covert recordings of tens of thousands of art pieces to the unwavering dedication of her and her fellow museum staff as they transported art from the Louvre using hundreds of trucks, thousands of boxes, and countless paintings, statues, and priceless masterpieces.

Alongside Rose's narrative, I felt compelled to weave in the story of a character whose quest revolved around a more personal journey. I wanted to integrate a single piece of artwork that bound a family together.

Writing Brigitte's story of an ordinary Jewish family under the threat of war broke my heart.

In the course of my research, I uncovered the tragic fate of eighty-four Jewish artists in Paris who perished during the Holocaust. Their stories are poignantly recounted in Hersh Fenster's book, *Our Martyr Artists*, and they served as a powerful inspiration for Brigitte's story.

Also, as I delved into the Resistance movement, I was fascinated by how the French worked to thwart their enemy. I wanted to include some of that historical information for the reader, like the creation of the Resistance newspaper *Libération*. However, I did take a little artistic licence as I introduced it in a chapter set in July 1940. Though, to be accurate, this newspaper didn't start producing papers until the following year.

As always when I write historical fiction, I love to create a story where ripples from the past come forward to inspire a present-day protagonist. From the very first moments of creating this book, Esther burst forth onto the pages, her voice strong and unwavering even before my pen met the page. As I crafted Esther's fate, I revelled in interweaving destinies, revealing how a seemingly small decision – keeping a painting – set into motion a chain of events that changed her life forever.

Bringing this book together was an absolute joy for me. It encompassed all the elements I adore: the enchanting backdrop of a beautiful city, three intertwined love stories, and the indomitable spirits of courageous women fighting for their beliefs. Thank you so much for coming on this journey with me and I really hope you enjoyed reading it as much as I adored writing it.

I hope you loved *The Last Day in Paris*, and if you did, I would be very grateful if you could write a review. It'd be great to hear what you think, and it makes such a difference helping new readers to discover one of my books for the first time.

I love hearing from my readers – you can get in touch with me on social media or through my website.

Thanks,

Suzanne

www.suzannekelmanauthor.com

facebook.com/suzkelman

x.com/suzkelman

ACKNOWLEDGMENTS

I am immensely grateful to Bookouture, my extraordinary publisher. I cannot thank them enough for the unwavering support and dedication of their exceptional team. A heartfelt thanks goes to my remarkable editor, Lydia Vassar-Smith, whose encouragement and amazing editing skills have been invaluable.

I also want to extend my thanks to the incredible team at Bookouture, including Jenny Geras, Peta Nightingale, Lizzie Brien, Mandy Kullar, Hannah Snetsinger, Occy Carr, Melanie Price, Alex Crow, Alba Proko, Sally Partington, Becca Allen, Richard King and all the others who have played a vital role in bringing my books to life. Also, Kim Nash, Noelle Holten, and Sarah Hardy, you are an absolute dream team! Your unwavering dedication to promoting my book, organizing blog tours, and seizing every opportunity to spread the word is truly commendable. Words cannot express how grateful I am for all of you.

A special, heartfelt thank you goes out to my amazing husband, Matthew Wilson. Your unwavering presence and support mean the world to me. I am forever grateful to have you by my side every day.

To my son, Christopher, you are such a blessing in my life. I am overflowing with pride to call myself your mother. Your genuine kindness, sharp mind, and profound wisdom continuously bring joy and happiness to me.

In addition to my immediate family, I am incredibly blessed to be surrounded by a chosen family of beloved friends who hold a special place in my heart. To my dearest friend Melinda

Mack, thank you for your kindness, compassion, and friendship. A big-hearted thank you also goes out to Eric Mulholland. I am so grateful to count you as a friend. To my beloved 'bezzie mate' Shauna Buchet, I cherish our sisterly bond. And to my number one writing buddy, K. J. Waters, thank you for being my biggest cheerleader. Your incredible support and friendship have meant the world to me over the years.

Lastly, I want to express my heartfelt appreciation to each and every one of you, my wonderful readers. Thank you for choosing my books amidst the overwhelming sea of choices out there. Your support and loyalty are invaluable to me. I am truly grateful for each and every one of you.